# A Woman of Style

# A WOMAN
# OF STYLE

*Colin McDowell*

ROWAN

A ROWAN BOOK

Published by Arrow Books Limited
20 Vauxhall Bridge Road, London SW1V 2SA

An imprint of the Random Century Group

London Melbourne Sydney Auckland Johannesburg
and agencies throughout the world

First published in Great Britain in 1991
by Random Century Group Ltd

Rowan edition 1992

1 3 5 7 9 10 8 6 4 2

Phototypeset by Intype, London
Printed and bound in Great Britain by
Cox & Wyman Ltd., Reading, Berkshire

ISBN 0 09 995720 5

For Laurie Purden

# CHAPTER 1

'Are bitches born or bred?' Constance asked on the night of her mother's funeral.

She and her Aunt Louise were sitting in her mother's living room, drinking sherry and feeling close, as old friends and allies do. Listening to the autumn wind moaning across this corner of the sparse Northumberland coastline a few miles south of Berwick-upon-Tweed, where Nora Simpson had lived for all of her married life, their memories of her were vivid. Constance wasn't thinking only of her mother. She was looking back over her own life. Bathed in the bright sun of Italy and glittering with social and commercial success, it seemed to her that it had always been menaced by dark shadows, many of which, Constance sometimes thought, had sprung up almost to punish her for leaving this remote area so early in her adult life. They were shadows that she could never have imagined when, as a young girl, she had run along the cold sands of Northumberland and watched the east wind flatten and fold the dunes as she dreamed of a bigger, more exciting world beyond – and away from her mother's influence.

She was brought back to the moment by Louise. 'Oh, darling, I think that's a little harsh.' Her aunt frowned slightly. 'Nora was very strong-willed, I know, but I don't think she was a *bitch*. She had a lot to contend with.'

'No, don't misunderstand me,' Constance went on. 'I was thinking more of myself than her. I know I'm a bitch and I do think Nora had a lot to do with it but I've often thought that it was – you know – in the genes.'

'Well,' Louise laughed, 'you certainly couldn't be mistaken for anything other than Nora Simpson's daughter, there's no doubt about that, but to be fair, my sweet, you've both had a lot to contend with. You've not had it easy, but *bitch* is far too unkind. You've had to be strong to *survive* – just as poor Nora had to be when your father died, and she was left on her own.'

Constance looked at her aunt – was she blaming her for Nora's lonely last years?

Louise Carter was a woman in her early eighties. White-haired and with make-up applied in the haphazard way that suggests no great interest in the face rather than a weakening of the critical faculties, Louise was still very much in charge of herself – her appearance, thought and manner. Constance looked at her fondly. Louise, who had been her comfort, buffer and rescuer so many times in the past; Louise, who had in so many ways been more of a mother to her than Nora; Louise, who even now had lost none of her vigour and strength of personality. You'd think that she was still in her sixties, Constance thought approvingly, as Louise took out a cigarette and, crossing her legs decisively, made herself comfortable on the sofa.

'You were closer to her than anyone,' Constance continued. 'Even before I went to Italy and married Ludo I never really knew her. Actually, she influenced every decision I ever made but I always felt she put a barrier between us. But I honestly don't know if it was deliberate, or just our chemistry. I've never understood it – probably because I've never really understood *her*.'

Constance slipped off her shoes and curled her feet under her. She was sitting on the opposite side of the grate and Louise Carter thought fleetingly how proud Nora had always been of her daughter even when they had been dramatically at loggerheads and how pleased she would be if she could see her now, in her elegant black dress and silver jewellery. Yes, my dear, she mused affectionately, Signora Villanuova you may well now be – and head of a fashion empire – but every attitude you've ever had came from Nora. She made you strong – and she was no more a bitch than you are.

Sensing that her aunt needed to talk, Constance poured more sherry.

'I understood her perfectly,' Louise said as she searched in her bag for her lighter. 'We were very close, you know. Much more than just cousins. I remember when she came from India after your grandmother died. She looked so strange. Tall, dark and gawky. She was very strong-willed. Couldn't be told *anything*. My father used to get so angry at her stubbornness – not at all like me, used to doing what I was told.'

There was a pause as she lit her cigarette.

'I got a shock yesterday when I went to the mortuary,' Constance said. 'I didn't realise that she'd let her hair grow out. She was quite white. I couldn't believe my eyes. And the nails on her right hand were filthy. I had to clean them.'

'Darling, how ghastly for you,' Louise commiserated, remembering how punctilious over her appearance her cousin Nora had always been. Her sophisticated turnout and stylish overdressing had made her a minor legend in this remote northern district.

'It was horrible,' Constance said. 'I had to lift her hand. It was so hard and stiff that I was frightened I would break the wrist. I don't know how I managed it. I had to bend over, parallel to the body, to get the nail file under the nails. I was frightened in case anyone came in. It would have looked so odd. But I had to do it. She was always so obsessed with her appearance, I couldn't let her go to her grave in that state . . . Her hand was so cold.' She shuddered at the recollection and continued. 'Then I combed her hair back. How wispy and thin it was.'

Louise was silent, then said, 'Poor Nora. That's why I was the only one she would allow to see her in hospital. You know how particular she was about dyeing her hair.

She wouldn't allow anyone else to do it and, of course, with her broken arm after the fall, she couldn't. She kept saying "Oh, the nurses don't matter and the doctors are afraid of me – I'll do it before I come out." Actually I preferred her with white hair.'

'Oh, I agree. After all, she was seventy-five. It was about time. But it was still a shock to see her like that, looking so old and spent.'

Constance hadn't seen her mother since her last visit to England over a year ago. She had been so busy with her dress house in Rome, coping with her designer, planning for the future and ensuring that everyone in the business was kept happy – each of which seemed a full-time job in itself – that she had hardly had time to spare for her three children, let alone her mother. Thinking now of the battles she had fought with her own children, especially her daughter, Margharita, she felt a pang of remorse over the woman she had buried a few hours earlier. Constance had also fought her mother all the way when she was young and her personality was still forming, and then had somehow abandoned her in later life, when the need to fight had gone. She felt guilty, but she could say with a clear conscience that her business was so demanding that she hardly had time to think of Northumberland although, in truth, as her successes and problems in Italy had increased, there seemed less and less reason to return to Nora. Her trips to see her mother had of necessity been brief. After two days even the smallest decision could become an exhausting battle of wills. The less they saw of each other, Constance had reluctantly accepted over the years, the better friends she and her mother were.

'She wasn't an easy character to love, you know,' she went on. 'Nora was admirable in many ways but no one could call her lovable.'

Louise frowned impatiently as Constance said, 'I suppose she lacked the maternal instinct. Rather like me, really.' She paused. 'In fact,' she murmured, 'she wasn't easy at all – any more than I am.'

'You never really knew her,' Louise replied.

'You're right,' Constance agreed. 'It's terribly sad but I don't think I ever really loved her, either. She wouldn't let me somehow. I needed to when I was a teenager. I had to face all my problems alone. She'd let me get half-way close and then she would push me away. I always felt that she cut me off just as we were becoming closer – and always when I most needed her.'

Louise smiled. 'That's exactly what she used to say. about you. She always felt that Miss Hatherby meant more to you than she did.'

'Miss Hatherby certainly influenced me, but not as a mother would. She was all intellect. I needed emotional support. No, Louise, no matter what you say, Nora kept me at arm's length.'

As Constance poured another glass of sherry for her aunt, Louise continued in a softer voice. 'I was the only one who really knew Nora – I could always tell what she was thinking. When she was first married, I was the only person she could turn to. Your father was such a disappointment to her, in so many ways. He had no imagination. Poor Will, he was the archetypal country doctor. So dull. Dull as his name. He never had an original idea in his life. You can't blame him – that's why he was a country doctor. They're *meant* to be dull. It isn't in the nature of doctors to be original or witty or *anything*. They have to be reliable, reliably *boring*. He was certainly that. Why they ever married I shall never know. I suppose she saw him as an escape.'

Louise lit another cigarette. 'Nora hated work. She had no money when she came from India, except for a little in bonds, or something, but not enough to live on. My father had managed to get her a job in a friend's office just off Hatton Garden. Not much money but things were different in the twenties. We didn't seem to need so much in those days. Of course, Nora felt being a typist was below her, and she couldn't *bear* the people she worked with. She was determined to get married and get out. In

11

those days married women didn't work, so for her it was the ideal solution. She wouldn't have to be dependent on my father any more and she would be free to live her own life. Work bored her – it was too predictable. Your mother had an amazing imagination – that's where yours comes from – she could have done so much better with her life . . .

'Anyhow, the problem was that we hardly ever saw any young men, so how on earth could she start courting? Of course, being the determined woman she was, Nora decided to take the bull by the horns and organise things for herself. We used to sit in the garden for hours going over her various plans to get married. She had a new one virtually every day. I just listened, there was absolutely no possibility of influencing her. I remember thinking how typical it was of her that she never thought of being wooed. She was like a huntress – in pursuit, in charge.'

'She always was,' Constance murmured to herself.

'She got the idea from a magazine story, of all things,' Louise continued, warming to the tale. 'She decided to go to a hotel – a grand one – and meet a man. You can't imagine how *bold* that was in those days. She decided against seaside hotels like the Metropole at Folkestone or the Imperial at Torquay. She was shrewd and quite calculating even then. She felt there would be too many families at the seaside and not enough single men. She wanted a *masculine* sort of hotel.

'So she chose Gleneagles, in Scotland, which was very new then, but already famous for golf. Nora calculated that there must be lots of single men up there so she decided it was ideal for the "manhunt", as we called it, even though the train fare was a serious consideration. I remember we went up to Euston together one Saturday morning, very excited, to buy the ticket in advance. It was a secret – if my parents had known she was going away alone they would have soon put the kybosh on it. No, she was supposed to be going to stay with a girlfriend from the India days who lived in Perthshire. Your mother

12

was always good with money – that's who you get it from. Will hadn't a *clue* – he couldn't have cared less! She worked the whole trip out, to the last farthing. I remember it vividly. A room without a bath was forty shillings a night. Gleneagles was ridiculously expensive in those days – still is, probably. I remember Nora's first postcard – which she sent in an envelope secretly to my office. She was so indignant. Breakfast cost five shillings and dinner, I think, about nine, but she knew that before she went. What infuriated her was that they charged three shillings for afternoon tea, so she decided to forgo it because she knew the men would still be out on the links.'

Louise chuckled at the recollection. 'We had a terrible check at Euston. We had to decide on travelling third or first class. I'd have just gone third but Nora looked ahead. She was worried about coming back. Going up to Scotland no one would know her so she could travel third but coming back, if the young man travelled with her – it never even entered her head that she wouldn't meet one – it could be embarrassing. It took us two turns through the arch before she decided. First-class return it would be. I remember her saying, slightly on the defensive, "It's an investment," and I thought, It's made her even more determined to succeed. Money always did that with your mother.

'Your father had only qualified from Edinburgh a couple of years before. He was the assistant doctor for the hotel – although a lot of guests brought their own in those days. Well, you've heard the story of how your mother got soaked on the third tee in a downpour. Of course, she wouldn't abandon the round. You know why? It was Saturday so they had put up the green fee from four and sixpence to seven and six and she couldn't *bear* to waste the money. She'd rather have caught pneumonia and died. As it was, she went down so badly with flu that she had to be confined to her room for the duration. She was *furious*. No wonder she was running a temperature! I'm sure most of it was caused by temper. That's when your father came in.' Louise chuckled. 'I remember her card: "I am being *very* attentively cared for by the hotel doctor, William Simpson." When he proposed to her on the last night I think she took him because, having been in her room for seven days, she'd met nobody else and couldn't bear to see her investment wasted.'

Both women smiled. 'Oh, I know,' said Constance, 'but it was more than that. It was a whirlwind affair. She thought it was romantic. I'm sure she had fallen in love.'

'I never understood it,' Louise reflected. 'It was so out of character for your father. He was very cautious – the last person to have a whirlwind *anything*, let alone romance.'

Thinking of her own marriage, Constance said, 'Maybe, but I think it was very much in character with my mother. Not that I'm in any position to pass judgement.'

Nora married William Simpson in November 1927 three scandalously short months after her Gleneagles trip. Louise's mother was shocked and felt guiltily conscious of failing to take proper care of her brother's daughter, but was glad to have the restless girl off her hands.

To Nora's barely hidden horror William had joined a partnership in Northumberland. It included a house in the tiny seaside village of Cramer, which clung low to the land in an attempt to avoid the rough seas and wild winds that buffeted the coast for what seemed to Nora most of the year.

'At first she hated it,' Louise continued, 'it seemed so remote and, in the thirties, of course, it *was*. And primitive after Surrey – I remember Nora saying she never knew how to dress. Your mother used to phone me, although trunk calls in those days were only for emergencies. She used to ring at nine thirty in the morning when Will was in surgery. If he walked in or the girl came to clean the grate, she'd pretend to be talking to a tradesman: "It really was more fat than lean. We threw away at least half," and she'd put the receiver down. I don't know what the girl must have thought. She probably told the whole village that the doctor's wife was always complaining to the local shopkeepers.' She chuckled. 'Not that Nora would care.'

Changing track, she went on. 'Your father wasn't interested in sex – strange for a doctor, really. He enjoyed a round of golf and playing cricket for the village and that was about it. Typical of thousands of boring husbands in the thirties. Nora and I used to say that the war did them all a power of good. Shocked them out of their complacency, gave them a bit of opposition. They had to start reacting the way women always have. Actually,' she said, warming to her subject, 'I think the war was a good thing for a *lot* of men. Of course, it was too late for your father. Your mother used to say men are such babies because they haven't *had* babies. We've all been through it and we know what pain's about.' Her voice was becoming sharper. 'I remember all the fuss when your Uncle Jim was dying of cancer. My dear, I could hardly keep my patience. He was always going on about how undignified and painful the examinations were. I used to think, That's a woman's lot – forever being prodded and poked and looked up by doctors who are total strangers. Men don't know the half of it.

'When your Uncle Jim died,' Louise continued, 'and I decided to retire up here, it seemed the most natural thing in the world that cousins should want to be close in their widowhood. I would have liked us to share a house but your mother preferred to be on her own.'

'She *would*,' Constance said, 'you know how she needed to rule the roost. Imagine sharing a kitchen with Nora!'

'You're right, my darling,' Louise laughed, 'it would have been a disaster.'

Suddenly Constance felt she didn't want to hear anything more about the past. Louise was so animated by now that she seemed to have forgotten that morning's funeral. Constance glanced at her watch. It was getting late and her youngest child, Tudor, who had accompanied

15

her to the funeral, and was now waiting for her in the local hotel, would be growing anxious.

'Louise, dear, I've just noticed the time. I ought to run you home. Tudor and I will stay in the hotel tonight but we'll call in to see you tomorrow.'

'Of course, darling, I understand,' said Louise huffily. 'You must be dead beat with everything – and me going on and on.'

Constance sensed that she had offended her aunt and she felt guilty. As she slipped her mink coat over her shoulders, she resolved to make up for it next day.

'You know, darling,' Louise said, as she was tying her scarf, 'you're very unfair to yourself and your mother. Having the courage and determination to live your life the way you want to is not being a *bitch*. You both married weak men. What else could you do but be strong enough to carry them? The fact that you were weak enough to choose them in the first place is another thing altogether,' she finished triumphantly.

By the time Constance had dropped off Louise, who was not mollified by being given a lift to her door, it was past six. She and Tudor were staying at the Black Boar, Chollerton's only hotel. As she walked into the Percy Bar the sight of her youngest son sitting in the corner raised Constance's spirits. He stood up as she walked towards him.

'Was it all right?' he asked anxiously. 'You look tired.'

'Yes, Tudor darling, I am, but it *was* all right. It was better for you not to come. We had a real trip down memory lane, talking about your grandmother as she was years ago. Louise needed to talk.'

Tudor smiled tentatively. Years at an English public school, punctuated by all-too-brief holidays in Italy, had made him almost a stranger within his family. Whereas his brother and sister, Manfredo and Margharita, had been brought up in Italy and educated to be Italians, he was a hybrid, with a mind trained to be English but emotions entirely Italian.

Constance said, 'It's a pity you didn't really know Nora. She was a very special character in so many ways. I admired the way she took on this part of the world and conquered it.'

Tudor looked puzzled.

'Oh, Tudor, this is a strange land,' Constance smiled. 'Northumberland is far removed from the civilised air of your school in the south, my darling. Surely you can sense that?'

Tudor moved uncomfortably in his seat and sipped his half pint self-consciously. He thought that his school was perhaps not quite as civilised as his mother cared to imagine but he remained silent.

'It *is* different here, you know,' Constance continued dreamily. 'This landscape. It's so uncompromising with humans. Picts, Scots, Romans – it's conquered them all. I never felt entirely at ease here when I was a little girl. It's such a male landscape. That's why Nora used to love it. There was something for her to *fight*. I love Italy, as you know, but nowhere has the brooding power of Northumberland. Nature has an aggression here that stiffens you and makes you strong. Do you know what I'm talking about?'

'Yes, I do,' Tudor replied. 'I think it's beautiful because it *is* so spare. I love the long bare hills with just the odd clump of trees. It's clean and uncluttered.'

'Before we return to the south,' Constance said enthusiastically, 'I'll show you this county. I want you to see how it formed my character! I'll take you to all the places I loved as a girl. You're old enough to understand now.'

'Understand?'

'Yes, Tudor darling, understand why this land is more wonderful than anywhere else in the world and why it is yours, just as much as it is mine. It is a birthright we share. I will show you my memories.'

# CHAPTER 2

Constance Simpson was an only child. She was brought up in Cramer, a coastal village a few miles from Dunstan-burgh. Although the village was tiny, her father's practice included a large area of the surrounding countryside as well as parts of Chollerton, the small country town three miles inland where he delivered her, in the Cottage Hospital, on 14 April 1929. The year is not significant but the month is. It was a testimony to her parents' efficiency. They knew how important it was for a baby to have fresh air and sun. They also knew how dark and long the northern winters could be. Priding themselves on being modern-minded about such things, they subjected passion to planning and decided to have a spring baby. The decision paid off. Constance was born healthy and remained so. By the time she was nine, she was tall, fair-haired, straight-backed and long-legged. Although she occasionally looked waif-like, there was a most unchildlike determination to her mouth and a look about her jawline that suggested that she would not be easily deflected from anything she had set her mind to, but otherwise her parents' pride in the perfection of their product was largely justified. She was an exemplary country lass and pleased her father very much for being so, although her mother was sometimes nervous. Even at that age, Constance seemed perhaps *too* self-willed and wild, like the country-side she roamed so freely.

It was the countryside that brought Constance close to

her father. Idealistic and romantic, Will Simpson responded to the beauty of nature almost as a duty and in strong contrast to his wife who found that it was always too cold and complained that the wind ruined her hair the moment she stepped out of the garden gate. He had a little book called *Blackie's Guide to Flowers of the Wayside*, and he and Constance always took it with them on their walks. They picked the flowers of the hedgerows and every new find had to be identified in *Blackie's*. It was Constance's favourite book. The paper was thick and textured, like felt. The illustrations were line drawings and she used to colour them in with crayons after each new plant had been correctly named. She would sit in the surgery in the evenings after the patients had gone and carefully shade in the colours. She did it for her father and liked to do so in the one part of the house that was totally his.

Constance and Will loved going for walks together. They walked regardless of the weather: on early spring mornings when the sky was remote and pale as a plover's egg; on stormy autumn afternoons when they felt they could reach up and touch the lowering clouds that covered the land like a bruise; and on frozen winter days when the sky was a white membrane stretched so tight that they could imagine it cracking with the cold. Constance always remembered the different skies but, in her memory, the colour of the Northumbrian landscape hardly changed with the seasons. It was always the softest grey-green, with sometimes a haze of yellow at the edges, sometimes a tinge of brown.

Always, as they walked they talked. Will Simpson was one of the new breed of educated men. His family background was humble but he had been brought up on the writings of Beatrice and Sidney Webb and the philosophies of George Bernard Shaw. He burned with a reforming zeal. Champion of the underdog and believer in the nobility of the common man, he lost no opportunity to teach his daughter the importance of never giving in

19

or allowing herself to be beaten by lack of courage. 'Try, Constance!' he would exhort, when she faltered before jumping a stream or climbing over a hedge. 'You can do it! I know you can! There's nothing to be afraid of.' His encouragement was always psychological, never physical. He willed her to overcome the problem – and she did so because she couldn't bear the thought of letting him down.

All through her life, even at moments when her difficulties seemed overwhelming, Constance would remember her father's words declaimed into the vast skies of Northumberland: 'Never be afraid, Constance. You can do anything you like, now and for ever. Nobody can stop you – only yourself.' Tightly clutching his hand and running to keep up, Constance had believed him. Years later, she acknowledged the debt she owed him for those early lessons in self-determination.

She and her father were out walking on the day he died. It was during the Easter holidays. Nora Simpson had taken the early bus to Chollerton to do her weekend shopping. Constance had walked to the bus-stop with her. The seasons are reluctant to let go in the North of England and, although it was early May, Nora wore her winter coat. It was a deep blue colour and had a matching hat like a tiny trilby, decorated with a feather. Constance thought that she looked very smart. She knew Nora thought so too. By the way her mother fiddled with the handle of her wicker basket Constance could tell that she was longing for the bus to come and take her to Chollerton where her beauty and style might stand some chance of being noticed. Rightly, Nora considered Cramer a wasteland as far as fashion was concerned. The wives of the village, who almost always wore black under their ubiquitous pinnies, looked askance at the doctor's wife and her parade of bonny colours. Constance didn't care – even when her friends made fun of her mother's elegance. She was proud of how Nora looked and loved to touch the material of her clothes. She intended to look just as smart when she grew up.

After the cream and brown Bedford bus had trundled away up the road Constance walked back to the house. She met her father coming out of the surgery.

'Mummy got off all right, did she?' he asked her. 'What are you going to do now? Very light surgery this morning: I haven't to be in Chollerton until two and I've only got a couple of calls to make. Fancy a walk?'

They strode down the drive and out of the gate and, once through the village, struck out for the Heights, as the long sea meadows between Cramer and Dunstanburgh were inappropriately called. To give the walk some point, Will Simpson had decided to call in to see a patient whose son farmed the fields beyond the Heights.

'I'll only be there for a minute, Constance, to see that things are all right. You can play with the puppies in the yard.'

To reach the farmhouse they could follow the muddy and pit-marked cart track between the fields or take the short cut across the meadow to the little wooden gate at the side of the garden. That morning, as it was dry underfoot, Will Simpson decided to take the short cut. As they climbed over the hedge, he was struck by the beauty of the day; the hedgerows were just coming into leaf and the meadow was dotted with buttercups and daisies. High above, the birds wheeled and dipped in the wind that blew the clouds across the huge sky. The field was empty except for a few ewes with young lambs. They panicked and moved away, complaining, as the two figures walked towards them. Suddenly their random bleating was joined by the rhythmic thud of drumming hooves. From the back of a barn three shire horses came thundering out – a stallion and two mares. Constance and her father stopped as the horses galloped furiously around the edge of the meadow, their enormous hooves kicking up great clods of earth as they went. The ground shook beneath the weight of their tread.

'Quick, Constance!' Will shouted. 'Run for the gate!'

She looked at her father in fright. He was white and

his eyes were anxiously watching the three horses, who had now separated. One of the mares galloped to the far end of the field where she stopped and started to crop. The other gambolled towards Will and Constance with the stallion by her side. Their eyes rolled and their manes tossed, as, snorting and whinnying, they tried to bite each other. The noise of their hooves boomed as they came closer. Pushed by her father, Constance started to run. The hoof sounds came nearer, irregular now as the two horses galloped together, rearing their heads and kicking out with their hind legs.

The beasts were almost on top of them. As Will turned and threw up his arms to head them off, Constance continued running. The stallion veered away and kicked out in an enormous arc. His hooves caught Will on the side of the head. Constance heard the crack of his skull and his cry of pain. She turned and saw him lying still, face down, as the horses careered away. Two farm hands came rushing out of the barn and ran across the field to the motionless figure. She too began to run towards the group huddled over her father's body. As she stopped a few feet away from them she saw that his cap had been knocked some distance from where he lay and the force of the blow, which had thrown him through the air, had dislodged his fountain pen from his pocket. Bending to pick it up, Constance saw her father's face framed by a farm worker's legs. It was grey. His hair was sticky with blood and a purple bruise was spreading across his temple. As she stared in terror, she heard one of the men say, 'He's gone.'

From the day of Will Simpson's death his wife and daughter lived a life incomplete. For the first few weeks their existence was bedraggled and formless. Although there was no dramatic change in their circumstances – no fear of eviction or drop in their standard of living – Constance felt rudderless. As she gazed forlornly at *Blackie's*, knowing that there would be no more collecting of specimens and no more colouring in, she felt guilt as well as resentment. Could she have averted the tragedy? Should she have stayed with her father? She sat for hours in her bedroom. Holding the red Conway Stewart pen she had picked up from the grass, she went over the scene again and again. Was it somehow her fault? Had she let him down? In bed at night, fear attacked her. What if anything happened to her mother? As she lay in the dark, listening to the moan of the wind above the crash of the waves, she slowly came to the realisation that, although she had lost her father, his spirit would give her strength to go on without him. Even so, in her darkest moments, wrong as she knew it to be, Constance could not stop herself thinking, If only it had been Mummy.

Despite her desolation, Nora Simpson was not the sort of woman to be beaten by a twist of fate. Throughout her life she had been a realist and a coper. In the evenings when Constance was in bed she sat in her husband's favourite chair and contemplated her lot. She never once gave way to despair or sentimentality. She had cried her personal tears before the funeral and that side of her grief was then over. Her job now was to plan the future. She spread out the balance sheet of her life rather as if she were playing Patience. There as no question of marrying again. There was no need to. Nora had no intention of having any more children and she was convinced that she and Constance would be better off alone. It was not that she couldn't contemplate marriage to anyone other than Will. It was merely that she had learned from her life with him that, like many married women, she didn't really *need* a husband. Even Will, she realised, for all his consideration, had subconsciously assumed that she was there solely to support him. 'Dancing attendance' was not one of Nora's expressions but she realised now that he was gone that she had done precisely that. She did not intend to do it again. From now on, her thoughts and efforts would be entirely for her daughter. Nora was determined that the tragedy would impinge as little as possible on Constance's life.

Louise came up for the funeral and stayed on for three weeks to give moral support. The two women quickly fell into a pattern. After supper, Louise would leave Nora to herself until the nine o'clock news and then she would join her for a nightcap. In those days villages like Cramer were silent and empty in the evenings. In the summer the villagers worked in their back gardens; in the winter, they snuggled indoors and closed the shutters against the wind and cold. At any time, very little visiting took place and the women were always alone.

One night, ten days after the funeral, as Louise was thinking of going up to bed, Nora began to talk about Constance and her future.

'I'm determined to make something of her, for poor Will's sake, if nothing else. I don't want her to end up with the sort of empty life I've got to look forward to. I want her to be independent. Able to stand on her own feet. I want her to *be* somebody.'

'I'm sure she will be,' Louise replied, non-committally. It was obvious to her that her niece already had the strength and resolution to ensure that she would make something of her life. 'However,' she continued, 'I think it's too early to think about it yet, Nora. When she gets to the grammar school her bent will come out.'

'Constance is artistic,' Nora replied firmly. 'I intend her to have something to do with the arts. You know, that's what I should have done. Not painting, or anything like that, but *something* creative. It's in my bones, but I've left it too late to do anything about it. I'm determined that Constance won't fall into the same trap.'

'Well,' said Louise gently, 'I'm sure that she'll have her own views when the time comes.'

Nora did not reply. She gazed ahead of her, her mind occupied in speculation.

*

Four months after Will's death, two things happened that helped Constance forget the past. War was declared and, more or less at the same time, her mother, who wished to distance her from the rough and ready children at the village school, arranged for her to have piano lessons.

The local gentry were Sir John and Lady Wardley, who lived at Seaton Cramer Hall, a large and dramatically sombre stately pile set in wooded grounds about two miles inland from Cramer. With them lived Miss Hatherby, Lady Wardley's sister. She had once studied to be a concert pianist and had been a pupil of Paderewski in Dresden in the summer of 1921. She now gave piano lessons, on a strictly limited basis, to suitable children. Her pupils were not entirely decided upon by Miss Hatherby. They were vetted by Lady Wardley, who prided herself on knowing all the Northumbrian families worth knowing. Constance was accepted because Nora was a pillar of the Women's Voluntary Service and worked closely with Lady Wardley in the war effort. Nora found Lady Wardley irritatingly superior but, as her junior in the W.V.S., had to submit to being patronised. The elevation of Constance was her reward.

Miss Hatherby was not like her sister. Although perfectly aware of her status in the county, she was not a snob. She welcomed Constance for her weekly lesson with genuine warmth. Her influence on the girl was soon considerable and Constance looked forward to her visits to the grim and rambling Gothic building. The villagers called it The Mansion and viewed it and its formal garden of still and silent yew trees with awe. Certainly, the house was grim, but Constance found its heavy extravagance rich and romantic. As she cycled up to the ornate porch she always thought of chivalrous knights attending maidens dressed in high, pointed hats and long sweeping gowns.

Whereas the house was darkly masculine in its Victorian confidence, Miss Hatherby's music room was so light and feminine that it seemed quite out of place in the general heaviness and gloom. It was a riot of colour and pattern.

The displays of china and silver-framed photographs and the arrangements of feathers and dried flowers would have made the atmosphere claustrophobic if the immense windows had not let in so much light. Everything in the room seemed to be clothed. Chairs and sofas wore lace antimacassars; tables had heavy fringed cloths that reached to the floor and even the carpets were covered with rugs. But the most enchanting thing in the room for Constance, apart from Miss Hatherby herself, was a large bamboo bird cage placed in the fireplace containing two brightly coloured and raucous cockatoos.

As Constance picked her way heavily across the minefield of the Minuet in G, her faltering efforts were greeted with screams and jeers from the birds who would not be silenced even when Miss Hatherby threw an enormous dust sheet over their cage. Although it was the size of a pantry, they endlessly clung to the bars and clamoured to be let out. At the end of one particularly painful lesson, Miss Hatherby *did* release them and they stalked the room stiffly, pecking at the furniture and flapping their wings, to Constance's great delight.

Her joy changed to alarm when Miss Hatherby said quietly, 'Come and sit down, Constance. I want to talk to you.'

Sensing the seriousness in her voice, Constance perched uneasily on the chair Miss Hatherby had indicated. A nervous lump came to her throat.

'Why do you wish to learn to play the piano, Constance?'

There was a silence. Constance had no idea how to answer. The truth was that she did *not* especially wish to learn. She had started the lessons because her mother had insisted and she now continued them because she loved being with Miss Hatherby.

'I would never discourage enthusiasm, no matter how lacking in talent,' Miss Hatherby continued, 'but, my dear, I'm afraid you have neither.'

The tone was gentle but the words were harsh and Constance wanted to cry. She felt ashamed of being such a failure.

As if she had read her thoughts, Miss Hatherby said, 'There is nothing to be ashamed of. The gift of music grows within. It cannot be grafted on to an alien stem. We mustn't allow your mother's money to be wasted in this way. I shall advise her that the lessons should cease.'

'Oh,' Constance cried. 'But what about . . .' She stopped. She had almost said 'us'.

'My dear Constance, I am not suggesting that you should no longer visit me. I merely propose that the charade of music lessons be terminated.' Trying to make light of it, she added, 'Why, even the birds think it a joke! I shall write to your mother.'

The next few days were agony for Constance, as she waited for the letter to arrive. As she feared, her mother took Miss Hatherby's decision as a social slap in the face and blamed her daughter for wasting an opportunity.

'I'm sick of your lack of co-operation, my girl,' she snapped over the breakfast table. 'How could you let me down like this after all the effort I've made? I can just imagine how that Wardley cow will be crowing. Do you never think about anything but yourself? Don't you imagine I deserve some consideration? You wouldn't dare behave like this if your father were still alive.'

Constance found her shame turning to anger. 'What a horrible thing to say! It isn't my fault. I've tried – I really have – but I don't have any aptitude for the piano! Ask Miss Hatherby. You know how much I've practised. I can't help it!'

She rushed out of the room and into the garden, determined not to return to the house until her mother had apologised.

The Northumbrian weather let her down. It seemed that in no time she was forced indoors by huge raindrops that appeared to have come from nowhere. She slunk in through the French windows, hoping to creep upstairs unseen. As she stepped indoors, she heard her mother's voice. She was in the hall, telephoning. Constance hovered indecisively. Her mother was speaking quietly, urgently, but sufficiently clearly for Constance to hear through the closed drawing-room door.

'But Louise,' she was saying, 'I can't imagine how that old maid up at the hall could have got to know. Who on earth ever talks to Miss Hatherby, for goodness' sake! It will be one of the W.V.S. lot, you mark my words, gossiping with that Wardley bitch. I've told you how they all toady to her. Someone must have seen me getting out of Philip Stacey's car one night.'

There was a pause. Constance tiptoed nearer the door.

'Louise,' her mother burst out in irritation, 'I will not be dictated to by that lot up at the Mansion. I shall have an affair with whoever I like. No, of course Constance has no idea. Give me credit for some discretion.'

Constance tiptoed back to the French windows. Her mind was racing. What was her mother talking about? Why had she mentioned Mr Stacey, the antique dealer in the square in Chollerton?

It was over a year since the war had started and, in that time, it had encroached even on remote Cramer. To Nora's intense annoyance she had been forced to take a lodger who was involved in essential war work. When she had protested to Lord Wardley, who was chief billeting officer for that part of Northumberland, he had referred her to a minion who, in turn, had taken great pleasure in pointing out that she could, if she preferred, have some evacuees from Gateshead but, either way, her spare room could not remain empty when everyone was required to make a war effort. Nora had bowed to the inevitable and accepted Mr Laker, a silent and sad Mancunian who worked as an inspector for the Ministry of Agriculture and Fisheries. Once a week, Mr Laker travelled to Chollerton to fulfil his night duties as an Air Raid Precaution officer. He shared a shift with Philip Stacey, the local antiques dealer, who was exempt on health grounds from active service. The two men had become friends and Philip Stacey frequently visited Cramer.

Constance remembered the many times she had seen her mother and him alone together either in the village street or at home; she had been uneasily aware of their absorption in each other. Only half understanding the significance of it, Constance realised as she stood watching the rain that her mother had a secret, separate life in a grown-up world from which she was excluded. She found it perplexing and wondered how it could have affected her lessons with Miss Hatherby.

The rain began to ease. Constance ran round the side of the house, and walking into the kitchen, slammed the door loudly behind her. As she was drying her hair on the kitchen towel, Nora appeared through the dining-room door.

Constance could not look at her mother. Throwing down the towel, she roughly pushed past her and ran upstairs. Safely in her room, she fell on her bed and began to cry. With a comprehension not entirely formed, she knew what the expression 'having an affair' meant, though the details of what her mother and Mr Stacey actually did together were hazy. Whatever it was, Constance knew it was a betrayal of her father's memory as well as being something of which Miss Hatherby could not approve. Would her mother's actions destroy the only friendship she had left now that her father was dead? She hated Nora for the double betrayal and swore that she would never forgive her. It was the first step in the emotional detachment that would dominate her relations with her mother for the rest of her life. As she lay, tense and isolated in her room, Constance longed for her mother to push open the door and come and talk to her, and tell her that her imaginings were all wrong. She couldn't bring herself to believe what she had overheard. Surely her mother and Aunt Louise would never betray her – and her father's memory – so coldly? Mr Stacey was nobody important, she tried to convince herself. He was only Mr Laker's friend. She was imagining things. Even as the thoughts entered her head, they were dismissed, because she knew that they were false comfort.

So, Constance decided, her friend had banished her because of her mother's behaviour. The letter must have said that she could not go to the Mansion again. Overwhelmed by the injustice of it all, she sat up. Why should she be the victim when she had done nothing wrong? Indignation gave her courage. As her tears dried, she began to understand why her mother had reacted so hysterically to Miss Hatherby's decision. It wasn't because she was angry: it was because she was guilty. This realisation gave Constance the strength she needed. She went into the bathroom and rinsed her face in cold water. Then she went downstairs to find her mother.

Nora was in the kitchen, washing the breakfast dishes. From the noise she made, it was clear that she was still angry but Constance wasn't frightened. She knew that *she* had no reason to feel ashamed. It was her mother who had done wrong. She stood in the kitchen doorway.

Sensing her presence, Nora turned. Her face looked troubled as well as angry.

'Well, my girl, I hope you're satisfied now you've had your little tantrum,' she said. 'If so, perhaps you can tell me what has been going on up at the Hall that has made Miss Hatherby stop your lessons.'

'Can I see the letter, please?' Constance asked.

For a moment she thought her mother would refuse but instead she merely said, 'It's on the hall table.'

The letter was short but perfectly polite. 'Dear Mrs Simpson,' Constance read:

Constance has tried so hard at her pianoforte lessons that I know you will share our disappointment at her lack of progress. After much thought, I have decided that it would be in everyone's interests to terminate the

30

lessons. I am sure that you will understand the reasons
for this.

Yours sincerely,<br>
Mildred Hatherby.

Could Miss Hatherby know of her mother's affair? Constance wondered. The letter did seem strange. After all,
she wasn't *that* bad at playing the piano. Putting the
envelope back on the hall table she went out to the shed
for her bike. In sharp contrast to her mood, the rain had
gone and the clouds were breaking up to reveal a blue
sky. Instead of another row with her mother, she had
decided that she must get to the bottom of things by going
up to the Hall and speaking to Miss Hatherby, and she
pedalled as fast as she could.

Constance was startled by Miss Hatherby's appearance
when she arrived at the Hall. She had never seen her in
the morning and she knew instinctively that she had made
a mistake in arriving without warning. It wasn't that Miss
Hatherby was in a state of undress, had her hair in curlers
or anything obviously embarrassing like that. The silk
shawl she draped over her shoulders winter and summer
was in place; her mother of pearl brooch was at her neck
as it should be and her shoes were shining as immaculately
as ever. But something in her demeanour was not composed to greet the outside world. She frowned with irritation but spoke with her usual friendliness as, walking
round the side of the house, she found Constance prop-
ping up her bike against the porch.

'Constance, my dear. What are you doing here? I didn't
expect you.'

The tone of the last sentence taught Constance a lesson
she never forgot. It was that disapproval could be con-
veyed without anger. She realised that she had imposed
on Miss Hatherby's kindness and she blushed for her lack
of consideration.

'Oh!' she blurted in confusion. 'I'm so sorry. I shouldn't have come but . . . I'm so frightened.'

She began to cry. Miss Hatherby was nonplussed. She had spent a lifetime obeying the rule of her childhood never to give way to her feelings in public, and like many members of her class, could not cope with displays of emotion.

'My dear child, stop!' she cried in agitation. 'You mustn't cry. Good gracious, you're not a baby any more. Come, sit down and tell me what is the cause of this extraordinary behaviour.'

Again, Constance could sense the disapproval. She began to feel foolish but she had to talk to somebody and Miss Hatherby was the only person to whom she could turn.

'Mummy had your letter this morning. She was so angry. Not really with me . . .' she paused and looked up into Miss Hatherby's troubled face '. . . she felt that you had done it because you didn't approve.'

'Approve?' Miss Hatherby asked in bewilderment.

Constance looked down at her feet and, blushing furiously, whispered, 'Of her gentleman friend.'

It was Miss Hatherby's turn to blush. More to give herself time to think than because she wished to know, she said to Constance, 'Perhaps you had better tell me right from the beginning, Constance.'

Only then did Constance realise how little she actually knew. Her voice squeaking with embarrassment, she told her friend what she had overheard her mother telling Louise.

'To eavesdrop is an unpardonable thing, Constance,' Miss Hatherby could not resist saying when she had finished.

Constance was furious. Was that all she could say? Why did everyone want to put her in the wrong when she had done nothing to deserve it? Frustration made her truculent. 'Is that why you've stopped my lessons?' she demanded.

'*We* decided to abandon the piano lessons, Constance,' Miss Hatherby chided, 'as you well recall, because we knew that progress was not being made. Your mother is quite mistaken to assume that there is any other motive except the evident fact that you are not musically endowed. Now,' she said decisively, 'you must go back to your mother and make that clear.'

'But what about me?' Constance cried in despair. 'What will happen to *me*? What about the man?'

Miss Hatherby was appalled. Throughout her life she had so successfully controlled her emotions that she was now capable of responding only to the demands of music. Faced by Constance's distress she felt utterly at sea and didn't know how to help her. She also found it distasteful to be discussing Nora's lover in this way.

'Did you know about him?' Constance almost shouted. 'Does everybody know but me?'

'Constance,' Miss Hatherby reproached her, 'I have no intention of becoming involved in your mother's business. I repeat, you must go back to her. Assure her that you are welcome here always – provided we have made arrangements – and please make her understand that there is no criticism – of anyone – to be inferred from our decision to stop your piano lessons.'

Constance knew that her friend had failed her. She looked across the terrace to the grim yew trees and thought, That's how they all expect me to be – silent and still. Well, I won't. I have as much right to know what's going on as they do.

'Come and see me on Thursday, as usual, my dear,' Miss Hatherby said as they walked back across the terrace. Climbing on her bicycle Constance looked directly at her and repeated the question. 'Did you know about my mother?'

Miss Hatherby looked down and shook her head before stepping into the house.

Constance felt let down but, more, she was overcome with indignant self-pity as she slowly cycled back along the drive that linked the Hall to the main road. The heavy boughs and dark leaves of the copper beech that spread over the drive perfectly suited her mood of despair. Once she had turned the corner and the house was hidden from view, she jumped off her bike and pushed it through the maze of potholes that pitted the drive as it meandered the half mile to the main gates. Just before she reached them she found a felled tree. Sitting down on it, she buried her head in her hands and burst into tears.

She had no idea how long she had been there when a movement in the undergrowth made her look up. At first, her eyes still full of tears, she couldn't make out the figure. Then it moved and a man stepped out in front of her. He was fat and dirty, with cunning eyes deep-set in his face. He was wearing uniform but his battledress jacket was unbuttoned and his tie was loose. Constance found him repulsive and she knew immediately that he was dangerous. She leapt up fearfully and said, 'What do you want? Who are you? This is private land!'

'Calm yourself, lassie,' the man replied, taking a step towards her. Suddenly, before she knew what was happening, he lunged forward and caught her wrist. Pulling her towards him, he snarled, 'I think you need something to cheer you up, lassie.' He pushed her against a tree and began pulling her skirt up over her knees. Constance struggled and tried to free her arms, but the man was too strong for her. She screamed as she felt his fingers pulling at her knickers. Letting go of her hands, the man hit her violently across the face.

'Shut it and keep it shut,' he growled. 'You're going to enjoy this.'

He tried to kiss her, pushing his face into hers. Wild with fear, Constance opened her mouth and bit his nose so hard that it hurt her teeth. The man reared back in pain and his hands went up to his face. For a split second, Constance failed to realise that he had released his grip on her. The realisation came at the same time to both of them. As he grabbed at her again she ducked under his arms and ran towards the gates. He tried to follow her but fell over her bike. As she dashed out into the road, where his camouflaged truck was parked, she was relieved that the only thing pursuing her was his curses.

Constance wanted to run home but she knew that she couldn't leave her bike. Hiding in the hedge a safe distance from the truck, she waited for the man to appear. Eventually he emerged, limping, through the gates. He looked up and down the road, saw nothing, climbed into his truck and drove off.

Constance realised that the soldier was not a local man. She could tell by the insignia of his uniform that he didn't belong to the regiment billeted at the Hall whose tents were visible at the far end of the park when she cycled up to the house. He must have stopped in order to relieve himself and, hearing her sobs in the silence of the wood, decided to investigate. She sat in the hedge for a long time. She felt calm but deeply guilty. Just as she felt ashamed and somehow responsible for the disgrace of her mother's lover so she felt that the man's attack had been her fault. Overcome with remorse, she wanted to die. I'll throw myself in front of the next car that comes, she decided.

Immediately she heard the Chollerton bus trundling towards her. She scrambled up out of the hedge and reached the roadside just as the bus rolled past. Furious, she sat down to wait for the next vehicle. Her mood changed from guilt to defiance. She determined to *show* her mother and Miss Hatherby *and* Aunt Louise. She imagined the remorse and guilt that would haunt them when she was dead. Well, it would serve them right for treating her like a baby. She continued to wait. The air was silent, the road deserted. 'Oh, *please* let something come,' she begged. Not a sound or movement answered her plea. 'It isn't fair.'

Suddenly she heard a car engine in the drive. It came closer, then stopped. She heard doors open. Slowly she walked back towards the gates of the Hall.

35

She stopped in horror at the sound of Lady Wardley's high querulous voice demanding, 'Who could have left it there? Poachers?'

'Can't say, m'lady.' Constance recognised the Wardley chauffeur's voice.

'Well,' Lady Wardley said, 'whoever it belongs to is a trespasser. After you've dropped me, come back and collect the bicycle and take it to the police. Come, or I shall be late.'

Constance scrambled back into the hedge and hid as the Daimler nosed out of the drive and turned into the main road, away from her, towards Alnwick. All thought of suicide had been knocked out of her head. She must get the bike before the car returned. She ran down the drive. The man's foot had broken a few spokes and the chain had come off, but there was no other damage. She pushed the bike out into the road and back to Cramer as quickly as she could.

For days afterwards, she couldn't rid herself of the guilty feeling that, somehow, she had brought the attack upon herself. She felt unclean and unworthy, rather as she hoped that her mother, in her dark moments, must feel about Mr Stacey – and she never told Nora of the incident. In fact, she told nobody until many years later, after her mother's death, when she confided in Louise. Guilt made her try to bury it deep in her subconscious.

Nora never mentioned Philip Stacey but she was certain that Constance had found out and half understood about the liaison. The knowledge caused her genuine distress and, in the face of Constance's increasing truculence, she turned to Louise for counsel.

'It isn't that Constance is naughty, or has tantrums,' she said to her cousin on the telephone, 'it's as if she has just turned her back on me. She is so cool and indifferent, so enclosed and private – when she's not openly defiant, that is. She's built a wall around herself. I don't know what to do.'

'Oh, Nora, darling, do think back,' Louise tried to soothe her. 'You know what we were like at that age. Always in a dream, cut off from the world – and forever being dreadfully wounded over the slightest thing. *Surely* you remember? It's perfectly natural. You're taking it far too seriously.'

'I feel so lonely,' Nora replied, 'so shut out. I can't bear it. She's all I have.'

'Stop worrying; it's only a phase.'

'She thinks more of that old maid up at the Hall than she does of me, her own mother, I can assure you of that.'

'Nonsense, darling,' Louise laughed, but she felt that it might possibly be true.

In fact, it was not. The idolisation of Miss Hatherby that had so annoyed Nora in the early days of the piano lessons had gone. Constance still respected her friend and had a certain detached affection for her. But since her failure to understand and help her over her mother's lover, Constance viewed Miss Hatherby rather as her mother described her: an old maid, unworldly, afraid of emotions and inexperienced in life. She still admired her education and artistic breadth but had come to realise that these were all Miss Hatherby could share with her. And, although she was still eager to learn from her, Constance needed more. Not that it stopped her from gobbling up every cultural titbit dropped before her. She was a willing ally in Miss Hatherby's ambitious project to educate Constance in the things she felt the girl should know. In Miss Hatherby's limited view this meant the arts. The Wardley family collection contained many treasures, including many Pre-Raphaelite paintings, and Miss Hatherby knew them all intimately. She intended to share her knowledge with her young pupil, who, like a sponge, was ready to absorb everything.

Stalking through the dark rooms she would suddenly stop and point to a fireplace – 'William de Morgan, those tiles. Remember the name. Much cleverer man than you would imagine by that livid green' – and then she would sail on, followed by Constance who, because she had rather liked the green, never forgot the name. Miss Hatherby showed Constance the treasures of the house. Together they looked at huge bound tomes which contained drawings by the Wardley ancestors on the Grand Tour – 'Great Uncle Charles, died of pneumonia in Genoa,' she snorted as she closed his sketchbook and picked up a folio of the architecture of Rome, Naples and the Campagna. 'Neopolitan mosquitoes are man-eaters, my dear; you cannot imagine how disagreeable they are.' Together they gazed at the family portraits and Miss Hatherby pointed out the niceties of her forefathers' dress – 'Folk would literally kill for shoe buckles of that quality. Gone. All gone now. God knows where.'

The Wardley family collection contained many treasures and Miss Hatherby knew them all intimately. Constance loved the pictures, but for her the most enchanting thing in the collection was a group of eighteenth century wax dolls dressed in the height of the day's fashion. Miss Hatherby explained in her dry, sibilant voice, that they were sent from Paris so that London ladies could know about the latest French fashions and have them copied. Constance spent hours drawing imaginary clothes for the mannequins and, encouraged by Miss Hatherby and her mother, made them dresses out of scraps of old material Miss Hatherby managed to find tucked away in the corners of Seaton Cramer Hall. Constance could not believe how beautiful they were. Their colours and patterns seemed as fresh as the day they were made and she was amazed at their richness compared with the wartime materials she was used to.

She worked very hard to get everything exactly right and would spend hours in her room sewing, unpicking and re-sewing until she felt that the clothes were perfect. Some of her happiest hours were passed in making these costumes and she found that time flew by – it seemed she had barely started before her mother was calling for her to have her bath and go to bed. Often, unable to bear leaving the dress until the next night, Constance would get up after Nora had closed the door and, placing her dressing gown at its foot so that no light would show, spend another hour or two at the work she loved. Like her mother, Constance was a perfectionist and devoted all her energies and efforts to making something she could show Nora with pride and, more importantly, present to Miss Hatherby with confidence.

Constance loved the days when her friend unpacked the boxes and trunks that contained dresses, shoes and bonnets which were often over a hundred years old. She adored the delicate materials with their strange names that Miss Hatherby always knew; the quaint shapes and the beautiful, faded colours. On one occasion they unearthed a blue taffeta ball dress with small bouquets of pink and cream brocade roses. Miss Hatherby swooped low over it and said, 'The Honourable Edwina Trevelyan! Come!' and, scooping up the dress, carried it through to the winter drawing room. To Constance's delight, there in the corner by the fireplace was a watercolour of a woman wearing the dress, and she was amazed by the similarity between her friend and the woman in the picture – they shared the same strongly determined mouth – even though Miss Hatherby was old and not pretty like the Honourable Miss Trevelyan, whose brown eyes possessed amazing richness and beauty.

For Constance, whose own home was sparsely furnished and contained no pictures apart from framed photographs of her father in a group of students and her parents' wedding photographs, the walls of Seaton Cramer Hall teemed with interest and life. Sir John's father had been a friend of Ruskin and the family collection contained several of his watercolours of Venice. 'All theory, that man,' Miss Hatherby declared. 'His drawing is pedestrian – although his mind was not. But these aren't Venice.

39

They are a cold, northern intellectual's idea of Venice.'
Then she would start to reminisce. On days when Miss
Hatherby felt expansive and inclined to talk, the whole of
Europe, its art and life, were presented to her pupil,
without compromise or condescension. Her reminiscences
were a delight to Constance and the things she learned
from her friend's rambling monologues stayed with her
for life. Constance cycled home from the Hall with her
head in the clouds and her imagination fired with images
conjured up by Miss Hatherby's memories. She could not
wait to rush up to her room to read the latest book her
friend had lent her – which could be anything from *The
Stones of Venice* to *The Prisoner of Zenda*.

Although the Wardley collection contained several huge
religious paintings from the Renaissance, Miss Hatherby
pronounced them 'doubtful'. Its real glory was in mid-
Victorian and Pre-Raphaelite paintings. Constance never
forgot standing in front of one on the main staircase. It
was full of knights, one of whom was dying in the arms
of a fair maiden. As she looked at the vast and busy
canvas, Miss Hatherby sensed she was finding it difficult
to take in and said, 'You know Constance, you cannot
look at a painting with the same eyes as you stare down
Chollerton High Street. Nothing as direct as that. Your
eye must take a painting by surprise. Quarter the canvas
and absorb all the details before putting it together again.'
She smiled fondly. 'That is how to look at pictures. I do
so want you to learn, my dear,' and, turning away, she
half whispered, 'There is so much pleasure, so much
pleasure to be gained by the informed.'

'There's a portrait up at the Hall of a woman wearing a
lovely dress,' Constance told her mother, as they were
both sewing in the drawing room. 'Blue, with roses.'
  'Who is it?' her mother asked.
  'The Honourable Miss Trevelyan. The family live near
Hexham somewhere and they have connections going back

to the early nineteenth century,' Constance said, quoting Miss Hatherby almost verbatim. 'It must be nice to have pictures of your family going back for years. All we've got is Daddy when he was a medical student – and your wedding pictures.'

'We never had the money for such things,' Nora replied. There was a sharpness in her tone that made Constance look up. 'There's no need to get angry,' she said, 'I'm only saying.'

'I've half a mind to stop her going up there,' Nora told Louise. 'Filling her head with such nonsense. She's beginning to think herself far too grand for us. The Honourable Miss Trevelyan! When they were swanning around looking pretty, our families were working their fingers to the bone for virtually nothing and now Miss High-and-Mighty thinks we should admire them. Poor Will would turn in his grave! Anyhow, I think that Hatherby woman has far too much influence on Constance.'

'Oh, come, darling,' Louise replied, taken aback by the injustice of Nora's remark. 'She has been *marvellous* for Constance. Think of how much she's taught her. She's given her a cultural background for life. That's a priceless gift. *Do* be fair.'

'She's turned her into a proper little snob!' Nora retorted. 'You don't understand how Constance has cut herself off from all her friends. She lives in her own world and is very secretive. I don't get to know half of what's going on. I know it sounds silly but I think Miss Hatherby is too interested in Constance. What can a woman of her age want with a young girl?'

Louise would have none of it. She was much more worldly than Nora and, having met Miss Hatherby, dismissed the slur out of hand.

'Nora, darling!' she laughed. 'You're becoming utterly ridiculous. Miss H. is no more a lesbian than you are, so stop being silly and just thank your lucky stars that she's teaching Constance so much.'

41

Nora felt ashamed. 'I just wish Constance would be more open. You've no idea how secretive she is. I don't like it. And,' she added, determined to have the last word, 'she *is* becoming far too toffee-nosed.'

Louise was right about Miss Hatherby. She was not a lesbian and it was Constance's mind that she wished to possess, not her body. Despite her remark, Nora knew this perfectly well and was determined not to allow it to happen. She lost no opportunity to diminish Miss Hatherby in her daughter's eyes and was always ready to ridicule her.

'Miss Hatherby! What on earth does she know about real life?' she would demand when Constance had quoted something her friend had said.

'I don't wish to criticise your friend but, when all is said and done, what does a half-mad old maid know about anything? I'm not blaming her, it isn't her fault, locked away up there, miles from anywhere but, I ask you, Constance, what can she possibly know about the realities of life in 1945? She's living in the past, poor dear.'

Through Miss Hatherby's dolls and pictures, Constance became increasingly interested in her own clothes – and had rows over them with her mother that often reverberated for days. Nora tried her best to get round the wartime restrictions so that Constance could be well dressed. In order to do so, she had no hesitation in breaking the law and regularly bought clothing coupons from the village women to supplement the meagre amount allocated to her and Constance by the Board of Trade. She spent hours unpicking her pre-war frocks in order to remake them for her daughter. She knew exactly how Constance should be dressed. Whatever she made was done to suit her taste. Constance was never consulted.

Coming back early from school one afternoon, she passed the dining-room window and saw her mother cutting something out on the table. She put her bike away and sauntered into the room. Nora was deep in concentration and the sudden appearance of her daughter startled her.

'What on earth are you doing home at this time?' she demanded.

'What are *you* doing?' Constance asked, looking with distaste at the pale green material on the table.

'Well,' Nora replied angrily, 'I was trying to give you a little surprise but you've spoiled that now.'

'Was that it?' Constance asked, fingering the fabric. 'More a shock than a surprise. If you think I'd be seen dead in that you must be mad. I'd rather walk down the road naked than put that thing on.'

'What on earth do you mean?' Nora asked in bewilderment.

Pulling it from the table and scattering pins across the floor, Constance held up the half-finished garment.

'Mummy!' she cried. 'It's a monstrosity! Surely you can see that! Not even Miss Hatherby would wear it! Where on earth did you get that material?'

'It was one of your father's *favourites*. You can't get material like this any more. I cannot believe that I've cut up the dress he used to love me to wear and all I get for thanks is cheek. You're becoming utterly spoiled by that wretched woman. Who do you think you are?'

'Somebody who has *some* taste at least,' Constance replied.

'Don't you speak to me in that way,' Nora retorted, 'or I'll box your ears, you ungrateful girl!' and they were into yet another quarrel.

It rumbled on for the rest of the week. Constance knew she had been insensitive, and was aware of how much she had hurt her mother. She even felt that, by her outburst, she had somehow insulted her father's memory. She wanted to make amends but didn't know how to. In desperation, she secretly telephoned Louise, something she had never done before.

'Aunt Louise,' she said, 'you understand, don't you? It isn't anything against Mummy. It's just that I don't have

43

the same taste as she does and she *always* wants me to have what she wants. I have fashion sense as well, you know. I'm sixteen. Don't you think it's time I was allowed to decide what I want to wear for myself?'

'Of course, darling, but you must be fair. You know how difficult it is to get your hands on *anything* these days – and your mother tries so hard to make you look nice. I always thought that green a very pretty colour. It suited your mother marvellously.'

'But that doesn't mean that it suits *me*, Aunt Louise. That's the whole problem. Mummy always thinks she knows best. And she doesn't – at least not for me. I have my own ideas but she won't listen.'

'She will, my dear, I *promise*, but you must give her a chance. Things haven't been easy for Nora since your father died.' Guilt swept over Constance but she felt like saying 'nor for me', as Louise went on, 'Just for me, darling, say you're sorry to your mother and then I'll sort something out. I promise. *Please!* There's a good girl.'

So Constance did. The dress was put in a drawer, unfinished but not forgotten about. It marked a vital staging post on Constance's path to independence and made clear to Nora that she was no longer dealing with a child. Her daughter was eagerly moving towards womanhood and would not be stopped.

It was inevitable that when Miss Hatherby introduced Constance to the Romantic poets she should fall heavily under the spell of Shelley and Keats. Unwisely, she repeated to her mother a remark Miss Hatherby had made about Keats in love.

'Love!' Nora exploded. 'I've never heard anything so ridiculous! A dried-up old spinster like that talking of love! I don't know which is worse – her drivel or you being daft enough to listen to it! Wait till you've had some experience before you start talking about love to a silly old virgin, that's my advice, my girl.'

'How do you know I haven't?' Constance replied provocatively.

'What do you mean?' Nora asked.

Enjoying the alarm in her mother's eyes, Constance replied, 'Nothing,' and left the room.

Nora could not allow it to end there. After supper when they were both knitting by the fire, she asked, 'Have you met a boy?'

Constance remained silent.

'If you're seeing somebody don't you think that, as your mother, I should know?'

'Just like you tell me all of your business,' Constance replied without looking up.

Sensing danger, Nora proceeded with caution. 'There is a difference,' she said. 'I'm an adult and you are a child. I am responsible for you, that's why I need to know what's going on.'

'I'll soon be seventeen.'

'Precisely. *Soon* be. That's why I want no secrets.'

'You keep things from me.'

'That is quite different.'

'All these little pieces of china we're getting. I know where they come from, you know. That shop in Chollerton.'

'Good heavens above,' Nora blustered. 'Can't I buy a few little pieces from Mr Stacey without asking your permission first?'

'Or are they presents for services rendered?' Constance asked, using an expression she had read in one of her mother's library books.

Nora instantly sprang from her chair and, before Constance could move, hit her hard across the face.

'How dare you speak to me like that?' she cried. 'You filthy-minded creature!'

The force of the blow almost lifted Constance out of her chair. She cowered in terror as Nora, beside herself with rage, raised her knitting needle. She brought the point down so hard it pierced Constance's shoulder.

45

Screaming, 'How dare you? How dare you speak to your mother like that?' she jabbed repeatedly until the sight of blood seeping through Constance's blouse stopped her short. Her eyes dilated with horror at what she had done. She embraced her sobbing daughter and clung to her in desperate shame.

'Your world is too enclosed, darling. It isn't natural, just the two of you up there alone,' Louise soothed Nora. 'She's almost a woman. You know how difficult it is for two women to live together, especially if they're mother and daughter. Poor Constance goes to a girls' school, comes home to her mother and visits a middle-aged woman about twice a week. And that's her life. The only man she ever sees is the wretched Mr Laker, to say "good morning" to. No wonder she's getting difficult.'

Nora wanted to say, 'It isn't her. It's me. I am so jealous and protective of her,' but, close as she was to Louise, she couldn't bring herself to admit what she saw as the black depths of her failure with her daughter.

Nora viewed her daughter's education at the Hall with ambivalence. Part of her was proud and delighted that Constance was learning so much but another, darker side was clouded by jealousy. Now the war was over she seriously thought that the answer might be to move from Cramer altogether. She toyed with the idea of Yorkshire or even further south but was persuaded by Louise that it would be a mistake to make Constance change schools at that point, just before her School Certificate examination. Also, she did not wish to leave Philip Stacey, so the idea came to nothing. Nevertheless, she continued to resent Miss Hatherby's influence as much as she feared it. She felt control of her daughter slipping from her.

'Miss Hatherby says that she can write to the principal of her college when I'm in the sixth form and see if they can give me a place,' Constance said casually when they were sitting on the lawn one afternoon.

'Really?' was the cold reply. 'Is that what you want?

To go to university? I can't see you being happy ending up like her, a frustrated old academic, reacting to other people's creativity. I thought you wanted to be a *real* person, creating, not criticising.'

Her daughter's reply stunned Nora. 'You have a very limited idea of creativity if you imagine that critics aren't real people. Think of Hazlitt.'

Nora realised how much ground she had lost to the attitudes of the Hall. She found the sheer sophistication of Constance's answer staggering, but managed to make a joke of it to Louise.

'My dear,' she laughed, 'talk about out of the mouths of babes and sucklings! I don't even know who Hazlitt *is*, let alone what he does! It's quite obvious I must cancel the *Express* and start taking *The Times*. Isn't it just coming to something when one has to try to keep up with one's daughter?'

Although the war had been over almost two years when Constance celebrated her eighteenth birthday in 1947, life was by no means back to normal. There were still restrictions on virtually every commodity and everything was in short supply – when it was available at all. Nora had wanted to take Constance down to Louise in Surrey for her birthday so that it could be a family celebration but she decided to wait until the start of the summer holidays in order that they might spend several weeks there. It seemed to her that the long war had been a form of imprisonment for the spirit as well as the body. Not only had travel been impossible, it felt like ages since she had seen any beautiful clothes or touched any rich materials. She knew that she and Constance both needed a real break in their routine. She was also determined to spend as much time in dress shops as she possibly could! She had made up her mind that her delayed birthday present to her daughter was to be a proper, shop-bought frock. She had been amassing clothing coupons for the last six months and was determined that Constance would have a magnificent dress from one of the London stores.

The last time Constance had visited London was in 1938. She and her parents had spent four unforgettable days seeing the Tower of London, the British Museum and as much as her father could pack in without exhausting her. Young as she was, everything had stayed in her memory – the sights, sounds and smells of the city. She was so excited to be returning that she was up before dawn and ready for the journey south long before the arrival of the taxi that was to take them to Berwick for the train to King's Cross. The journey was slow and subject to inexplicable stops in mid-country; although the war in Europe was over, the carriages were still full of men in uniform; there were long queues for the tea trolleys at York and Grantham but Constance arrived in London that evening with her excitement undimmed. The Underground took them to Waterloo and another train carried them to Woking where they were met by Louise's husband, Jim.

'You poor darlings! You must be *exhausted*!' Louise cried as Constance and Nora staggered into the hall with their heavy cases. Suddenly, Constance realised that she actually was very tired – but not too tired to notice with pleasure the warm wood panelling, the Turkey-red stair carpet and the clean smell of polish which all added up to an atmosphere of richness and opulence quite foreign to her mother's sparse house in Northumberland.

She loved her little bedroom. It had a painted chest of drawers and tiny wardrobe and she fell asleep enjoying their shapes in the fading light. When she woke the next morning, she found them even more entrancing. The house was silent and she had no idea of the time but, as it was light, she got up, dressed and went downstairs.

She slipped out into the garden. Like the house, it was neat, friendly and immaculately kept. Tall fir trees grew at the bottom by the boundary fence, casting long early-morning shadows across the lawn and the laurel hedges which enclosed it. As she walked down the crazy-pavement paths to the lily pond, Constance was struck by the blackbirds hopping around in the sun. They seemed so much less menacing than the crows that pecked and fought in the newly harvested fields at home.

From that first morning, Constance felt happy in the south. She loved its warmth and was amazed at its lack of wind. She was delighted with the high trees, privet and rhododendrons that protected and sheltered the houses. She sniffed with pleasure the fresh, clinical smell of the Scots pines and the newly creosoted palings. Surrey was the first landscape she had experienced that could be called feminine. Its softly rounded and gently coloured contours, dotted with lush trees and russet houses, set comfortably into the landscape like plump and cosy chickens, were in strong contrast to coastal Northumberland which so often looked scoured and rough. Many years later Constance changed her view of the southern landscape. For her it became a cloying and pallid countryside, tamed and weakened by man's attempts to prettify nature but, in 1947, she thought it the pleasantest spot in the world and she was delighted to be there.

After only a brief time in this balmy atmosphere, Constance knew that she must stay. Going to the local shops with her aunt one afternoon, she broached the subject that had been on her mind for days. 'I love it down here. I don't want to go back to the north. Please, Aunt Louise, you must help me. Can you talk to Mummy for me?'

'But what do you want to do with your life, my darling? You must have some sort of a career. Have you thought of nursing?'

'Oh, Aunt Louise! I couldn't bear it!'

'There's nothing wrong with nursing, Constance,' Louise replied sharply as they walked into the butcher's. 'Think of where we would have been without nurses during the war.'

'I know, but I must do something more creative. I want to create beautiful things – and I know I could.'

'Of *course* you could, my sweet,' Louise replied. A plan was forming in her head but she was not prepared to make it public yet.

# CHAPTER 3

'But darling, she's only just eighteen,' Nora said to Louise, 'and she's not trained for anything. Who would employ her and how would she hold down a job? It's awfully generous of you to offer to have her, but I don't want her hanging around, getting under your feet all day.'

'I think you're being far too pessimistic,' her cousin replied firmly. 'Can't you see, my dear? She's ready. She must be allowed to spread her wings and open up. She needs to meet sophisticated young people.'

Afraid that she might have hurt Nora, who was sitting very quietly, Louise added, 'Of course, she'll miss you but I do think she could stay on for a *little* longer, to see what might happen.'

Louise had secretly appointed herself champion and orchestrator of Constance's half-articulated hopes for the future. Much as she loved Nora, she was sufficiently realistic about her cousin to know that whatever was beginning to develop in her niece would be much more likely to come to something if Constance remained with her in Surrey than if she returned to the north. 'They'll get on each other's nerves,' she said to herself, 'they'll do nothing but fight. I'm determined that Constance will be given a chance.' Subtle pressure prevailed. Nora agreed that Constance could stay in Surrey for another month.

Her agreement was not only a reflection of Louise's powers of persuasion. It was an acknowledgement of the need for both mother and daughter to have a breathing space. The tension and frustration that had built up in the claustrophobic atmosphere of their life in Northumberland had finally spilt over when Louise had taken them both to the West End to buy the birthday dress. Nora had insisted that they 'do' every shop in Oxford Street, starting at Marble Arch, but they had only reached Selfridges when the impracticality of the scheme became obvious. There simply wasn't enough stock in the shops to give them any real choice. Nora had been harbouring dreams of pre-war munificence, and she was bitterly disappointed – as became increasingly apparent in her short-tempered exchanges with Constance.

'I'm afraid stocks are still pathetically low,' Louise said as they looked at the half dozen dresses that were the only ones the assistant had in Constance's size.

'You can say that again!' Nora retorted.

'They're all horrible in any case,' Constance murmured, disappointment making her sulky.

'What on earth do you mean?' asked her mother aggressively, picking up the nearest dress to hand. 'What's wrong with this, I'd like to know!'

She tried to hold it up against Constance who pulled away and said loudly, 'Yellow! Mummy, you must be mad if you think I would be seen dead in a yellow frock! I'd be a laughing stock!'

Looking around, anxious in case the assistant had heard, Nora retorted, 'Don't you take that tone with me, young lady. How dare you speak to me like that in public!'

'Don't worry!' Louise said lightly, 'the day is yet young! We've plenty of places to go to yet. Why don't we abandon the original plan and go straight to Debenham and Freebody, as we're so close. They've usually got a very good selection.' Sounding much more confident than she felt, she led mother and daughter from the store.

Louise kept up a flow of bright chatter as they set off for Wigmore Street. She did not dare stop talking because she knew that Constance wasn't speaking to her mother and that Nora would be unable to resist goading her

daughter with a volley of questions. Louise realised that
Nora wanted a fight in order to clear her growing frustration – and she was determined not to give her the
opportunity.

Things began much more successfully at Debenham
and Freebody. The range was wider, as Louise had predicted, although Nora pointed out that the clothes were
much 'pricier' than elsewhere. Nora chose a blue cotton
dress with lots of tiny buttons covered in maroon imitation
silk. Constance tried it on.

'Now, you really look very nice in that!' Nora said,
beaming with self-vindication. 'You'll get years of wear
out of it.'

'It's boring,' Constance said flatly. 'Can I try that one,
please?' She pointed to a black and white print dress that
the assistant had brought in whilst she was changing into
the blue.

'Far too grown-up,' Nora said crossly. '*And* too dramatic. You'd be bored with it in no time – and so would
everybody else. Chollerton is a very small town,
remember.'

'I'm not going to be spending the rest of my life in
Chollerton, Mummy,' Constance replied.

'And you're not having this dress,' Nora said, bending
down to look at the price tag. 'It's two and a half guineas!'
she hissed at Louise, who could tell that she was genuinely
appalled.

'Then I won't bother with anything,' Constance said.
'Come on, Aunt Louise, we're wasting our time here.'

As she turned back to the changing room, Nora caught
her arm. 'Listen to me, young lady,' she said under her
breath, 'I'm not putting up with any tantrums. That dress
is too old for you, and *that* is *that*.'

'All right,' Constance replied, breaking from her
mother's grip. 'You and Aunt Louise decide! Don't bother
to ask me! I only have to wear the damned thing!' Bursting
into tears, she rushed into the changing room.

53

Nora was mortified. She could not believe that her daughter would let her down by swearing in public.

'Wait!' Louise said, restraining her cousin and following Constance into the changing room.

'Darling!' she said, over Constance's sobs, 'Don't get upset. Mummy's right. It *is* too dramatic. There's nothing wrong with your taste. It's a stunning dress but it's meant for a woman with lots of clothes to ring the changes. Honestly, you *would* soon be bored to tears with it.'

'Oh, Aunt Louise, it's always the same. She always thinks that she knows best. I'm the one who has to wear it. What's the point of buying a dress that I don't like, just to please Mummy?'

'None whatsoever,' Louise said cheerfully, 'and that certainly is not what your mother wants. Of *course* we'll find one that you like – that we *all* like. Now, dry your face and we'll go down Regent Street. Swan and Edgar are sure to have something.'

And, to everyone's relief, they did. Louise picked out a pretty little pink dress that nobody could possibly take exception to and so honour was satisfied. But it was a tense trio that made its way back to Surrey.

When Constance had gone to bed that night, Louise made her suggestion that Nora leave the girl behind for a while longer. She knew that Nora was sufficiently demoralised to take the idea seriously and agree with little fuss.

Over breakfast on the day following Nora's departure, Louise tried to encourage her niece. 'So, my darling,' she said, 'the big adventure beginneth! We have one month to prove to your mother that you are a grown up. How shall we do it?'

Constance went pink – with pleasure and uncertainty. 'Do you think that she'll let me stay for good? It would be so marvellous if she would.'

'Well,' Louise replied, 'You know your mother as well as I do. She certainly won't be happy if she thinks you're just hanging around down here and not getting anywhere. That's why we *must* have a plan.' She waited expectantly. Constance blushed even harder as the silence grew.

'Your mother has always wanted you to do what *you* want but she will insist that you can only stay here if you have a job. Any job would do, to begin with. What about working in a shop? You know, a shoe shop in Richmond or something like that.'

'I wouldn't mind a dress shop but I don't think it would be very nice to help people try on shoes all day.'

'No, you're probably right. A *hat* shop would be fun.'

'Oh! Aunt Louise! What a super idea! That would be lovely!'

'Wouldn't it. We'll just have to wait and see.'

Louise had her clothes made for her: not by one of the grand West End couturiers such as Hartnell or Lachasse, whose prices were far beyond her, but by Paul de Levantière, a Belgian who, because his salon was in unfashionable Chelsea, charged much less. He had been her dressmaker since the early thirties and they knew each other very well. He allowed her more freedom of choice than many of his clients who were perhaps a better advertisement for his dressmaking skills. Although he always sent her out with new clothes that should have made her embody his idea of elegance, he was resigned to the fact that she would return in a version far removed from his original concept. Louise was, in fact, that curse of the couturier, a woman with a mind of her own and a strongly individual fashion intelligence.

Plump, bespectacled and usually shining with perspiration, Paul de Levantière would try very hard to be the Grand Couturier with Louise in the fitting room – but he was a gentle man and her firm independence always routed him.

'Madam Carter will, of course, require grey gloves with this suit,' he would purr, using his very best couturier's tone. It was to no avail.

'Oh, I should not imagine so, Monsieur Paul,' Louise would say lightly, conscious of the devastation she was about to cause. 'I absolutely *loathe* grey gloves, as you well know by now! They are the height of vulgarity. How could you suggest such a thing? Do you want to ruin your beautiful suit? No, I shall wear brown. That's what this needs.' And Paul de Levantière would sigh, turn with a resigned expression to his fitter and ask for the next outfit to be tried on.

Paul de Levantière adored Louise, as she well knew. He loved her humour and the fact that she treated him as an equal, although their business was always conducted on the most formal lines. He was prepared to forgive – and grant favours.

Shortly after Norah's departure, Louise was fitted for her autumn suits. She was excited because this was the first time that de Levantière had followed the New Look that was capturing the world but was still hard to come by in England because of clothes rationing. Louise loved the huge sweeping skirts and tightly cinched waists.

'Oh!' she cried as she twirled around in front of the mirror. 'It is just *so* romantic – like before the war! I feel like an Edwardian princess or something! I can't tell you how feminine this line makes me feel!'

De Levantière beamed with pleasure. He loved working with a woman who understood clothes. He was even happy to agree when Louise suggested that the buttons on the jacket were not quite right. As he repositioned the pins, she suddenly decided to take the opportunity to mention Constance and her plans for her.

'I have this niece,' she said, 'who should have a job. She's very creative. Do you know any milliners who might need a sales assistant? She's tall and has a good figure. Her manner is a little diffident as yet, but she'll soon come out of her shell with the right encouragement. The money is not so important. It's the experience she needs.'

Paul de Levantière continued to pin in silence. He had

heard this request a thousand times. 'How old is she?' he asked.

'Eighteen.'

'Could you imagine her working here?'

'Here?'

'Yes, I am looking for a receptionist. You know, somebody to answer the phone and post letters.'

Louise was overjoyed with the suggestion. 'I think she would love to work here, my dear Monsieur de Levantière – absolutely *love* it!'

He beamed and wiped his brow with a large white handerkerchief. 'Why not bring her to next week's fashion show and introduce her to me?' he suggested.

The salon was small and exceedingly hot. The air was heavy with perfume and the little gold chairs were jammed tightly together in an attempt to seat everyone. Constance thought the audience the most elegant crowd of people she had ever seen. Mainly middle-aged women with their daughters, they all wore hats and gloves; everyone seemed to know everyone else and the chattering and laughter only subsided into an expectant hush after the chief vendeuse had discreetly clapped her hands twice. The gold satin curtain at the end of the cat walk parted and out stepped Paul de Levantière. Smiling at the round of applause from his audience, he took his seat on the front chaise longue and the show began.

Constance leaned forward eagerly.

'Model number one,' the vendeuse said, as a mannequin appeared in a slate grey tweed suit, ' "The Pennines", an informal suit equally at ease for drinks at Claridges or walks in the hills.'

There was a scattering of ragged applause as the model walked slowly through the audience, pausing to undo her jacket. 'The blouse in pink crepe de chine is fastened by three mother-of-pearl buttons at the neck.'

And so it continued. Constance was in seventh heaven. The dresses, the hats, the model girls – everything appeared perfect to her. It seemed no time at all until the last model, wearing a mauve duchesse evening dress called 'Tour d'Eiffel', had swished back through the gold curtain and Paul de Levantière was standing to acknowledge the enthusiastic applause.

'Did you enjoy it, darling?' asked Louise.

'It was *wonderful*!' Constance replied, her eyes shining with excitement.

As she looked at her niece's radiant face, Louise felt sure that she had been right to approach Monsieur de Levantière.

Three days later Constance was back in the salon with Louise, gazing in amazement at the transformation. The elegant chairs and sofas had gone; there was not a flower to be seen and, where the gold curtain had been, there was a very ordinary and rather battered door, through which they were taken to Paul de Levantière's tiny, chaotic office.

An agreement was quickly reached. Constance would work for de Levantière answering the telephone, opening the mail and doing any other chores that arose. Constance was so thrilled at the idea of working in such a glamorous world that she would have agreed to anything in order to have the job. She bubbled with excitement on the train down to Surrey.

'Oh, Aunt Louise, you are marvellous! I can't wait to start on Monday! Mr Levantière really seemed to like me. He's so nice, I know I'm going to love working there.'

'Darling, you'll do marvellously. I know that he took to you and I'm sure you'll learn an awful lot – and you'll meet such interesting people!' replied Louise, equally thrilled.

Constance was worried about her clothes, but Louise took her on a very practical shopping spree and they bought two simple skirts and three blouses.

'You can ring the changes but always look business-like,' she said brightly.

Although Constance soon learned that life in a couture house was more about hard work than glamour, she loved Maison de Levantière. A more sophisticated girl would have realised that her enthusiasm was being ruthlessly exploited as the tasks she was given became broader and more demanding, but Constance happily did everything she was told. Monsieur de Levantière smiled benignly, thrilled at the unique combination of willingness, reliability and intelligence that became increasingly apparent in his protégé.

Constance had been there just under three weeks when she was called into the fitting room by the vendeuse. The house model had gone home feeling sick and there were customer appointments. Constance would have to show a couple of dresses. She almost fainted with shock, but had already learned that the edicts of the couturier (one of the last true autocrats of the Western world) were not to be questioned. With a sinking feeling, she went to the dressing room to get ready.

'There's nothing to it. Honest, lovey,' the dresser said as she helped Constance into the first dress. 'Just look straight ahead and smile. Then turn around and show the back and that's it. A kid of ten could do it.' She stood back and gave Constance an appraising look.

'There,' she said approvingly, 'You look smashing.'

And so it happened. Constance stepped out wearing her first dress, called 'Charming Surprise', a name she never forgot. Walking forward, face scarlet, legs turned to jelly and arms stiff and awkward, she felt like a marionette, but by the time she had shown the third model, 'Wicked Lady', she had begun almost to enjoy herself.

'I don't know how I managed it,' Constance told Louise that night, excited and proud of her achievement. 'It was terrible! They were all sitting there staring at me and Monsieur de Levantière said, 'This is Constance, who has kindly stepped in at the last moment.' I thought I would *die* at the start but, actually, once I got into the swing of it all it was rather fun.'

The following day, she was called into Monsieur de Levantière's office. He beamed with pleasure as she walked in.

'Ah,' he said, 'The saviour of the House! Sit down, my dear, I'd like to have a little chat with you. I noticed how well you did yesterday.' Constance blushed with pleasure.

'It was not only that you looked so well in the clothes. It was the way you showed them. With intelligence. Almost as if you understood what was in my mind when I designed them.' Paul de Levantière rubbed his pencil up the side of his nose in a thoughtful gesture. 'Do you like clothes?' he asked.

'Oh, yes!' Constance replied eagerly.

'Well, liking clothes is not enough. Any foolish young woman can like clothes. You have to teach yourself to understand them. You have a great opportunity here, my dear, if you care to take it. Learn to observe. Train your eyes not merely to look but also to see. Notice our customers. Some of the most elegant women in London come through these doors. Understand how they dress. Taste is inborn, little can be learned without it, but everything can be developed if you have it *and* the discipline to train your eye. That is all I need to tell you.' As Constance walked to the door, he added, 'Thank you for yesterday. Tell your aunt that I am very pleased with you.' Constance could have wept with happiness.

Every Wednesday Louise played bridge with a group of women friends. Her turn to act as hostess came up a month after Nora had returned to Northumberland. Constance helped by serving tea and passing sandwiches and cakes. She was in the kitchen washing up when she heard a car coming up the drive. To her surprise, a red M.G. swung to a halt below the open kitchen window. The driver gracefully unwound himself from the low-slung vehicle and stood up, stretching his back, unaware that he was being watched. He was tall and thin but his most striking feature was his long, softly curling brown hair.

Although he was wearing an old check shirt and dirty cricket flannels that stopped above his ankles, Constance thought him the most elegantly handsome man she had ever seen. He had a superior air of self-confidence that reminded her of portraits of eighteenth-century land owners striding their acres surrounded by dogs. Suddenly becoming aware of her gaze, the object of her speculations stopped in mid stretch and moved languidly to the window.

'Hello' he said. 'You're new. Do you work here?'

'No, I do not,' Constance blushed with indignation. 'I'm Mrs Carter's niece. Who are you?'

'Oh,' he said, wearily, 'I've come to collect my mother. Are they in the drawing room? I'll go round to the front.' And he walked away. Constance was stunned by his arrogance.

'Cheek!' she said, in a voice she hoped was loud enough to be heard. Less than a minute later noise erupted from the drawing room and excited voices drifted down the hall. Laughing and chattering, Louise walked into the kitchen, holding the young man by the hand.

'Constance!' she cried. 'This is someone I've been longing for you to meet. Nicky is Mrs Scott Wilson's son. I've known him since he was a little boy. He's very naughty and breaks everyone's heart – don't you darling – but we all love him.' She turned, eyes flashing flirtatiously and pushed back his hair from his forehead. 'When he's cleaned up a bit, he can look quite presentable,' she laughed.

Constance stood awkwardly by the sink. Her aunt's antics embarrassed her and she could feel herself blushing.

'We're just finishing a rubber, Nicky, my sweet, we won't be long,' Louise said. 'Constance, you'll look after Nicky, won't you? A cup of tea perhaps?' And she was gone.

There was a silence. Constance could think of nothing to say. She could almost *feel* her head emptying of thoughts. It seemed that she stood there for an age before Nicky said, 'A cup of tea *would* be rather nice.'

As she made the tea, he stood by the window, gazing across the garden, conscious of her resentment.

'I'm surprised I haven't heard about you on the grapevine. How long have you been here?'

'Three weeks.'

'God! I *am* slipping! How long are you staying?'

'I don't know. It hasn't been decided yet.'

'Whose decision? Yours or Louise's?' Constance was so appalled at his forwardness that she burst out, 'Don't be cheeky! Asking personal questions! Who do you think you are?'

To her fury, he laughed and said, 'You'll do.'

Standing by the sink, slurping his tea and nibbling a slice of fruit cake, Nicky Scott Wilson continued his questions. Although flattered by his interest, Constance was not overwhelmed. By the time Louise returned to the kitchen to tell him that his mother was ready to go home Constance felt that he knew absolutely everything about her, but had revealed nothing of himself.

'Nicky's such a sweetie, don't you think?' Louise said, as they were re-arranging the drawing room when everyone had gone. 'He always reminds me of those marvellous cavaliers, with all that hair.'

'Or a King Charles Spaniel,' muttered Constance, puffing as she pushed the sofa against the wall.

Louise stopped, crestfallen. 'Oh, didn't you like him, darling? I felt sure that he would be absolutely your cup of tea. After all, he is quite the most handsome young man in Surrey.'

'Yes,' Constance agreed, 'I'm sure he thinks so, too.'

From the beginning, Constance felt ambivalent about Nicky Scott Wilson. She found him physically attractive, but his languid, elegant and mannered demeanour irritated her. It made him seem weak to her robust northern eyes. Despite his charm and looks, she was determined not to fall all over him because she sensed immediately that that was what he expected. Their relationship was characterized by a battle of wills that Constancé always made sure to win. Nicky approached her with the assumption that men are naturally right and it is the role of women to follow their lead. Constance, whose confidence was growing daily, was not prepared to give in to Nicky's wishes merely because of his sex. If she felt he was right, then she agreed with him. If, as happened more frequently, she did not, she let her view be known, even though it almost always led to a quarrel.

Nicky was assured – even worldly – and, in the early stages of their friendship, used his confidence to put Constance in her place – not because of any particular need to bully her but merely because that was how he had always treated his girlfriends. He assumed that he could come and go as he wanted, without worrying over-much about their opinions or needs. He worked at Sotheby's and, as Louise gushingly pointed out to Constance after their first meeting, 'He knows absolutely *everybody*, darling. His mother tells me he is out every night at some 'do' or other. He's always in great demand.'

'Well, I don't suppose he'll want to bother with *me* then,' Constance replied. But she did not believe it. She knew that she had made an impression on Nicky, simply by the way he had looked at her when he and his mother had said goodbye. Although she had not been prepared for his barrage of questions and had answered them almost truculently, she had made Nicky think twice about her simply because she seemed more direct and independent than most of the girls he knew. To say that he viewed her as a challenge would be absurd – Nicky Scott Wilson and his type were far too assured to think of life in terms of challenges. But he did find her sufficiently different to wish he knew her better.

Nevertheless, it was over a week before he contacted Constance. Even Louise, who had begun by confidently predicting how well he and Constance would get on, had stopped referring to him. Constance found Nicky more attractive as the days passed with no word from or of him. Then, one afternoon, she stepped out of the side entrance of Maison Levantière to find Nicky standing in the rain, waiting for her.

'Oh! Hello,' she said in surprise.

'I thought you might fancy a drink,' he said, without preamble.

'You must be mad,' Constance replied. 'I've just come from work. My aunt's expecting me. Anyhow, I'm under-age. I'm not allowed in pubs.'

'Oh, I know a private club,' Nicky replied airily. 'There isn't any problem.'

'That's what you think,' Constance said, starting to walk up the street. 'I'm on my way home. I wouldn't dream of being late for Aunt Louise.'

'A cup of tea?' Nicky said, catching up with her. She stopped and faced him.

'Are you joking? You pop up out of the blue and expect me to drop everything, just like that. I'm sorry, Nicky Scott Wilson, but if you want to see me you'd better make proper arrangements.'

'By appointment only? Like the Queen?' Nicky asked, with heavy irony.

'Yes, if you like,' Constance replied sharply. 'I'm not a push-over you know. Even if your other girl friends are.'

Nicky burst out laughing. 'You northern girls,' he said. 'Talk about blunt! I like it!'

'Look,' Constance said crossly, 'I'm not standing around getting soaked to the skin, talking to you. I *must* go or I'll miss my train.' Nicky caught her wrist.

'When can I see you? I really want to.'

'Oh, well . . . ' Constance was at a loss. 'Why don't you ring me?'

'It's for you,' Louise said, with a conspiratorial smile.

She handed the phone to Constance, who immediately recognised Nicky Scott Wilson's languid voice.

'Hello,' he said, without saying who he was. 'Do you play tennis? I thought I'd give you a game tonight. Six o'clock, all right? Fine. I'll collect you.'

'Short and sweet,' Louise said.

'He's so full of himself,' Constance complained. 'He thinks he can get away with anything.'

'Boys as handsome as Nicky usually *can*, darling.'

'Well, not with me.'

'Aren't you going?' Louise asked in alarm.

Constance blushed. 'Yes. This time. But I'm not going to be taken for granted again. I don't care how handsome he is.'

Nicky was much more impressed by Constance's figure than her skill at tennis. He could not resist showing off, hitting the ball all over the court and making her run around until she was pink with the effort and furious with herself for getting into such an undignified situation. Every time she missed the ball – which was most of the time – she became more angry.

Hot, sticky and uncomfortable, she let a particularly easy shot past and angrily threw her racket on the ground.

'That's it!' she cried. 'I've had enough of you making a fool of me, Nicky Scott Wilson! I'm not playing any more,' and she stormed off the court, convinced that everyone at the club house was laughing at her.

Nicky caught up with her.

'Oh, come on, old girl, it's only a *game*,' he said banteringly. Constance turned on him.

'I suppose you think you're clever, making me look a fool in front of everyone,' she cried. 'Well, *I* don't.'

Nicky laughed.

'It isn't funny,' she said, holding back tears of frustration. 'Just take me home, please.'

'Don't take it like that. It's only a bit of fun. You did very well. After all, I *am* a good player. What do you expect?'

'You would be, wouldn't you? Nicky Scott Wilson is good at *everything*, isn't he? Well, see if I care. *Never* ask me to play tennis with you again. Now, take me home please.'

As they walked to the car, Nicky tried to slip his arm around her waist. Constance indignantly moved away, shocked by his forwardness.

'What's wrong,' he asked. 'Afraid I'm going to take advantage of you?'

'Not at all,' Constance replied as calmly as she could. 'It would take more than *you* to take advantage of me. Just remember, when I want you to be familiar, I'll let you know. Until then, keep your hands to yourself.'


If things were not always plain sailing in her developing relationship with Nicky, her days at Maison de Levantière were an increasing pleasure for Constance. She could hardly keep her patience if the train was delayed and she arrived late. The hours flew by and it seemed no time at all until she was back on the train, reliving every moment as she travelled home. She enjoyed all aspects of life at the salon but, as she was increasingly called upon to show clothes, Constance began to love the opportunities for discreetly showing off. More important, she found it fascinating to put Monsieur de Levantière's advice into practice. She learned the arts of dress and make-up by looking at the clients of the House. She soon realised that what he had said was true: taste and style *were* inborn. The couturier could only give so much. The crucial ingredient that turned his clothes into something outstandingly elegant always came from the woman wearing them.

Monsieur de Levantière decided that, as a reward for modelling, Constance could buy at cost two of the previous season's models. She spent hours in the stockroom, trying everything on so that she could describe each dress to Louise. Finally, she chose a navy and white spotted silk with a square neckline and a slim draped skirt, and a grey linen shirtwaister with a full skirt and patch pockets. They made her feel very sophisticated.

Although she enjoyed the modelling, Constance was at her happiest sitting next to Monsieur de Levantière in his hot little office, taking notes as he worked on his collection. He was impressed by her intelligence and, on the few occasions when he asked her opinion, by the growing assurance of her taste. Very soon, she had become a sort of personal assistant, helping him select fabrics, cost dresses and choose accessories.

Louis was delighted at Constance's progess.

'Transformed, my darling, absolutely *transformed*!' she told Nora over the phone. 'You'll be proud when you see her. She's so assured and modern. And her clothes sense! She dresses marvellously now. I think you'll be very impressed indeed. De Levantière has had her hair cut and it makes her look very sophisticated. How wise you were to let her stay, darling.'

Each evening she and Constance would go over the day at Maison de Levantière, talking about the customers, fitting-room gossip and the new fabric deliveries. Louise enjoyed it all every bit as much as Constance. One night, Constance hugged her and said, 'Thank you for being so marvellous. Mummy would never have understood like you have.'

'Oh, I'm sure she would, darling,' Louise said loyally. 'But I'm just so glad that you enjoy modelling. I knew you would.'

'Oh,' Constance said, 'that's alright, but it isn't the best part. What I love is looking at the designs and helping choose the fabrics – and working out how much to charge!'

'Does Monsieur Levantière let you do that?' Louise asked, impressed.

'Well, I only write down the figures, really, but I do find it fascinating.'

'How interesting. I never imagined that the business side would appeal to you at all. I thought you would enjoy the glamour.'

'But that *is* the glamour,' Constance replied. 'In a way. I mean, it *is* marvellous wearing Monsieur's beautiful clothes and having my hair done and everything, but modelling is very boring after a while, Aunt Louise, because it is so very easy.'

Louise's face fell. 'But you've always said you loved it.'

'Oh, I *do*,' Constance replied hastily. 'But it is *too* easy, somehow. There's nothing to do. You just walk out, stand and smile.' She stopped. She knew that belittling modelling was not being honest. She loved it. But she loved the other aspects more. 'It's difficult to explain. I feel I'm in charge when I'm helping Monsieur – and that's what I really like.'

Louise smiled. 'Like mother, like daughter,' she thought to herself.


Although Constance was proud to be seen with Nicky and loved it when he took her out, she was determined not to be taken for granted. Their evenings were frequently marred by rows, started by Constance in response to what she saw as slights on Nicky's part. She was not always right. Underneath the aloof and patrician air of not being involved with life, Nicky was a warm and open young man. He was also much more vulnerable than Constance dreamed of, and was frequently hurt by what he saw as her deliberate hostility.

'I don't understand you northern girls,' he would say. Constance, who felt that he had said this a thousand times before, usually shrugged impatiently.

'It has nothing to do with North or South, Nicky. It's about self-respect. Why should girls give in to boys all the time? You're no better than we are, even if you are stronger. I don't know why you think you have the right to boss us around. We have a right to our opinions as well, you know.' And Nicky would nod unhappily, although he did not really comprehend. His upbringing, education and training had been based on the assumption that in any situation his class were the natural leaders. The idea of bossing anybody around was as alien to him as it was distasteful in his mind. For him, life was simple. He decided what he wanted and others – regardless of sex – followed his lead, without needing to be bossed.

'That's the trouble with Nicky,' Constance told Louise after she had returned from yet another evening that had ended with a quarrel. 'He thinks he can do what he wants and the rest of the world should line up behind him and follow. I won't do it – because I know it's wrong.'

'Oh dear,' Louise said, unhappily, 'I did *so* hope that you two would make a go of it, but with all the rows I don't really know, I'm sure . . .'

'But don't you and Uncle Jim ever disagree?'

'Yes of course, darling, but you know, each sex has its different strengths. Men are *meant* to lead, Constance.'

'Why?' Constance demanded, indignantly. 'Who said so? It isn't true, Aunt Louise. Honestly, it isn't true!'

Louise thought how like Nora Constance sounded.

'Don't you like Nicky?' she asked.

Constance paused, blushing.

'Yes I do. But not when he's taking me for granted. When he just decides something without even *thinking* of me, I hate him, I really do! I'm just as good as he is, even if I didn't go to Eton.'

Louise laughed. 'Of course you are darling,' she said, but she was unnerved. She felt that, even by Nora's standards, Constance was too headstrong for romantic liaisons.

There were times when Constance loved Nicky and times when she hated him, but her overall emotion was liking. She liked his company. He was full of inconsequential but amusing chatter and Louise had been right when she said that he knew everybody. He went to all the openings, parties and dinners that he wanted to and frequently did not see Constance for several days. To begin with, she did not mind. She found his sophistication so overwhelming that she needed a space in order to assimilate all the things he was introducing into her life. Besides, although she was still finding life at Levantière exciting, it was also exhausting. She was perfectly happy most nights to return home, gossip with Aunt Louise, lay out her clothes ready for the next day (which she did religiously, come what may) and then go to bed.

But it was not enough for long. She felt that the 'on-off' nature of their relationship – when he was here today but not tomorrow, or even the next day – was all part of Nicky's habit of taking her for granted. She determined that *she*, not he, would decide how often they saw each other and how they would occupy their time together. Although she was nervous of putting him to the test, she knew that, sooner or later, she must. She spent hours trying to decide whether or not he loved her. Was she just convenient? Did he *need* her? Whenever the question of whether or not she *needed* him popped into her head, Constance conveniently ducked it. She simply did not know, although deep in her heart she feared that what she felt for Nicky Scott Wilson was not true love. How could she love someone who considered himself so superior to her?

Sexually, their relationship was frequently charged, but rarely physical. After his early rebuff at the tennis court Nicky had, if anything, treated Constance with almost too much respect. At the cinema, under cover of darkness, he put his arm around her tentatively, but was always ready for rejection, and he had only twice kissed her. Constance could not decide whether or not his diffidence sprang from fear or indifference, and she found it puzzling that someone as confident as Nicky in every other area of his life should be so timid when it came to love.

She finally spoke to Louise.

'How do you know, *really* know, when someone loves you, Aunt Louise?'

Louise laughed to cover her embarrassment. 'Oh! Good Heavens, Constance! What a question! I have no idea.'

'But you *must* have,' Constance pressed. 'How did you know with Uncle Jim?'

'Oh, I don't know *how*, but you just do,' her aunt replied, blushing. 'It's just something that happens between two people. Why do you ask? Not more problems with Nicky, I hope?'

'No,' Constance replied, tentatively. 'Not *problems* exactly. It's just that I don't know if he loves me – or even cares. He is so funny. *You* know how many times he doesn't phone. And I can't phone *him*.'

'Certainly not,' her aunt agreed. There was silence.

'Do you think that you love *him?*' Louise asked, gently.

'Oh, Aunt Louise, I don't know. Isn't that awful?'

'Does he . . . er . . . show much affection?'

'Not really. He treats me like a sister.'

'Oh well,' Louise replied, secretly rather relieved. 'I should give it time, darling. It doesn't do to make yourself cheap. I'm sure that everything will be alright.' And there she thought it best to let the matter rest.

It was precisely because he was finding Constance more frequently in his thoughts than any other girlfriend that Nicky was so tentative. He felt differently about her. When she argued with him – so cogently and logically – he felt proud of her; when he saw her walking towards him – so jaunty and enthusiastic – he was overcome with tenderness. He liked the fact that she was different from anyone else in his life. But it bewildered him and, in a sense, made him resentful. Why should she have this power over him? Other girls did what he wanted – why couldn't she? But he knew, deep down, that her attraction was the very fact that she did not. Like many people for whom life presented no challenges, Nicky Scott Wilson, for all his assurance, was a coward. He did not want to take life seriously, and he felt his relationship with Constance – and her independence – were forcing him to do so.

The thing that Constance loved perhaps more than anything else about living in the south was the sun. After the

71

cold of the north, so frequently scoured by winds and battered by rain, she could not believe how frequently it shone – or how hot it became. Whereas in Northumberland it rarely lasted for a whole day and almost never appeared on consecutive days, in London and Surrey it seemed to shine uninterrupted for weeks at a time. Like a cat, Constance luxuriated in its sensual heat. It gave her a marvellous feeling of having escaped the cold clutches of the north and all her unhappiness there. She was determined not to return.

'I always want to live where the sun shines,' she told Louise. 'It makes me feel alive. I can't bear grey skies.'

'Oh, we get plenty of those as well, you know,' her aunt laughed. 'Just wait and see when we get to November. No sun then, I can tell you!'

Constance smiled. She was not entirely convinced – surely London could never have weather as dreary as a northern winter?

'I love it here, Aunt Louise,' she said, feelingly.

'I know you do, my darling, and we love having you. It has all turned out so much better than I dared hope for.'

Constance smiled. She was not all that sure that things were turning out so well with Nicky, but she was ready to admit that everything else about the south was idyllic. Sitting in the garden on that warm summer evening, neither woman knew how soon the idyll was to end.

Constance and Nicky had walked for what seemed miles in the heavy air of the beechwood. The huge trees offered shade from the sun, but their deep sprays of leaves seemed to trap and intensify the heat of the day. It was swelteringly hot and Constance could feel her dress sticking to her back as she walked. Brushing past the tall ferns, she noticed that the halo of flies buzzing around her head had increased, and she swatted them angrily as they landed on her face and arms.

They came to a clearing and Nicky slumped on to the

72

trunk of a felled tree, shaded by the overhanging branches that almost covered the space it had made.

'God! I'm so hot!' he groaned. 'Let's rest for a minute.'

Constance sat on the stump of the tree, just above Nicky's head.

'Well, only for a minute,' she said. 'The flies are driving me mad.'

She looked down at Nicky, lying perfectly still before her with his eyes closed. With his fine features and pale face he looked like a carved medieval figure on a tomb, and Constance was overwhelmed by his beauty. She could see the sweat on the fine hairs above his upper lip. The air was still and the flies seemed to have gone. There was no movement except for the tiny spider that was crawling up Nicky's arm. There was no sound, except the occasional click of a twig falling to the ground. They both remained totally motionless in the heat.

Constance felt perfectly happy. Leaning forward, she gently kissed Nicky's forehead. His eyes jerked open.

'Nice,' he smiled.

She leaned over him more closely and kissed his lips. Nicky lay perfectly still. He moaned slightly with pleasure as she kissed him again.

Constance could not help herself. Overcome by the romance of the setting, she did what she had always promised herself she would not, until Nicky had done so first. She told him how she felt.

'I love you,' she whispered.

'I know,' he replied.

Constance sat up, disconcerted. That was not the reply she had expected. Nicky rolled off the tree trunk and, offering her his hand, said 'Come on. We'd better get back.'

Constance felt hurt and betrayed. Why was he avoiding saying that he loved *her*? Perhaps he didn't? Before she could say anything, Nicky had begun to walk away. When she caught up with him the bombshell came.

'You know how you are always talking about Miss

73

Hatherby?' Nicky asked conversationally. 'Well, I've been meaning to tell you for ages. She's my great aunt.'

All thoughts of romance were banished from Constance's head. She was so shocked by what Nicky had said that she could not believe it.

'What do you mean?' she cried, grabbing at his arm to make him stop walking. 'What on *earth* do you mean?'

Alarmed by her vehemence, Nicky replied, 'I've been meaning to tell you for ages. But the time was never right, somehow.'

'*Meaning* to tell me? Why didn't you tell me straight away? How could you keep it a secret – after all I've told you?'

Bursting into tears, she turned and ran back through the wood, pushing blindly through the ferns, stumbling, hot and panting, determined to get away from Nicky so that she could try to think straight.

He ran after her, calling her name, but she ignored him and kept running until she reached the road. She could not believe his secrecy. When he had caught up with her and gasped, 'Constance, I'm sorry, I really am sorry,' she rounded on him.

'Why did you keep it a secret?' she cried through her tears. '*Why*? You *know* how much I love Miss Hatherby. Didn't you think I would want to know? How *could* you not tell me?'

Nicky remained silent. He had not told her initially because he was by no means sure that she would be anything more than just another fling and, in his quest for an easy life, did not want to complicate things by admitting the relationship. As time had gone by, and Constance's conversation had made clear the depth of her friendship with his great aunt, he had been afraid to tell her, fearing exactly the reaction he had now received.

'I don't know,' he whispered. 'I don't know. It was silly, I know . . . '

'Take me home,' Constance demanded. 'Take me home now.'

They drove back in silence. When they arrived at the gate, Nicky said, 'Please let me try to explain, Constance.'

'There is nothing to explain,' she said coldly as she stepped out of the car.

Luckily, her aunt was playing bridge so the house was silent and deserted. Rushing up to her room, Constance flung herself on the bed and tried to cry. But she couldn't. Her mind was racing too fast. Why had Nicky behaved so extraordinarily? Surely, it could mean only one thing. She was nothing to him – just another girl to have fun with but not take into his life. Well, that may be good enough for other girls, but not for her. If Nicky Scott Wilson wanted to keep his life secret, that was fine by her; but he needn't expect her to be a part of it, in that case.

Her thoughts were interrupted by Louise calling her name.

'Constance,' she cried from the foot of the stairs. 'Come down quickly. I have some marvellous news!'

Constance reluctantly slid from her bed. She went to the bathroom and washed her face in cold water. Looking at herself in the mirror she saw that her eyes were swollen and her face blotchy. What would Aunt Louise think?

Louise, however, was in such a state of excitement that initially she did not notice anything wrong.

'Darling,' she cried. 'Such news! I couldn't wait to get home to tell you.'

Constance stared at her blankly. Could Louise have heard about Nicky and his deceit? Surely not.

'Your uncle has taken a job in Italy,' Louise said momentously. 'In Rome! Can you imagine! He phoned to tell me that he had it shortly after you and Nicky had left. Isn't it marvellous?'

Suddenly, she realised the state Constance was in.

'Darling, whatever is wrong? You look dreadful.'

Constance burst into tears and rushed into Louise's arms.

'Oh, Aunt Louise! It's dreadful! I've quarrelled with Nicky!'

Louise rose to the occasion. Suppressing her excitement at her own news, she was all concern for Constance. She listened sympathetically as Constance told her of Nicky's revelation. Shocked as she was, Louise felt it unwise to take sides.

'Oh, I'm sure there is a perfectly simple explanation. It's clearly a misunderstanding,' she said soothingly.

'Do you think so?' Constance asked, clinging briefly to a hope she did not really believe in.

'Of course, darling. I really shouldn't worry. He'll be on the phone to you in no time.'

Later, she told Constance all about Jim's new job.

'The United Nations Food and Agricultural Organisation is moving from Quebec and the new headquarters are to be in Rome. They need all sorts of experts – including lawyers. Isn't it exciting? We're going so soon. I shall never be ready in time. It's a nightmare!'

'What about me?' Constance asked in a quiet voice. Louise took Constance into her arms.

'You're coming as well, silly. That is, if you want to. How could we abandon you? I had a long talk with Nora this morning. I didn't know how you'd feel about leaving Nicky, but after this I suppose. . . . '

What she was saying finally sunk into Constance's confused brain.

'Oh, Aunt Louise! How super!' she screamed. 'I can't believe it! I can't believe it!' Her mind flew to Miss Hatherby. Once again she heard her friend's voice, 'Rome . . . It is the most human city in the world.'

Suddenly, all thoughts of Nicky forgotten, she was the happiest girl in the world.

Constance heard Louise on the telephone and knew she was talking to Nora.

'I'm sure that Jim will be able to get her some sort of job but, to begin with, she can treat it like a little holiday, until she sees if she likes it.' She paused. 'Oh, yes, that's a good idea. We'll need a couple of weeks to settle in before she comes. Anyhow, she will want to say goodbye to everyone in Northumberland. My dear, it is *such* a rush. . . .'

Constance thought of Nicky. Would he phone? If he did, would she tell him the news? Her first thought was simply to disappear without telling him anything. Then she realised that Louise would have already broken the news to the bridge party. No doubt Mrs Scott Wilson had already told Nicky. Well, she would wait. She was determined not to make the first move.

Louise called her to the phone to speak to Nora.

'Everything's fine, my darling,' she whispered, giving Constance a little pat as she handed her the telephone.

'You are a very lucky girl,' Nora began. 'And I hope you've said thank you to Aunt Louise properly. It's a great opportunity and I hope you appreciate it.'

'Mummy, would you believe it? Nicky is related to Miss Hatherby.'

There was a silence. The news did not please Nora. She felt that the Hatherby influence on Constance in the past had been too great. In fact, one of the things that had pleased her about her daughter staying in London was that it kept her away from Seaton Cramer Hall. She did not want the relationship to start up again.

'Why haven't you told me before?' she asked.

'Oh, I kept forgetting,' Constance lied. She was not prepared to give her mother the satisfaction of knowing that Nicky had deceived her.

'Well,' Nora said, 'I hope he won't be following you up here when Louise has gone to Italy. I don't think I could stand any more Hatherby nonsense.'

'Oh, don't worry,' Constance replied, confidently 'He won't.'

As Constance had suspected, Nicky did not have the courage to approach her. He had heard about Louise's move and the thought of losing Constance had affected him more than he had imagined possible. Upset as she was, Constance had no intention of contacting *him*. The stalemate might have continued had Louise not needed to go to Rome to look at apartments and make arrangements.

'We'll only be away for four nights,' she explained to Constance. 'Can you cope here alone, or would you like to go home?'

Constance was far too involved in Maison Levantière, quite apart from enjoying her freedom from Nora, to want to return to Northumberland. Besides, she still hoped to hear from Nicky.

'Oh, I can manage,' she replied positively, although she was apprehensive of being alone in the house. 'I've the dog for company. Don't worry.'

'Well,' Louise replied, 'if you're sure . . . In any case, I'll have to talk to your mother.'

To everyone's relief, Nora agreed.

Louise lost no time in telling Constance that she did not need to return to Northumberland.

'Well, my darling. It's all settled. You can stay here and look after the place whilst we're gone. I don't want you to be lonely so I've spoken to Mrs Scott Wilson. She's invited you to have dinner with them the night we leave. Nicky will come and collect you. It's high time you two were friends again. Perhaps he'll take you out somewhere later in the week.'

'Oh, Aunt Louise,' Constance cried, 'I do wish you hadn't. I don't want to have Nicky Scott Wilson fussing round me like a wretched nanny while you're away. I'm perfectly capable of existing without *him*, you know.'

'I'm quite sure that you are, Constance,' Louise retorted. 'But that is not the point. Now *do* co-operate for my sake – or I won't have a moment's peace in Rome. At least go to dinner. That won't hurt you.'

Dinner, however, was agony. After the easygoing ways at Louise's table, she could not believe the stiff formality at the Scott Wilsons'. Nicky's parents were much older than Uncle Jim and Aunt Louise. His father was an ex-general who had retired long before the war, and the life he and his wife led was essentially an upper-class thirties one. Constance was not experienced enough to appreciate this. She was surprised that Colonel Scott Wilson wore a dinner jacket. She was amazed that the food was served by a maid and was appalled at the stiffness and formality of the conversation.

'Your aunt will find it hard to leave Surrey,' Mrs Scott Wilson stated. Constance could think of no intelligent reply.

'Rome is, of course, so primitive,' Mrs Scott Wilson continued.

'Drains,' her husband said. 'No drains. Filthy beggars, the Italians.'

Constance was indignant. She was sure that Miss Hatherby's view of Rome was the right one, but was frightened to say so.

Nicky shuffled awkwardly. He was more ill at ease than Constance would have thought possible. He was also more formal than she had ever seen him, his suit and stiff collar making him look quite different. He had barely spoken. Now, he cleared his throat and said, 'Constance is going to Rome herself.'

'Unwise,' his father said. 'Most unwise for a young girl. I don't know what the Carters can be thinking of.'

Constance longed to tell him to mind his own business, but she kept silent and forced herself to smile.

Finally the ordeal was over and Nicky drove her home.

'I'm sorry that you are leaving,' he said formally.

'Are you?'

'Yes. I'll miss you very much.'

'Oh, I expect you'll survive,' Constance said, coolly. Discouraged by her tone, Nicky hesitated.

'Can I see you before you go back to Northumberland?' he asked, at length.

'Yes. You know you only have to phone.'

As they drove up to the house Constance thought that it looked very dark and silent. Stopping the car by the front door, Nicky said, 'I'd better come in – at least until you get the lights on.'

'No,' she said firmly. 'There's absolutely no need. But if you'd wait until I switch on the hall light. . . .'

Nicky looked at her. Even in the dark, she could tell that he was disappointed.

'Are you sure?'

'Yes, I'm perfectly all right.'

'OK,' he replied. 'Another time.'

She turned at the door to wave but the car was already in gear and accelerating down the drive. Though she clearly had made him angry, Constance knew that her decision had been right. Once indoors, she had a glass of water and began to feel better.

She seemed to lie in bed for a long time before falling asleep. Seeing Nicky again had been an unsettling experience, for two reasons. She realised that not having spoken to him for ten days had given her a perspective she had not previously had – a perspective on herself as well as him. She knew that she did not love him but, more, she knew that despite his sophistication, he was not enough for her. He lacked a driving force, though Constance was not sophisticated enough to put it that way. All she felt as she lay in the dark was that Nicky could not satisfy her. The other revelation was more unsettling. She had enjoyed watching Nicky longing for encouragement tonight. Like a little puppy dog, he had waited for a sign that he was forgiven. She had enjoyed witholding the sign. For the first time in her life, she felt her power as a woman.

Suddenly, she knew that her aunt's news had come at the perfect time. She realised that she had become increasingly frustrated and dissatisfied with her life with Nicky . . . maybe even with Surrey . . . perhaps even with Maison de Levantière. As she drifted into sleep, she knew she was ready for Rome.

How long she had slept before the sound woke her she had no idea, but suddenly she was wide awake. There was a bang on the window. Constance jerked up in bed clutching her throat in terror. Someone was throwing gravel at the glass! Trying not to scream, she sat up and, without putting on the light, looked at the illuminated face of the alarm clock. It was 12.20. She sat there for a few seconds, then heard a voice softly calling her name. Rigid with fear, she remained silent. The voice came again: 'Constance.' She thought quickly. The noise had definitely come from outside. Nobody was in the house. But why wasn't the dog barking? Was it someone she knew? Without putting on the light, she slipped out of bed and tiptoed to the window.

'Constance, stop being such a bore. Open the window, for God's sake!'

It was Nicky. She pulled back the curtains and leaned out.

'What's happened?' she called.

'Happened?' he repeated, gazing up in puzzlement. 'What do you mean?'

'What have you come for?'

'I wanted to see *you*.'

Her relief released her anger. 'What do you mean, you wanted to see *me*?' she hissed. 'Do you know what time it is?'

'Did I give you a fright?' He grinned. Constance noticed that he was swaying slightly.

'You're drunk!' she said.

'Nonsense!' He staggered back and raised his voice. 'Just a little tipsy. Let me in. Want to talk.'

'Are you mad? It's gone midnight.'

'Just a little talk,' Nicky pleaded.

'Go home before you wake the neighbours.'

'Please!'

'I'm not listening to any more of this,' and she closed the window and climbed back into bed. More gravel hit the glass, her name was called more loudly, but she ignored it and pulled the bedclothes over her head. The calling continued for a few moments and then, with a cry of 'bitch', to her horror, Nicky Scott Wilson began to make the most blood-curdling noise as he bayed her name to the night sky, like a wolf.

Constance was incensed. Leaping out of bed, she threw the window open and yelled, 'Stop that noise or you'll wake the neighbours and Aunt Louise will be *furious* when she hears about it. *Stop it*, I say!'

Nicky grinned up at her. 'Only if you let me in,' he slurred. 'Need to talk. Only five minutes.'

'You're drunk,' Constance repeated self-righteously. 'Go home. We'll talk tomorrow.'

In reply, Nicky threw back his head and made the dreadful noise again. To Constance, it seemed even louder than before. A light went on in the house opposite.

'Alright,' she cried. 'But only for a moment. Wait until I get dressed – and *please* be quiet.'

As she struggled into her clothes, she could hear Nicky softly singing 'Constance, Constance, *talk* to me, my Constance, or I shall end my life!' as if he were an opera singer. Anxious as she was about the neighbours, she couldn't help laughing as she hurried downstairs.

As he stepped into the light from the open door, Constance realised that Nicky was indeed very drunk. He staggered forward into her arms and almost fell, taking her with him. Half dragging and half carrying him, she managed to get his inert body into the drawing room and onto the sofa. Breathless, she straightened up and said fiercely, 'You can only stay for a minute and then you must *promise* to go.'

'Please, Constance,' Nicky pleaded. 'Don't send me away. Can't you see how I feel about you?'

'You're drunk. There's no point in talking to you now. You *must* go home.'

Nicky slid off the sofa and clung to her legs.

'Please, please,' he begged.

Constance tried to stand up. 'This is ridiculous!' she cried. 'Nicky, you *must* go home!'

All his pleading was in vain. She was determined. It took a long time, but she finally got the drunken figure out of the door and closed it firmly behind him. Leaning against it, she waited for the car to start. Nothing happened. She gently opened the door and peeped out.

The light from the hall illuminated the scene. Nicky was sitting in the driver's seat, sound asleep. Although she had no experience of drunks, a sixth sense convinced Constance that he would sleep all night. She tiptoed out with a blanket and tucked it around him. Looking at his handsome face, she felt a pang for what might have been. She went back into the house and locked the door behind her. At dawn she was woken briefly by the sound of the sports car going down the drive. She did not get out of bed to look. She knew that Nicky was really nothing to her now.

The next afternoon, Constance was sitting in the garden with the dog when she heard the sound of Nicky's car. She remained in her deckchair. He walked across the lawn towards her, sheepishly holding a bunch of yellow roses.

'Hello,' he said gently. 'Are you speaking to me? I wouldn't blame you if you weren't.'

Constance had never been given flowers before and she beamed with pleasure.

'I'm sorry,' he said, 'I don't know what came over me. All I wanted to do was talk. Forgive me for keeping you up all night. I hope the neighbours didn't complain about all the racket I made.'

'There's a time and a place,' she replied. 'Fancy making all that noise. And *singing* as well.'

'Singing? What do you mean – singing?'

Although she remembered the words perfectly well, Constance merely said, 'Oh, nothing, it was just part of your general racket.' She looked down at the roses.

'Anyhow,' she added, 'If you want to talk, there's plenty of time now. Go ahead. I'm not stopping you.'

Nicky looked away. 'You know, you're quite a cracker. I'm very keen on you.' She was silent.

'Look, why don't we go for a drink tonight and then we'll talk.'

'I don't see why not,' she answered, although a little bit of Nora in her made her add, 'provided you keep sober.'

'Don't worry, I will,' he replied ruefully.


'You're an enigma,' Nicky said portentously after his fourth drink.

'What on earth do you mean – an enigma? There's nothing strange about me.'

'You're mysterious. You change.'

'In what way?'

'Well,' Nicky slouched back in his chair and lit a cigarette. 'Half the time you have this little-girl-lost look – like when we walked into this bar tonight – and then suddenly you look all determined and hard.'

'Hard?' Constance was affronted. 'How dare you call me hard?' Nicky sat up, afraid he had put his foot in it.

'No, not hard. That's the wrong word. . . .' He cast around desperately. 'Capable. In charge. I don't know. Anyhow, there's something spooky about it. It suddenly makes you look much older.'

There was nothing that Constance wanted more than to look older and more sophisticated. She was intrigued.

'In what way?'

'I don't know. It's difficult to say. You look very businesslike. As if nothing could beat you once you'd made up your mind.'

'I'd like to be a businesswoman.'

'Really? God, how boring!'

'I don't think it's boring at all,' Constance replied, her mood immediately changed by his complacency. 'You don't understand what it's like for a woman. It gives you

84

confidence when you are in charge. Anyhow, why should the men make all the decisions?'

'Because we're trained to.'

'I've never heard anything so ridiculous. It's because you're frightened to let us, in case our decisions are better – which they would be.' Nicky looked crestfallen but did not dare argue with Constance when she was in this mood.

The time to leave Maison de Levantière came soon enough. The farewell was surprisingly emotional. Constance and Monsieur de Levantière suddenly realised how much they had come to rely upon each other in the time that she had worked there. 'Now listen to me, Constance,' he said. 'You have talent – real talent. You're practical *and* creative and that's a rare combination, believe me. If you want, you could go far in this business. Not that I am encouraging you, mind. I would never do that. This is a hard and uncertain way of earning a living. Nothing comes easy in the fashion world, but I'm sure you have what it takes if you fancy trying it some day.'

Constance was lost for words, overwhelmed that her worth had been recognised.

Nora was longing to see the new Constance and proudly show her off a little around the neighbourhood. Certainly, she decided, she would take her into Chollerton and maybe even Alnwick – although she would make sure they kept well away from the antique shop. Constance, on her side, had become sufficiently worldly to know what was expected of her when she returned home. She knew that she would be flaunted before the whole of Northumberland if her mother had her way, so, although aware that good form dictated that she should dress down in the country, she took a deep breath and faced the fact that, for their first few outings at least, she would have to wear what Nora called her 'dressy' clothes. In full make-up and wearing the latest style, she felt slightly self-conscious at Chollerton bus station, but was prepared to play the game for the evident enjoyment it brought her mother. However, when she went to visit Miss Hatherby, she wore her simplest frock and no make-up, despite her mother's protests.

She felt guilty about Miss Hatherby, having written to her only once, in the first week after her arrival in Surrey. Her friend greeted her as if she had never been away, so the guilt evaporated and she began to talk about Nicky.

Miss Hatherby smiled.

'My great-nephew Nicholas! Fancy your meeting him. I haven't seen him since he was a baby. How is he? I understand that they think very highly of him at Sotheby's.'

'He's nice,' Constance said guardedly. 'He's taken me to lots of places. He knows everybody.'

'He would,' Miss Hatherby chuckled, and they spent the next half hour discussing him.

Talking to her dearest friend about Nicky helped Constance a great deal. The more she thought about him, the warmer she felt. She now knew that he could never satisfy her, but was not prepared to dislike him just for that. She was glad that she was going to Rome as it brought their relationship to an end, cleanly and conclusively. 'I'll always think of him as a friend,' she thought.

Then she told Miss Hatherby the news.

'Rome!' her friend exclaimed. 'How thrilling, Constance! My dear, what discoveries you will make! Now,' she leaned forward urgently, 'promise me that you will use your eyes, your ears and your *brain* to the maximum. Be alert to everything, let nothing escape you, and you will soon have a true education for life. Now promise me that you will be *alive* out there, Constance. Alive and alert at all times.'

'I will, I will, I know I will,' said Constance, fervently.

# CHAPTER 4

As the train trundled out of Paris, Constance snuggled into her corner feeling almost ridiculously happy, proud and capable. For the first time in her life she was conscious of being independent and in charge. It was a feeling she liked very much indeed. It stayed with her throughout the long and endlessly delayed journey across France. The difficulty in sleeping, the lack of food, even the primitive lavatory, couldn't dim her happiness. At midnight, twenty-four hours after leaving Calais, she finally arrived in Milan where she had to change trains. The September night was hot and humid but it did not perturb Constance as she struggled through the crowds of noisy, gesticulating passengers purposefully carrying cardboard boxes, mattresses and crates of chickens down the long platform. She was delighted with their movements and their language. She watched with amazement as goats were pushed into guards' vans; she gazed with awe at the rough, dark faces that loomed in front of her out of the steam. It seemed to her that she had never seen so many people as there were on that platform, waiting for the Rome express to arrive.

She was thankful that Louise had insisted that she travel first class. When the train pulled in there was a rush for the doors. People fought to be first on, children were lifted through windows; the scene was frighteningly chaotic. Constance squeezed her way down the platform looking for the first-class carriages. Eventually she found them but couldn't get near – the crowds were as dense further up and, push as she might, she could not make a parting for herself. She began to panic. It seemed that the train would pull out leaving her and the hundreds of milling travellers still shoving each other back and forth across the dimly lit platform.

Suddenly Constance became aware of someone tugging at her case. She turned in panic.

'Signorina,' a young man said to her urgently, 'I'll take it. You follow me.'

Before she had time to think he had wrenched her case from her and, pushing it in front of him, used the sharp ends as a battering ram to force his way through the crowds. Constance followed close behind, clutching at his shirt in her terror that they might be separated in the crush. Jabbed by elbows, trodden on, even spat at by an old man, Constance slowly pushed through the crowd, cleaved for her by her unknown protector. It took several minutes but they finally boarded the train, fought their way down the corridor and collapsed into the relative calm of a first-class carriage.

As she flopped down in a corner seat, Constance looked at the man pushing her case on to the rack opposite. She noticed his broad shoulders and muscular back. As he turned round and smiled at her, she was struck by his looks. To Constance's English eyes, his skin was so brown he might have been an Indian. His dark eyes lit up as he grinned and said, in only faintly accented English, 'We are lucky that the penalties for travelling in a first-class carriage on a third-class ticket are so severe or we would not have got on.'

Constance suddenly felt shy. For a second, she was tongue-tied. 'How did you know I was English?' she asked.

He grinned again, repeated her question and said, 'You could be nothing else. You looked like a piece of English lavender surrounded by rough grass. I knew at once.'

Constance was enchanted. As he settled into the seat

opposite, he leaned forward and, formally extending his hand, said, 'Excuse me. I am Ludovico Castelfranco di Villanuova. I am delighted to meet you. *Parla Italiano?* No? So, have you just arrived? Tell me.''

Constance felt swamped. She suddenly realised how tired she was, but she made an effort and told him that she was travelling to Rome to join her aunt and uncle.

'You have a long journey, signorina,' her companion told her. 'The lines are not fully repaired after the war. We go to Florence via Genoa and La Spezia. It takes much time. But you are tired. You must sleep. You are safe now. It might be long before we start. In Italy these days nothing is certain.'

Constance had been sound asleep for an hour before the double-engined train began to jerk laboriously out of the station, leaving many travellers on the platform to wait who knew how long for the next express. As her mouth fell innocently open and her body relaxed, Ludovico Castelfranco examined her closely. He could hardly believe how young and inexperienced she seemed. There was something vulnerable in her as she slept that contradicted the determination in her face when she was awake. He thought how very English she looked. Although he had only caught a glimpse of her blonde head above the milling crowds on the platform, he hadn't even briefly mistaken her for a German or Scandinavian. As he looked at her, slumped awkwardly in sleep, he tried without success to put his finger on that indefinable something which made this girl so totally English. Ludovico found her very attractive. His eyes roved boldly over her sleeping body. She was wearing a grey dress with a wide skirt. Her hat was a pale pink straw and her sandals had grey wedge heels. Everything matched perfectly, even her pink beads. He noticed that her figure was good and that her legs and ankles were very much better than those of the girls he remembered from his days in London before the war. He and his friends had always agreed that English women's legs were the disaster of Europe but, he was pleased to see, this girl's were different.

As the train chugged slowly forward, stopping inexplicably for long periods and even occasionally travelling backwards, Ludovico enjoyed the luxury of being able to examine his travelling companion openly while she slept. He assessed everything about her, from her clothes and shoes to her luggage and hairstyle. He knew merely from her appearance, in a way that Italian men always do, that she was a virgin. The knowledge excited as much as it intrigued him. Thinking about it and its possible implications, he drifted into a fitful doze, a gentle smile on his face.

When Constance woke up, he was sound asleep and it was her turn to stare. His chin was resting on his shoulder and his face was in profile to her. She had never seen such perfect features. His brow, nose, lips and chin were in exact proportion, like a sculpted Roman head. His wavy black hair curled behind his ears so thickly that she was reminded of an Ingres portrait of a nobleman she had seen in one of Miss Hatherby's books. Constance thought Ludovico the most romantic man she had ever seen but what intrigued her most were his luxuriantly long eyelashes. On any other than his strongly classical face, they would have looked disturbingly effeminate. Although she had to admit his lack of height, Constance had noticed that he was muscular. How old he was she wasn't sure, but he was certainly older than Nicky, she decided, and much more mature.

Constance fell into a second sleep as the train continued on its slow path to Genoa. She was vaguely conscious of passing through occasional stations but she didn't wake up until a soft shaking of her shoulder gently brought her to life. She opened her eyes and looked straight into the beautiful face of the Italian. It was dawn and he pointed to the window.

'Look,' he said quietly so that the others in the carriage would not wake. 'Look. The Mediterranean.'

Constance looked. She had never seen anything so ethereal as the scene that slid slowly past her eyes. The sea was covered with a mist that hovered above its surface, like a cloud. It was the most delicate shade of creamy blue and out of it floated the masts and superstructures of fishing boats, riding silently at anchor. The tranquillity and gentleness of the scene reminded her of Japanese paintings. The mist changed to a warm pink and began to disperse as the sun rose above the horizon. The surface of the sea became glossy, like copper. Constance was mesmerised. Neither she nor Ludovico said a word for many minutes. Then he pointed to the window on the other side of the carriage.

'Look,' he whispered, touching her arm to gain her attention. Heavily wooded hills climbed high above the railway line, dotted with small villages just beginning to be bathed in the warm light of the rising sun. Constance was thrilled at her first sight of the red terracotta tiles of Italy, glowing in the morning air as above them the pale blue sky deepened. 'We will soon be in La Spezia,' Ludovico said.

At La Spezia, he pushed his way down the crowded corridor, looking for a refreshment trolley. He was away so long that Constance began to feel nervous. He finally returned with two chunks of roughly cut bread, a slab of cheese and a tiny tin jug of milk.

'All I could get,' he apologised. Constance was perfectly happy. She had not eaten since Paris and nothing had ever tasted so good to her as this rough peasant fare. As the train left La Spezia, she was so enjoying her adventure that she laughed out loud. It was the beginning of a love affair – with the man and his country.

'And now,' he said, 'you are rested and fed and – how do you English say? – watered, so it is time to learn of each other.'

Constance laughed again and said, 'I think I am going to love Italy.'

He looked into her eyes and said, 'I *know* you are going to love Italy. I can see it in you already.'

'How old are you?' Constance asked boldly.

'I am twenty-five. You are from London? I was there in nineteen thirty-eight. Do you know Halkin Street? That is where we lived. London is a beautiful city – so confident, so assured.'

Constance was intrigued by the 'we'. 'Who lived at Halkin Street?' she asked.

'My father and I.'

She was relieved, but she wondered how she could manoeuvre the conversation in order to find out if he was married. He was wearing a ring but she did not know on which hand a wedding ring would be worn in Italy.

There was a slight pause. Constance looked out of the window. Ludovico suddenly said, 'I *like* English girls. They are always so clean and uncomplicated – no?'

It seemed to Constance that he had paid her a very oblique kind of compliment but, in order to take the lead he had given her, she decided to ignore the suggestion that she and her countrywomen might be boring in comparison with Italian women.

'Do you know many English girls?' she asked.

It was his turn to gaze out of the window. Constance could see that he was calculating how much to tell.

'No,' he replied carefully, 'not *many* – but some. When I visited London.'

'And all you can remember is their cleanliness?'

'Cleanliness? Please – what is?'

Constance laughed, unaware that he was playing for time. 'Not dirty – clean,' she explained.

Ludovico laughed uneasily. 'I say something silly – no?'

'No, not at all. It just seems a very negative compliment. It's rather boring to be clean.'

He looked at her in surprise. 'You like to be dirty? I do not *think* so!'

Oh dear, Constance thought, we're getting into heavy weather here. I wish I'd never started this.

His next remark made her blush.

'You know,' he said, leaning across to her and almost whispering, 'like under your arms. You English girls are always so smooth and clean. Italian girls are hairy. I do not like that hairy. It smells.'

Constance was deeply embarrassed at the intimate turn the conversation had taken. It was perfectly obvious that this man had been allowed to get very close to both English and Italian girls and, she decided, had probably known a great many of both. He's obviously an almighty flirt, she thought. Despite her embarrassment, it made him seem even more attractive. It also reassured her: surely no *married* man – not even an Italian married man – would talk so boldly, almost sexually, to a total stranger?

If Constance thought she was learning things about Ludovico, it was nothing compared with what he was gleaning from her. His eyes sparkled with delight as her mannerisms and voice reminded him of just how attractive he found Englishwomen. As her confidence grew, Constance began to talk with animation about her job at Maison de Levantière, life with Louise and even some of her difficulties with her mother. Ludovico lay back in his seat and smiled. Her innocence and enthusiasm captivated him. As the train was on the final run towards Florence, he leaned forward urgently. 'Come with me when we get to Florence,' he said. 'I want to show you Italy's fairest city.'

After a moment's hesitation, Constance said yes.

On the first day, Ludovico murmured, 'Constance . . . Constanza . . . you are a Constance. It is the perfect name for you,' as they lay on the grass in the Boboli Gardens, sheltering under the trees from the fierce afternoon sun. Since leaving the train at eleven o'clock that morning, so much had changed in her life that Constance felt dazed. They had sent a telegram to Louise (Constance could not pluck up the courage to speak to her); Ludovico had telephoned a friend about somewhere for them to stay and they had eaten what to Constance, used to English food, seemed the most delicious lunch she had ever tasted. As she lay in the heat, she felt drowsy and at the same time tinglingly alive.

'Talk to me,' she said.

'What do you want me to say, you funny English girl?' he asked as he rolled over on his stomach and began to tickle her neck with a blade of grass.

'Tell me about you.'

'About me?' he chuckled. 'OK. I am Ludovico Castel-franco di Villanuova. I am twenty-five. I stand five feet ten inches, I have brown eyes, black hair . . . all my teeth.' He paused. 'You can see how I am, but the parts you cannot see are even better.'

Constance grinned: Ludovico was exactly the way she had always imagined an Italian would be. As if he had read her thoughts, he said, 'I am – how do you say? – I am your typical Italian: generous, warm, passionate and very' – he rolled the 'r' like a music-hall opera singer – '*very* jealous.'

Constance sat up and hugged her knees. 'How very disagreeable,' she said. 'Tell me more.'

'I am a poor orphan boy. My father is dead for many years.'

'Brothers and sisters?' cried Constance.

He paused, distracted by the interruption. 'Brothers and sisters? None. I am the only child.'

A sadness seemed to cross his face for a second but Constance was barely conscious of it.

'Your mother?' she asked. She was beginning to enjoy herself.

'Oh,' he said sadly, 'she is a sick, lonely woman, as Italian mothers always are.'

'Where?'

'Way up in the hills . . .'

'The old woman who lived in the hills,' Constance cried in delight.

Ludovico was not pleased at the interruptions. 'English

94

girls always drink too much wine,' he said with mock severity. 'Where was I? Oh, yes, my mother. My mother is a saint – very religious – very devoted to the memory of my poor father. She surrounds herself with priests. She prays all day. Very Italian; very devout. I worship her for her piety.'

'Tell me about your home.'

'Alas,' he joked, pretending to cry, 'I have no home. My mother's house up in the hills is so,' he searched for the word, 'away . . .'

'Remote,' Constance corrected.

'Yes, so remote, that I must live with friends wherever I am – Rome, Naples, even here, in Florence.'

'Like a gypsy,' Constance laughed.

'Exactly,' he agreed.

Constance searched for something more to ask.

'Tell me about your loves.'

'None,' he lied. 'I am a *scholar* gypsy. I love my books, I love my library. After that, there is nothing.'

'Liar,' she laughed.

'No, seriously,' he said.

She put her hands round his neck and pretended to strangle him. 'Don't tell me all these lies,' she laughed.

'Let me go!' he cried, then he suddenly leaned forward and kissed her.

Constance was not ready for it and rolled away on the grass.

Her mood changed. 'Why do you lie?' she asked pensively.

'All right,' Ludovico cried, determined that the atmosphere should not be lost, 'now I tell true. I have hundreds, no thousands, of girlfriends. They never leave me alone. They telephone all day; they run after me in the streets; they bribe my barber for locks of my hair; they make my life unbearable. And I love them all.'

Sitting up, Constance roared with delight. 'You are naughty, wicked and bad,' she cried as she pretended to hit him over the head. He ducked the blows, and holding her tight, said, 'I love you. *Only* you.'

The apartment Ludovico took Constance to was at the top of an old palazzo in Via Santo Spirito, a dark street dominated by the cupola of Chiesa Santo Spirito, the vast Renaissance church at the end of the road. It was tiny and not terribly clean, but it entranced Constance. Without waiting to be shown, she walked through the primitive kitchen and on to a small balcony perched perilously above the red-tiled roofs of the houses below. From it, she could see the narrow street and the small square where the traders were dismantling their stalls. The sounds, the heat, the smell were all marvellous to her. 'Oh, Ludovico,' she cried. 'It's just perfect! Perfect! It's exactly how I always imagined Italy would be.'

Ludovico found the area squalid and dirty but he pretended to share her enthusiasm. Catching her by the arm, he said, 'Come. I have something else to show.'

He led her through the kitchen to a darkened room. Constance could see nothing. He opened the shutters. It was a bedroom, containing the largest bed she had ever seen. It filled the room, leaving only inches on each side between it and the walls.

'*Ecco!*' Ludovico cried theatrically as he gestured towards it. 'Here it is. The *Matrimoniale* – our own double bed!'

The bed was in the worst nineteenth-century taste. The bedhead was florid and overblown, its shiny walnut carvings reaching almost to the ceiling. And what carvings! Madonnas, cherubs, birds, fauns and flowers crowded and pushed each other in a design that defied logic and allowed no place for the eye to rest. Constance had never seen anything so complicated. As she gazed at it she became embarrassed. Ludovico's arm crept round her waist. She could feel his breath on her neck. Suddenly she felt shy and nervous. Gently pulling away, she said in a slightly strained voice, 'More! Show me more. What else is there to see?'

'Nothing; this is the apartment. You don't like?' Ludovico's face puckered with anxiety.

'I love it,' she smiled. 'Now please show me more of marvellous Florence.'

As they rushed, laughing, through the side streets and played hopscotch across the squares, Constance was increasingly aware of time passing. The thought of the night terrified and thrilled her. Ludovico's physicality was already overwhelming. He embraced her in bars without any embarrassment and stole kisses in shop doorways, no matter who was passing by. His bodily presence seemed to be submerging hers and making them one. He endlessly touched her, and the physical thrill made her tingle. But, despite the excitement growing inside her, Constance felt ill at ease. Her conscience wouldn't let her be happy. She knew that she must speak to Louise.

When she told Ludovico, he frowned and said, 'That is not possible, my darling.'

'Why not?'

'Telephoning here in Italy is very difficult. Half the lines are still down since the war. Don't worry. She will have the telegram by now.'

Something within Constance strengthened. She knew she was falling in love with this man; she felt certain that she couldn't resist him; but she also knew that she couldn't treat Louise in this way. Could not and would not.

She looked Ludovico in the eyes and said, 'I must, Ludovico – I absolutely *must* – speak to my aunt before we go back to the flat.'

He looked back at her and knew the strength of her will. 'Stay here,' he said and slipped out of the bar.

'This is the palazzo of a friend of mine. It is not necessary for you to meet him at the moment – in fact, he is not here right at this moment – but you may use the telephone. Give me the number. I will dial.'

'Then wait outside, please.'

'Aunt Louise? Did you get the telegram?'

'Constance! Where on earth are you? Your uncle and I have been worried to death! I haven't dared contact your mother! What *are* you doing?'

Constance wilted. She had never heard Louise speak in this tone of voice before. It was obvious that she was very upset and alarmed.

Trying to keep her voice calm, and almost choking on the tears of guilt that had come to her eyes the moment she heard her aunt speak, Constance said, 'Oh, Aunt Louise, I've met a boy . . . no, not really a boy . . . a young man' – and she began to sob.

There was a silence and then her aunt cried, 'But what are you *doing*? Where is he taking you? Why did you get off the train?'

Through her tears, Constance began to tell the dreadful story – and, hearing it with her aunt's ears, she saw that it was indeed dreadful. It took a long time because Louise kept interrupting with questions that Constance couldn't answer and which seemed irrelevant beside the tremendous fact that Ludovico was waiting for her and she longed to run to him.

'I don't know what to *do*,' Louise wailed.

'Please don't do anything yet,' Constance pleaded. 'I'll ring you in a couple of days. I am perfectly safe. He is a gentleman. I *know* that no harm will come to me – and so would you if you could only see him. You'd love him, you honestly would. Please, Aunt Louise, *trust* me!'

It was midnight when Ludovico and Constance finally climbed the stairs to the apartment. They had reached the first landing when Constance stopped.

'Wait,' she cried, pulling Ludovico back, 'I want to count.'

'Count?'

'Yes, I want to know how many steps there are to the top.' She turned and began to run down the stairs. 'Come!' she cried.

'Come back, Constanza!' Ludovico called.

She took no notice. Angry that she had defied him and yet delighted at her little-girl behaviour, he reluctantly followed, then, holding her very close, walked her back up the stairs as they counted each step in unison.

'. . . ninety-four!' Constance gasped as they reached the door of the apartment. 'How do you say that in Italian?'

'*Novantaquattro*,' Ludovico groaned, as he wrestled with the huge lock. In the half-light from the single landing bulb, he took what seemed to Constance an age to open it. Finally, he stepped inside, groping for the light switch. There was no bulb in the hall light. As Ludovico shuffled into the kitchen, Constance waited fearfully on the landing. She heard Ludovico stumble, curse and then light a match. As he came back into the hall, his face irregularly illuminated by its flame, she was overwhelmed by the dramatic beauty of his features. He disappeared into the bedroom, where the match went out.

'Oh no!' he cried. 'There are no bulbs in any of the lights. I should have known. In Italy when people move out they take everything – and I mean everything. I'm amazed that they have left the fittings!'

'I don't believe it!' Constance said.

'It is true, my darling. Come.' He stepped forward and pulled her into the apartment. Closing the door, he said, 'There is nothing to do but go immediately to bed. Follow,' and, holding her hand, he led her into the bedroom. Constance was glad of the dark but was pleased, as Ludovico held her tight and started passionately kissing her face and neck, that there was sufficient light from the street for her to see him.

As she was swept up in his passion she forgot everything except her need for him. He undressed her slowly and with infinite gentleness, as if she were a peach he could not bear to bruise, and then guided her shaking hands as she undressed him. She had never touched a naked man before. Ludovico slowly slid her down his body and she kissed the skin of his torso, excited by its masculine smell. He straddled his legs, and guiding her head with both hands, tried to make her take him into her mouth.

She pulled away. 'No!' she gasped.

'*Yes*,' he whispered urgently, as he slowly pushed her head down again. She had no choice. His firm prick forced her to open her lips and take him into her mouth.

It was the most marvellous feeling Constance had ever experienced.

After a few minutes, he raised her to her feet, and gently pushed her back on the bed. Immediately, springs began to groan. The slightest movement caused them to twang and reverberate through the silent apartment. For all her excitement, Constance could not resist laughing. As her body began to shake with mirth, Ludovico raised himself up in dismay and cried, 'What do I do wrong? Why do you laugh at me?'

'Not at you, Ludovico,' she gasped, 'at us and this ridiculous bed. Listen to the noise it's making.'

He pulled himself away and sat on the edge of the bed. She knew he was angry.

'It's nothing to do with you, Ludovico,' she said, gently stretching forward to touch him. He shrugged her off.

'You laugh!' he said. 'How can you laugh at such a moment! You destroy everything.'

She sat up in horror. 'Oh! Ludo, please! Don't be like that. Please don't be angry. I'm sorry.'

'I am failed. I am failed as a man. How can you do this to me?'

'Oh, Ludo, don't be silly.'

'Silly! Silly! You call silly the most sacred moment between a man and a woman? Do you say this to your English men?'

Constance smiled in the dark as she thought of the

chaste kisses she had allowed Nicky. 'There are no English men,' she whispered. 'You are the first.'

There was a silence and then he turned. 'I know, my little virgin. I know.'

There was something dismissive in his tone that irritated Constance. 'How do you know?' she asked indignantly. 'What have I done wrong?'

'You laughed,' he retorted.

Somehow her insecurity changed his mood. She could see that he was smiling.

'Look!' he cried, beginning to bounce up and down. 'Listen to the noise. Get used to it. It will sing its song to the rhythm of our love. You must enjoy it. Do not let it distract you again,' and he pulled her towards him. His passion was so strong that Constance was overwhelmed. She heard nothing more than his urgent whisperings, half Italian, half English, his groans and her cries accompanied by the futile protests of the bed as he took her, slowly, confidently and with an expertise she was too inexperienced to appreciate.

Constance lay awake long after Ludovico had fallen into a heavy sleep. It wasn't just the slight pain that stopped her sleeping, it was also the mental shock of what she had done. She couldn't imagine why she had behaved as she had. You don't know him, she thought, desolately. He might wake up and walk out and you'll never see him again. She imagined how Nora would react if she knew. Who is he? she mused. Is he telling the truth about his ancestors? Were they really ruling huge areas of land when my family's ambitions were for nothing grander than the next meal and the work to pay for it? Or was it all a pack of lies to make me give in? In her heart, she knew that the speculation was unfair. She had given in because she found him irresistible and, looking at his strong brown back in the first grey light of dawn, she still found him so. She longed to wake him so that they could make love again but did not dare to because, for all the intimacy of the previous hours, Constance knew that she was lying next to a virtual stranger.

It was broad daylight when she woke. It was hot, her skin was clammy and she felt sick. She rolled over to touch him. He was not in the bed. Sitting up, she looked round the bedroom. He was gone. Nervously she whispered, 'Ludo?' There was no reply. The apartment was silent, its air of abandonment only emphasised by the cries and noises from the street below. She knew she was alone. She slid off the edge of the bed. The floor tiles were cold but she hardly noticed as she tiptoed to the door and looked into the kitchen. No note. None of his clothes left. Nothing. She shuffled across the kitchen to the sink. He's gone! she thought. He's had his fun and now he's run away. I'll never see him again. What will I do?

Leaning on the sink, she began to sob, overcome by the hopelessness of her situation and guilt at her behaviour.

Suddenly, she heard the front door click. She turned and ran into the hall, already beginning to laugh at her foolishness. 'Oh, what a shock you gave me,' she said as the door slowly opened. A thin, wiry old woman, grey-haired and dressed in black, stepped inside. *'Buon giorno, signora,'* she said croakily and began to talk very quickly in Italian. Constance understood nothing. Still talking, the woman went into the kitchen and, standing on a chair, screwed a light bulb into the fitting above the table.

'Signor Ludovico, where is he?'

*'Mi dispiace, signora, non parlo inglese.'*

'Ludovico, Lud-o-vi-co, where is he?' she cried in desperation.

'Here he is!' a voice called in English. She turned. To her relief, Ludovico walked in through the open front door, carrying two enormous brown paper bags.

She rushed towards him. 'Oh, Ludovico! Thank God. I didn't know where you were. I was terrified!' She tried to kiss him.

'Wait! Wait!' he laughed as he pushed past her into the

kitchen and put the bags on the table. 'I've just been down to the market. I thought you would still be asleep.'

Her relief at his return made Constance angry. 'How could you do such a thing?' she demanded. 'Never give me a shock like that again.'

'No, Constanza,' Ludovico replied, 'I did not give you a shock. You gave it to yourself – because you do not trust me. If you are to love me you must believe in my honour. Now, we talk no more of this seriousness.'

Constance cooed with delight as Ludovico unpacked the bags. Coffee, oranges, apples, fresh warm bread, thick creamy milk – she couldn't believe the luxury of it all. They ate on the terrace and Constance found it almost as sensual and satisfying an experience as the previous night's love-making. She sat back in the sun and closed her eyes. Sensations rushed in: the cries of the traders in the street below them mixed with the screams of the swallows that swished low across the roofs; the dark aroma of the strong coffee mingled with the fresh smell of the bread.

Her dreaming was interrupted by Ludovico who knelt before her and slid his hand between her legs. She groaned voluptuously at his touch. He gently pulled her out of the chair and, kissing her, said, 'Come to bed.'

'What about the woman?'

'She has gone. We are alone.'

He led her into the bedroom, which was glowing with an intense white light like nothing she had ever seen in England. Without bothering to close the door, Ludovico began to make long and passionate love to her, teaching her how to take and give pleasure in ways she had never dreamed of. They remained there all day.

On the second day, she wrote Louise a letter that she knew was inadequate but told all that she felt capable of confiding for the moment. Writing it reinforced her conviction that she had been right to stay in Florence. Ludovico was the only man she would ever love.

On the same day she discovered the Italian willingness

to make love anywhere. In her innocence, Constance had always assumed that it was an activity that took place in bed. When Ludovico came back to the apartment with food for lunch and found her stripped to the waist, washing herself in the cracked kitchen sink, he immediately started making love to her, pushing her back until the taps dug into her. She was as thrilled by his daring as by his actions. Apart from anything else, it was only eleven thirty in the morning.

On the third day, Ludovico spoke to the Principe di Savognia, his tennis partner and the owner of the flat they were staying in. He wanted to discuss this English girl with his oldest friend. Giancarlo Battista di Savognia had known Ludovico since he was a boy. After the death of Ludovico's father, Giancarlo had become his closest confidant. Ludovico had no secrets from him. He had told him of the English girl on that first day when he had asked for the loan of the flat and permission for Constance to telephone from his palazzo. Giancarlo had agreed instantly to both requests and then forgotten about them. It was not particularly unusual for somebody to borrow the flat. Many of his young friends still lived at home under the watchful eyes of their mothers and needed a place to take their mistresses. The attic apartment perfectly fitted the bill and was much in demand.

The Principe di Savognia was typical of his class. Bathed in a delicate self-importance, he held himself in high esteem as the bearer of one of Italy's oldest titles. He listened, but he did not involve himself in the affairs of his friends, except on the level of gossip. Ludo's brief romance with an English girl was so run-of-the-mill that it hardly warranted mention at dinner parties, let alone gossip. However, when Ludovico told him that he wished to marry Constance, that was a different story, worthy of gossip indeed. Savognia was incredulous.

'But you know nothing of her,' he pointed out. 'You must wait. It is too soon to think of such things. Perhaps in a few months' time it will be different. Or you may have moved on by then.' He looked closely at Ludovico. His friend, he could tell, was serious. Nevertheless, he was surprised by the vehemence of his reply.

'Are you crazy? Months! I mean today . . . tomorrow . . . before the weekend.'

'My dear Ludo, what are you talking about? Have you gone mad, talking of marrying a total stranger – and a foreigner – after five minutes? What would your mother say? Besides, you have her already, there is no need.'

As he spoke, he looked at Ludovico, who was furiously plucking at the strings of his racket and gazing at the ground. Savognia was exceptionally tall for an Italian and stood well above Ludovico. He took a slight step forward and, taking his friend's chin in his hand, lifted his face so that Ludovico was forced to look up into his eyes.

'Ludo,' he said softly. 'You have been this way before. Don't be silly about this girl. It is an infatuation – and one I understand, believe me. She is foreign and beautiful, I am sure. You have awakened her to passion and taken her virginity. It is all very agreeable but please, my dear boy, don't allow yourself to take it seriously. You can only be hurt if you do – and you will surely hurt her. Believe me, I know you. I know your . . . enthusiasms. By all means enjoy an autumn romance but do not think of it as anything more than that.'

Ludovico scowled at him, then jerked his head away. Looking at the ground, he said, 'You know me better than anyone, Giancarlo, but this you do not understand.'

'How can I?' his friend quickly broke in. 'It is all so new and, in any case, I haven't seen the girl. In fact,' he added softly, 'it is all so new that not even you can know her.'

He was aware that he was infuriating Ludovico by his opposition to the plan but everything he knew about his friend convinced him that the idea of a whirlwind marriage was wrong and could end only in disaster.

Savognia had been brought up in an anglicised fashion. Looked after by an English nanny, he had frequently spoken English at home with his parents. Later, he had spent a year at Cambridge after graduating from the University of Bologna. He felt that he knew the English character and, although he wouldn't hurt Ludovico by articulating it, he was sure that the sort of English girl who would get off a train and move in with a stranger would very soon be travelling on.

Giancarlo Savognia had always allowed his intellect to rule his emotions. That is why he underestimated Constance and misunderstood Ludovico. He could not imagine how an intelligent person (as Ludo insisted this girl was) would behave as Constance had, unless there were some emotional flaw in her. Giancarlo had never known passion, and had only occasionally felt the pull of lust. Nevertheless, he felt that intellectually he understood both emotions better than his friend. When they parted, he was sure that he had given Ludovico serious pause for thought.

He was wrong. Ludovico went straight to the Via Santo Spirito, strode purposefully through the leafy courtyard, and ran up the broad shallow stairs to the top floor. He burst into the apartment, woke Constance from her doze, and fell upon her, greedy and desperate to prove to himself that he was right and his friend was wrong. Constance was overwhelmed by his urgency. Afterwards, they lay silently together and as he thought of the recent conversation with Giancarlo he slowly ran his finger along her hip-bone and down towards her inner thigh. For him this was the most beautiful part of her body. Her flesh was so creamy-white and fine that he could trace the blue veins under it. The concavity beneath the hip-bone reminded him of a little valley high in the hills of Tuscany or Sicily, bare, smooth and satisfying. He loved to lie next to her and kiss it and then to stretch flat and look up at her hips. The gentle curve of her body was like a piece of rock smoothed by the sea. He marvelled at how soft her skin felt to his touch. It was of a different, finer, texture than the skin of an Italian woman. He was determined that she would belong to him, exclusively and permanently.

On the fourth morning Ludovico sat on the bed beside her. 'We are to marry,' he said. 'I make arrangements. OK? We can go this afternoon. It is easy.'

Constance was overcome; she couldn't look at him. She focused on the cigarette held lightly in his hand. She knew by looking at his fingers that he was completely relaxed. She thought, He is utterly confident that I will say yes – if not today, then another time. And he was. He was also confident that they would marry that afternoon, after tennis, but her silence troubled him.

'You *do* want?' he asked. It was barely a question.

She finally looked at him. 'Of course I do. You know I do. But so much has happened . . . so quickly.'

'And?' he interrupted.

'And there are so many questions unanswered.'

'Such as?'

'Well, for a start, I'm not a Catholic.'

'I will tell the priest that you are. There is not a problem.'

'Ludovico, I cannot do that. It is wrong.'

'Wrong?'

'It would be a sin. We can't start our life like that. I don't want to marry in a Catholic church. Surely there's an Anglican one here?'

'Constanza, you cannot ask that of me! For a Catholic to be married in an Anglican church . . . is . . . well, it would mean that we were not married.' He paused. 'We will have a civil wedding. That is the answer. It is so easy – religion doesn't come into it.'

Constance had always thought registry marriages pedestrian and lacking in commitment, but before she could say any more Ludovico slipped from the bed and made for the door, saying, 'You rest, Constanza, I am going to arrange.'

She heard his feet bouncing down the palazzo steps and

107

then his whistle as he crossed the courtyard. In the silence that followed, she placed her arms over her bare breasts and, pushing them up, bent her head and smelt them. They still retained the faint aroma of Ludovico's body. She loved the smell of his flesh and was happy to have it lingering on her. She lay there rocking gently back and forward, thinking, If that is what he wants . . . She felt as if she were floating in limbo, beyond conscience, beyond responsibility and even beyond reality. But she also knew that he was right. She wanted to marry him and she could see no reason to delay simply because of religious differences. Should she tell her mother – and would he tell his? She decided not, in both cases. Bald information was all it could be: the statement of a fact, far beyond parental agreement or approval. Strangely, although Nora was in her mind, Constance realised that she hadn't thought of Nicky since she had left Northumberland.

Golden morning light bathed the apartment as she slipped into a gentle sleep. When Ludo returned, he found her still dreamily lying on the bed. He was so angry and frustrated that he hardly noticed she was not yet dressed. The registry office couldn't marry them at such short notice and they must wait until the following day. As he paced up and down the narrow kitchen, shouting curses through the bedroom door, Constance smiled. How emotionally extravagant the Italians are, she thought fondly as, calming down, he returned to bed and gently made love to her.

On the fifth day, they married. Ludovico was intent on keeping it a secret, so the ceremony was empty and impersonal. The witnesses were people who worked at the registry office. Constance felt a pang of sadness as she walked into the building on Ludovico's arm, thinking that no one in the world who cared for them knew what was happening. The previous night she had spoken again to Louise – an anguished conversation, that ended with her aunt insisting that Nora be told that Constance was not in Rome.

Even to think of Nora was a sort of agony for Constance. Over the past two days she had managed to convince herself that her mother was a different person from the one she knew. She had even begun to believe that Nora would understand this grand passion. Listening to Louise's agitation, Constance was amazed at her own naiveté. Hope had betrayed her into thinking dreams could become reality. She realised that there would be no light-hearted understanding in Cramer of actions for which she herself could find no easily articulated justification.

'Oh, my God!' Louise had cried. 'Why on earth haven't you phoned her yet? I don't know what she'll say. She'll go absolutely demented! Really, Constance, I can't *believe* what you've done! To get off a train with a total stranger . . . I really cannot . . . well, words fail me. What sort of a man is he? No, don't tell me! I *don't* wish to know. Now listen to me, Constance, you *must* phone your mother. I won't do it for you!'

Constance promised that she would, but she was so afraid of the outcome that she knew she couldn't, not until she and Ludovico had been married and she was beyond her mother's power.

Kissing Ludovico in the cramped registry office, in front of strangers, she wished that her mother, Louise, Miss Hatherby and so many others could have been there with them. After the ceremony, she and Ludovico went to Chiesa Santo Spirito, at the end of their road, where Ludovico had arranged for them to be blessed, explaining to her that it had no religious significance and did not endanger her non-Catholic soul. As she stood in the dark chapel, listening to the priest's murmured prayers, the empty, depressed feeling intensified. When she had lost her virginity four nights earlier, Constance had been elated; but now she felt as she had always understood women did on their bridal night: deeply upset and even slightly resentful at what had happened. She was coming down to earth. The romantic fantasy world that she had entered when she left the train with Ludo was dissolving in the light of reality. As they walked into the trattoria opposite their palazzo for the wedding breakfast to which nobody had been invited, she shivered slightly. What did she know of this man who was now her husband, and what was to become of them, two strangers who had begun to be familiar with each other's bodies but knew nothing of the thoughts and emotions that lay within.

Ludovico called exuberantly for champagne but it was unobtainable, so he settled for a sweet fizzy wine instead. He wanted to cheer Constance up but it had the opposite effect. As the courses came and went, she could only toy with her food.

Eventually, Ludovico said, 'It has been a mistake, no? You do not wish to be my wife? I do not please you.'

She looked up, struck by his desolate tone. His eyes were full of tears.

'Oh, Ludo,' she cried, 'please don't cry. I couldn't bear it!'

'I want only you,' he replied, rubbing his eyes with the back of his hand, 'but you do not want me. How could you let me do this to us? Why didn't you say? Why, Constanza? What can we do? I cannot live without you but marriage without love is insupportable. Please, please, you *must* learn to love me!'

Tears were rolling down his cheeks. To Constance, he looked like a little lost boy.

'Oh, Ludo, I can't bear to see you cry. I love you, I really do. I'm *happy* that we are married. It's just that I feel so cheap. In England registry office weddings are for girls who have got themselves into trouble. I wish we had waited and done it properly – with our relations and friends. A real wedding.'

'No,' he replied, 'that wouldn't have worked. We are married in the only way we can be married, believe me. That is not the problem. What I do not understand is why you don't love me.'

'Ludovico,' Constance said, placing his hand on the ring on her finger, 'I love you more than anybody in the world and I always will. That's why I wanted something to be proud of.'

Ludovico brightened. 'But you have something. You have us. Are you not proud of us? We are so young and beautiful. We make love like no one ever has in the whole world – the whole *history* of the world – we are better than Antony and Cleopatra,' his voice began to rise with his spirits, 'Romeo and Juliet, Paolo and Francesca, Beatrice and Dante,' he was lost for words, 'better than . . . better than . . . Fred Astaire and Ginger Rogers! Nobody has even been better in bed than Constanza and Ludovico.'

He stood up, grinning, and held his glass high. '*Ragazzi!* Boys!' he shouted to draw the attention of everyone in the trattoria to their table. '*Ragazzi!* We are the greatest lovers in the world. Nobody has ever loved as we have!' There was a great round of applause. 'And,' Ludovico cried, 'we are just married!'

It seemed to Constance that the room exploded with noise. There was cheering, clapping, stamping on the floor and banging on the tables, as everyone in the restaurant crowded round them. 'You want family?' Ludovico shouted above the noise. 'You got family. The Italian nation. They are your family!' and, to even greater cheers, he kissed her long and hard. More wine was brought, an accordionist appeared from nowhere and everybody began to sing while she and Ludovico danced their first dance in the hastily cleared space in the middle of the floor. Then the celebration began. People crowded in from the streets, everybody danced and sang and drank and laughed. It was the most marvellous party Constance had ever been to.

As she lay in bed that night, she was unable to sleep for the excitement of it all. Scenes from the evening flashed before her eyes: the dignity of the old man to whom Ludovico had gently presented her and with whom she had performed a stately dance, delicately held in his wizened old arms; the young men who had made a ring around her and Ludo before lifting them on to their shoulders and carrying them back to Santo Spirito; the women who had caressed her blonde hair and whispered, '*Bella! Bella! che bella ragazza!*' Above all, she recalled the pride and happiness in Ludovico's eyes as they met hers in the swirling crowd. It had been a marvellous wedding party and it was followed by a wedding night that she knew she would never forget. Despite the heat, Ludovico's passion had taken her to heights she had not dreamed were possible. Now, although it was past two, sweat was still running between her breasts and trickling over her stomach. She silently slid out of bed and stood by the window. The linen curtain fell inert across it. There was no breeze to lighten the atmosphere.

Her mood changed suddenly and completely. Once again, she felt lonely and cast out. Cool Northumberland seemed so far away. She began to cry. She longed to be close to her mother, or talking to Louise or cycling up the drive towards the grim yews of Seaton Cramer Hall and the warm welcome of Miss Hatherby. When she thought of her old friend, she felt ashamed. That dignified woman would never have acted as she had: so selfishly and unthinkingly. I have behaved like a spoilt child wanting its own way, she said to herself. How am I ever going to tell my mother and Louise? And how could she keep her shameful marriage from Miss Hatherby? She thought of the inevitable disdain with which her friend would react to the news that Constance had been seduced into a reckless marriage with a virtual stranger.

She crept back to bed and lay next to her husband, taking care to leave a space between their bodies.

The next day, Constance had regained her equilibrium. She knew perfectly well that she and Ludo were right for each other. Happy when they were together, when she was left alone she fretted, missing his presence and the way the light moved round his body as he enthusiastically used every inch of it to express the slightest emotion. She felt she would never tire of the way Ludo demonstrated each change in his mood. She already knew his movements off by heart: the way he rubbed the bridge of his nose when he made fun of her; how his upper lip crinkled as he laughed; his habit of pulling his ear as he made a point he thought important. Above all, she loved his Italian mannerisms: hands cupped together in a pleading gesture when she was slow to understand something or arms flailing in the air as he enthused about the beauty of Capri, the magnificence of St Peter's – anything, so long as it was Italian. His Mediterranean vibrancy excited and stimulated her. She compared him with Nicky. How could she ever have thought that his negligent self-involvement would be enough for her?

Constance knew the time had come to face the music and speak to Nora. But she also felt a compulsion to talk to Louise. She couldn't bear the rift that had come between her and the aunt who had always understood and helped her; who had so many times stood between her and her mother as faithful friend wanting the best for them both and who was now so alienated from her. She rang her first.

Louise's tone was placatory.

'Your uncle and I think you should get on a train and come down to us right away, darling,' she said. 'If you mean anything to this young man, I'm sure he will understand. He can come and visit you some time later.'

'I can't do that, Louise.'

'Why on earth not? Is there something wrong with you? Oh, my *God*! He isn't holding you against your will? Tell me, Constance, *for God's sake, why can't you leave?*'

Constance began to whimper.

'Oh, Aunt Louise, I'm married.'

There was silence at the other end. Plucking up her courage, Constance took advantage of it and plunged ahead. 'You don't understand what it's like, Aunt Louise. He's lovely. And he loves me. Oh, Aunt Louise, *do* try to understand. I *really* love him, I really, really do. I'm so happy. I can't bear to think of you thinking that he's

113

bad. He isn't. He didn't make me do anything I didn't want to. I did it because I love him. I will always love him.'

As she spoke she suddenly realised that the whole thing made sense simply because of that, the only thing that mattered. Why should she cry? She wasn't ashamed of Ludovico or her marriage. She was immediately calmer.

'I'm all right,' she said. 'You and Uncle Jim mustn't worry. Everything is fine.'

And she knew that it was. Ludovico was the most beautiful man she had ever seen. He was the kindest man she had ever met. He was the most romantic man she had ever known – and the most exciting. Despite her negligible experience of men before she met him, she was convinced that Ludovico was as near to perfection as any man could be.

Her courage flooded back; but not sufficiently for her to be ready to talk directly to her mother.

'Aunt Louise, please, please will you talk to Mummy and warn her?'

'*Warn* her?' Louise echoed in alarm. 'What can I tell her? *You* must face the music, darling. I can't do it for you. How can I just ring her out of the blue and tell her that her daughter has married the first Italian she's met, without telling any of us?'

'Well,' Constance wheedled, 'tell her I'll be ringing with some news. You don't need to go further than that. Please, Louise, just for me?' In her confusion, she forgot to call her 'Aunt'.

Reluctantly Louise agreed. Pouring herself a large brandy, she booked a call to Northumberland, hoping that Nora would be out. For the first time since she arrived in Rome, the connection came up immediately and she could hear Nora's voice, distant but clear, at the other end. Inevitably, Nora had the whole story within minutes. Her reaction surprised Louise.

'Well,' she said, 'you know who I blame for all this, don't you?'

Louise was relieved when she went on, 'Nicky Scott Wilson. I knew she'd have to find some way of getting over him but I didn't expect anything as drastic as this.'

Her matter-of-fact tone surprised Louise. 'Constance has done this on the rebound,' Nora continued. 'She cannot love this man, no matter what she says. Good heavens, she only left here a week ago! How can she possibly know somebody well enough to get married, the little ninny! Where were they married – a church or a registry office? How easily can marriages be annulled in Italy?'

Nora's realism and level-headed assessment of the situation made Louise ashamed of her own emotional reaction to the news.

Nora Simpson didn't believe in crying over spilt milk. She couldn't rail into thin air. As she sat with a whisky and waited for Constance's call, she listened to the autumn wind tugging at the corners of the austere house. It drowned the roar of the waves which she knew would be crashing on to the beach in impotent and seemingly endless fury. She suddenly felt terribly alone and isolated in this remote corner of England. Whereas summer still lingered in Florence, winter had already taken hold in Cramer. The night was cold and draughts swept round the room. Nora thought of Will. How would he have taken the news of this sneaky, hole-in-the-corner business? As she sipped the scotch, she reflected that if he were still alive he would no doubt be bringing the full force of his liberal rationalism to bear on the problem right now. She had to admit that he would almost certainly not see the situation as an unmitigated disaster. After all, Constance was respectably and correctly married, was she not? Presumably she loved the man and he loved her. Dismissing fears that her daughter might have been tricked into a fake marriage by a man determined to ruin her, Nora tried to think more positively, but her brain persistently returned to the appalling question, 'Why an *Italian*, for God's sake?'

By the time the call came both women were calm. Nora was determined not to make a scene; Constance was resolved not to cry. They both lived up to their intentions.

'Mummy?' Constance asked timidly when she heard the voice at the other end.

'Constance, are you all right?'

The voice sounded reassuringly calm.

'Mummy, there's nothing to worry about, honestly.'

'*I'll* decide that, when I've heard what you have to say for yourself. You'd better start at the beginning.'

So Constance told her mother everything. Nora reacted with masterly self-control.

'Well, Constance,' she said, 'I don't know whether you're right or wrong. It could be as marvellous as you think it will be or it could be a total disaster. Only time will tell. All I'll say is that you must be honest and, if it's wrong and this man is a mistake, you must have the courage to tell me. That is all I ask.'

When Nora had put down the receiver, she thought ruefully, She's a chip off the old block. Who am I to complain? I hardly knew Will much better when we were married. Truth to tell, I made my decision within a week, as well. It must be a family failing. And she went to bed thinking of that amazing week at Gleneagles. Somehow, it made Italy seem less far away and her daughter's behaviour there much less reprehensible.

Although she knew that, at best, her mother's approval was qualified, Constance derived strength from the fact that at least she now knew. While Ludovico was playing tennis, she sat on the balcony and wrote Nora a letter.

Dear Mummy,

I know how disappointed and unhappy you must feel and I know you think I've behaved badly. I suppose I have but that doesn't make my behaviour wrong. I'm going to tell you right away that, although I wasn't a virgin when we married, I was until I left the train

116

with Ludovico. I could have resisted him until we were married, and I know he would have waited, but it was me who didn't want to wait. I loved him so much that I knew it would be all right. I haven't made a mistake. He is everything I want and will always want. If you really care about my happiness, you will be pleased at what has happened. I have never been so happy in my life and I know that it will go on for ever. When you meet Ludovico I'm sure you'll understand. You'll love him. Promise me you won't worry but, especially, promise you won't make up your mind until you see him. Please try to understand.

love,<br>Constance

★

'Giancarlo has invited us for lunch on Sunday, at his villa in Fiesole. It will be fun. You will meet lots of my good friends.' Ludo smiled with delight. He couldn't wait to show off his bride. The news of his marriage had spread like wildfire through Florence. All his friends would be at the Villa Battista to see him and Constance for themselves.

Constance bit her lip. 'What will I say to them?' she asked nervously. 'How many will speak English?'

'All! All!' Ludovico replied flamboyantly. 'There will be no problem with that, believe me. Besides, I shall be with you to translate if necessary. Do not worry.'

He could see that the news had alarmed her. He took her hands in his. 'Look, they are my friends. They will like you. They want to like you – because they like me. Be just as you are now and you'll be fine.'

Ludovico had all the confidence of the good-looking young man who knows that his charm and social position make him welcome everywhere. He had told her he was an only child like her, but Constance knew that being an only child in Italy was different. There had been nothing solitary about Ludovico's life. He had rolled through childhood in a warm cocoon of love provided by endless cousins, uncles, aunts and servants. Feeling that the world liked him, he liked the world and faced it, relaxed and open. Constance had been brought up much less extravagantly. Self-confidence had not been part of her education so, despite her brief period of employment at de Levantière's, she felt insecure and nervous when she met new people. The idea of a luncheon party full of unknown Italians rather terrified her. Ludo's stories about the life he had led convinced her that all his friends would be sophisticated and worldly. She knew she would be gauche and awkward. Constance was especially nervous of meeting the women. She had already noticed on the streets of Florence how pretty the girls were – and how well dressed – and she made up her mind to look just as good.

'Do you think you can borrow an iron for me?' she asked, determined to make sure that her appearance would not let Ludovico down.

They went to lunch at Fiesole on a perfect autumn day. As the taxi climbed away from the city, Constance was enchanted by the morning bells ringing out from all the churches in Florence. She looked at the Duomo shimmering in the haze below them. She thought it majestic, dominating the city without overwhelming it. It has very good manners, she said to herself fancifully. Although her stomach was churning at the thought of the coming ordeal, she was determined to appear at ease so as not to let Ludo down. She gazed out of the window, rehearsing conversational gambits.

Ludovico was uncharacteristically silent. He too was feeling nervous. It was important to him that his friends should like his wife, especially the two or three who, like Savognia, were close to him. It was also essential that Constance should learn to like Italians and the Italian life. He didn't want a wife who stood on the periphery of his existence, always the foreigner, never involved with Italy. He had seen that happen before in Florence with what some of his friends referred to dismissively as 'half marriages'. He was determined that they would not say that of his.

As they walked down the drive, Constance was surprised at how cool it was under the pines. Drawing nearer, she could hear the noise of laughter from the terrace. They walked round the side of the house and her step faltered. Her nervousness was forgotten. Spread before her was the whole of Florence. She had never seen a view so beautiful.

'Oh!' she gasped. 'Ludo, look!'

Although he had marvelled at it many times, Ludovico had never become blasé about the stupendous vista from the Villa Battista and its famous terrace that ran the whole length of the low, pale yellow house. He was delighted at Constance's reaction.

'Come to the edge,' he said, grasping her hand excitedly. He took her to the balustrade. Before them was a landscape that could have come straight from the brush of Giotto. Immediately below them were vines, their leaves turning scarlet above the purple grapes. They gave way to blackened and gnarled olive trees that rhythmically criss-crossed the sweep of the valley.

'What are those trees?' Constance asked.

'Olives. Older than time. They are the blood of the Mediterranean,' Ludovico answered theatrically.

'Oh, Ludovico, what a romantic place to live,' she sighed, 'I'd give anything to have a view like this.'

'For how long are we to be deprived of the company of the lovely new bride?' a voice spoke silkily behind them.

They spun round. Standing a few feet away, with a glass in his hand, was their host.

'Giancarlo! *Ciao! Come stai?* How are you?' Ludo said delightedly.

'*Benvenuti!* Welcome to you both!' his friend replied with a slight smile.

'Let me introduce you to Constanza, my wife,' Ludo said triumphantly.

'I am delighted to meet you.' Giancarlo bowed slightly

119

as he took Constance's hand and pressed his lips to it. The formal gesture, chivalrous and yet intimidating, was like a bucket of cold water thrown over Constance's confidence. She felt her face go hot with embarrassment as he straightened up and gave her a piercing look that took in everything about her appearance. He had not yet decided whether she would be friend or enemy, so his eyes were distant – and she knew it.

'You must come and join the others. They are all eagerly awaiting the guest of honour.'

Giancarlo's smile did not reassure Constance. She could feel her heart thumping and was sure that people would see its movement beneath her dress. She knew that at least the dress – given to her by Monsieur de Levantière as a farewell gift – looked right. In beige shantung, with a full skirt cinched with a wide belt in grey suede, it was very sophisticated and was made more so by her long grey gloves and tiny grey hat. It gave her confidence and she felt sure that she could hold her own against the Italian guests.

Her thoughts were interrupted by Giancarlo. He was talking to her.

'The vulgar think that Venice is the most romantic city in the world,' he was saying, 'but its charms are too obvious. Florence is much more romantic, but the most beautiful city in Italy is Bologna. Do you know it, Constanza?'

Constance had barely heard of it but said, with much more confidence than she was feeling, 'No, but I hope Ludo will take me there soon.'

She looked at Giancarlo. He was fine-featured and his dress and movements had a fastidiousness that made Ludo's appearance seem almost earthy. His receding hair exposed a noble curved brow. His dark eyes were serious but it was his mouth that made Constance hopeful. It was sensitive and humorous at the same time. He was wearing a sports coat which had obviously been tailored in London, suede shoes, a striped tie and a beige waistcoat.

He looked as if he had just stepped out of a drawing room in the shires. Constance thought it extraordinary that this English-looking body could be topped off by such an Italian face. Somehow, it was as if he were playing a part.

'Of course,' he was saying urbanely, 'the most magnificent cities are in England. Cambridge, Oxford, York. So full of chivalry, so . . . how can I say it? So confidently upper-class. They are totally elegant. Italian cities are so coarse when you lift their skirts.'

He smiled directly at her and she smiled back to hide her slight embarrassment at the sexuality in the comment, knowing that a few weeks earlier she would have blushed at it. She felt that the remark was an acknowledgement that, young though she was, she would be accepted in Italy as a mature and grown-up woman. The thought gave her confidence and she managed to relax slightly. This man would be a friend, she was sure. She already felt safe in his company as he went on talking effortlessly.

They were now on the terrace proper. The silence of curiosity descended on the guests as Giancarlo said, '*Finalmente!* They have arrived! Ludo never could get out of bed in the morning!' Everyone laughed. The tension was eased. A white-gloved servant came forward with a tray of drinks, which he offered Constance.

'Signorina,' he said as he lifted the tray towards her.

'No, no! Enzo,' said Giancarlo, wagging his finger with mock severity. '*Signora!*'

Everyone laughed again. The ice was broken. Constance relaxed a little more. Ludo was right. These faces, behind the curiosity, were friendly. As Giancarlo took her round his guests, formally making introductions, Constance knew that she could fit into this world of refinement, privilege and elegance – and that she wanted to. She coped with the frankly curious looks of the men, one of whom made her blush as he kissed her hand by saying, 'No wonder Ludo does not get out of bed in the morning.' She even survived the appraising looks of the women and smiled when she heard one of them say after she had

121

passed, 'What beautiful English skin.' Constance realised why she could hold her own in this elegant crowd: she was different because she was foreign but, more important, admirable because she was British.

'We must start without Gioella,' Giancarlo said to his guests, in Italian. Constance did not understand him but the last word, strangely rhythmic and warm to her ears, stuck in her mind.

Giancarlo took her arm courteously as if he had known her for years, and, followed by his guests, led her out of the sun on the terrace and into the shade at the side of the house. There, in a raised garden overlooking the drive, and sheltered by umbrella pines, the servants were waiting to serve food at little tables scattered around haphazardly.

Constance had lost Ludo – something she had been dreading on the journey up from Florence – but she was not alarmed. She and Giancarlo sat at a table with a distinguished-looking woman in her fifties, whose name Constance could not remember but who was referred to by everyone as Contessa, and her son, Pino, who laughed a lot and told Constance anecdotes about the other guests. Like everyone else, it seemed, he spoke English impeccably. After a particularly silly piece of gossip, his mother leant forward. '*Basta, Pino, cattivo ragazzo!* Stop it, you naughty boy!' she said in a harsh voice which, years later, Constance was to learn was typically Milanese.

The Contessa turned to her with a smile. 'Signora. Listen to no more of his nonsense, I beg you! He will destroy the reputation of everyone in Florence, if he has a chance.' Pino wriggled flirtatiously and grinned at Constance, who laughed at him. His mother obviously adored him and merely said with unconvincing sincerity, 'Now, Pino, mind what I say.'

At that moment, there came a *phut-phut-phut* from the drive below as a tiny Fiat Topolino chugged towards the house. There was a lull in the conversation and then somebody said that word 'Gioella' again. Constance detected a change in the atmosphere as Giancarlo excused himself and walked down the steps to greet his last guest. The mood was now one of tingling anticipation. Pino smiled and said, 'Have you met Gioella yet?'

'Pino, please!' his mother said sharply, in a tone that puzzled Constance. It was severe and almost panicky, she thought.

A lively and rather loud woman's voice could be heard below them in the drive, speaking to Giancarlo in very quick Italian. Constance had no time to assess the bewildering exchange of tone that the lunch party had taken before Giancarlo was walking towards her with a vivacious woman by his side who was busily blowing kisses and calling *Ciao* to the tables she passed.

'Constanza,' Giancarlo said with all the formality of their first encounter before lunch, 'allow me to present Signora de Grignano. Gioella, this is Constanza, Ludovico's English wife.'

Constance looked at Gioella and calculated she must be in her early thirties. She had thick black hair, cut short, enormous dark eyes that were never still, and large, very scarlet lips. She was wearing a jade-green dress that Constance realised, from her days at Paul de Levantière, was exceedingly expensive despite its simplicity, and a pair of tiny gold slippers. She was the epitome of fashionable glamour and, merely looking at her, Constance felt swamped.

'How do you do?' Gioella said, in heavily accented English. Her voice was deep and had a sardonic, mocking tone that frightened Constance. She could think of nothing to say. The tension was broken by Pino.

'Gioella, you witch!' he screamed. 'Where did you get those divine sandals? They must be Ferragamo!'

'*Naturalmente, tesoro!* Of course, darling!' Gioella said with a sharp emphasis on the last word. She looked round the group. 'Ludo!' she called, as Ludovico moved towards her. 'How clever you are to find the perfect English rose of your dreams. But how naughty of you to pluck her and set her in a vase that only you see! Why didn't you invite us to the wedding, you bad man?'

Ludo grinned sheepishly. 'But you have been in Monte-catini,' he countered. 'You couldn't have come in any case. I know how you would let nothing interrupt the cure.'

The cure? Constance thought, looking in surprise at this woman who seemed so radiant with health.

Gioella smiled. 'I can lose a few centimetres from my waist *any* time, darling! For this I would most certainly cross oceans, let alone forgo a couple of treatments. After all, Ludo, darling, who can resist the making of history, no matter how briefly?'

She took his arm with an easy familiarity and, turning away from Constance, led him back to his table saying, 'Now, you darling man, tell me how such a *bizarre* thing happened.'

Constance was stunned. The hostile tone of Gioella's last comment shook her. Even worse was the way she had been abandoned without a thought by her husband. She was not sophisticated enough to hide her bewilderment and in order to cover her embarrassment the Contessa said quickly, 'They are like brother and sister, signora. They have known each other since they were children.'

Constance watched Ludo and Gioella laughing at some private joke, and hated them both. Her thoughts were interrupted by Giancarlo. 'Contessa,' he was saying, 'if you will excuse us we will take some lunch. Come, Con-stanza.'

Savognia helped Constance to the delicious buffet. There were lobster, turkey and wild boar salads, wonder-ful vegetables and mountains of fruit. Thinking of the austere rations back in Britain, Constance was uneasy at such luxury. Quite apart from the self-indulgence, she wondered where it all came from. Was Savognia in the black market? She smiled at her naiveté. How could he be – he was a prince, wasn't he?

The wine was pink and slightly fizzy. Constance loved

it and drank freely to keep up her courage. Gradually, she relaxed sufficiently for Savognia to feel able to leave her and join his other guests. She slowly walked towards Ludovico and Gioella. Although she felt like a little girl who had gone into the wrong party room, she was determined that this woman would not keep her away from her husband. Gioella's eyes flashed with amusement as she pushed a chair towards her and said, 'Constance, what a very sophisticated dress. Do come and tell me all about the latest fashions in London.'

It was meant as a challenge, to expose her gaucherie, but Constance grabbed it as a lifeline.

'Which ones?' she asked demurely as she ignored the proffered chair and placed herself between Gioella and Ludovico. 'Are you thinking of Hartnell or Creed – or maybe Stiebel?'

Gioella was immediately alert. So, she thought, you are not so simple as you look. You do know something, after all.

'Actually,' she replied with a smile, 'I buy Hardy Amies. I think he has more French style than the others.'

'How funny to come to London for French style,' Constance replied sweetly.

'Constance was a model, you know, Gioella,' Ludovico interrupted enthusiastically, unaware of the battle of wills that was developing between the women.

There was a long pause. Gioella looked Constance up and down and said, 'Really? With anyone I would know?'

'Oh, I shouldn't think so,' Constance replied. 'What a delicious lunch this is,' she went on, changing the subject dramatically in her determination to keep the ball in her court. 'I really don't know how you Italians do it, so soon after the war. It isn't like this in England.'

'How old did you say you were, Constance?' Gioella asked.

'Oh,' Constance blushed, 'eighteen.'

'How *sweet*,' Gioella smiled, knowing that she had reasserted herself. She tweaked Ludovico's ear. 'Ludo, you are too naughty. What could you have been thinking of, you bad man?'

Constance wanted to shout, 'How dare you touch my husband?' but before she had time to react they were joined by Pino.

'*Ciao*,' he said casually as he sat next to Gioella. His rehearsed words froze on his lips as he became aware of the tension between the women. Thinking quickly he said, 'I love English women in beige. It goes so well with their pale skin and light hair. They look like deliciously glamorous mice, don't you agree, Ludo? Look at Constance. Isn't she just like a lovely little mouse, so sweet you could eat her?'

Constance blushed as the others laughed.

'And what about Italian women, Pino?' Gioella asked.

'They are very different,' he replied as he leaned forward and toyed with her necklace. 'They are from the land of green ginger. They are strong and powerful, but not to everybody's taste.'

'They are *in* the land of green ginger,' Ludovico said, 'Italy is that land. It has everything marvellous within its shores, everything a man could need.'

'Except the perfect woman,' Pino interrupted gallantly. 'She has come from the cool north.'

Gioella impatiently removed his hand from her necklace and, standing up, said, 'Come, Constance, let us leave these silly men. When Pino starts talking about his ideal woman we know we're more likely in a fantasy land than a green ginger one.'

Constance was appalled at the thought of being alone with her but rose helplessly as Gioella stretched out her hand. Casting an agonised glance of appeal at Ludovico, who failed to notice it, she was led off along the terrace, away from the tables and chairs.

'So, my dear,' Gioella said, 'you have fallen for the charms of the most charming man in Florence.'

It was as much a statement as a question. Constance noticed Gioella's mouth. Despite its generous proportions,

126

it had a downturning discontented twist as she talked. She laughed harshly. 'By marrying him, you will have made enemies of women you do not even know,' she continued. 'Ludo was very popular as a bachelor. It will be interesting to see how his popularity will survive when he appears with a bride. It will do him good if it slumps a little. You do not know Italian men yet, my dear, but I can tell you they are all – without exception – unbearably vain. It starts in the cradle.'

Constance could not fail to detect the bitterness in the voice, belying the smile on the lips. She didn't know how to reply.

'Where are you living?' Gioella asked.

Something in her tone convinced Constance that the answer was already known and she said, 'Santo Spirito.'

To her surprise, Gioella laughed and said, 'Really, that's too bad of Ludovico. Fancy taking you to that tired old love nest. It's been used a thousand times already, as I gather the bed makes clear. It's Florence's most famous musical bed.' She laughed gaily. 'But I'm sure you've already found out all about that, if I know Ludo. He and Carlo . . .' She stopped abruptly.

'Who is that?' Constance asked.

'Oh,' Gioella said dismissively, 'just someone from the far past. Nobody, really. I suppose we should rejoin the others. Don't you find them terribly provincial after London? I mean, I adore Florence and the people are delightful but, oh dear, they are so inward-looking. They know nothing but Florence and, worse, they don't care about anything that's not to do with them and their boringly perfect city.'

'What is Ferragamo?' Constance asked Ludovico, as they were going to bed that night.

'He is a shoemaker here. Gioella spends a fortune with him.'

He had already told her that Gioella's husband, Signor de Grignano, was a very rich industrialist in Milan who

127

had managed to treble his already substantial fortune during the war. He and Gioella lived between Milan and Capri but she was known by everybody in Italy because she was, as Ludovico said, *'sempre in giro* – always moving around'. She disliked Milan's climate and saw no reason why she should spend all her time in that city merely because her husband needed to be there for business.

'How old is she?' Constance asked.

'Oh, much younger than him,' Ludo replied, 'about thirty-three, perhaps.'

'She is very beautiful and elegant,' Constance ventured.

'Yes, I suppose so,' he answered vaguely.

'Have you known her long?'

'Oh, for ever. Gioella is the sort of person everyone has known for ever. She's always turning up.'

Like a bad penny, Constance thought viciously, saying nothing. Her silence surprised Ludovico.

'Don't you like her?' he asked.

'Oh,' she said, flustered. 'Yes, of course. I just find her a little . . . well, a little hard. But I'm sure that she's very nice when you get to know her.'

It wasn't true. From the moment she had met Gioella, Constance had seen a jealousy in her that was frightening. She knew that she was unhappy that Ludovico had married.

Ludo took Constance in his arms. 'You don't need to get to know her if you do not wish to. No one knows her. She is like a butterfly. She flits in and out of people's lives and never stays long enough to *allow* anyone to get to know her. Anyhow,' he ended, 'she is nothing to you. In fact, she is nothing to us, my darling. We do not need to worry about Gioella di Grignano. I don't want to think of her any more.'

Constance couldn't sleep. The events of the luncheon party swam before her eyes. She knew that she had been a success and that Ludo was proud of her. She also knew that, after some initial reservations, Giancarlo had taken to her. What concerned her was the strange attitude of Gioella. Constance felt it was important that she and this woman get on. Gioella was obviously the centre of the social life of Ludo's circle – probably the whole of Italy's, she thought nervously – and a close friend of Giancarlo as well. Constance wanted to avoid a confrontation with her. It was obvious that she hadn't managed that on their first encounter. Gioella had been irritated by her and, in revenge, had set out to make her feel like a schoolgirl – not only by action and word, but simply by being effortlessly in charge of everyone, with the possible exception of the Principe di Savognia. Constance could not get out of her mind the careless way Gioella had completely taken over Ludovico, excluding her as if she mattered not at all.

At breakfast the next morning, Constance said, 'Ludo, I think I must have some new clothes.'

'Of course,' he replied enthusiastically. 'Why don't you speak to Gioella? She is always so chic. She knows all the best dressmakers in Italy. She will advise you.'

Taking advice from Gioella di Grignano was the last thing Constance intended to do, but she replied sweetly, 'Oh, that isn't necessary. *I* will find some shops that suit me.'

There was a pause.

'But I will need some money.'

Ludovico looked at her sharply. 'Did you come to Italy without money?' he asked in surprise.

'No, of course not, but I didn't bring much. I was going to stay with my aunt. I certainly didn't bring enough to buy a new wardrobe – or even a couple of frocks, if it comes to that.'

'Then you must send to England for some,' Ludovico replied reasonably, returning to his newspaper.

Constance looked at him in indignation. She could feel herself going pink.

'What on earth do you mean?' she demanded. 'Aren't you intending to give me a dress allowance?'

Ludovico threw back his head and roared with laughter.

'What on earth is wrong with you?' she asked.

'My darling Constanza,' he said, 'I do not *have* any money. How can I give you a dress allowance when I cannot even afford to pay the rent on this flat?'

Constance looked at him in bewilderment. 'What do you mean?' she asked in a small voice.

'Exactly what I say, my darling,' Ludovico replied good-naturedly.

Constance went cold with fear. 'But how are we going to live?' she said.

There was silence as they looked at each other across the table. Constance's bourgeoise terror of being penniless was met by Ludovico's aristocratic disdain for money and the means of acquiring it. While her eyes glazed with panic, his sparkled ironically. Their attitudes were so different, they could have come from separate planets.

'What are we to do?' she pursued. 'How can we exist?' Then, clutching at a straw, 'What about your job?'

'Darling, don't be silly,' he replied indulgently.

'What's silly about it?' she demanded shrilly.

'I don't have a job.'

'Why not?'

Ludovico folded his newspaper and turned away in exasperation. 'No Villanuova has *ever* had a job, that's why,' he replied as if he were talking to a child. 'There is no job for people of our class in Italy. *Life* is our job.'

Constance had never heard anything so arrogantly decadent. She was blazing with middle-class righteousness.

'Well, you'll have to do *something*,' she answered sharply, 'unless we are to starve to death.'

Ludovico folded his arms and leaned on the table. His smile irritated her. It was so complacent.

'What there is to smile about I can't imagine,' she cried.

'You, my darling. You.'

'In what way?' she asked coldly.

'We are talking about a couple of frocks. Nothing more

130

serious than that. Why do you think of starving? You English are so extravagant. You exaggerate everything.'

'I find that very funny coming from an Italian,' Constance replied. 'Do we have any money or not?'

'Do *you* have any money, my darling?'

'Of course not. You know I haven't.'

'Then we have no money.'

'What on earth do you mean?' she cried in frustration. 'What about the land and the castle you told me about? Was that all a pack of lies? You *can't* be penniless if it's true.'

'The money is my mother's,' Ludovico replied. 'She gives me a small allowance. I am well enough known in Italy not to need money. There is not a problem.'

'So you have to ask your mother when you want money?'

'Yes,' Ludovico replied blandly.

'Well, that *is* the problem,' Constance retorted. 'You are a married man. You can't live on handouts from your mother. You have a duty to me. She doesn't even know of my existence yet.'

'Oh yes she does. I am sure. Italy is a village. Someone must have told her.'

Gossipy Pino or Gioella, Constance thought. 'Anyhow,' she went on, 'as a married man you must face up to your responsibilities. You must start working. Surely you can do *something*.'

Ludovico passed his hand over his eyes in mock weariness and said, 'Nothing, my darling, except make love.' He grinned. 'And you've spoilt that.'

'What do you mean?'

'Married gigolos are not in demand and, anyhow, who could possibly measure up to you?' He leaned over and grabbed her. 'No more of this nonsense,' he whispered. 'Come. Come to our bed.'

As he undressed her, Constance tried one more time.

'Ludovico,' she said earnestly, 'you must get a job. We must have a regular income. Besides, it isn't right for a man to be idle.' Although conscious of how like her mother she sounded she could not help herself. 'Surely you can find *something*.'

Ludovico stopped removing her clothes and sat down on the bed.

'Now listen, my darling,' he said quietly. 'I am a Castelfranco di Villanuova. I do not work. What you are saying is ridiculous. It is like an Englishman telling your Princess Margaret to find work as a waitress. Even if she tried, nobody would employ her – because she is Princess Margaret. That is exactly the same as people like me in Italy. So, *basta*, Constanza. We talk no more of this foolishness.'

As the plane from London bounced along the runway at Ciampino airport, Nora congratulated herself on not having been sick, even during the bumpy moments as they flew over the Alps. Looking out of the tiny window, she was disappointed. She had expected a deep blue Mediterranean sky. Instead, there was a thick haze on this October morning. It seemed to her that Rome was as grey as Northumberland and she felt slightly cheated. But when the door of the aeroplane was opened and the passengers stepped out, she was amazed at how muggy the temperature was. Smells like thunder, she thought, as she walked across the tarmac. She had decided to come to Italy knowing that she wouldn't rest until she had seen the situation for herself. Louise had agreed it was essential that Nora and Constance should meet and that Nora should talk to Ludovico. Louise was equally anxious to see this man who had had the power to persuade her niece to go against her upbringing and character and behave so recklessly after such a brief acquaintance. Waiting in the airport she was suddenly aware of Nora striding towards her. She was impressed by how elegant she looked, and could tell by her cousin's walk that Nora also felt that she was looking good. Her soft brown wool suit and velvet Vandyke cap perfectly complemented her auburn hair. She was delighted to be abroad – for the first time in her life – and pleased to see Louise again. In the first few minutes of their greetings, the real purpose of Nora's trip was forgotten by them both.

'My dear, you look marvellous!' Louise cried. 'What a wonderful hat. Where did you get it?'

'Marshall and Snelgrove,' Nora replied. 'I bought it yesterday. It cost seven guineas but I think it was worth it.'

'That's *outrageous*!' Louise laughed with delight. 'Jim would have a fit.'

As the taxi sped them into Rome, Nora had no chance to look at the view; she was kept busy listening to Louise, who was giving her assessment of the situation.

'She's obviously perfectly happy. There's no doubt of that at all. Jim has made some enquiries through Italian legal colleagues and by all accounts the man does come from a very good family – very good indeed – so at least he hasn't told her a tissue of lies about his background.'

She paused and smiled conspiratorially at Nora. 'His mother is a *princess*, my dear. Imagine!'

Nora was not nearly so impressed by that sort of thing as her cousin but she admitted to herself that it was unlikely a man from such a background would be deceiving Constance.

'The family is very well known in Italy, apparently,' Louise continued. 'Jim says the father is dead and there is some mystery about the mother. She lives in the depths of the country and is a little eccentric, so they say. Anyhow, Ludovico – ' she laughed – 'these Italians all have such priceless names my dear – Ludovico is coming down from Florence with Constance. I insisted. Of course, Constance has no idea that you'll be here. She thinks that she's merely bringing him down to meet Jim and me.'

'Does he have any money?' Nora interrupted.

'Oh, I'm *sure* he does, dear. After all, he *is* nobility, when all's said and done.'

Nora felt slightly mollified. At least her daughter wouldn't starve.

# CHAPTER 5

Although she was delighted that Louise had invited her and Ludovico to Rome, Constance was still nervous. Inconceivable as it seemed to her, she was terrified that Louise and Ludovico might not like each other.

'You'll adore Louise,' she told Ludovico, as they travelled to Rome. 'She's such fun and loves a joke. She was marvellous to me in London and she's always been able to get round Mummy for me. Once Louise has met you and told Mummy all about you, everything will be all right, I know.'

'And then?'

'And then we can go to England and you will meet Mummy. She'll have got used to the idea by then. After that, I think that I must meet *your* mother!'

'*Basta!*' Ludovico cried in mock exasperation. 'No more mothers, Constance, please! We have too many mothers in our marriage!'

In all her life, Nora had never felt so nervous as she did on the afternoon that she waited for Constance's arrival. The meeting had been cunningly orchestrated and she was alone in the flat. Louise was due to come in later – by which time, as she had said to Jim, she hoped that the dust would have settled. Nora was shaking, despite the fact that she had put on her new hat to bolster her resolve.

Constance was also shaking as the rickety lift slowly winched up to the third-floor apartment, but it was with

134

anticipation, not fear. She was looking forward to seeing Louise again and desperately in need of her approbation for her husband. As she straightened Ludovico's tie and smoothed his hair, she said, 'Now, just remember to be yourself. Act naturally and she will adore you.' She rang the bell and held his hand proudly as they waited. Footsteps echoed in the hall inside. A bolt was drawn back and the door began to open.

Constance's smile froze. Nora was standing before her, face grim beneath her new velvet hat.

'Mummy!' Constance gasped. 'What on earth are *you* doing here?'

'You might well ask, my girl! I'm here to get to the bottom of this nonsense!'

Nora held open the door and, despite the fact that Constance's legs had turned to jelly, she and Ludovico stepped nervously inside.

For several seconds nobody spoke. Nora was taken by surprise at the extraordinary good looks of the man who stood in front of her, although, characteristically, she noted that he was short – not quite as tall as her daughter. Constance was tongue-tied with fear. Before Nora knew what was happening, Ludovico stepped forward and took her hand. Bending low, he kissed it. Nora blushed with embarrassment and said falteringly, 'You'd better come in.'

As they followed her along the corridor, Ludovico squeezed Constance's hand. She looked at him in gratitude. She knew how much his action had thrown Nora off guard and felt sure that he had saved the day.

She was right. Nora was discomfited – but she was not routed. She had come to Rome to say certain things and she was determined to do so.

'I cannot imagine why you've come all this way,' Constance said. 'Everything is fine.'

Nora recovered. 'I wanted to speak to you,' she replied with dignity, 'and to see the man you are calling your husband.'

There was a silence. 'After all,' she went on, 'he *is* my son-in-law, apparently. Don't you think I have a right to know what he looks like, at least?'

Constance felt guilty. Her mother's words made her feel selfish and uncaring. To reassert her authority, she said, 'You don't have to worry, you know, I'm not going to ask you for money or anything. Ludovico and I are quite capable of supporting ourselves. And I can't imagine why you're suggesting that we're not properly married. We are – and we intend to stay that way.'

'I think you had better tell me about this whole business from the beginning – and don't leave anything out.'

As she listened, Nora was incredulous at the tone that Constance was taking. If she had not been in such an emotional state she would have realised that it was terror that was making her daughter defiant – terror that her mother might try to find some way to separate her from Ludovico and drag her back to England. Like an animal trapped in a corner, Constance could only attack and wound her tormentor.

'You've never cared about me, or my happiness,' she said, 'you've always wanted your own way in everything. You always tried to stop me doing things. Look how you hated Miss Hatherby, and Nicky . . .'

'Nicky?' her mother echoed sarcastically. 'Well, my girl, you certainly showed marvellous judgement with him, didn't you? I just hope, for your sake, that you've made a more sensible choice this time.' She paced the room in frustration. 'That is exactly what worries me, you silly girl. Can't you see? I don't want to stand in the way of your happiness but I know how immature you are and what a mess you could be making of your life. Anyone with any sense would at least have waited. Good God, how can you possibly know this man? He's not even English. What do you know about Italians?'

Constance hated her mother for behaving as if Ludovico didn't exist, and speaking as if he weren't standing there with them.

'Signora,' Ludovico replied, 'Italians are the same as the English when they fall in love.'

'Love? She's too young to know the meaning of the word! She's just a child.'

'You're jealous,' Constance replied. 'You can't bear to think that you've lost your influence over me. You can't accept that I have my own life now. You always wanted to keep me in your pocket. Well, it's too late. The bird has flown and won't be coming back.'

Something snapped inside Nora.

'You little trollop,' she cried. 'You fall into bed with the first man who comes along and expect it to last! You must be mad! Men tire of your kind very quickly, Italians or no, I can assure you of that. There are plenty more like you waiting to be picked up like some common tart! You haven't even the sense to see that, you little fool!' and, overcome with frustration and anger, she raised her hand, ready to strike her daughter.

Ludovico stepped between them and, with the greatest dignity, said to Nora, 'Signora, please do not speak to my wife in that way.'

The shock of his intervention stopped both women. Constance was filled with strength. She was his wife and that single, marvellous fact was all that mattered, whether her mother gave her approval or not.

Nora softened at Ludovico's protective gesture. Bitter pill that it was to swallow, she knew that she had to accept him or be alienated from her daughter for ever.

Louise arrived at that moment, making the maximum noise with her key in the door. She burst in, radiating positive good humour. By now she had decided to accept the marriage for the *fait accompli* it undoubtedly was. It was part of her conciliation plan that, having allowed her cousin to let off steam, friendly relations between mother and daughter should be firmly re-established as soon as possible. Louise knew and loved them both better than either realised and she was determined that they should be estranged no longer. Her presence changed the atmosphere immediately. After the hugs and kisses from Constance – who had never been more grateful to see anybody – and the formal introduction to Ludovico, there was a pause.

'Well,' Louise said brightly, looking round at them all, 'I expect you've had your little chat, so why don't we all go round to Caffè Greco and have a drink to celebrate the fact that Constance is now a married woman?'

Giving Constance a large smile and avoiding Nora's eye, she went on, 'And to *such* a handsome man!'

Faced with such a determined attitude, Nora could only capitulate. Later that evening, when the cousins were discussing the events of the day, Nora had to agree that Ludovico seemed charming and that Constance was clearly very happy. However, being Nora, her approval was not unqualified. She described the first seconds of the confrontation.

'I was shaking like a leaf and my head was splitting. God knows what I looked like. He stepped forward and kissed my hand – can you imagine – and then said in that funny broken accent, "Mrs Simpson, I am so happy for this day." My dear, I could have died. "*So happy*," and he'd only clapped eyes on me a minute before. These people! They're so theatrical!'

'He's very handsome, don't you think?' asked Louise, who had been unable to keep her eyes off Ludovico at Caffè Greco. 'And that *voice!* Like Charles Boyer!'

'Charles Boyer is *French*, Louise,' Nora corrected her, not entirely happy with her cousin's obvious enthusiasm for Ludovico. 'But I know what you mean. I can see how he could sweep an inexperienced girl like Constance off her feet, but that is the problem. I think he's a rogue – a charming rogue. He's a womaniser, mark my words.'

'Oh, Nora!' her cousin replied. 'How can you possibly say that?'

'He has far too much charm. I don't know much about Italians but I know enough about men to know that the

138

way he was buttering us up isn't natural. And he's got a roving eye. Constance is not the first, I'm sure.'

'Well,' Louise conceded, 'I expect he's had *some* experience but I wouldn't like to go further than that.'

'If he hasn't got a mistress tucked away somewhere I shall be very surprised,' Nora said. 'But the deed is done now and it's too late to try to interfere. I just hope that Constance doesn't get hurt. I could shake her, I really could. She's so headstrong. She's given no thought to the future. I mean, let's be honest: he's aristocratic, charming and good-looking, I accept all that. But then what? He has no job. He doesn't even have a profession. They have nowhere to live – although why that should be so if there's a huge castle somewhere with just his mother in it, I don't know – and I simply don't see them surviving.'

The letter was expressed in formal terms. Ludovico translated it for Constance. His mother had written to him enquiring if there was any truth behind the preposterous rumour that he was married and living with a wife in Florence. She went on to order him to visit her immediately, as she required an explanation directly from his own lips.

Ludovico had told Constance very little of his mother. She knew that the Principessa Maria-Angelina was a widow and lived a remote and reclusive life in Castello Castelfranco di Villanuova, in the Marche on the Eastern side of Italy, where the family had its estate. She also knew, because he had told her several times since their first day in the Boboli Gardens, that religion was the mainstay of the life of the woman who was now her mother-in-law. Some years ago, shortly after the sudden death of her husband, Maria-Angelina had convinced herself that she had felt the hand of death gently pressing her shoulder. Her life since then had been one of waiting, and preparing herself for the moment that could come at any time. Austerity – of thought, emotion and living – characterised the life at Castello Castelfranco di

Villanuova. The atmosphere surrounding the Principessa was anathema to Ludovico and he kept away from the castle as much as possible. He knew, however, that he could not avoid this visit. He went immediately to see Giancarlo in order to arrange the loan of a car.

'Did the letter sound very angry?' his friend asked.

'Giancarlo, you know my mother,' Ludovico replied. 'Of course it didn't. She has far too much dignity and self-control for that. It was formal, correct and uncompromising. Just as she is.'

Giancarlo chuckled. 'I know,' he said, 'but you mustn't be afraid. Surely it can hardly have been a surprise? You have been married almost two weeks, after all. You can never have imagined that you could keep it from her for ever. Actually, I'm surprised that it has taken this long.'

'Anyhow, it's a good thing in one way,' Ludovico said cheerfully. 'At least I shall be able to ask about some money. I can't go on borrowing from you.'

Giancarlo gave a shrug.

'No, I mean it,' Ludovico continued. 'You've been very kind, but I must face up to the problem. The difficulty is that I don't care. How can anyone imagine that money is important enough to worry about?'

He ran his hands ruefully through his hair and, looking up at Giancarlo, said, 'But I must do something for Constanza's sake. It upsets her so much. I cannot understand why. Is it typical of the English to have this obsession with money? I mean, quite honestly, it is a little vulgar, no?'

Giancarlo laughed. 'Oh, Ludo, you are comical. Of course it isn't an English obsession. Do you think they are a nation of bourgeoisie? Anyhow, who is more careful about money than an Italian? Think of your farmers in the Marche!'

'That's different,' Ludovico smiled. 'They are peasants.'

'No, it's not. You lived a life of privilege, then the war came and since then you've been playing. But you know,'

Giancarlo said kindly, 'it is time to grow up. Your childhood is over and you must face your responsibilities. Go up to the castle and arrange your affairs.'

'You mean find a job – as Constanza is always telling me?'

'Don't be silly,' Giancarlo replied affably. 'What on earth can you do? You know nothing and have no training. No one would employ you. Anyhow, your name is too grand to appear on a payroll. It would merely make the others feel insecure. No, my dear friend, you must face the fact that you are useless. Your only value is hierarchical and that is something that Constanza should understand. You must get your mother to settle an allowance on you against the estate so that you can live properly. You cannot expect Constanza to stay in that one-roomed apartment much longer, as I'm sure you know.'

Ludovico understood everything his friend was saying and he knew that the advice was sound.

'Do you think I should take Constanza?' he asked as they parted.

'Certainly,' said his friend, who was not always entirely without malice.


Constance marvelled at how the little black Fiat kept on the road that twisted and swung around and over the hills as they laboured their way towards the castle. At each turn, the villages down in the plain looked even more like tiny toys. She was relieved when they crossed over the top of the hills and began to drop down again.

'This is our valley,' Ludovico said proudly, with a proprietorial sweep of the hand. Constance was both impressed and bewildered. How could a man who laid claim to all of this be so short of money that he couldn't afford to buy her a frock?

Suddenly, Ludovico stopped the car on a bend and said, 'Come.' He walked her to the edge of the steep drop at the side of the road. 'There it is.' He pointed.

On the other side of the valley, halfway up the hill,

stood a grey building. It was large and rambling, and Constance found it slightly disappointing. It didn't look in the least like a castle, except in its grimness and what appeared to be a total lack of windows. She had been expecting a lofty, airy structure with pinnacles and turrets thrusting up to the sky, a sort of Gothic folly. This building looked far too workaday and down-to-earth for a castle. Ludovico was unaware of her disappointment as he pointed out the extent of their land and named the little villages that clung to the hilltops. If Constance had been disconcerted at the appearance of the castle, that of the land revitalised her. The rolling hills, the tight little woods and the tidy farms and villages pleased her eye enormously.

'What a beautiful landscape,' she said.

'Yes,' Ludovico replied, 'it is all split up between peasant farmers who pay us rent and a tithe on their produce. They work very hard. It is cooler here than in Florence and so the fields are always green. Mind you, we have harsh winters. No one imagines it of Italy. They think the sun shines all the time but in winter there is frost and snow here. When I was little I used to break the ice and on that hill above the castle I tried to teach myself to ski.'

He put his arm round Constance and pointed. 'Do you see down there, just below the wood, before you come to the road? That is where I used to ride my pony.'

His eyes were alight with enthusiasm as he remembered his childhood. The memory excited him and he could not wait to get back home. 'Come on!' he said. 'Let's hurry.'

Momentarily he had forgotten the bizarre woman waiting for them across the valley.

As the car chugged up the last mile in the afternoon sun, Principessa Maria-Angelina, alerted by the noise, shifted in her chair and reached for her bell. In instant response, the door of the room opened and a tiny woman entered. She shuffled awkwardly across the highly polished floor, then made her laborious way to an enormous writing desk

142

that stood in the middle of the room. Rolling back the top drawer, she removed an inlaid silver glove box. Opening it, she took out a set of ivory stretchers and carefully stretched each of the fingers of the grey chamois gloves she had also taken out. Placing them on a silver tray, she returned to her still-silent mistress. The Principessa took them up carefully, put them on and, delicately passing her fingers under her nose, sniffed them before saying to the woman, 'You may go.' Only after the door was closed did the princess rise.

She was a woman in her fifties but from her appearance she might have been in her seventies. Her skin was crazed with lines and her bones looked brittle and dry. Nevertheless, her back was still held sternly upright and her narrow body moved across the room with some vigour as she stepped towards a tiny antechamber which was built into the corner opposite the door. It was screened from the main room by a heavy brocade curtain. Inside, the tiny space was divided equally between the Principessa's spiritual and temporal needs. Immediately in front of her stood a small altar with a crucifix, a kneeling pad before it; to the side was a folding dressing table, with a mirror and a silver-backed hairbrush tied to it with black silk ribbon. On top of the table was a black straw hat with a heavy veil. The Principessa put it on, adjusted her hair and returned to her seat, confident that virtually no part of her flesh could now be seen. The veil came to just below her nose, her black dress had sleeves cut to the wrist and her skirt fell below her anklebone. Taking another sniff of her fingers, the Principessa sat upright, alert and waiting.

The Principessa Maria-Angelina was a woman of strong views. Shortly before her husband died she had become convinced that Mediterranean light was too intense for the refined eye. Whereas the peasants in the fields could be expected to cope with it, she could not. She had ordered all the curtains in her portion of the castle to be sewn together and, from that day, they had never been drawn apart. She spent her time in semi-gloom, reading the Bible and doing her unique jigsaw puzzles.

Ten years previously she had been passing from her sitting room to her bedroom along the wide, parquet-floored corridor that linked the two when quite suddenly she was struck by the dangers of temporal pride and the error of storing up riches. She looked at the paintings that lined the wall. Heavy in their pompous gilt frames, they had been part of the Villanuova treasure for generations. They were portraits and religious scenes by minor but worthwhile painters of the calibre of Cima da Conegliano, Catena and Aretino Spinello and were almost all painted on wood. The Principessa closed her bedroom door thoughtfully.

The next day, she called in the estate carpenter. She explained her requirements carefully. He was a man too stupid and too afraid to be appalled by what he was ordered to do. Since then, it had become the Principessa's habit to do a jigsaw puzzle for two hours each morning. As she picked up the carefully sawn pieces of the Old Masters, her servant waited to be handed them with instructions as to where they were to be placed. The jigsaws were so large that the Principessa had to sit on a specially constructed platform at the end of the room in order to see exactly where to instruct the servant at her feet to place each piece. The Principessa had used fourteen pictures for her complete set of puzzles so she ran no risk of becoming bored through repetition.

Just as Maria-Angelina feared light and eschewed temporal pride, so she hated noise. Her servant, who had been in her service since the Principessa was married, wore slippers wrapped in wool so that her footsteps made no sound on the parquet floors. No one else entered the Principessa's apartments. Very soon after her marriage, which had been a great disappointment, she had become addicted to the juice of the white poppy. Every day, in the early afternoon, her servant brought her a pair of new gloves that had been exquisitely scented with opium. With their aid, Maria-Angelina managed to get through the day. She sniffed softly at them now, as she heard footsteps crossing the great courtyard below.

Ludovico felt very nervous as they walked along the parquet corridor, their shoes making a shockingly unfamiliar noise that echoed through the silent building. He was nervous not for himself but for Constance. He had told her nothing about his mother's eccentricities and now regretted that she was to meet her with no preparation. Well, it's too late now, he thought, but he did not say it out loud. Instead, as the door loomed larger, he gave Constance a brief warning.

'You might find that my mother has funny ways, but do not let them worry you.'

Constance looked at him in alarm but before she could speak the servant was knocking gently on the vast double doors of the drawing room, the grand *salotto*. Constance's heart leapt in horror as they stepped inside. In the semi-gloom, the Principessa, swathed in black and sitting bolt upright, looked like a spider or a mummified body. Constance's mouth was dry as she heard her husband say, 'Mother, this is my wife, Constanza.'

The Principessa raised her hand and beckoned them forward. Her voice was deep and amazingly powerful.

'Ludovico, I will not tell you how disgraceful I find your behaviour. It is sufficient for you to know that you have held the name of Castelfranco di Villanuova to ridicule throughout Italy.'

Her voice rose slightly. 'Ridicule, I say. From Val d'Aosta to Palermo people are laughing at your folly. It means nothing to me,' she ended magisterially, 'I wait only for death.'

'Why have you called me here, Mother?' Ludovico asked quietly.

There was a long pause, of unbroken silence. The only movement was of the Principessa's fingers which were passed delicately beneath her nose.

145

'I have called you here to confirm that your foolish youth is over.' She paused and looked hard at Constance. 'You and your *bride*,' she said with heavy irony, 'cannot continue to live in servants' quarters under the gift of Savognia. You may be prepared to allow Italy to continue to laugh, but I am not. You will return here to live and start tending the estate that only too soon will be your own.'

'Mother! That is impossible!' Ludovico interjected.

'You will not live with me, of course,' the Principessa continued. 'I shall retain these apartments and the rest of the castle will be yours.' She waved her hand in dismissal. 'Tomorrow you will come to me and say when you shall arrive so that arrangements can be made.'

As they left the *salotto*, Constance was shaking. Walking down the staircase she turned to Ludovico. 'So what was that all about?' she asked.

He translated briefly. She was horrified at his cowardice. He had said nothing to counter his mother's proposal. It seemed he was prepared to accept her ruling without consulting his wife in any way. They dropped down into the courtyard without saying a word. It was only when they were in Ludovico's apartments – smelling dank and unused – that she spoke.

'We're not going to live here!'

Constance was furious. Ludovico, who had lost all his exuberant nonchalance, remonstrated with her.

'Please, Constanza, do not become angry.'

'Who does she think she is? How dare she talk to you like that? You're not a child! You are twenty-five!'

Ludovico wearily passed his hand down his face. 'I warned you she was a strange woman,' he said lamely. 'What alternative do we have? You demand money and she is the only person who has it. If we don't move up here, even my small allowance will cease. That I know. She is that sort of woman. Good God! Do you think I want to be buried alive out here until she dies, but what alternative can you offer, that's what I'd like to know?'

And, of course, she could offer none.

Constance was sure of only one thing. As long as they stayed in the castle, the power emanating from Maria-Angelina's apartments would prevent them making any real decision about their future together. Ludovico seemed totally subdued by his mother's aura, and Constance felt that she had to get him away immediately.

Ludovico demurred, as she knew he would. 'Constance, don't be silly,' he pleaded, 'it is almost six o'clock. Where could we go? We have to stay until the morning.'

Constance felt possessed of a strength she had never felt before. She knew that their very future was under threat and she said urgently, 'We are going, and we are going *now*. I don't care where to. We can sleep in the *car* for all I care but we are not staying the night up here. Take me away from this hateful place . . . now!'

As she heard the car pull out of the courtyard, the Principessa smiled to herself. What was he doing, this wayward son of hers? Gently passing her fingers under her nose, she answered her question.

'So, my little Ludovico who will never grow up,' she murmured to herself, 'you are doing what you have always done when things do not go your way, trying to run from the problem. Just like your father – and just like him, you never understand that problems run faster than you do.'

The Principessa Maria-Angelina Castelfranco di Villanuova loved Ludovico with the passionate intensity that Italian women can bring to their relationship with a male child but she was an intelligent woman of shrewd judgement. She could not blind herself to his faults.

All his life, he had been weak. She knew it and it hurt her. But there was nothing she could do. His charm and his beauty had been fatal to his character. Unlike another person in her thoughts Ludovico had never had to face a check or accept a defeat and now he was incapable of doing so. He merely turned his back and walked away when things became difficult. When did it start? she mused. Was it in the cradle or was it with the priests? Much as she would have liked to, Maria-Angelina had too much respect for truth to blame it on her husband. She knew that her son's character was formed long before he came under his father's influence . . .

Ludovico had been adored from the day of his birth on an airless, humid morning in mid-June. Maria-Angelina had gone into labour just before midnight and had struggled through the small hours. Release had come at about four thirty. The peasant women attending her managed to make mother and son comfortable before the first long rays of the sun began to spill down across the valley and it was time to pray. Apart from her servants, Maria-Angelina was alone. Her husband was in Rome attending to business. Ludovico had appeared ten days before his calculated time.

The castle had no telephone. By the time the telegram had been sent to Rome and her husband had travelled home a space of almost three days had elapsed. In that space, a bond had been forged between mother and son which ensured the effective exclusion of the father. The Principe did not particularly care. He was delighted that the baby was healthy and relieved that it was a boy, but his interests lay elsewhere. Already, after only four years of marriage, he found his wife's lack of passion too constraining and preferred the more abandoned love-making he enjoyed with his mistress. He felt imprisoned by the narrow country life of the castle and was much happier in Rome . . . or Florence . . . or anywhere. As a prominent landowner, he could find infinite reasons and excuses for spending time in Rome, supposedly taking care of regional issues with members of the government, and had installed himself and his servant in a small flat in a palazzo just round the corner from Piazza Repubblica. Here he entertained his mistress, a coarse and vulgar Neapolitan woman who made no demands but would go to any length to satisfy any he made of her. Their relationship was based entirely on lust. Il Principe Castelfranco di Villanuova did not require love. His self-esteem provided enough of that. All he cared for was the availability of sex when he required it. This his mistress gave generously – and cheaply. It was a great comfort to Villanuova that his sexual luxury cost him remarkably little money.

Having ascertained that wife and baby were well, he decided to return to Rome as soon as possible. His son was surrounded by flouncy, feminine fuss, day in and day out; the Principe hated this domestic, women's world encased in prayer. It seemed in its wholesomeness to reproach him for his irregular life and he knew that, at this stage, Maria-Angelina and her motherly love were all that were required. His time would come a few years hence, when he would teach the boy the skills required of a gentleman – shooting, hunting and sporting. So the Principe reasoned with himself as he drove back to Rome, knowing that it would be several months before he came to the castle again.

Maria-Angelina was relieved at the sudden departure. She knew about her husband's mistress, as Italian women always do, and accepted the situation as being, if not normal, certainly common. She no longer loved her husband, in fact, she disliked him, and his attitudes were anathema to her. She was largely indifferent to his behaviour in Rome, although, of course, she heard all about it. Remote as the castle was in the twenties, her family and friends wrote regularly and hardly a letter arrived without news of the Principe's doings. Nothing they told her could upset her any more, because she had taken comfort and refuge in religion.

All Italians were brought up to be devout in those days. They were expected to give the Church a commitment that suffused their whole life. For many it did but for many more, especially in Maria-Angelina's class, religion got in the way of pleasure. The Italian aristocracy was the least religious section of Italian society. The young in particular turned their backs on the Church at least thirty years before their compatriots in less privileged social positions dared to do so. Even Maria-Angelina's devotion had wavered when she first entered society. Dancing late and praying early cannot exist together for long and, as with her friends, it was the Church that suffered.

Only when she realised how insubstantial her marriage was did Maria-Angelina begin to look round for solace. It was out of the question for her to take a lover, so she took to religion instead. By doing so, she ensured that her husband would never be close to her again. He loathed the constricting attitudes of the Church and was indifferent to its threats of hellfire for transgressors such as himself. Transgressor he certainly was. Fornication was the driving force of his life. He could resist it with no woman, at no time.

From the beginning, Ludovico was an enchanting child. His prettiness was merely part of the overall charm. His dark eyes sparkled mischievously; he rarely if ever cried – as, indeed, why should he? He was equally as rarely crossed, thwarted or checked. The castle echoed to his demands, his wishes, his needs. A small army of servants pampered and protected him. Only his gaiety and charm prevented him from becoming a brat. Nobody brought an iota of critical faculty to bear on the life of the boy, except his mother. The Principessa was indulgent but not foolish. She had no intention of allowing her son to follow the same hedonistic path as his father. Ludovico's life of unchecked pleasure and rampant self-will was sharply curtailed when he turned eight. At that stage Maria-Angelina called in the priests. They were not merely to inculcate the discipline of devotion; they were to teach him the literature, history and knowledge of art essential for a boy of his class.

She had left it too late. Ludovico was addicted to pleasure (just like his father) and had become self-indulgent (exactly like his mother) and he was not prepared to have his enjoyments cut across so ruthlessly. He hated the priests and their lessons. He failed to appear in the little schoolroom that had been made in an antechamber next to the chapel; when punishment loomed, he ran away, well aware that one or other of the servants would shelter and entertain him until the trouble blew over. He was content to idle away his days in the stables . . . the dairy . . . with the housemaids as they cleaned the bedrooms . . . and especially out in the fields with the peasants, playing around them as they laboured in the scorching heat.

And he always got away with it. He was such a beautiful boy, with his dancing eyes and dazzling smile, that no one could deny him anything. He would have undoubtedly grown up to be a monster if his father had not decided to step in. The Principe now spent most of his time in Rome, but from his brief, infrequent visits and the reports he regularly received from his estate manager, he began to suspect that religious mania was slowly driving his wife mad. Her obsession with light had become common knowledge, although her opium habit was a secret known only to her closest house servants. Her husband was determined to introduce wider influences into his son's life and to break the emotional hold his wife had over the boy.

A chance meeting at a dinner party in Florence provided the solution. Amongst the guests was his old friend the Principessa di Savognia. As he settled himself next to her, he said gallantly, 'My dear, you grow more attractive every time I see you.'

The princess, who was fifteen years his senior and had never looked at any man but her husband, shook out her napkin, laughed indulgently and said, 'Save your kind words for the pretty young girls who want to believe such rubbish.' She picked up the gold place marker in front of her plate and, pretending to hit him with it, cried, 'Are we not, just for once, to have a serious conversation?'

And they did. They talked exclusively of the problem of Ludovico – and the Principessa di Savognia gave it all her attention. After all, no topic is of more interest to an Italian woman than that of children and it becomes even more compulsive when the child is masculine.

'He needs to spend some time away from the castle . . . and his mother . . . He is too much the little master of his kingdom there,' she advised. 'Why don't you bring him to Florence? He can come and visit my son Giancarlo.'

That dinner party changed Ludovico's life. Three days after the conversation with the Principessa di Savognia, his father left Florence and drove up to the Marche. He had not informed his wife, but had decided on an impulse that morning to pay a visit to the castle. He was prepared to remain as long as necessary but he was determined that he would not return to Florence without Ludovico. It was mid-afternoon by the time he drove down into the valley, and the sun dazzled his eyes as he pulled up the other side towards the castle. He noticed that the workers had returned to the fields after the siesta and men, women and children were pitching in to their tasks, hampered by the dogs that kept getting underfoot. He had just turned the last corner before the final steep climb to the castle gate when two dogs ran across his path. Blinded by the sun, he failed to see them but heard the thump as he hit the second one. As the animal lay in the road, howling, he was aware of another dark shape about to follow it under his wheels.

Jamming on his brakes, he managed to avoid it. As the car skidded past the figure, the Principe was shocked to see it was a child. Stepping from the car, he was horrified when he recognised his son. Ignoring the frightened peasants who clustered round, he swept Ludovico up in his arms and, dumping him in the seat next to him, accelerated angrily for home.

It was the best piece of luck he had ever had. He knew it and was aware of exactly how to exploit it to his maximum advantage. Striding across the courtyard with the boy in his arms, he shouted for his butler in a voice that clearly echoed his towering rage. The man came running out of his pantry, his eyes wide with shock at seeing the prince back home. 'Find the Principessa immediately,' he was ordered, 'and conduct her to my study. And I mean now, no matter what she is doing.'

Maria-Angelina had heard the arrival and was ready when the butler appeared. When her husband's voice had first shattered the afternoon calm of the castle, she had been in her anteroom, brushing her hair after her devotions. She was so alarmed by all the commotion that she was still clutching the silver-backed brush as she followed the butler to the study.

She entered the room silently. The Principe was standing before the fireplace with Ludovico in his arms. The boy lay rigid with fear, his enormous eyes looking at his mother beseechingly. Before she could speak, her husband said, 'Do you see what I have in my arms? It could have been a corpse for all the care you take of my son.'

Maria-Angelina gasped in horror and crossed herself.

'So,' he continued, 'this is how you look after my child – allowing him to run wild like an animal.'

He held up the terrified boy before his mother's eyes. 'This is a son of the Villanuovas, let me remind you.' He paced angrily before her. 'He is filthy and smells like a peasant. Why? Because you, whom I left as his guardian, are so obsessed with the odour of stale incense that it takes the place of everything else; because you, who should be aware of his movements every minute of the day, think only of your own genuflections before the Madonna; because you, the woman with whom I shared my bed, are no woman at all but a dried-up, sterile wreck fit only for prayer. You dare to call yourself a mother? You are not worthy of the name.'

Trembling with shock, anger and disdain, Maria-Angelina lifted her head haughtily and replied, 'How dare you take that tone with me? You, the father, who has shown no interest in your son's welfare, education or even existence, you have been so busy serving your lusts elsewhere. You have the nerve to come here and criticise me when you haven't been near the place – or him – for over a year – how dare you?' As she spoke she walked over to the bellpull and tugged it sharply. The door opened almost instantly.

'Take the boy to the priests,' she ordered, 'and tell them to keep him there until I come.'

Then the real row began. Both tempers flared as they shouted at each other, accusing, goading and dragging up all the little pinpricks of the years of their marriage. They were no longer arguing about their child. They were fighting about themselves, and the hatred, disappointment, frustration and futility that had gripped their lives.

'You are a madwoman!' he shouted. 'Fit for nothing but a life on your knees before your beloved priests!'

With a strangled scream, Maria-Angelina rushed at him and began to viciously beat his chest with her hairbrush as he struggled to capture her flailing arms. When he had overpowered her and thrown her on a sofa, the Principe said in a deadly voice, shaking with anger, 'You have had your last of him,' and strode from the room, leaving his wife sobbing with rage.

And to all real intents, she had. Her influence over Ludovico had been swept away that afternoon, although her love remained undiminished. In barely an hour, all her plans had evaporated. The next day, Ludovico and his personal servant left the castle with the Principe, not to return for several years. By that time, his confidence had developed to such an extent that his mother accepted that he lived an independent life, largely outside her influence.

Despite the split between his parents – never to be repaired – Ludovico was not allowed to feel deprived or lonely. He spent a great deal of his time with cousins, aunts and uncles as well as travelling with his father. The Principe not only took him round Italy but they also visited Paris, London and the South of France together. By the time he was fourteen, Ludovico was sophisticated, worldly and urbane. His looks, which had blossomed into a teenage voluptuousness, ensured that he was adored everywhere, and his father paraded him with increasing pride.

The idyll ended abruptly. The Principe Castelfranco di Villanuova suffered a fatal heart attack in the dining car of the Florence express when Ludovico was only seventeen. Ludovico returned to Castello Castelfranco to attend his father's funeral, and saw his mother again. He was now sufficiently au fait to realise that she had changed. Remote and distant, it was as if she had placed a layer of fine glass between herself and the world. She could see it and it could see her but they could not touch. Contact with everybody but her and servants had almost ceased. Her eyes dilated with horror at the number of mourners who arrived on the dull November morning of the funeral. After they had departed, she and her son had to learn how to come to terms with each other, conscious that over the years they had become virtual strangers.

They did so, surprisingly well, largely by not interrupting each other's lives. His mother had long ago convinced herself that having Ludovico snatched from her so brutally was a test presented to her by God. She accepted this and loved her son with a deeper and less selfish love as a result. Sadly, the hedonism he had inherited from his father prevented Ludovico from seeing either the depth of the sacrifice or the intensity of her love.

# CHAPTER 6

Stunned by Constance's insistence that they leave the castle and his mother's influence that very night, Ludovico steered the car out of the courtyard and set off down the hill, not knowing where to go or what to do. As they nosed a path through the villagers returning from the fields, Constance was struck by the way the peasants, when they realised who was driving the car, doffed their hats and bowed deferentially. Then she noticed the hats. Made of bleached straw, they had large brims and beautifully moulded crowns. Constance thought the proportions perfect. The simple elegance of the shapes impressed her. She hadn't spoken to Ludovico since they had driven through the castle gate but now she turned to him and said, 'Ludo, where do they get those beautiful hats?'

'I have no idea,' he replied shortly.

'Well,' she said, 'why don't you stop and ask them?'

He looked at her as if she had gone mad. 'What on earth for? I can buy a hat for you in Florence.'

'Not like that you can't,' she replied decisively. 'Please, Ludo, do stop and ask.'

Encouraged by the conciliatory tone of her voice, Ludovico pulled to a halt before a group of peasants leading home their mules.

Constance leapt out of the car, the anger and frustration which had engulfed her at the castle now forgotten in her growing excitement.

'Ask them where they get them from,' she repeated. 'Go on!'

The peasants had stopped in a fearful cluster, wondering what they had done wrong. The men respectfully removed their hats as Ludovico walked towards them.

'*Buona sera*,' he said. '*Come sta?* How are things? Work is going well?'

'*Sì, sì, Principe*,' the leader of the group replied. 'The weather has been good. We have an excellent harvest this year.' He paused, smiling expectantly, wondering what Ludovico wanted.

'These hats you wear,' Ludovico said, 'where do they come from? My wife would like to know.'

The atmosphere changed. The peasants looked at each other warily. Dropping his voice, the leader said, 'Giulio, Principe. In Trapena.'

He looked away shiftily. At the mention of the name, two of the older women crossed themselves. With a curt 'thank you', Ludovico turned away and walked back to the car. Constance followed, puzzled by the grim look on his face.

'What is Trapena?' she asked.

'The next village up the valley,' he replied. 'But we are not going there. You must forget about hats. We'll find some in Florence. Come, we must get on.'

Constance wasn't prepared to be fobbed off.

'What is the matter, Ludovico? Why won't you take me to see this man? What's wrong with him?'

'Look, my darling, just believe me when I say that it is not possible. Trust me. You must forget about the hats.'

She was angry. She knew that something had been said during their encounter with the peasants, something from which she was being excluded.

'No, Ludo, I won't forget the hats. Not until you tell me what the mystery is.'

He looked at her in despair. 'He's an idiot,' he said, 'that's all. A hideous, shambling wreck who the villagers

157

think has the evil eye. I cannot have you mixed up with someone like that.'

'Oh,' she cried in relief, 'is that all? That's no problem. Good heavens, all we want to do is look at some hats. Please, darling,' she wheedled, 'it's a very *little* detour. It will only take a few minutes.'

They found the house of Giulio without difficulty. As they walked up to the door, chained dogs barked viciously in the barn. The whole atmosphere felt menacing to Constance, and she was conscious of Ludovico's tension. She knew he resented her determination but she felt sure that there was more to his anger than that. He had only been persuaded to drive to Trapena because he knew that she would not be gainsaid. His every move made it clear that he was ill at ease. Constance realised that he was dismayed at her determination to have her own way over something apparently as trivial as a new hat but, for her, it was much more than that. It was part of a plan forming in her head – a plan that could remove the pernicious influence of the woman at the castle for ever. As the sound of his banging on the door echoed through the silent streets of Trapena, Constance wondered what horror dwelt in this house that made Ludovico so unhappy to be here.

The door opened fractionally. A woman's face scowled at them, middle-aged and wizened. To Constance she looked like a witch. The door opened a little more, revealing some of the woman's black-clad body, every inch of which was tense with suspicion. '*Si?*' she asked, holding the door ready to slam in their faces.

'*Scusi*, signora,' Ludovico began, and explained what they wanted. Her face remained impassive and hostile.

'Signora,' Ludovico encouraged her, 'I am the son of the Principessa Maria-Angelina. I wish to speak to Giulio.'

She relaxed fractionally and said, 'It is with me you must talk. *I* look after the business. Come. I will show you.' She led the way past the barn, oblivious of the demented barking of the dogs, and stopped before a small tumbledown shed.

'Giulio,' she cried, banging on the door, 'open up immediately.'

There was the sound of someone laboriously moving round inside, bolts were withdrawn and the door swung slowly outwards. Constance gasped. Standing in the doorway was a huge man – a hulk. She stepped back in fear as the woman said dismissively to Ludovico, 'As you see, signore, the devil has given me an idiot to care for.'

The man slavered and made a strange unearthly noise. Constance shivered. She wanted to turn and run away but Ludovico had started to talk to the woman again.

'Can he speak?' he asked.

'He can listen,' she replied. 'But do not waste your time with him. Giulio,' she said harshly, 'get out of the way. Come into the yard and let us get in.'

The man shambled forward, past Constance. She shuddered, and quickly followed Ludovico and the woman into the hut where she was almost overcome by the odour that hit her as soon as she stepped inside.

'*Scusi*, signore,' the woman said, 'be careful where you walk.' She indicated buckets by the door, from which the smell rose.

'You wait outside, Constanza,' Ludovico said, 'I'll bring a hat out to you.'

She ignored him. She had no intention of going out into the yard with that shambling hulk, no matter how strong the smell. In any case, she wanted to see how the hats were made. As her eyes became accustomed to the dark, she saw a pile of straw and, in front of it, a bench on which stood a shaped block of wood, crowned with a half-made hat. Several finished hats were stacked on the floor next to Giulio's three-legged stool.

She stepped forward and fingered the hat on the stand. It was damp. Only then did she notice beyond the table a tin bath in which lengths of straw were steeping, covered by a golden-brown liquid. The woman was talking fast, using the local patois. Unable to follow, Constance turned to the finished hats. She tried one on. It felt perfect. She

159

realised that there were three basic styles. Holding them up, she said to Ludovico, 'These are *divine*! They are so elegant. I can hardly believe it.'

'Which one do you want?' he asked.

'All of them,' she replied.

'What? All three of them?'

'No,' she said impatiently. 'All that she has.'

'Constanza, are you mad? There must be at least fifteen hats lying around!'

'Please, Ludo,' she replied, 'don't argue. I'll explain later.'

He turned to the signora. As he talked, her face remained impassive and then she smiled briefly as he named a price.

As they drove away, Ludovico said slightly petulantly, 'I can't imagine what you're going to do with so many identical hats.'

'They're not identical,' she corrected.

'Well,' he answered, 'I don't know where you're going to wear them.'

'Oh, Ludo,' she said, 'don't sound so cross. Have you no faith in my judgement? I'll tell you what I'm going to do with them. I have no intention of wearing them all myself. I'm going to sell them.'

Ludovico was shocked. 'Sell them? Who to? Who on earth would buy peasant hats?'

'They won't *be* peasant hats when I've finished with them. I'm going to trim them and make them very chic. We are, my darling, going to make some money so that we can be independent and do what *we* want, not what your mother commands. I'm going to have a hat shop. The Straw Hat shop.'

'You're mad,' he interrupted, 'totally mad. Nobody's going to buy hats worn by peasants in the fields.'

'Just you wait and see. By the time I've finished they won't even know that they *are* peasant hats.'

'Do you know how they're made?' Ludovico asked. 'Do you know what that smell was?'

Constance shook her head.

'Piss, my darling. Human piss. That was what was in those buckets. That is what they use to soften the straw so that they can shape it. Who is going to buy a hat smelling of piss?'

Constance was intrigued. 'Why do they do that? Where does it come from?' she asked.

'They collect it from the villagers, she told me – though I think most of it probably comes from that monster.'

Constance shivered in distaste but she was not prepared to be put off. She knew that she had found a solution to their problem and she had no intention of being deflected.

'We'll spray them with eau de Cologne before we put them in the shop,' she replied.

Back in Florence, Constance's enthusiasm blossomed.

'You know, Ludo,' she said, 'there isn't any reason why these hats shouldn't be shaped in all sorts of different ways. I'm sure it depends on what you do when the straw is malleable, on the block. I wonder how skilled that Giulio man is?'

'He's an idiot, Constanza. He won't have any skill at all. It will be the mother who does the skilled part.'

'I'm not sure that you're right,' she replied. 'It's people like that who are often extraordinarily clever with their hands.'

She suddenly pushed Ludovico's newspaper aside and said, 'Take me up to Trapena.'

'When? What for?' he asked in alarm.

'Now. Today. I want to talk to that woman.'

'Constanza, are you mad? We cannot go chasing up there just like that. What if we go all that way and they aren't there?'

'People like that are *always* there,' she replied, and he knew that she was right.

'I don't know if Giancarlo needs the car,' he said.

'Look, get dressed and go and find out.'

Ludovico was distressed at the idea, Constance could

161

see, but she was determined that her plan should go ahead. He put down his newspaper and said, 'Constanza, forget this crazy scheme, I beg you. There are things up in Trapena that you do not understand. Please listen to me when I say that we should not get involved with the people up there. It can come to no good.'

'Why? You must tell me why! You're hiding something from me, I know. Why do you have secrets from me? Is this how Italian men treat their wives – because, if it is, you'd better know *now* that I am English and I won't stand for it.'

In no time, they were having their first quarrel. And although Ludovico finally gave way and agreed to take her back to the castle, Constance was distressed that she couldn't persuade him to tell her why he viewed Trapena and its madman with such revulsion.


As they accelerated up the hills and away from Florence, Constance said, 'What is her name?'

'Whose?'

'The mother's.'

'What did the villagers say? I can't remember.'

He knew that she was aware he was lying so after a moment he said, 'I don't think we'll get any co-operation from her. She's as hard as nails. I can't see her giving away all her trade secrets to a rival.'

'Not rival,' Constance corrected, 'colleague.'

'Colleague? What on earth are you planning?' Ludovico demanded.

'Well, darling, it's really very simple. This is my plan. I design the hats, they make them and we sell them. Surely that'll keep her happy? We'll pay the correct price for them, of course. How can she object to that? It will give her a regular income all year round as well as keeping her son occupied.'


'No.' Signora Rosina's face reflected her irritation. 'The signora does not understand. Only Giulio makes the hats.

162

I have no skills. God was kind even in His cruelty and although he is only a poor idiot Giulio was given the fingers of an artist. He can do anything with straw. I can do nothing.' She shrugged.

Ludovico translated for Constance and ended by saying, 'So that's it. There's nothing to be done.'

'Whatever do you mean?' she asked.

'You cannot work with that animal. I will not let him near you.'

Constance wasn't prepared to let go of her scheme so easily. She turned to Ludovico.

'Ask her to take us to the shed,' she told him.

As the door swung open and Giulio stood blinking in the sunlight Constance put her hand on Ludovico's arm to restrain him.

'No,' she said, 'you stay here. The signora and I must go in alone.'

'But you won't understand them,' he protested.

'Yes, I will,' she replied. 'If he and I are to get through to each other we'll do it with our hands, not words. Don't worry, I'll be perfectly safe. I'm not afraid,' she lied. 'Just tell her that I want her son to show me exactly how he makes a hat. All I want to do is watch him.' She managed a smile. 'Don't look so unhappy. Sit in the shade and have a cigarette.'

In the dark shed she watched, fascinated, as Giulio's hands played with the straw, pulling, plaiting and weaving it with deft, quick movements. He grunted with pleasure as a hat began to take shape. As she stood next to him, Constance noticed how sensitive his fingers were. Despite his bulk, they were delicate, almost feminine. She began to lose her fear. Those hands would never do anything violent, she thought. His mother is right. He is an artist.

Two hours later, she ran across the yard, holding the still-wet hat. Ludovico was sitting under a tree. He looked up sulkily.

'Isn't it amazing!' she called enthusiastically.

'Do you know how long you've been in there?' he asked.

'Oh, never mind about that. Look at *this*,' she said, waving the hat in front of him. 'Isn't it an absolute miracle of chic? Don't you adore it? He's so clever! You must tell the signora that I can work with her son perfectly well. There will be no language problem. We'll communicate with sign language. Ludo, my darling,' she pulled him up on his feet, ignoring his reluctance, 'we're going to be all right. Isn't it marvellous? I know it'll work. Smile, please, Ludo. Don't you understand? We're going to be all right!'

And she began to dance him round the yard, impervious to the coolly laconic gaze of Signora Rosina, who stood in the doorway with Giulio, open-mouthed, beside her.

Nora's emergency trip had inevitably been extended into a real holiday.

'Do you realise that I've been away for three weeks?' she asked Louise.

'I know, darling, but it's been such fun!'

'I must get back. This is my last week. I would like to have Constance here for a couple of days if that's all right by you.'

'Darling, don't be silly! Of course it's all right. And Ludovico?'

'No, I want to be able to talk sense to her!'

Constance was so confident in her new venture that she arrived in Rome blooming with happiness.

'Marriage certainly seems to suit her,' Louise said fondly.

'At the moment,' was Nora's grim reply, but even she sat up and started to take notice when Constance began to talk about her business hopes.

'I *knew*!' Louise said when she and Nora were alone together, 'I always knew she would do something in fashion.'

'Do something in fashion? Really, Louise, do talk sense. She's not doing anything in fashion! She's trimming a few peasant hats!'

164

'Well,' Louise said cautiously, 'it's a *beginning*, after all. I think it's rather a good idea.'

'Who can make a living out of trimming hats, for God's sake?' Nora burst out in frustration. 'It's Victorian! That's just so typical of Constance. You'd think she was a character in *Cranford*, instead of a married woman in a foreign country, facing the breadline because she has a lazy husband too grand to find work! It's like *La Bohème* or something!'

'There must be a limit to the number of trimmed straw hats people are prepared to buy,' Louise conceded, 'and of course, they're very seasonal. But I do think that Constance has a talent in that direction.'

'Of course she has. She's artistic, like me. That's who she gets it from but she certainly hasn't inherited my practical streak.'

'Oh, I don't know,' Louise said. 'It's early days yet.'

She thought, Well, she's inherited your determination, at least.

'Of course,' Nora concluded, 'talent is all right but these things need money and experience and Constance has neither. That's why she'll be back home, tail between her legs, before the New Year, you mark my words.'

One of the things Nora Simpson prided herself on was practical northern common sense. She felt sure that the chances of her daughter's little business – as she dismissively thought of it – actually surviving were slim. Nevertheless, she wanted to see it succeed – as a matter of family pride, if nothing else. She accepted that for the time being her daughter was on her own but she still wished to retain a measure of influence and involvement with her.

Constance, on her part, had felt a new confidence in relation to her mother since their confrontation in Louise's flat. The scene with Nora had violently wrenched her out of childhood and into womanhood. She no longer saw her relationship with Nora as one of mother and daughter. They were now two women, equal in judgement and equally strong. She realised how afraid she had been of her mother and how much she had needed her approval. That had now changed and, as a result, Nora's approval came with a generosity that Constance would never have expected.

Over lunch in Louise's apartment, before Constance was due to return to Florence, Nora suddenly said, 'Now, Constance, I want to get some things settled before you go.'

Constance's heart sank.

'I think you have talent,' her mother went on. 'In fact, I know, and have always known, that you do. Talent, however, is never enough. It must be backed. I don't know where this hat business could lead – if anywhere – but I do know that it cannot survive without money. I am arranging to transfer two hundred pounds from England for you.'

Constance was speechless.

'It's only a loan, mind you,' her mother went on, 'against the money your father left you. That won't come to you until you are twenty-one and you need the money now, it seems to me, if this crazy marriage stands any chance of surviving. You know what I think about that and I'm not going to repeat it now. I just hope I'm wrong. But at least you'll have some cash to get things going. Then it's up to you.'

Constance was struck by her mother's no-nonsense practicality but before she had time to thank her Louise chimed in. 'We're all certain that you'll make a success of everything, darling, but your mother is right. Nothing can be achieved without money. Your Uncle Jim and I are going to lend you a hundred pounds. You can pay it back when you are able.'

Tears came to Constance's eyes but before she could say anything all sentimentality was swept away by Nora.

'And if that husband of yours is any sort of man, he'll get on to that mother of his and see what *she* can cough up, if they're so damned well-off!' she said, concluding the conversation.

'She seems quite determined.' Giancarlo di Savognia was speaking on the telephone to his friend, Bettina Bonoccorsi. It was eleven o'clock and the morning sun filtered through the shutters, laid itself in long bars across his abandoned breakfast tray and crept up his fingers as he aimlessly coiled and uncoiled the flex of the telephone. Although still in bed – his first appointment was for lunch at two – Giancarlo had not been idle. He had spoken to several people on the telephone, as was his normal morning habit when he was in Florence. He had started a letter. It lay unfinished on the linen pillow next to him. But above all, he had been thinking – about Ludovico and Constanza. He was sure that their idea was crazy but he wished to help them.

'She is quite different from Ludo, you know,' he went on. 'She has a remarkably intelligent eye and a lot of drive. He, poor dear, is as weak as ever but she is not the same at all. She is learning Italian very well.'

'Darling, whatever for?' Bettina asked. 'No one speaks Italian. What could she possibly do with it?'

'Because she is a determined woman, that's why,' Giancarlo replied. 'I'm sure that she intends to become multilingual.'

'Oh, God! No!' laughed Bettina. 'I'm sick of meeting people who speak twenty languages and haven't a worthwhile thought to express in any. English is all that is required now.'

Giancarlo smiled at the irony of Bettina's observation. She spoke four languages fluently and, even this morning, to amuse themselves, they were talking in French – flawlessly.

'Anyhow, tell me how she coped with that old madwoman at the castle,' Bettina demanded.

'Well, the interview was apparently very short and not at all sweet,' Giancarlo replied as he settled down for a good gossip. 'Ludo tells me that the old woman was even more difficult than usual. She accused him of making the family name a joke throughout Italy . . .'

'His father did that years ago,' Bettina interrupted. 'Surely she hasn't forgotten?'

'I'm sure she hasn't,' Giancarlo continued, 'if I know her she'll be only too conscious of poor old Carlo and his antics. You know the Villanuovas, Bettina, their fatal flaw has always been women. They've all been prepared to throw away everything for a woman.'

'Is this Constanza a gold-digger then?'

'Oh, absolutely categorically not. She isn't at all like that. This is what I am telling you. She is an extremely serious woman. She has that northern gravity, if you know what I mean.'

'You do make her sound a tiny bit bourgeoise and earnest, darling,' Bettina murmured down the telephone, 'I would imagine that Ludo might regret his impetuosity soon enough. He likes women who are *fun*. You know how utterly unserious he is. It sounds to me as if it won't be long before she's moved on and he'll be running back to mama for another handout.'

'You couldn't be more wrong, Bettina,' Savognia corrected her. 'Constanza is resolved that there won't be any need for handouts in the future. That, my dear, is the whole point of the enterprise. She's going to make Ludo independent.'

Bettina laughed. 'Well,' she said, 'I don't know what she'll achieve financially but I'm quite certain that she's wasting her time if she thinks she can get Ludo psychologically independent of that old witch. You know as well as I do, Giancarlo, that she's ruled him with a rod of iron ever since his father died. She'll never let him out of her clutches. He's the only Villanuova she has ever been able to bend to her will.'

Savognia was becoming increasingly angry. He had not telephoned Bettina to hear all this. He had done so in order to enlist her help. He held the receiver away from his ear as her spiteful tirade continued. He knew how much Bettina hated the Villanuovas – and not without cause, he was prepared to admit – but he also knew that, like most women of her age, she had a soft spot for Ludo and he was determined to tap it, knowing how much help she could give the new business if she wished, and how much harm she could do if she did not.

Bettina Bonoccorsi was a malcontent and a dangerous gossip. Her friends treated her with caution, except when they wanted a rumour spread quickly and efficiently. She was known to everybody in the fashionable world of Rome and had been tripping lightly from one fashion house to another as long as anyone could remember. She relayed tittle-tattle about each and every one. Her visits were always welcome because, although much of what she said was either unimportant trivia or old news, every now and again she unearthed a nugget of information about an unfortunate couturier which could be of value to his competitors. Personal gossip about sexual peccadilloes or financial chicanery was loved by everyone in Rome although it was not taken too seriously. It made people laugh for a day or two but soon slipped out of currency. Not that it was forgotten. The Roman aristocracy who were central to that city's world of fashion never forgot personal gossip of any kind, as Bettina knew to her cost.

Couturiers were always nervous about Bettina's little visits because they knew that, given half a chance, she would spy on their secrets for next season and then tell the world. Bettina had no loyalty to anyone. She had been born of a sprig of a noble Tuscan family which had made a fortune from its red wines. Unfortunately, Bettina's branch of the Bonoccorsis had little money. The small amount of not very productive land which surrounded their family castle had to support the two sons of the family. The two daughters, it had been understood from an early age, would have to fend for themselves. Bettina was the elder and plainer of the two. Her sister married young, having been courted with admirable determination by the local doctor. Bettina made mistakes, confused pleasure with progress and suddenly knew by her twenty-sixth birthday that she was on the shelf. Barring a miracle, she would never marry. Not that life was therefore savourless for her. The branch of the Bonoccorsi dynasty that she came from might not be wealthy but it retained its nobility and the attributes of that nobility. The palazzo that Bettina was sitting in this morning was one of them. Palazzo Tronci had been in the family since the days when the Bonoccorsis had been part of the Roman nobility and it had remained in their possession through the move to Tuscany and the venture into commerce that had made one side of the family powerful while Bettina's branch became the poor relations. Bettina's apartment in Palazzo Tronci, which had belonged to her great-great-great-grandmother, was not on the *piano nobile*, but it was on the floor immediately above and was well proportioned and light. Bettina found it the ideal base for those visits to friends in the country or other cities which were essential if she were to keep down her costs.

She wriggled slightly on the tiny overpadded satin boudoir chair to look at her watch. She must finish this conversation, but first she must fully understand what Giancarlo was saying.

'So,' she ruthlessly cut across him, 'they want people to buy hats that were made for peasants in the fields? Oh, darling, *really*! It's the most preposterous idea I've heard. Only an Englishwoman . . .'

'Now, listen, Bettina,' Giancarlo interrupted, 'I want you to talk to the couturiers in Rome; you know, the Fontanas or Simonetta, and be positive about the hats. You're wrong to think of them as only suitable for peasants. Constanza has done beautiful things with them. They're very chic. They would look lovely with summer dresses. They really would.'

He was pleading much more strongly than he felt. The hats were pretty but he knew that they would require a lot of hard work if they were to be taken seriously by the likes of Bettina. He was prepared to put in that hard work (indeed he had been doing so that morning), not only because he wanted to help Ludovico but also because he felt an increasing respect for Constance. He knew that his voice alone, however, was not enough. It was vitally important that Bettina should start talking about them.

'You know you can trust me, Bettina, my dear,' he added. 'Please have faith in my judgement until you can get up here to see for yourself. Don't forget, I've booked you for a weekend.'

Bettina noted the bribe with satisfaction. All right, she thought, as she put down the receiver, I'll tell people about them. Why not?

Bettina Bonoccorsi respected Savognia's judgement. He was a man of taste, in fashion as in everything else. His studies, especially his deep involvement with Italian painting and architecture, had refined an already shrewd eye. He understood fashion in the instinctive way of certain Frenchmen. He could sit in Christian Dior's salon alongside Cocteau and Berard and be as fully aware as they of the subtleties of cut and the balance of shapes even though he had never attempted to design anything in his life. Bettina knew, as did all his friends, that Giancarlo had huge creative talents in him. He could draw with a high degree of fluency but, although competent, the work was always flawed by a facile slickness. He was moved deeply and passionately by beauty on all levels, but his tragedy was that his abilities came to nothing because he could not find the connection between the depths of his soul and the skill of his hands. His personality condemned him to be the eternal critic, informed and intuitive, but ultimately sterile.

Giancarlo was not going out on a limb for Constance. He could see a strong talent at work in her. Or so he convinced himself as he languidly set about dressing for lunch. He took a great deal of care over the choice of his clothes and spent several anxious moments on his receding hair before he was satisfied with his appearance. As he walked towards the door, his servant silently stepped forward from the shadows of the hall and handed him his grey kid gloves, which Giancarlo put on, his Malacca cane and his grey Borsalino, both of which he carried in the same hand as he stepped into the courtyard and out into the Florentine sun.

Giancarlo had chosen one of Florence's good but not grand restaurants. He had made his choice very precisely. He wanted a venue that was sufficiently impressive without seeming intimidating. As he stepped through the door he was greeted with the effusiveness that people of his title always receive in Italy.

'Has my guest arrived, Mauro?' he asked as he removed his gloves.

'No, not yet, Principe,' the maître d'hôtel replied, with a slight bow.

Giancarlo was not surprised. He had timed his arrival impeccably. It was exactly four minutes to two.

'I shall wait here at the door,' he said decisively as Mauro was about to lead him to his table.

'*Si, si*, Principe,' the man replied, trying to hide his surprise. To cover his confusion he clicked his fingers at a passing waiter and said, 'Bring a chair immediately,' and, smiling, bowed out of Giancarlo's presence.

Giancarlo was concerned that his guest might find it overwhelming to walk into a strange restaurant alone. As he was determined that this lunch should be a success, he was prepared to commit the social solecism of hanging round the door even though it had so obviously discomfited Mauro. He hadn't long to wait. Even as the waiter approached with a chair for him, Constance appeared. Giancarlo stepped forward to greet her and was struck by how handsome she looked. He noticed that she was wearing the same dress that she had worn at the Fiesole lunch and he thought how well its colour suited her pale northern colouring. Constance blushed as she noticed his glance sweep over her. She knew that Giancarlo remembered every detail of the frock and she wished she had chosen her spotted navy. However, her embarrassment quickly changed to delight. Noticing the hat she was carrying, his face lit up.

'So,' he said, 'you have a new hat. Please, why do you carry it? Put it on.'

'Oh, no,' she said in panic, 'I couldn't walk into a restaurant wearing it, but . . .' she held it before her, 'I thought you would like to see.'

Giancarlo took it from her and, holding it up at arm's length, exclaimed, 'Constanza, this is lovely! Where did you find these little pink beads?'

Thrilled by his unaffected enthusiasm, she explained that they were, in fact, pre-war. 'I was keen to have really unusual trimmings that would be a strong feature without overwhelming the design of the hat,' she said, as they settled at their table. 'I searched everywhere but couldn't find what I wanted. Then Ludovico suddenly remembered his mother's old dressmaker, who had a shop on the corner of Borgo Ognissanti and Via de' Fossi, near Piazza Goldoni. So we went to find her and she was still there.'

As she talked the scene came back vividly to Constance . . .


'Signora? Signora Annunziata?' Ludovico pushed open the heavy door and ushered Constance into the dusty shop. 'She must be here,' he whispered, 'or the door would have been locked.'

'Who is it?' a voice croaked from somewhere at the back of the shop and a tiny woman festooned in tape measures, with an enormous pin cushion pinned to her left breast, squeezed through the narrow gap at the end of the counter.

'Signora Annunziata!' Ludovico said enthusiastically. 'Do you remember me? I used to come here with my mother when I was a little boy.'

The old woman squinted up at him through her glasses,

one lens of which was broken and held together with discoloured sticking plaster. She stared at him fiercely for a few seconds and then, turning away, said, 'No.'

'The Principessa Villanuova,' Ludovico said.

The woman's whole demeanour changed. 'Oh,' she said in delight, 'the Principessa! I have not seen her for years. What a holy woman! A true walking saint. How sad she always was. But you are her son, you say? Which one?'

Ludovico looked startled. 'Signora,' he smiled, 'your memory is going. I was the only child who ever came with my mother.'

The old woman gave him a quizzical look and said, 'Va bene. You are right. My brain is going the same way as my eyes. Why are you here?'

'Signora, let me introduce my wife. She is English.'

The old woman gave Constance a long look and said, 'I can see.'

As Ludovico explained what they were looking for, Constance gazed round the shop. Small and cramped, it was piled high with battered shoeboxes, old hatboxes, biscuit tins and even a wooden chest. Slowly, the old woman began to open them tó reveal her treasures. She had supplies of everything: mother-of-pearl buttons; artificial violets; yellowing lace collars and cuffs; fur trims; brass hooks and eyes. As Ludovico, who had climbed the stepladder to reach the top shelves, handed down the boxes, Constance became increasingly excited. She had never seen so many marvellous things. The old woman said something.

'She wants you to see her beads,' Ludovico translated. Box after box was opened, revealing beads of every size and shade. It was like an Aladdin's cave . . .

'It was incredible,' Constance told Savognia. 'You would never find anything like that in London. Everything was so old and so . . . untouched. Things were still in their original wrappers. One packet was marked 1903, can you imagine! She let us have so many marvellous things for

174

the hats.' She settled back in her chair as the waiter brought the menu.

After they had ordered, Giancarlo lit a Camel and, blowing the smoke through his nose, said, 'So, Constanza. Your little venture is now under way.'

She grimaced. 'Well, it's just beginning,' she said, 'but I think it will be all right.'

'I am sure it will,' he replied. 'I must tell you, my dear, that we all admire you very much. So much courage . . . and so very young. I am certain – absolutely, categorically certain – that you will succeed in your little hat-trimming enterprise but tell me, my dear, have you any business experience at all?'

'Oh, yes,' Constance replied confidently.

'Really?' Giancarlo raised his eyebrows.

Constance told him about her few weeks with Monsieur de Levantière and how fascinating she had found the business of ordering fabrics and working out costs.

'That sort of thing interests you, does it?'

'Oh, very much. Some day I would like to have a small business of some sort, something to do with fashion.'

'How very interesting. What does Ludovico think of that?'

Constance smiled. 'I haven't mentioned it to him. He often finds it hard enough to be interested in the hats, let alone anything else.' They both laughed and although Constance felt disloyal to Ludovico, it was what was required to properly relax the atmosphere between Giancarlo and herself.

Though Constance hadn't seen Giancarlo since his luncheon party in Fiesole she felt that she knew him much better now. Ludovico had talked about him at great length. It was obvious that the older man had an enormous influence over her husband but this didn't worry Constance. She knew how deeply Ludovico loved her.

During lunch they talked of Florence. Giancarlo promised to take her to the art galleries and suggested furthermore that she might also like to see some of the family collections still in private hands. They had been hidden away during the war and were now being reinstated in the galleries of the great palazzi of the city. Constance thought of Miss Hatherby and was thrilled. She found it so easy to talk to Giancarlo that she told him all about her friend at Seaton Cramer Hall and the Pre-Raphaelite pictures and other treasures there.

'So,' he said, 'that is where your taste comes from with these hats. It all becomes clear.'

'Oh, not just there. I learned so much at Monsieur de Levantière's – about taste and elegance.'

'Really?' Savognia said, intrigued. 'Tell me more.'

As Constance recounted her experiences, he looked at her face, flushed with happiness, and thought of Ludovico's description of her when she abandoned herself to passion – because, as is the way with Italian men, Ludovico had told Giancarlo everything about their love-making. Giancarlo watched her as she talked animatedly. He began to see why his friend had been captivated. There was an extraordinary undercurrent of sensuality in this cool blonde northern woman. He knew why Ludovico was so passionately in love with her.

Wishing to move the conversation on to a more intimate level, Giancarlo said, 'Constanza, I want you to know – as one of Ludo's oldest friends – how grateful I am that you have made him so happy. You know, I am sure, that he adores . . . how do you say in English? . . . adores . . . yes, that's it . . . adores the ground you walk on? I cannot believe the change in him. I must be honest: when he first told me about you and asked if he should marry you, I said no.'

Constance was shocked – not at Giancarlo's negative reply but because Ludovico had discussed something so personal to them with anybody else, even his best friend. Giancarlo, noticing and misunderstanding her expression, went on quickly, 'It was, of course, nothing against you. It was just that it seemed so unexpected. The meeting on the train; the fact that you were . . .' he paused delicately

'. . . not Italian. His financial situation. Oh! There were lots of reasons to urge caution but, my dear,' he smiled, 'you had so ensnared him that he wouldn't listen. I think he was absolutely right not to,' he went on hastily, 'but it was a shock.'

Constance remained silent for a moment as Giancarlo methodically stubbed out his cigarette by folding it over and pressing it down firmly.

'You know Ludo very well.' She asked tentatively.

'Very,' Giancarlo replied. 'We have been intimate for years.'

Constance was startled. For her, being intimate meant only one thing – but she could not believe it of Ludo.

'How do you mean . . . intimate?' she asked awkwardly.

'He first came to me when he was a little boy, as you know. We did everything together. *Everything*. We are like brothers of the blood. We have no secrets. I love Ludo more than I love myself.'

Giancarlo dropped his voice. 'I think I might even kill for him,' he added passionately.

Constance was disconcerted. What was Giancarlo trying to say to her?

'It is possible for a man to have that love for his friend,' Giancarlo said conversationally, as he lit another Camel.

Constance's mind was racing. Had he and Ludo been lovers? She felt sick at the thought. Savognia could see her distress.

'Have I said something to offend you?' he asked politely.

Constance blushed with embarrassment. 'No,' she lied. 'I just didn't realise how much you and Ludo cared for each other.'

'Oh, yes,' he went on, making matters worse, 'in our innermost souls we are one. There is no part of either of us untouched by the other.'

So, she thought in despair, it's true. This is why he has invited me here. To tell me. Ludovico must have asked him to because he isn't man enough to tell me himself. She felt she would go mad if she had to sit there and listen to any further confidences, but she didn't know how to leave. She could hardly just walk out.

The silence began to embarrass Savognia. Looking at Constance's face, he leaned forward and said, 'Are you feeling unwell?'

'Yes,' she said, grasping at the straw. 'I feel sick. Please excuse me. I must leave.'

She stood up. 'I'm sorry but I can't stay here any longer. I'm sorry,' and she turned and fled.

'Constanza!' he called after her, picking up the hat that she had left on the table. She did not stop. She ran from the restaurant and headed for the apartment. By the time she reached Via Santo Spirito, tears were streaming down her face.

She burst into the apartment. Ludovico was lying on the bed. He leapt up when he saw her face.

'Darling,' he cried, 'what is wrong?'

'What is Giancarlo to you?' Her voice shook.

'What do you mean?' Ludovico countered.

Sobbing in her distress, Constance told him of the conversation in the restaurant. Ludovico fell back on the bed with a roar of laughter.

'What are you laughing at? It isn't funny,' Constance said, her voice rising.

Ludovico's laughter became even more helpless. She was bewildered by his reaction. To cover her embarrassment, she walked over to him and said awkwardly, 'Ludo, why are you laughing at me? Have I said something funny?'

'Oh, my darling,' he sat upright and pulled her down by his side, 'you most certainly have. What do you take me for? Giancarlo is my best friend – *basta*! We are Italian men, not English. How could you imagine such a thing?' He put his arms round her. 'To go to bed with Giancarlo? What a preposterous idea!'

'But he said he would kill for you,' Constance said defensively.

'So he would,' Ludovico agreed, 'and I would for him – but that doesn't make us lovers! It is nothing to do with sex. It is about honour.'

Within minutes they were making love so wildly that Constance knew she had been mistaken but, lying on the bed after he had left for the tennis court, she still felt uneasy about the intimacy between the two men. Did it mean that Ludo told Giancarlo about their own private world?

'She is very young to be thinking of having her own business, I must say,' Savognia said to Ludovico.

The two men were changing after tennis and, as his friend seemed so relaxed, Ludovico had raised the question of Constance's hopes – while making perfectly clear his own lack of enthusiasm.

'It's this obsession with money,' he groaned, 'and her absolute determination to try to make us financially independent of my mother.'

'Well, there's nothing wrong with either ambition,' Savognia replied, 'but can she do it? You know how difficult it is for a woman to do anything in business in this country.'

'She has asked me to find a small shop for her here in Florence,' Ludovico went on in despair.

Savognia thought for a moment. 'I have just the place,' he said, 'in Via Tornabuoni. It has been empty for years. Constance can have that.'

Constance was so excited at the news that even Ludovico found himself becoming enthusiastic.

'How quickly can I have the keys so that I can get in and start decorating?' Constance asked.

'Decorating?'

'Yes, if it has been empty for all the war years it will be in a terrible state. I must start work immediately.'

'Start work? You? Constance, what on earth do you mean? Savognia's men will look after all that.'

179

'But I don't want them to! It is *my* shop! *I* want to do every thing so that I know it has been done properly.'

'Are you suggesting that you will actually physically work on the redecorating?' Ludovico asked faintly.

'Of course! Why ever not?'

'I will tell you why not! You are a Villanuova now and I will not hear of such a thing. You must put it out of your head immediately. How can you imagine that somebody of your class could be seen working with peasants? Really, my darling, there are times when I think you are quite crazy! Maybe that's why I love you, eh?'

'Constanza Castelfranco?' Ludovico's voice cracked with horror. 'Are you out of your mind? Do you really suggest that my family name be put on a sign outside a *hat* shop? Really, Constance, this is too much!'

'Why not?' she asked truculently. 'It's my name as well, isn't it? What else should I call my business?'

'Why must it have your name on at all? That's what I do not understand.'

'Because it *is* mine and I am proud of my name *and* my shop.'

'It is absolutely out of the question, my darling. We would be the laughing stock of Florence. No, of the whole of Italy. You must think of something else.'

Constance knew that there was no point in attempting to push Ludovico on the subject. She thought for a moment.

'Can we call it Constanza? That doesn't involve your precious family name but everybody will still know that it is me . . . and that is very important, not just for the business, but also for me.'

'Ludovico, I must learn to drive.'

'Why? We don't have a car.'

'Not at the moment, but we will soon. Once we really get things going with Giulio I shall need to go up there at least once a week.'

'Well, I can drive you.'

180

Constance was determined to have the freedom to go to the Marche whenever she wanted, without having to persuade Ludovico to drive her, but she was beginning to learn to read his moods and could tell that he had closed his mind. She said nothing more of it to him.

'Constance, my dear, you are very young and a little inclined to be headstrong. I wonder if you have fully thought of the difficulties involved in even the simplest business transaction here in Italy.'

'Oh, Giancarlo! Of course I have! I know it will be difficult but that isn't a reason for not doing it. All I need is a little car to go and collect the hats once a week, a girl in the shop to serve and help me trim the hats, and my business has begun! What is so difficult about that? I really wonder sometimes if there is a plot by Italian men to stop women achieving *anything* on their own initiative, I really do!' Savognia laughed rather uneasily. 'I will teach you to drive,' he said, 'I promise. We cannot have the wishes of the *donna inglese* thwarted, can we?'

Although she knew that she was being patronised, Constance smiled – as she knew she must if she were to keep her most powerful ally.

# CHAPTER 7

Savognia insisted upon an official opening for the hat shop. Although he was extremely reluctant to draw attention to it, Ludovico knew that he had no choice but to agree. In fact, he had begun to be swept up in the momentum of the enterprise. Now that it was a *fait accompli* he found himself carried away on the crest of Constance's enthusiasm to such an extent that he was actually enjoying himself – although he dreaded his mother's reaction when she found out.

The opening was the gesture of confidence that Constance needed. Unlike Ludovico, she wanted everyone to know about the shop and her hats.

As the shop was so tiny and Giancarlo's list of guests so long, the reception was held in his palazzo. As she walked through its magnificent rooms before the guests arrived, wearing her navy spotted silk, Constance regretted not having invited Louise. She knew that her aunt would have loved it.

Constance marvelled at how much her life had changed in the few months since she had left the train at Florence with Ludovico. It was as if she had grown up overnight. She recognised that since her marriage her confidence had increased at a pace she could hardly keep up with. Her mother's visit had also helped. It had acted as a blessing on her marriage. She no longer felt embarrassed, as if she had done a shameful thing. She was ready to proudly face the world as Ludovico's lawful wife.

As Savognia had known, they needed all the space they could find for the guests. Everybody had accepted; gate-crashers in their hundreds had wheedled a way in and people had even come from Milan and Rome, so much gossip had been engendered by the whirlwind romance, the stories of the strange young bride and the speculation over how the mad old Principessa was taking it all. The impressive turnout was a manifestation of curiosity fuelled by gossip. Everybody wanted to see Constance.

She knew it and she didn't care. In fact, she gloried in it. As Ludovico took her round, introducing her, she was impressed that he knew absolutely everybody in the crowded rooms. Intrigued by the envious looks that some of the women gave her, she was sure that at least half the females in the room were in love with her husband. And she was pleased.

Suddenly they were face to face with a dark-skinned woman with a mischievous air. Constance noticed how her eyes glinted as she bent forward and kissed Ludovico.

'Bettina, *cara mia*,' Ludovico said, 'how good to see you again. It seems so long.'

'It *is*, darling. Capri in May. An awful lot has happened since then. Not least, your little escapade. Who would have thought it? Married before any of us could turn round! And into trade now, as I believe your wife's nation would say.'

Ludovico introduced Constance who was subjected to that instant head-to-toe sweep of the eye she was learning Italian women were so good at. So good that many people failed to notice. She did, however, and she knew that Bettina realised it.

'So, my dear,' Bettina laughed, 'what do you make of this impossible man?'

Constance put her arm round Ludovico's neck and said, 'I think he's lovely.'

'Oh, he's certainly *that*,' Bettina agreed, 'it's a Villan-uova trait. Remind me to tell you all about this wild lot, some day. You'd be surprised at what they get up to!'

Ludovico laughed and blushed. '*Basta*, Bettina. Do you want my wife to leave me before the month is out? I can see I must keep you two apart.'

Constance laughed at the joke; Bettina did not. Giving Constance a sharp look, she said to Ludovico, 'So, your wings have finally been clipped. No one has heard a thing about you for weeks. You have been very naughty, neglecting your friends.'

She smiled at Constance. 'Your husband, my dear Constanza, is quite ruthless with his friends. He only sees them when he needs them. He never thinks that they might need him.'

Turning to Ludovico, she went on, 'Where is Savognia? He is almost as elusive as you – although I do at least speak to him on the telephone occasionally. I can't imagine how I will track him down in all this crush!' She looked around in a perfunctory way and then said, 'Do you see anything of Gioella?'

'Of course not,' Ludovico answered quickly, 'how could I?' He paused. 'I think she's still in Switzerland, at one of those clinics.'

Bettina smiled and said to Constance, 'She will not leave her body alone. She is always having some new treatment or other to make her more irresistible to men. It certainly seems to work, wouldn't you agree, Ludo darling – speaking as a respectably married man, of course, viewing from the sidelines?'

Not waiting for a reply, she took Constance by the arm and said, 'I must part you newlyweds, or tomorrow everyone will be talking! Come and tell me about your hats, Constanza, and this little shop you've opened. *Too* amusing, my dear! Where did you get such an *original* idea?' and she led her into the *salotto* where the buffet was spread out.

As Constance talked, Bettina ate, to Constance's fascination. Without seeming to take her eyes off her plate, she was able to detect just when the waiter was near enough for her to snatch another titbit from his salver. She reminded Constance of an octopus.

'You know, my dear,' Bettina told her, 'You might just be able to do something big with these hats, if Ludo will let you.'

'Let me? Why on earth should he stop me?'

Bettina quickly changed the subject. 'Do you know Monica Peterson?'

Constance did not.

'She is an American. She comes frequently to Italy. I know her very well – and so does Ludo. She must talk to you next time she is here. To be successful you must sell in America. That is the grand *mercato* of the moment. I'll speak to her myself – she will know how to help you.'

Constance was overcome with gratitude at Bettina's confidence in the hats. Selling in America was something she had never contemplated even in her wildest dreams. The idea went straight to her head and she smiled warmly at Bettina.

'I think I've made my first female friend,' she told Ludovico, as they were preparing for bed. She was sitting on the bed as he brushed her hair. It was a ritual that had developed almost unnoticed over the weeks and it gave them both a great deal of sensual pleasure. His strong arm faltered in mid-sweep. He did not particularly want Constance to become friends with any of what he felt was the pack of self-involved harpies at the party that night.

'Who?' he asked casually.

'Why, Bettina, of course,' Constance replied. Half closing her eyes, she leaned back as Ludovico continued brushing, so she didn't see his face darken as he looked at their reflection in the mirror.

'Really?' he said calmly. 'What makes you think that?'

'She was so sweet about the hats. She's promised to introduce me to people. She's sure that we could sell in America. She obviously knows everyone. Do you know someone called Monica?'

185

Ludovico abruptly stopped brushing. 'I'm tired. Let's go to bed,' he said brusquely. 'We can talk in the morning.'

Constance was surprised at his change of mood. Lying in the dark, she asked quietly, 'Don't you like Bettina?'

He took a long time to reply.

'Of course I do, but there's no point in trying to become too close to her. She only rarely comes to Florence. Also, I think she's rather too old for you.'

'I think she's very sweet,' Bettina told Giancarlo on the telephone the next morning, 'but I cannot see it lasting. She will not satisfy him for long. He has too much of the Villanuova blood in him. He is a sexual gypsy.'

Her words stung Giancarlo. Sitting bolt upright in bed, he spoke firmly. 'Bettina, don't talk rubbish. You don't know anything about them. I hope that you won't go round Rome saying such foolish, demeaning things or I shall be very disappointed in you.'

Why are you so keen on it lasting? Bettina asked herself, but she said aloud, 'Don't be silly. I wouldn't dream of it. I talk between two friends. I hope you are right. Ludo should be ready to settle down by now. But, seriously, *caro*, can you see her coming to terms with Italy and all us dreadful Italians? She seems so Anglo-Saxon, and uncomplicated. You know what I mean, I'm sure.'

'Didn't you think her attractive – in a classic way?' Giancarlo asked.

'Well,' Bettina replied, 'she has a good figure, and marvellous legs, but I thought her face too severe. Not plain, exactly, but lacking sensuality . . . and you know how important *that* is to Ludo.'

'Well, I don't think Ludo is complaining.'

'Giancarlo, I cannot bear it when you pretend to be naive! Of *course* Ludo won't complain. He'll merely slope off to his old friends when he begins to find the time dragging with his little English mouse.'

'Bettina, I will not listen to this rubbish. Now, tell me, what did you really think of her?'

She was not to be drawn. 'That shoulder-length hair looks rather démodé now, don't you think?' she said brightly.

Ludovico was amazed and slightly alarmed at the new purposefulness in Constance. Already, she no longer needed to speak through him. She was picking up Italian at extraordinary speed and could easily communicate on a rudimentary level with the stallholders in Via Santo Spirito. Her growing assurance pleased him on one level and worried him on another. He liked the idea of having an accomplished wife; he welcomed the fact that he didn't have to spend time on the boring and tiring business of translating and yet he missed the softly pliable woman who, in their first few days, had lain in his bed like his own odalisque awaiting his return. That woman had gone, superceded by someone much tougher, less pliant and more independent. Ludovico was forced to accept that there had been a shift in emphasis in their relationship. From their very first day together in Florence he had subconsciously approached Constance as if she were a mistress – someone to be cosseted, adored and used, but not to be considered. Even though that she commanded his love in a way that no mistress ever could. He was besotted with her. She was, he felt sure, the only woman who would ever seriously engage his emotions and his soul – and yet he had been guilty of viewing her in a traditional Italian way. Her attitude towards the hats had forced him to change his approach. Ludovico now realised that his wife was a partner in his life, not an adjunct to it. He had to accept that she was strong in a way that he was not. She had a streak of reckless determination that explained why she had broken her journey and followed him at Florence. He knew it was something he would not control.

Constance was in a permanent state of alert receptiveness. She was learning so much about herself, about Ludo-

187

vico, their relationship and their marriage. There was no doubt in her mind that she could make the marriage a success and she increasingly felt fewer doubts about their ability to build a business. She even felt hopeful about her mother-in-law. Constance knew that the Principessa Maria-Angelina represented her biggest challenge. Underneath the austere and ironic façade, Maria-Angelina was as self-indulgent as her husband had been. Ludovico was her joy, her sole interest, apart from her religion, and her intellectual plaything. As she had her servant move round the huge jigsaw pieces, she thought of him; as she passed her gloved fingers beneath her nose, she pictured him. Constance knew that Maria-Angelina would not give up Ludovico without an enormous struggle because she needed him to fill an empty life while she awaited the death for which she daily prepared herself.

Despite her love for him – a love so powerful that his presence actually affected her physically: even in a crowded room, she could find herself shivering with desire if his hand lightly brushed hers – Constance was becoming increasingly aware of Ludovico's inadequacies. In her heart of hearts she was a little shocked at his fecklessness. His upbringing, it seemed to her, had been designed expressly to protect him from having to face any of the problems of life. She still found it hard to accept that he had never had a job – nor, indeed, had ever contemplated having one. To her, it seemed an utterly immoral way to live. She knew that if the hat business were to have any chance it would have to be engineered by her. Even if the shop became an enormous success, she recognised that she could never entirely share it with Ludo; quite apart from his indifference, it already meant too much to her. In a way, she thought fancifully, it's our very first baby, so *I* have to carry it and make it strong.

The car climbed up into the hills. Constance was thrilled by the fresh coolness in the air as it blew through the open window and ruffled her hair. It was like a tonic after the debilitating closeness of Florence. Even in the autumn, the city still seemed dusty and airless to her northern lungs. She recalled the cold sharpness of North-umberland mornings when the day was bitter-sweet and the air, tangy with the threat of foul weather, encouraged activity; here in the hills, she felt there was at least a chance of recovering some of that energy. For her heat meant loss of hope, lack of purpose and subliminal depression while cold meant determination, direction and decisiveness. She turned and smiled at Ludovico.

'Thank you for bringing me,' she said.

'No, no, signora, he is telling you with his hands. Loop before the plait. You must or the hat will not have the strength.'

Signora Rosina was attempting to be patient but it was trying to have to interpret her son's grunts so that the Englishwoman could understand. Constance bit her lip in frustration. Giulio worked so quickly and deftly he made her feel that she was all thumbs. Then without a word, he placed his hands on hers and guided them. His touch was extraordinary. His fingers were as soft as a woman's and yet she could feel the strength of the craftsman in them. She felt that in some mysterious way he was trans-ferring his skill to her, and she was thrilled.

It was her second day of working in the little hut. Already she was pleased by the unspoken rapport that was building up between her and Giulio. She even thought she detected a slight softening in his mother's attitude towards her. It hadn't been easy to persuade her to allow Constance to come and learn from her son – although her opposition had been nothing compared with Ludovico's.

'Constanza, you are being ridiculous,' he had said when she first suggested it. 'You cannot work alongside peas-ants. They will lose all respect for you. It would be as bad as me joining them in the fields. I will not allow it.'

She bridled, but kept her temper. 'Ludo,' she said evenly, 'it is *you* who are ridiculous. I can't begin to run a business if I don't know the processes myself: I can think of no quicker way to lose my mother's money. Giulio is the man with the skill – the magic in his fingers – I *have* to learn from him if our hats are to be the very best available. Surely you can see that? It isn't as if I shall be alone with him. His mother will be there.'

'I cannot believe that a wife of mine is prepared to go back to that foul-smelling piss-hole. It's disgusting. You'll faint from the fumes.'

'*You* might, Ludovico, but I most certainly won't. Now, please, talk to Signora Rosina and arrange things. You know that there's no other way.'

Ludovico had shown his disapproval by refusing to stay with her while she learnt the trade. In the morning, he dropped her in the square at Trapena and drove off, returning only to collect her in the evening. As she walked up to the hatmaker's that first day, Constance was conscious of being watched by dark, suspicious eyes peeping through the shutters of the hovels. She didn't care. It was only on the second day, when a woman threw a stone at her, that she realised how seriously she had disrupted the social order. She didn't dare tell Ludovico. On the third day she was bombarded by a hail of sharp objects accompanied by shouted insults and high-pitched whistling from behind the farm walls. As she began to run towards Signora Rosina's house, dodging the missiles, she thought, My God, these people are stoning me!

She arrived at the door. It was closed. She banged desperately on the shutters. Signora Rosina didn't appear. 'Please, please! Let me in!' Constance cried. Suddenly, a huge hand caught hold of her arm and dragged her from the door. Turning in dismay, she saw it was Giulio. As he pulled her towards the shed, using his body to shield her from the stones, Constance caught a glimpse of Signora Rosina standing impassively behind the shutters. She knew with a horrible certainty that the woman would have done nothing to help her, even if the villagers had stoned her to death.

Constance was terrified of telling Ludovico but knew that she must, that very evening. As she unfolded the ghastly tale, she began to cry with delayed shock. She shook with fear as she explained the spine-chilling behaviour of Signora Rosina and she longed for Ludo to take her in his arms and comfort her. For all her distress, Ludovico offered her no sympathy. As she talked, he let her know, without saying a word, that what she had suffered had been her own fault.

'I think Signora Rosina hates me,' Constance wept.

'Of course she does,' Ludovico said. 'They all do. What do you expect? You come up here and imagine that you can overturn the natural order of centuries in a few days? I warned you of this but you wouldn't listen. This land is primitive. The people are ignorant and backward. You are the first non-Italian woman they have ever seen, for God's sake! And yet in your foreign arrogance you assume that they should think exactly as you do! *You* are the primitive one, not them, primitive because you can see things only in your way. They watch your extraordinary behaviour and they think you are a witch. They know – they have always believed, since time began – that an idiot is the devil's son. When they see you joining him in his hut, of *course* they are frightened. Who wouldn't be? Theirs is perfectly natural behaviour. *You* are the unnatural one. They are superstitious and illiterate. How could they not be terrified of a witch and a devil's son working together behind closed doors? Can't you see what your arrogance has done to them? They are simple people frightened of the unknown. How the hell did you *expect* them to react?'

'This is ridiculous!' Constance retorted. 'We're living in the twentieth century, for God's sake. This is the age of cars, aeroplanes, wirelesses.'

'Wirelesses!' Ludovico burst in. 'They've never seen a wireless, let alone listened to one. What do they know about cars and aeroplanes? They ride on mules and have never even been out of the valley. You are mad if you

191

think they can understand your ways. Listen,' he went on urgently, 'I will tell you what I should have told you before. That house is damned. It is considered evil ground. No one goes there except the whore Maria, who collects the hats. When Signora Rosina walks the street, people run indoors and lock their shutters. They think she has held hands with the devil. That is why she didn't come to your aid. They would have killed her had she done so. He, poor hulk, is not even allowed into the street. Now do you see why you should have listened to me? You have destroyed my position – and that of my family. It will take years to rebuild. You are a destructive force here. You must never return to that house.'

Constance agreed, as she knew she must, that they would return to Florence the next day. For Ludovico, she was aware, the whole episode was now over. She would visit Trapena no more. She was determined, however, that after a decent period she would drive up from Florence alone and take up where she had been forced to let go.

As they sat in Ludovico's gloomy apartments that night there came a knock on the door. It was the estate factor. He talked to Ludovico in whispers at the door. Ludovico turned to Constance and said in a voice full of animosity, 'I must go. I am needed in the village.' Before she could say anything he had left with the factor.

She waited restlessly for his return and as the time passed she became impatient. Drifting into the study, she sat at Ludovico's desk. Absently she tried the drawer, but it was locked. She pushed back her chair so abruptly that she jolted the desk. A key clattered to the floor. As she bent to pick it up she saw its hook underneath the desk. She was about to replace it but, instead, decided to try it in the lock of the drawer. It turned smoothly.

She paused, debating whether to open the drawer, then, relocking it, she walked back into the *salotto*. Ludovico had been away almost an hour. What was she supposed to do, sitting here all alone with no one to talk to? She crossed to the window and looked down into the courtyard. Nothing moved, except the big light above the castle door. As it swung to and fro, it cast fantastic shadows on the walls around. Constance thought she had never seen anything so desolate as the scene below. Silent and sombre, it looked to her as if it hadn't changed since Renaissance times. Feeling excluded and abandoned, she moved away from the window.

She was hardly conscious that she had returned to the study. Idly, she turned the key in the drawer once more. Again, it moved smoothly and efficiently. She gripped the handle and pulled. The drawer slid out an inch. She pushed it back. She leapt back in shock as she heard a door bang somewhere below her in the castle. It was followed by an even deeper silence than before. Slowly, she edged forward to the desk once more and pulled open the drawer. It was empty except for one small book, bound in dark green leather. Constance picked it up. It was an address book. As she flicked through the pages, a photograph fell out. It was of three teenage boys, dressed for tennis and holding up their rackets to make a triangle. Each one had signed his name across his image. 'Ludovico', 'Giancarlo' and 'Carlo'. Constance was delighted at how pretty Ludovico had looked as a boy and thought that she detected Giancarlo's customary seriousness behind his smile, but it was the third boy who intrigued her. 'Carlo' was so like a slightly older version of Ludovico that she knew he must be a cousin. How odd that Ludovico had never mentioned him. She would ask him when he returned.

Suddenly she heard Ludovico's car pulling into the courtyard. She quickly replaced the book and locked the drawer. The key was back on its hook and she was sitting in the *salotto* by the time Ludovico came in. One look at his face banished all thoughts of the address book. She knew immediately that something was terribly wrong.

'Where have you been?' she questioned. 'What has happened?'

He passed his hand wearily across his eyes but made no reply.

'Ludo,' she asked in alarm, 'is everything all right?'

'No,' he turned savagely upon her. 'No, it is not. Thanks to you.'

Her heart sank. 'What is it? What is wrong? Tell me!'

He sat down heavily. 'I have just come from Trapena.'

She waited, too frightened to speak.

'Giulio is dead,' he said flatly, 'they've killed him.'

'Who?' she cried in terror. 'Who have killed him?'

He gave her a pitying look. 'Are you mad? Do you think we're ever going to find that out? That's a secret that will never come out of the village.'

'What happened?'

'Somebody burned down his shed. He is locked in at night. With all the straw it was an inferno in seconds.'

'What about his mother?'

'She just stood at her window and watched. No one would go to help him. They thought he was the devil, returned to his flames.'

'It isn't the end you know,' Constance said when they had returned to Florence. 'I mean to continue. I have to continue, for the memory of that poor, gentle man.'

She stopped Ludovico's attempted interruption. 'No, please let me tell you. You'll think this silly but I know I can make hats as well as Giulio did. It's as if his strength has passed to me. I'm going to use my mother's money to set up a little industry in Castelfranco. I will train the young girls of the village to make hats.'

'Don't you think you've done enough damage? You can't set foot in Trapena now. Are you going to do the same with my village?'

'No, of course not. It will all be open and above board. I shall ask your mother's factor to organise it.'

'Not in Castelfranco, Constance.'

'So where?'

'I don't know. Maybe another village, away from my mother.'

Constance was keen to have her business as far from Maria-Angelina and her spies as possible and was happy with Ludovico's suggestion of Biaggibonsi, a larger village further down the valley. She knew that he was still uneasy about the whole enterprise and was grateful that he was at least trying to be positive and practical.

'Please trust me, Ludovico,' she said. 'I know it will work.'

He said nothing.

'But you must have some sort of business plan, Constance,' Giancarlo said patiently.

She had turned to him for advice, not because she felt that she needed it but because she wished to try out her ideas on somebody and she knew that although Ludovico would listen he would not become involved with any of the practicalities.

'By what you've described, you'll need perhaps six girls. Who will oversee them? You can't spend all your time up in the Marche, after all.'

'Well,' she replied uncertainly, 'I suppose we'll have to put one of them in charge when I'm not there.'

'Absolutely, categorically not! Nothing will be done! The moment you leave, they'll be off home or working in the fields. You need a man to supervise them.'

Constance was determined to ignore the unquestioned Italian attitude that automatically assumed that only a man could bear authority.

'A woman would be better,' she said.

'I assume you are aware that there is not a literate woman in the village? There must be paperwork – who on earth will do it?'

Constance bit her lip. She hadn't thought of that but rather than admit the fact she said, 'Look, why don't we go up there and *see*? You never know.'

195

Savognia was delighted to be so closely involved. 'I'll drive us up tomorrow,' he said.

'No,' she corrected, '*I'll* drive us up. You can show me what I do wrong. Don't look so frightened. I won't kill us!'

'I'm impressed,' Savognia told Ludovico later that day. 'She has definite business skills, there is no doubt. She is so intelligent. She picks things up very quickly. Mind you, she has a will of her own. I do hope she's not going to be stubborn about the overseer. You know as well as I, Ludovico, that only a man can do a job like that. She must understand that, if she is to have any hope of success.'

'She will surely listen to you. She so wants the business to do well that she will certainly take your advice.'

Neither man was convinced.

Finding willing girls was no problem. Constance chose an initial workforce of eight. She insisted on training them herself so that she knew they would be working to her standards and would be aware of what quality of workmanship she expected. On the question of the overseer she was stubborn. Having spoken to the Principessa's factor, she was determined not to employ him.

'Really, Constance!' Savognia burst out impatiently. 'I simply cannot understand your objection.'

'Well, Giancarlo, let me spell it out for you. Firstly, I don't see why I can't have a woman – and you have given me no valid reason to change my view. Secondly, I don't wish to employ anybody who has anything to do with Maria-Angelina. I will not have every detail of my business retailed to her – and you know perfectly well that that is precisely what would happen if I employed her factor.'

They were walking through Biaggibonsi's village square on their way to the car, parked in the shadow of the church. It was late afternoon and the men were sitting round the fountain. Not a woman in sight, Constance thought, how typical of Italy!

At that moment, a loud cry split the air. Suddenly, a large woman burst from one of the side streets and strode across the square. Pushing through the knot of men at the fountain, she grabbed a man even bigger than herself. Pulling him by the ear, she dragged him from the crowd and berated him in a non-stop flow of curses. Finally, pushing him ahead of her, she literally kicked him across the square as the men cheered and clapped.

'Who on earth is that?' Constance asked in delight.

'My dear Constance, I have absolutely no idea,' Savognia replied with a fastidious little shiver.

'Oh, do find out, please!'

Reluctantly, Savognia joined the still-laughing men and began to make enquiries. His presence instantly cut across the mirth. Fearfully, the men answered his questions, wondering why such a grand man should be interested in a hoyden like the notorious Milva.

He rejoined Constance by the car. 'Well,' he said, 'she is the village harridan, as her behaviour has just made amply clear. That poor unfortunate was her feckless brother, who had failed to do something she demanded. I gather that the disgraceful scene we witnessed is quite a frequent little performance.'

'So,' Constance said in admiration, 'there are *some* women in Italy who are not prepared to let men push them around all the time. Find out where she lives, Giancarlo. I want to meet Milva.'

And, despite his protests, she did.

The first thing that struck Constance was that, despite her size, Milva had a firm young body and a beautiful face. The second was the fact that she looked boldly and directly at Savognia as he spoke to her. The third – and by far the most important – was that her dark eyes were as intelligent as they were fearless. Constance knew that she had found her overseer. This woman would not be intimidated by men, would not be cowed by the castle and would command loyalty and respect from any work-force. No strikes with her around, Constance thought cheerfully, looking at the woman's strong and honest expression.

Driving back to Florence, Constance at the wheel, she and Savognia had their first outright disagreement.

'In my opinion the woman is a slut,' he said crossly, 'but quite apart from that, she is clearly illiterate. How on earth can she be expected to cope in your absence?'

'Did you see her eyes?'

'Eyes?'

'Yes. They were brimming with intelligence. She will soon learn to deal with the small amount of paperwork required. She is a born leader, and that is much more important to me.'

'I can see that she has a natural authority but that also means she could be a troublemaker.'

'I don't think so. Anyhow, I'm going to give her a chance.'


'Surely Ludovico knew that the idiot was his half-brother?' Monica Peterson asked Bettina, as they sat late over her first lunch since she had arrived in Italy from New York.

'Ludovico knows nothing about his father's indiscretions,' Bettina replied. 'He has no idea that he littered the Marche with bastards.'

Monica thought this rich coming from Bettina, whose cupboard also contained a few skeletons, but made no comment. 'Well, he need never know now,' she said, after a pause. 'The evidence has been destroyed. Who was the mother?'

'My dear, you know what a lustful old goat the father was! She was the village whore. When the child was born, Maria-Angelina paid one of her field servants to take him on as her own. She gave her the money to go and live in Trapena. Then she conveniently forgot all about her husband's little indiscretion. As the child grew, she paid for him to be trained in hatmaking. Poor Maria-Angelina! I actually feel sorry for her. She thought that everything was neatly parcelled up and safely stowed away at the back of the cupboard and now this happens!'

'But surely it won't come out?'

'Oh, I think so. There has to be an inquest. I don't see how it can be kept quiet.'

Monica smiled. 'Don't underestimate the power of the Principessa Maria-Angelina! She has managed to keep plenty of silent secrets before now. I'm sure she will do so this time. Discussion of parentage is not normally part of an inquest on someone who has died in a fire, I would have thought.'

The two women eyed each other. Although they would, without hesitation, claim to be friends, they nevertheless viewed each other warily. Monica Peterson had lived in the cut and thrust of New York society long enough to be on her guard with a woman like Bettina and Bettina knew that Monica, as an ex-journalist and a fully paid-up member of the international chattering classes, needed to be approached with caution. It was symptomatic of their respect for each other – and their interdependence – that Bettina was the first person Monica had seen since arriving the day before. She knew that all the catching-up she needed to do would be achieved in one luncheon with La Bonoccorsi, as she always referred to her friend.

Monica Peterson straddled the international world with a success rare in Americans. She felt at home in France and Italy in a way that most of her fellow countrymen did not. Although her parents had been Scottish, her husband was an Italian. Not that he played a part in her life any more. She had dumped him by the wayside soon after the marriage and had set out alone to make a life for herself, using her maiden name, in New York. She had been helped by an easy, outgoing personality, a sense of humour and a spectacularly feminine figure. Monica was big and saw no point in trying to hide it. Because she radiated health and energy she never appeared to be fat –

199

although she was certainly overweight. She had large, pendulous breasts that drove many men crazy, trim ankles that by right belonged to a slim woman, and a mane of dramatic orange hair that reminded people of Rita Hayworth. Her voice – basically Brooklyn – was resonant with vitality. As Bettina looked at her, half approvingly and half enviously, she thought how impossible it would be for Monica ever to be anonymous. Her presence and her personality seemed to spread around her. She engulfed everyone in her zest and good humour.

'And Carlo?' Monica asked suddenly.

Bettina lit a cigarette and looked away. 'Of course, he knows. When did he not know everything? He was worldly even in his cradle. He's a very different story.'

'Do you see him at all?'

'Sometimes – across a crowded room, as the song goes,' Bettina replied guardedly.

Monica knew that there was no point in continuing. 'So, tell me more about this Constance,' she said, changing the subject. 'How on earth is she managing to hold Ludo's interest?'

'*That*, my dear,' Bettina replied, relieved that the subject had changed, 'is the great question. However, she seems to be doing so very successfully. He goes nowhere without her. In fact, they rarely go anywhere. They're hardly ever seen in Florence and have only been down to Rome once.'

'How is Gioella?' Monica asked.

'She's been on one of her health cures,' Bettina replied, 'so nobody's seen her for some time. I'm sure she's just biding her time until things cool off. She's certainly not the sort to accept a situation like this and quietly walk away, is she? She's very bitchy about Constance. Calls her the white mouse. I gather she and Pino gossip for hours on the telephone – it's his job to keep her informed of developments.'

'Little bastard,' Monica said contemptuously. 'I bet he loathes Constance. He's had a crush on the Villanuovas

200

for years so he'll make as much mischief as he can, I'm sure.'

'Yes,' Bettina replied, 'but who takes any notice of Pino? Nobody in Rome, I can assure you.'

'What about Savognia?'

'My dear,' Bettina laughed, 'Constance has had the most extraordinary effect on him. Of course, he adores the English so perhaps it isn't so surprising after all. He's eating out of her hand. And protective! He's like a mother hen! The slightest word of criticism of the *donna inglese* and he's up in arms immediately. I'm frightened to even open my mouth!'

Monica smiled at the unlikeliness of this but allowed her friend to continue.

'He's pushing us all to do something for her and the wretched hats. And I mean pushing! He's ruthless. I've heard a rumour that he put some money in the business but I don't know if it's true. Her mother certainly did. Maria-Angelina most certainly did not!'

'Surprise, surprise!' Monica said, and they both laughed.

'They've opened a small factory up near the castle,' Bettina went on. 'Not in Trapena, of course. She wanted it in Castelfranco, can you imagine! Naturally, Ludo stopped that. His mother would have gone mad! So it's in Biaggibonsi, further down the valley. They employ a few girls from the village. She learnt to make the hats by watching Giulio before the tragedy and apparently picked it up very quickly.' She lowered her voice, 'That's what caused all the trouble. The villagers thought she was a witch.'

She told Monica the details. 'So you see,' she ended, 'it was murder. And she's the one responsible.'

'Poor darling,' said Monica, 'what a thing to have on her conscience.'

'Oh, I don't think she understands what she's done at all!' replied Bettina.

Bettina was wrong. Constance knew only too well the role she had played in the death of Giulio. She was also aware that there were dark secrets surrounding the idiot about which she was sure Ludovico knew nothing. The more time she spent at the castle the uneasier she felt about everything that concerned Maria-Angelina, Castelfranco and Trapena, and she was increasingly curious about the true background of her husband's family. Who was the mysterious Carlo whose photograph she had found? As she'd been snooping, she couldn't confront Ludo directly with her discovery, but she was convinced that his identity was important. Constance wished she had the courage to ask Maria-Angelina but in none of their trips to Castelfranco had she and Ludo once seen her. They might have been alone in the castle but for the brooding presence of the Principessa, which for Constance was almost tangible.

Although Ludovico came up to Castelfranco with her happily enough, he left the organisation of the girls in Biaggibonsi entirely to Constance. He loved her, so much that he was prepared to indulge her whim even though he couldn't understand it. His mother had always given him money; why should he refuse to take it now? There was no financial need for his wife to behave in this way. But he had enjoyed the days when Constance trimmed the hats in their tiny flat in Florence and he could see that it was fun for her. He was even reconciled to the hat shop, particularly as Savognia had ensured that the sign was so discreet that only clients would notice it, but he couldn't understand Constance's growing obsession with the little factory – actually, a large room in the cellars of the local *osteria* – where the hats were made.

Constance arrived to open up each morning promptly at eight and rarely left before six. The time flew by for her and, though the girls took a brief afternoon siesta, she always found something to do that prevented her from having a break. All the time she worked, she thought of two men: her father, whose admonition – *Nobody can stop you, Constance, except yourself* – was always in her head when she hit difficulties; and Giulio, whose gentle hands guiding hers had first taught her the excitement of creativity.

The girls found her puzzling. Aged between seventeen and nineteen, they were aware that, despite her authority, Constance was still a young woman, like themselves. For that reason, their respect for her was reluctant, though they gave her it wholeheartedly as the one who paid their wages. Constance was as conscious of her youth as they were and, like them, found herself turning to Milva as the natural authority. To give herself stature in their eyes, and to bolster her confidence, she made a point of always wearing make-up and a hat to work, just like the saleswomen and office staff at Maison de Levantière. She loved working with her team and was gratified to see that her choice had been sound. They picked up the various processes with amazing speed.

'You know,' she said to Ludovico one night, 'the attitude to women here in Italy is so wasteful. My girls are so quick and intelligent it's disgraceful that if I hadn't come along, they would have been wasted in the fields.'

'Hardly wasted, Constance. We need grain in order to survive. Somebody must produce the harvest.'

'Oh, I know all that! What I'm objecting to is the way men won't give women a chance. Look at Milva. If I'd listened to Giancarlo, I would have ended up with that fat and boring factor. As it is, Milva is worth all the men of this village put together.'

The relationship between the two women was guarded. Strong-willed and used to having their own way, they could easily have clashed over many little points but did not because of a mutual respect. Milva Pecoraro was twenty-six. One of a large family, she had learned to be in charge of her life at an early age. She loved the position of authority her new job had given her in the village and she was determined to help Constance in any way she could. She was as keen as her boss that the hat business

203

should flourish. As they began to understand each other's way of working, their respect grew into something like affection and they were sufficiently relaxed with each other to enjoy an occasional joke.

Constance found Milva formidable. There were days when a black mood descended on her that affected the whole factory. On those days all gossip and laughter would cease and the girls would work fearfully and quietly, afraid to speak in anything above a whisper. Try as she might, Constance could not break the tension and was forced to admit that her inexperience put her in the power of Milva's personality.

It was on such a day that Constance had the first and only challenge to her authority. One of the quickest and most skilled of the girls was Concetta, a gypsy-dark Sicilian whose parents had drifted north during the war. Her temperament was fiery and she frequently quarrelled with the other girls, who were jealous of her speed. On Savognia's advice, Constance had initiated a scheme whereby the girl who produced the highest number of hats each week was given a small bonus. Concetta had won it for three consecutive weeks and fully expected to do so again. The other girls were all working as hard as they could to overtake her.

Constance had been counting their totals and came out of the corner that passed as her office. Holding up her tally sheet, she cried, 'Concetta, this week you have a rival. Assunta has produced exactly the same number of hats as you. So, it all depends on today's total.'

Concetta said nothing. She gave Assunta a villainous look and continued working feverishly.

'This is your great chance, Assunta!' Constance said lightly as she passed by on her way to Milva at the end of the room.

To her surprise, Milva said urgently, 'We must speak, signora. Outside.' Her tone had an authority that was not to be questioned.

'Signora Constanza,' she said grimly the moment they were out of the door, 'you have done a very wrong thing.'

'Wrong thing? What on earth do you mean?'

'You must never play two southern girls off against each other, no matter how keen you are to keep production high.'

Constance was stung. 'It has nothing to do with production! I was just having fun and making some healthy rivalry.'

'Rivalry in Sicily is *never* healthy, signora. Surely you know that?'

'But Concetta and Assunta are friends! It was a joke!'

'The poor do not joke, signora. That bonus is desperately needed by their families. Do you know what happens to the girls who leave here without it every week? They are beaten by their brothers while their fathers look on and their mothers spit at them. That is how amusing your joke is.'

Their conversation was interrupted by a hideous scream from inside the factory. Before Constance had fully registered it, Milva had leapt for the door and left her, bemused, outside.

Recovering quickly, she followed Milva inside. She was striding towards the central workbench and for a second, her back blocked Constance's view. Then she saw. Concetta and Assunta were rolling on the floor, biting, scratching and pulling each other's hair while the other girls looked on. Milva stepped up to them and, with enormous force, pulled them apart by the hair. But she had separated them a split second too late. Assunta had managed to pull out a small knife with which she slashed wildly at Concetta. Missing her face by inches, she gashed her rival's arm. As the blood poured out, Concetta fainted.

Catching her before she fell, Milva gave Constance a look of contemptuous fury and said, 'Go back to your castle, signora. There has been enough mischief for one day. I will deal with this.'

Constance had never suffered such a total rejection. The

curtly authoritative dismissal had put her in her place. As she walked across the square, she realised how much she still had to learn before she was worthy of working with this peasant woman who was so much wiser in the ways of the world.

I'll show them all that I can learn, she thought. I'm not a poor little rich girl playing at factories. This is what I want to do and this is what I *will* do, and nobody is going to stop me! And I *can* learn. I'll learn from Milva. I *have* to! I won't let this business fail!

She knew she must apologise to Milva. Early the next morning, she called her outside, uncertain how to do so. In Italy, people like Milva were automatically denied such a civility because of their class.

After a moment's hesitation, she realised that a direct approach was best. 'Thank you for your quick action yesterday, Milva,' she said.

The woman's face relaxed slightly. So, maybe she wasn't going to be dismissed after all, despite her hasty words.

'I want to apologise,' Constance continued in a rush of words, 'for putting you in that position through my own thoughtlessness.'

'Signora, you do not apologise to me. You are the padrona. You do what you wish and Milva helps.'

'Oh, Milva, I'm so keen to make a success of it – and I need your strength to help me.'

'You need no strength from me. You have the fire – the fire in your eyes – and nothing will stop you. That, signora, is why I work for you.'

'So, you won't leave me?'

Milva smiled and, looking directly into Constance's eyes, said, 'Never.'

# CHAPTER 8

'When you were young did you have many friends up here?' Constance asked Ludovico on the night before they were due to return to Florence. She wanted to know more of the third boy in the photograph.

He gave her a guarded look. 'No,' he replied, 'why do you ask?'

'Oh, no reason,' she replied lightly, 'I just wondered what you did up here all the time?'

'Well,' Ludovico's voice relaxed. 'When I was very little I just played with the peasant boys in the village but when I moved into Florence Giancarlo was my friend. I came up here very rarely and when I did I spent most of my time riding.'

Constance pictured him, silhouetted against the lonely sky as he urged his pony on, and thought romantically of how Byronic he must have looked.

'Did you have many cousins?' she continued.

He laughed. 'Am I Italian? I had so many cousins that I would need ten hands to count them!'

'No,' she went on, 'I know that all Italian families are huge. I mean a special cousin, a friend – to compensate for having no brothers and sisters,' she added artlessly.

Ludovico frowned and seemed to be thinking deeply.

'No,' he replied, 'no one in particular. Giancarlo was my friend – and my brother. As he still is. There was nobody else.'

Constance did not have the courage to probe further.

'We've been invited to spend a weekend at Giancarlo's house on Capri,' Ludovico told Constance as she drove him back to Florence. 'You want to go, I assume? You'll love Capri.'

Ludovico and Constance took the train to Naples on Thursday afternoon. Giancarlo had asked them to arrive before the other guests so that he could catch up on their news including life at the castle and developments in the hat business, as well as giving himself the time to assess how this unlikely marriage was going. He wanted to be primed and knowledgeable when the rest of his guests arrived on Friday. It was raining in Naples as they boarded the family motorboat that Savognia sent to collect them. As they pulled away into the bay, Constance felt her spirits rise. The sea was ominously dark; the sky was a raw, rough grey and the rain was becoming heavier as they moved from the shore. It was the first time since she had arrived in Italy that the elements had produced anything approximating to what she considered to be northern weather. She loved it. Stormy as it was, the day wasn't cold and she stood next to Ludo as the little boat pushed its way across the water. She let the rain pour down her face, refreshing and invigorating her. Ludo suddenly removed his arm from her shoulder and pointed.

'Look,' he said, 'the island of Paradise. Even in the rain, it is beautiful, yes?'

Constance was entranced. Through the rain they could make out the tiny quayside, with the town nestling on the cliffs above. The tops of the houses were stranded in low-lying cloud and the whole scene was awash with a blue-grey light that removed all colour – except from the sea. As the boat entered the harbour, overhung by its high black cliffs, she noticed the deep green of the water, heaving and rolling as the rain spattered its surface. Its rich greenness reminded her, absurdly, of ginger beer bottles.

'There he is,' Ludovico cried and Constance saw the tall, elegant figure of Savognia standing still and patrician among the scurrying men working on the quayside. He wore a long, enveloping mackintosh and carried a very large umbrella. He not only looked as if he were from a different race from the men around him, he could have come from a different planet.

As she was handed out of the boat, which heaved alarmingly in the swell, Constance couldn't help saying to Giancarlo in reply to his greeting, 'What a beautiful coat.'

'Oh,' he laughed, 'it's a thousand years old. It was the motoring coat of some member of the family, long before the First World War. It came here to die, as most things in our family do, but somehow it has managed to hang on. It really is the most practical thing on the island.'

He took her arm and lifted the umbrella high. 'Except for this,' he said proudly. 'It came from the Vatican. Only Popes ever have umbrellas big enough to protect them from the wrath of God!'

Constance could tell that he was in the highest of spirits, despite the rain. As they toiled up to the town, she felt sure that this was to be a happy weekend.

The Villa Savognia would be passed unnoticed by the average visitor to Capri. Its door presented an anonymous face to the narrow street leading from the main square and it seemed perfectly at home with the shops of the grocer, ironmonger and butcher that jostled on either side of it. Once the door was closed on the noisy, bustling street, the visitor's privileged entry into the cultured and confident world of the Savognia family was immediately apparent. In the centre of the small marble hall stood a large silver font, ornately chased and embellished with cherubs moulded in the round. It was as magnificent in its workmanship as it was in its vulgarity, but what was more significant for any Italian visitor was that it placed the Savognias, precisely and obviously, in their southern Italian context, which was easily forgotten by those who saw them only in their Florentine manifestation. The font, garish as it was, was French and had been made for Joseph

Napoleon to mark the occasion when he was made King of Naples by the Emperor Bonaparte.

The font set the tone for the whole villa. Every room was floridly overdecorated, with far too much gilding, excessively elaborate curtaining and, as Giancarlo casually told Constance, as he led her from one room to another, 'a complete lack of taste quite breathtaking in its confidence. My mother,' he went on, 'hated every inch of this place but my father wouldn't let her lay a finger on it. As a result she hardly ever came here and the whole place has remained a monument to our family's early vulgarity. Actually I wouldn't change it for anything now. To me it is all tinsel and glitter, like a fairground or a circus and, in a way, I love it. If it were larger, it would make the perfect setting for a fashion show, don't you agree, Constanza, my dear?'

They were walking across the elaborately patterned parquet floor of the garden drawing room and she watched with amusement the antics of Giancarlo's two King Charles spaniels as they slid around on its highly polished surface. She couldn't entirely agree with Giancarlo. She found this sumptuous, jewel-like house rather satisfying in its richness and was amazed that such a building – almost a miniature palace, she thought – could be hidden behind such a very plain door in such a very ordinary street.

'It's probably our grandest house,' Giancarlo continued, as they looked out into the garden, ' – we keep it shut up for most of the year. I never come near Capri in the summer; it's far too hot, and I don't get down half as much in the winter as we did before the war, after my mother's death. My father died here, you know. He's buried in Naples, but his last years were spent here very happily with his first mistress.'

'You Italians!' Constance burst in with a laugh.

'No, really! It was very beautiful. She was older than him and years before – oh, I don't know, maybe sixty years earlier – she had first introduced him to love. Then,

210

when my mother died, they came together again, after years of not seeing each other, and she was with him to the end. It was lovely, don't you think?'

She smiled in agreement as they joined Ludovico in the drawing room. To Constance's surprise he was flicking through *Country Life*. 'My father used to have it sent out here and I've never cancelled the order,' Giancarlo explained. As the three of them took tea, served by an old man in black, wearing startlingly white gloves, Constance thought how amazing this Savognia was. He was every bit as unexpected and bizarre as the surroundings she now saw him in. As he and Ludo argued animatedly about nothing, as Constance had already discovered all Italians could do for hours, she watched them fondly. Sprawled across the huge and overstuffed sofa, they reminded her of Landseer's 'Dignity and Impudence', the picture that was on the lid of the biscuit tin in her mother's kitchen in Cramer. Ludovico was perky and lively in his old corduroys (bought in London just before the war), and a pair of rather battered shoes. Giancarlo's long legs, beautifully encased in well-pressed flannel, stretched out in front of him and ended in a perfectly polished pair of brogues which, she knew, must have been handmade for him by one of his Florentine craftsmen. She had a great affection for them both and felt honoured to be welcomed into this privileged circle.

At dinner that night, in the intimacy of the small family dining room, Constance allowed herself to be provoked into her first public quarrel with Ludovico. It was about nothing and everything. The two men had become increasingly animated in their discussion of the merits of Fiat and Ford cars. She was not in the least interested in their endlessly reiterated opinions which in her view had gone round in circles for far too long. In exasperation, she attempted to stop the argument by saying sharply to Ludovico, 'Well, Giancarlo should know. At least he *has* a car, which is more than you do.'

Both men were shocked. They had been so engrossed that they had almost forgotten she was there.

'*Giusto. Brava!*' Giancarlo said triumphantly. Ludovico looked at her in horror. His eyes showed his feeling of betrayal.

'*And* he's been to America,' Constance plunged on, desperately trying to dispel the silence and change the expression in Ludovico's eyes.

'*Ecco*,' said Giancarlo, decisively. 'Now tell me, Constanza, who is likely to know more about cars – the Ford company, with all their money, or Fiat, who are tiny by comparison and sell only in Italy? I ask you!'

Giancarlo's strong loyalty to everything American or British and his contempt for what he felt were the tinpot attitudes of his own country, which he had never forgiven for falling for the idiotic fallacies of Mussolini, were well known to Constance but she thought his views, in this case, were correct. Unlike an Italian wife in such a situation, she remained true to her intelligence and said, reasonably, 'He's right, Ludo. Don't be silly.'

Ludovico was furious. Throwing down his napkin, he rounded on her.

'How dare you say that to me?' he shouted. 'How dare you speak to your husband like that?'

Constance went hot as he continued shouting, 'What do you know about it? What do you know about anything? You are just an ignorant Englishwoman!'

All the tension and frustration that had been building up since Constance had begun her hat business broke out in his voice. She was dismayed and embarrassed by his outburst in front of Savognia, but she wouldn't kowtow to him.

'I know just as much as you,' she replied. 'At least we could afford a car, which is more than you can say.'

She had hit at one of Ludovico's most deep-seated insecurities – the fact that because he had no income of his own and was reliant on his mother for everything, he had few of the possessions his contemporaries took for granted. He was still young enough to find most galling the fact that he had no car.

The argument would have continued if Giancarlo, who was startled by Ludovico's vehemence, had not said, '*Basta*. It is not important. We can't afford Ford cars here anyhow. Come, let us take coffee in the *salotto* and then go to bed.'

Despite his friend's efforts to get the atmosphere back to normal, Ludovico was still seething with rage when they said goodnight. The row continued, as Giancarlo had known it would, almost as soon as the bedroom door was closed. To Constance's astonishment and anger, Ludovico began by attacking her relationship with Giancarlo.

'You seem to have forgotten whose wife you are,' he said angrily. 'Even if he does have more money than I do, it is to me you are married.'

'What on earth do you mean?'

'Do you think I haven't noticed the looks you give each other or the way you go off together whenever you can?'

Constance thought what he was saying so preposterous that she laughed. 'Ludo, are you crazy?' she asked.

He suddenly moved over to her and, gripping her arm, almost growled, 'You are mine, not his. And you should remember that.'

As she wrenched from his grasp, Constance surprised herself by replying fiercely, 'No, Ludovico, you are wrong. I am mine; not yours, not his, not anybody's.'

She suddenly saw what Ludovico's anger was all about. It had nothing to do with Giancarlo – it had to do with her, and her independence. More, it had to do with her upbringing. She had not been trained to be a wife in the Italian mode, she thought viciously, ready to creep around apologising for her very existence and frightened to cross her husband in anything.

'You are my husband, Ludo,' she said quietly, 'not my lord and master. We are equal partners. There is no other basis for a marriage.'

Constance realised how carefully she would have to

tread to help Ludovico overcome his vulnerability and uncertainties. How could she show him that she would never look at another man, that she was interested in no one but him and that she loved him so deeply that she would do anything for him – except submerge her personality? That, she was incapable of doing. She was too strong to be humiliated in that way, even had she wished it. Constance understood sexual jealousy, as all women do, no matter how inexperienced and youthful. What she didn't know – and didn't even consider – was how threatened Ludovico felt by her plans for the hat business; a business in which he knew he had no part and could play no role; a business which he thought might endanger their marriage. He could fight another man, but he could not compete with his wife's increasing ambition to be successful in a field that he found alien and unimportant. He had a terrible dream that night: he was trying to put his arms round Constance but she backed away, laughing, as a huge straw hat, the brim of which turned to knives, swung between them and cut off his outstretched arms, leaving him with bloody stumps as she faded from his view.

'How close are Giancarlo and Gioella?' Constance asked Ludovico the next morning over breakfast in their bedroom. The atmosphere between them was still tense and she knew that she must talk it away before the other guests arrived.

'I don't know,' he replied sharply. 'Ask Giancarlo.'

'Is she coming this weekend?'

'No.'

'How do you know?'

'Giancarlo told me, of course. He told me everybody who is coming.'

'I'm very surprised,' she persisted. 'I thought she went everywhere. She can't *still* be taking the cure, surely?'

'Why ask me? How do I know what she's doing? Why

214

are you so obsessed with Gioella and her comings and goings?'

'I'm not obsessed. It just seems that she is never seen anywhere.'

'Why should she be?'

'Well, it was you who told me she went to everything.'

'Things change,' he said as he walked into the bathroom for his shower.

The other guests began arriving soon after breakfast and the stream kept up all day. Constance noticed that only Bettina and Monica were as privileged as she and Ludo had been, to be collected in Savognia's smart little speedboat, with its richly polished mahogany and sparkling brass.

Bettina lost no time in introducing Constance to Monica.

'I hear you are going to be Italy's greatest milliner,' Monica laughed, not unkindly. 'And what does Ludo feel about it?'

'I think he's in shock, poor darling,' Bettina chipped in before Constance had a chance to reply.

'*Au contraire*,' Savognia said, 'you're very proud, aren't you, Ludovico?'

Ludovico knew that this was his chance to undo the damage of the previous night's quarrel.

'I am the luckiest man in the world,' he said, raising his voice slightly so that he could be heard by everybody in the room. 'I am married to the most beautiful woman and now I discover that she is talented as well. What do you think I feel?'

Walking over to Constance, he put his arms around her and kissed her on the brow. Everybody clapped as her eyes misted with tears of happiness.

The rest of Savognia's guests crossed from the mainland on the public ferry. As they appeared throughout the day Constance began to understand the appeal that exclusive clubs must have for men. Everybody knew everybody and even she recognised virtually all the newcomers as having

215

been at Giancarlo's launch party for the hat shop. In its cosy familiarity it was just like being in a large family, or attending a school reunion.

The last arrivals included Pino and his mother, the Contessa. Pino greeted Constance with a gratifying enthusiasm.

'*Ciao*, Constanza,' he cried, leaping across the dogs in order to be kissed. 'How are you? It has been so long and I have so much to talk about' – and he proceeded to do so with a great deal of giggling and whispering until Constance felt drained.

'*Basta Pino*,' his mother said good-naturedly. 'Signora, you must not allow him to exhaust you with his boring rubbish.'

But Constance had not been bored. As she went up to run her bath she thought of something Pino had said. It was not the words that had upset her, but the tone he had adopted. Half conspiratorially, he had asked if she had heard of the quarrel between Savognia and Gioella di Grignano.

'They were very angry,' he whispered, 'he told her that she would come to no more of his parties – because of her behaviour.'

'What behaviour?' Constance asked.

'Oh,' he said slyly, looking over at his mother, 'I don't know.'

Constance knew that he did know and, although she realised it would be a mistake, she was prepared to put herself in his power by asking more.

'When did they have their row?' she asked.

Pino looked genuinely surprised at the question. 'Why, after his luncheon in Fiesole, when we all met you, of course.'

'What was wrong with her behaviour?' Constance asked. She was mystified.

Pino looked uncomfortable. 'I don't know,' he lied, as he looked round for an escape.

Constance plucked up courage and asked the direct question. 'Was it about me?'

'I must go and unpack.'

She laid her hand on his knee to restrain him. 'Pino,' she repeated, 'was it about me?'

'*Si*,' he said quietly, without looking at her.


'Why did Giancarlo quarrel with Gioella?' she asked Ludovico when they were alone in their room. He looked at her with hostile eyes.

'Not Gioella again! I really cannot stand this, Constanza. What has happened to make you so obsessed with this woman?'

She ignored his question and repeated hers.

'Have you been talking to Bettina?' he asked.

'No, I have not,' she replied indignantly.

'Then who is filling your head with all this nonsense?'

It suddenly dawned on him. 'Don't tell me you've been listening to that vicious little queen Pino?'

She was silent.

'I cannot believe it! That a wife of mine should waste her time with somebody like that!'

'You can say what you like but they *have* quarrelled, haven't they? That's why she isn't here this weekend – for the first time ever, Pino says.'

'Pino knows nothing,' Ludovico retorted. 'Gioella is in South Africa with her husband. There is no mystery. Now, put her out of your mind and get dressed or we shall be late for dinner.'


Bettina and Monica went to the bar in the square next morning. 'I'm so glad to be out of there,' Bettina said as they ordered their cappuccino, 'it's like a morgue without Gioella to keep us lively. How do you think Constance is looking?'

'I think she's OK,' Monica replied, 'but beneath that cutesie exterior there is one tough lady.'

'And very single-minded,' continued Bettina. 'I cannot

217

,imagine how long Ludo will put up with her – once the novelty of his oh-so-English bride has worn off. He and Giancarlo are besotted with her, it seems to me. I can't get over how she's captivated Savognia. Did you see the fuss he was making of her last night? Talk about visiting royalty! I thought I detected a slight rush of passion after the pudding but I was probably wrong. That glazed look about the eyes often comes from indigestion, I believe. Anyhow, there's no question about it: he's putty in her hands. He'd quarrel with anybody over her – as we know,' she ended darkly.

Monica was barely listening and, fortified by her cappuccino, she was in any case inclined to be generous.

'Look, it's only decent that in the changed circumstances some people should back off and I don't think they should hang around to be pushed. Anyhow, I've told Constance that I'll look at her hats when I pass through Florence. They must have something because one thing about Savognia, he does have taste. I don't know why, but I'd like to see her succeed.'

'Oh! So would I,' Bettina quickly agreed, 'if only to shake up the men a little – although I don't know whether Ludo's ready for it.'

'Oh, come, darling,' her friend replied, 'Ludo's a playboy. He'll never be ready for it.'

'She's too serious for him,' Bettina said, 'she's got real ambition. He doesn't know the meaning of the word. It won't take him long to start to slide back to his old ways. Matter of fact,' she looked quickly round the bar, 'I don't think he's looking so happy this weekend. You sat next to him at dinner last night. What did you think?'

'Oh, we talked about *her* most of the night and he seems pretty much taken up with her to me.'

'Well, we'll see. We've not seen the end of Gioella yet, of that I *am* certain.'

There was a pause. Monica was not in the mood for Bettina's gossip. 'I guess we'd better mosey back to the ranch,' she drawled, 'I feel better for that coffee and some fresh air.'

As the two women passed under the windows of the Villa Savognia they heard angry voices, which they both recognised immediately. With a single significant look they stood silently below Savognia's study window and shamelessly eavesdropped. Savognia was speaking.

'How dare you burst in here when I've told you that I didn't want to see you on Capri this weekend? You didn't even telephone first.'

'Telephone?' a woman's voice interrupted. 'Do you think you own this damned island? I can come and go here exactly as I wish and I don't have to ask *your* permission before doing so.'

'You are so selfish,' Savognia replied, 'you think you can do exactly as you please. What gives you the right to embarrass me and my guests in this way?'

'So – ' The woman's voice was deep with emotion. 'I am an embarrassment now, after all these years?'

'Gioella – ' his voice was pleading – 'I don't wish to quarrel with you, my dear, but he is married now. You must behave with some discretion. She is English. If she discovered your relationship with Ludo, it would be the end. All you need to do is wait until things have settled down and she becomes involved with her business. Then he'll have all the time in the world for you. That little enterprise won't hold his interest, as you well know. With her, it will become an obsession. So, the problem will be solved. But you must give it time. Please listen to me. Don't think that I'm trying to split you and Ludo up but I insist on discretion. And that means that you cannot appear at lunch. You must have been mad to come over without speaking to me first.'

His voice softened. 'Gioella, we have been friends too long to quarrel now. Go back to Naples. I'll arrange for the boat to take you. Please don't make me angry.'

'I have come to see him and I won't go until I have,' Gioella replied.

'Don't make me order you out of my home, Gioella,' Savognia pleaded.

'I only wish to talk to him,' she insisted.

'He's here with his wife, for God's sake! What can I do to make you understand?'

'You don't have to do anything. I understand only too well. Now, what you *had* better do – and pretty damned quickly – is find a way for me to speak to him alone. Then I'll leave and no one will be embarrassed. Least of all your precious little white mouse.'

The listening women knew that it was time. They rang the bell aggressively and, when they were admitted, swept past the font and into the *salotto* with maximum force and noisy exuberance to join the other guests. Within a few minutes Giancarlo appeared, looking slightly pink but quite composed.

'Now,' he cried enthusiastically, 'I'm sure you're all more than ready for lunch.'

After lunch, the sun came out and Giancarlo announced that they would take an impromptu trip to Anacapri to Axel Munthe's villa, to see the view of the Bay of Naples from the spectacularly positioned garden. His guests were enthusiastic and he telephoned to make arrangements.

'I won't come myself,' he said, 'I've seen the view a thousand times and Monica knows the garden well so there is no problem.'

He turned a deaf ear to the cries of protest. 'No,' he said adamantly, 'you all go off and have fun. I have things to organise here.'

Constance was disconcerted when Ludovico turned to her and said, 'Do you mind if I don't come either, darling? I've been there so many times before and I think it would be good for me to stay and keep Giancarlo company. Bettina and Monica will look after you.'

She wanted to be selfish and insist on his coming, but

feeling that he wanted to be alone with Giancarlo to smooth away the slight coldness that she detected still existed between them, she reluctantly agreed to go without him.

As she and Bettina walked along the narrow paths of Munthe's garden and leant over the balustrade to admire the view of Vesuvius across the bay, Constance felt sufficiently relaxed to tell her why she felt Ludovico had stayed behind. Bettina was intrigued and began to question her closely about the argument between the two men.

'Of course,' she said, when Constance had told her everything, 'Giancarlo is a funny sort of man. Always has been.' She gave Constance a sidelong look. 'But I don't suppose he's allowed you to see that side of him yet. He can be very difficult. Lots of people think he's manipulative of his friends. I don't see enough of him to know,' she went on hastily, 'but there's no doubt that he's had an enormous influence on Ludo ever since they were boys. He's probably frustrated now that you've come along and Ludo listens to you instead.'

'Oh, I don't think he does,' Constance laughed ingenuously, 'Ludo makes up his own mind on most things.'

Bettina was stunned. Could this intelligent woman really be so blind to her husband's weakness or was she playing games with her?

'Well, my dear,' she replied, her eyes half closing in her puffy face, 'he certainly must have changed, if that's the case. He used to follow Giancarlo round everywhere like a little lamb, doing everything he was told. We all adore Ludo – ' she made a sound that was half laugh, half snort – 'but nobody would try to pretend that he was strong-willed. After all, darling, look at the way he lets his mother go on – treating him like a simpleton, giving him no money, keeping him away from the estate. It's pathetic really,' she ended venomously, 'I'd love to think that you had given him a little backbone but I have to say that I find it unlikely. His life before you came along

221

was hardly the history of a strong man, as anybody can confirm.'

Constance burned with indignation. How dare you be so spiteful about my husband! she thought angrily. She wanted to hurt Bettina but was frightened of annoying her.

'Ludovico is a very good husband,' she replied lamely.

'Ludo is *marvellous* with women, darling,' Bettina said, looking hard at her. 'That's his one skill. He's renowned for it.' Her voice dropped patronisingly. 'I'm sure he'll have no difficulty in keeping you happy. You're lucky. There are lots of women in Italy who would be thrilled to be in your shoes. Despite his faults, none of them would accuse him of inadequacy in *that* area, I can assure you.'

The innuendo was not lost on Constance. I'm not listening any more to this vulgar woman, she thought, and turning away from the view she said, 'I think we should catch up with the others, don't you?'

She tried to sound distant and grand. For a split second she felt like Miss Hatherby issuing one of her chilly rebukes.

Bettina was angry. This young Englishwoman had goaded her into being unpleasant, even indiscreet, and yet the icy superiority of her Englishness had given her the last word.

Back in the town, fate came to Bettina's rescue and gave her back the upper hand. As the group of guests passed through the square, she suddenly said loudly, 'Monica, isn't that Ludo over there?'

Constance had just time to recognise Ludo's back as he turned down a side street. She felt a frisson of fear. In that brief instant she saw that he was not alone, and that his companion was not Giancarlo.

# CHAPTER 9

'What is wrong?' Ludovico asked Constance two days after they had returned to Florence. The atmosphere between them was so tense that he could bear it no longer.

'With what?' she answered coldly.

He ignored her and went on, 'Are you still angry about that foolish quarrel at Giancarlo's? I've said that I'm sorry. What more do you want?'

Constance felt deeply uncomfortable. She knew that fate had put them into a strange reversal of roles. She hadn't sulked since the days in Northumberland, after the numerous quarrels with her mother, and now she was doing so with Ludovico of all people, who Giancarlo had once told her was notorious for it. She knew that it was a ridiculous situation but could see no dignified way of getting out of it.

'Why didn't you tell me about your affairs?' she countered.

'What affairs?' he asked, playing for time and wondering how much Constance knew. She told him about her conversation with Bettina. Ludovico laughed.

'Did you expect me to be a virgin?' he asked. 'Are Englishmen still virgins when they get married? I don't really think so.' His relief at the vagueness of the question made him feel almost relaxed. 'Do you think it would have been as good for you if I had been?' he murmured intimately as he slyly slipped his arm round her shoulder and nuzzled the nape of her neck.

She softened at his touch but was determined not to be sidetracked.

'Of course I expected you to have some experience but it was the way Bettina said it . . . as if you were notorious for having affairs. I don't know . . . it made me feel so cheap . . . I don't know why,' she finished lamely.

They were strolling listlessly in the Boboli Gardens. Thinking back to the first day when Ludovico had brought her here, Constance was overcome with sadness at how quickly the carefree joy of their love seemed to have clouded over.

'Let's stop for a moment.' Ludovico motioned towards a stone bench between two classical statues on heavy, weather-worn plinths. She sat down heavily. They were silent. They were strangers to each other – and, for the first time since they had met, foreigners.

Constance stared at the mirror-image of the seats and statues on the other side of the gravel walk. Trying to keep her voice level she plucked up courage to ask the question that she knew she must.

'Did you see Gioella on Capri?'

His reply was instant and aggressive. 'Yes. Why?'

'Why didn't you tell me?'

He was silent.

'Didn't you want me to know?' she said wretchedly. 'Didn't you think I ought to know?'

Ludovico stood up and began pacing up and down the gravel path in front of her, swinging his arms in agitation.

'Listen, Constanza,' he said, 'Gioella is an old friend – a very old friend – we have known each other for years . . .'

'Gioella is a married woman,' Constance interrupted, 'and you are a married man!'

'Does marriage destroy friendship in England?' he countered angrily. 'Because it certainly doesn't here! Am I to become a recluse because I am married to an English-woman? Why don't you put me in a cage and lock me up? Constanza, you are being ridiculous!'

She bit her lip in anger. He had put her in the wrong and made her seem petulant and unreasonable and yet she knew there was more to his relationship with Gioella than he was prepared to admit. She wanted to cry but she was still her mother's daughter. Instead, she looked directly at him and asked, 'If seeing her was so open and above board why keep it a secret?'

'It was not a secret.'

'Then I'd like to know what it was. Nobody even told me she was on the island. Pino was right. Giancarlo and she don't speak to each other any more, do they?'

Ludovico turned angrily away. 'You know why, don't you? Because of you. A friendship of years – since childhood – and you destroyed it at your first meeting with the woman.'

'What did I do?' Constance pleaded. 'For God's sake, why won't anyone tell me what I did? I cannot stand this!'

'Don't play the little miss innocent with me, Constanza. You have so bewitched Savognia that he sees insults and slights everywhere. Your behaviour is a disgrace.'

Constance was shocked. 'My behaviour? I've done nothing wrong. What are you suggesting – that I've flirted with Giancarlo? How can you be so stupid – or are you accusing me in order to cover your own guilt? Was she your mistress?'

Ludovico was given courage by the tense. He looked quickly to each side of him, and said defiantly, 'Yes, but only for a time.'

'After she was married?'

There was a silence. Constance watched two little boys chasing each other round the plinth opposite, each of them twisting and turning in an effort not to be caught.

Ludovico finally spoke. 'Yes.'

Constance suddenly felt exhausted. She wished to hear no more. 'Take me home,' she said quietly.

They walked back to Via Santo Spirito in silence. At the door, he said brusquely, 'I have to see Giancarlo. I won't be long,' and left her to let herself in. She heard his heavy footsteps crossing the courtyard below and was overcome with misery. Then she raised her head defiantly. How dare he have secret meetings with another woman? He was hers and she would not share him with anyone.

It was dark when the telephone rang and Constance was nearly asleep. It startled her out of the reverie that had kept her unaware of the passing of time or the fading of the day. She propped herself up. Should she pick up the phone or let it ring? She picked it up.

'Hello,' she said flatly.

'Constanza, my dear.'

It was Giancarlo. She sat upright and unconsciously began to smooth her hair as he went on, 'Are you free to have supper with me tonight? I thought it would be a good thing for us to get together – just the two of us, for a *tête-à-tête*.'

'Where is my husband?'

'I was just going to tell you. He has borrowed the car because he had to go up to the castle. Money, you know. He'll be back in Florence tomorrow.'

Warming to his theme and gaining courage from her silence, he went on, 'So, Constanza my dear, I thought it was a marvellous opportunity for a quiet evening's chat. Of course, Ludovico asked me to make sure that you were all right . . .'

Constance was stunned. All she could think of was: He's left me.

'. . . if you're too tired, but I think it too good a chance to miss,' Giancarlo was saying, in his most persuasive tones, 'we have so much gossip to exchange.'

The very thought of gossip sickened Constance but she wearily agreed to meet him for dinner at Sabatini in Via de' Panzani, because it was nearby and she was so tired that to give reasons why they shouldn't see each other seemed more daunting than doing so.

'He hasn't run away, my dear. What a preposterous idea!

226

He needed money and you know that he never gets any unless he goes up there in person. Be reasonable.'

'Reasonable? You cannot be serious! My husband leaves me saying he won't be long and then his friend rings and says he's left Florence – without a goodbye or even a word – and you tell me to be *reasonable*! Are you suggesting that this is normal behaviour in Italian marriages?'

'He was upset, I admit, but that was by the way. I think he felt it would be easier for you both if you had – how can we say – a breathing space. It's only twenty-four hours, after all, Constanza.'

He took a slow sip of wine and looked at her plate. She was eating remarkably healthily, he thought cynically, for a woman distraught at her husband's disappearance. Constance intercepted the look and blushed. She felt ravenous, as she always did these days. She put down her fork.

'You have no reason for jealousy, Constanza,' Giancarlo resumed. 'Look, I'm not here to plead for Ludovico. He doesn't need that. You know how much he loves you. You must trust him and believe in him.'

He lit a cigarette and looked beyond her shoulder at the waiters standing at the back of the restaurant.

'But you must know that you are not married to a saint. Ludovico is a man. At his age you expect some indiscretions in his past – some skeletons at the back of his cupboard. It is his past that makes his present. You are an intelligent woman. You do not think that Englishmen have lovers in their past? Of course they do. The only difference is that they are more secretive.'

'And Gioella?'

Giancarlo's eyes moved slowly back to her face. He looked at her directly. He knew what he had to say – precisely what he and Ludovico had agreed. 'Of course,' he said, 'but it meant nothing. He was very young when it started. Her husband is a very boring man. His only interest is money. Gioella needed some excitement in her life. It is not so unusual, Constanza, my dear, not even in your country. Underneath those immaculate Savile Row suits there surely beats a little passion. Here in Italy, it is normal and even right for a man to have a mistress – especially a young man like Ludo. It is almost an extension of friendship. Oh, how can I make you understand?'

His fingers drummed lightly on the edge of the table. 'It is a relationship about passion, not love. That is why, even if it were still happening – which I can assure you absolutely categorically it is not – you would have nothing to be jealous of. And, certainly, to be jealous of past affairs is ridiculous. You must understand, Constanza, that here in Italy what happens in the marriage bed is sacred and what takes place in other beds is utterly unimportant and not even to be considered. It is merely a little indulgence of the flesh. In other countries men take to gluttony or drunkenness but Italian men take to the bed.'

'Why are they still seeing each other?' she asked sharply, continuing quickly, before he had time to speak, 'and please don't pretend that they aren't, Giancarlo, because I know that they are – and did, on Capri. When you had safely sent us all to Anacapri.'

He was caught off guard. 'How?' he asked.

She ignored his question. 'Did you invite her to Capri so that they could meet behind my back?'

Giancarlo was stung. 'Of course I didn't. What do you think I am – a conspirator? Nobody invited Gioella. She just appeared – without any warning to me, Ludovico or anyone. And that is the truth.'

She knew it from his tone.

'Ludovico saw her merely to tell her that it was over. Nothing else. She was with him for less than ten minutes. Nothing happened that could make you jealous. They had a cappuccino in the square and talked, and that was all. Then that *idiota*, Monica, brought you all through the town. Gioella fled. That was all there was to it.'

'Do you think it is easy for me?' Ludovico asked as he stretched out to touch her naked body.

She rolled away from his grasp and buried her head in the pillow.

'Gioella! Please! You must listen to me. We don't have much time. Giancarlo will return soon. You know that I love you. How many times do I have to prove it? But I'm married now – and so are you. We must be discreet.'

He could hardly believe that he was talking in this way. While his best friend was deliberately keeping his wife occupied in the restaurant, he had made love repeatedly to the mistress he had sworn never to see again. He felt weak-willed and cheap and yet, as he looked at Gioella's beautiful back, he knew that he could swear as much as he liked but he would always break his oath.

When he had arrived at Giancarlo's palazzo after quarelling with Constance, his friend had told him that Gioella was calling in on her way to Milan. Ludovico could not credit the irony of it. His first reaction was to leave immediately, but Giancarlo had persuaded him that fate had played Gioella into his hands. Now was the perfect opportunity to tell her, conclusively, that the affair was ended. Buoyed up by Giancarlo's resolution, Ludovico had agreed to stay and talk to his mistress, though he was secretly unconvinced that it would bring the desired result.

Gioella was ushered into Savognia's study by his major domo. Ludovico sat in a corner. For a split second, the evening sun slanting through the wooden blinds laid bars of light across his body and she thought how appropriately like a prisoner he looked. She showed no flicker of surprise as she kissed Giancarlo, but merely smiled and said *'Ciao'* to Ludovico before sitting down on the huge tapestry-covered sofa. Both men were impressed by her aplomb although Giancarlo noted how she instantly began to search in her handbag for her cigarettes.

Ludovico was aware only of her beauty. As she pulled back her head and dragged heavily on the cigarette, the light caught the colour of her apricot silk suit and reflected it on to her face. It gave her lips an intensity which he found both exciting and alarming. Giancarlo noticed how even Gioella's elegant couture clothes could not disguise the sheer animal vitality of her body, as she took off her hat and shook out her black hair with an urgent gesture of her hand, while holding the cigarette between her lips.

Gioella was nervous but even in the seconds that it had taken her to light the cigarette she knew that she was in command. The space between her and the two men was hers alone. Although she was amazed to see Ludovico – was his presence another example of Giancarlo's duplicity? – she was pleased because she knew that he would be forced to listen. She would talk and they would not interrupt. She glanced from one to another, and thought how like erring schoolboys they looked.

'Well, Ludo, this *is* a surprise,' she said, with a tight smile, as she flicked her cigarette with an impatient thumb. 'So, your English mouse *does* allow you out alone occasionally. Or is she also here?' She turned quickly to Giancarlo. 'Hiding behind the sofa or running along the skirting board? No? What a pity! I feel she could have learned a thing or two.' She dragged heavily on her cigarette. 'Oh, for God's sake, the pair of you, stop looking so crestfallen. I'm the one who's been ambushed, not you.'

She turned to Savognia. 'Why didn't you tell me that Ludo would be here? Did you think it needed the strength of two men to put me in my place? Don't tell me that you're losing your powers, Giancarlo. Can't you organise people on your own these days? What do you think you're both going to achieve? You expect me to be dropped – discarded – used and then forgotten – tossed aside like some common whore on the banks of the Arno merely because Ludovico Castelfranco di Villanuova has married an Englishwoman? Well, I'm sorry, *ragazzi*,' she almost snarled, 'but it doesn't happen that way. We're far too well known – and so is our affair – for us to take that line. We are not the sort of people to have no past, no history, and as for your preposterous idea of excluding me from society, Savognia, it shows just how out of touch with reality you have become. What gives you the right to interfere in my affairs? This business is nothing to do with you and unless you have anything to say that is more constructive than your previous comments, I would prefer you to leave. It is our problem, not yours.'

She looked across at Giancarlo whose face was suffused with anger. Flicking her ash on to the floor with a contemptuous gesture, she paused. Neither man spoke. Ludovico gazed admiringly at her. She was as magnificently sexual as a tigress, and he longed to have her again. Giancarlo's lip curled. How dare this insufferable woman dismiss him from his own *salotto*, like some servant?

Gioella continued to look at him, defying him to remain. She was enjoying his discomfort. Still nobody spoke. Giancarlo rose and, with the greatest dignity, walked silently from the room. The tension left with him. As the door closed, Ludovico stood up and reaching Gioella in one swift stride, took her in his arms and covered her face with urgent kisses. She made no resistance.

'Discreet?' Gioella ran her hand down her stomach, still wet with the sweat of their passion, and smiled sardonically. 'Oh, Ludo, *caro mio*,' she murmured, 'don't you understand? Discretion has nothing to do with it. Of *course* we can be discreet – though I won't be bullied into allowing Giancarlo to decide where and when I'm permitted to be seen. No, my darling, what you must understand is our need for each other. You think it would be nice if your pale Englishwoman could reform you and make you good so that your eye never wanders and your feet never stray.' She chuckled. 'You will never be good. You will always need me – just as I will always want you.'

She ran her fingers gently up his tumescent penis. 'Do you think I can live without him?' she whispered huskily. 'Do you think he can live without me? Little miss mouse's white thighs will never satisfy this boy. And you know it.'

Ludovico tried to push her head down on him but she jerked away and sat up.

'Oh God!' she cried. 'How could you be so damned stupid? You've spoiled everything! Why did you have to marry her? Couldn't you see the effects it would have?'

'I love her.'

'No you don't!' She shook him by the shoulders. 'No you don't! You love me and only me! I will not let you give up our happiness for her.'

A door slammed downstairs. With a guilty start, Ludovico leapt from the bed and began to dress.

'Giancarlo mustn't find us in his bed,' he said as he struggled into his clothes, 'he will go mad. Quickly, you must get up!'

Gioella laughed mockingly. 'Do you think I'm going to put my clothes on when I'm in this state?' she asked. 'You must be crazy. I need a shower,' and, sliding deftly from the bed, she ran into Giancarlo's bathroom and closed the door behind her.

Pulling up his trousers, Ludovico rushed for the door. Just before he reached it he heard the lock turn. He hissed through the keyhole, 'Gioella! Come out this minute! Giancarlo mustn't find you here! Open the door! Open it at once! You cannot do this to me.'

His voice rose urgently. 'Gioella! Please!' He heard her laugh from behind the door. 'You whore!' he cried. 'I'll never forgive you for this.'

He heard the splash of water and then, to his horror and disbelief, Gioella began singing at the top of her voice. 'Love and marriage, Love and marriage; Go together like a horse and carriage; this, I tell you, brother: you can't have one without the other.'

With a slight groan, he turned and leaned against the door. What could he say to Giancarlo?

Minutes later, Ludovico crossed the darkened hall towards the light that shone from the open door of the study. Stepping inside, he found Giancarlo sitting at his desk, his fingers drumming on his cigarette case. He looked up and smiled as his friend walked in.

'So,' he said, 'we are rid of that vulgar shrew. I hope you have left her in no doubt about the situation.'

He stopped as he became aware of the expression on Ludovico's face. 'You *have* sent her packing, no?'

In answer, Ludovico beckoned him into the hall. The strong tones of Gioella's singing drifted down the stairs.

'Get her out of this house. Now,' Giancarlo said, 'and make it clear that she will never return.'

Constance heard the clock of Chiesa Santo Spirito as she surfaced from her uneasy sleep. It struck three. She thought the night would never end. She had tossed and turned, unable to sleep in the vast empty bed that seemed so unfamiliar without Ludovico. All night her imagination had raced. Had Giancarlo lied about Ludo? Would he return? Was he spending the night with Gioella? Above all, as the hours crawled by she reproached herself. Why had she allowed her resentment of his secretive behaviour on Capri to build up and prevent her from telling Ludo that she was pregnant? Although she hadn't yet seen a doctor, she knew with absolute certainty that it was so. But she felt no joy. What sort of a father would a philandering husband be? Lying in the smothering silence she was conscious of how she had taken for granted the comforting little sounds and movements of Ludovico as he lay asleep by her side. She missed them.

'Oh, please God,' she murmured, as the square of the window began to lighten with the first hint of dawn, 'please let him come back. Please don't let Giancarlo have been lying to me. I forgive him. I'm being ridiculous with all my suspicions. Of course it's all over with Gioella.'

The next time Constance woke it was broad daylight. She looked at her watch. Eleven o'clock. She felt ghastly but she forced herself to get up and look at her face in the mirror. 'Oh, God,' she groaned. Her skin was blotchy, there were shadows under her eyes and her hair was lank and greasy. He mustn't see me like this, she thought, or he'll run a mile and never come back again.

Ludovico did not return to the apartment until the afternoon. Letting himself in apprehensively, he found Constance sitting in the kitchen. She looked up and asked, with what she hoped was heavy sarcasm, 'Was your mother well?'

'I didn't go,' he answered simply, 'I stayed with Giancarlo. I needed time to think.'

Constance had a ludicrous but overwhelming feeling that the whole of Italy was plotting against her. Pushing back her chair, she walked to the window and looked out across the terrace, to the rooftops glowing in the afternoon sun.

'And . . . ?'

'This foolishness must cease,' Ludovico said, following the lines he and Giancarlo had rehearsed over lunch. 'You know that I love you. You are my wife and there is no one else who means anything to me. You are the only one. Please believe me, Constanza. I am sorry that my past makes you unhappy but I ask you to remember that it is truly that – my past. Now there is only you.'

Constance turned towards him. 'And Gioella?' she asked.

There was the minutest pause before Ludovico said, 'She is finished. All that is over.'

'So you won't see her again?'

'Absolutely categorically not,' Ludovico said, moving towards her.

Constance stiffened. The expression was one of Giancarlo's favourites – he had used it just last night at dinner. Whose words was Ludovico using? She pushed his hand away as he made to touch her.

'Do you expect me to believe that?' she asked sharply.

Ludovico was unnerved. 'Is there any reason why you shouldn't?' he countered.

'Only you can answer that,' she replied.

'Constanza, for God's sake, what is the matter with you?' Ludovico raised his voice in frustration. 'Why can't you believe me? Why don't you trust me?'

Constance made no reply for some seconds. She felt trapped and wanted to run – but where? Suddenly, she knew where she must go.

'Will you borrow Giancarlo's car? I want to drive to Biaggibonsi – today, this afternoon.'

She knew that she needed contact with her little factory and, above all, Milva, to put her thoughts in order.

She left without telling Ludovico about the baby.

Milva had decided not to sack Assunta – she was far too good a worker to lose – and, since the bonus scheme had been dropped, things had gone well in the factory. She felt that as the girls were now working as a team, they should have some sort of productivity bonus and she was determined to convince Constance of the wisdom of the idea.

She was delighted to arrive early in the morning and find Constance already there, checking the books.

'Signora!' she cried. 'Welcome back to Biaggibonsi. The books are in order, yes?'

Constance smiled at her with pleasure. 'I have missed you, Milva. Is everything going well? How are the girls?'

'Signora,' Milva blushed, 'I owe you an apology. I have changed the work pattern a little.'

Constance frowned. 'In what way?'

'I have put the girls to work in pairs. One quick girl like Assunta with one of the slower ones like Rosa. It keeps production up without too much rivalry.'

It was Constance's turn to blush at the memory of her bonus scheme.

'You see, signora, rivalry does not work; teamwork does. You wouldn't know that but I do because I am a peasant, and that is how we do it in the fields. Without co-operation there can be no harvest. You are very young, signora, and have much to learn. Listen to Milva. She will teach you.'

Constance knew that she should not allow a peasant woman to talk to her like this but she listened eagerly.

'You can make a success of this business, signora, if you really want to, but only if we all work as a team. Is it success you need, my little one? Is that what will bring a light to your eyes? Milva sees a sadness in them now that was not there before.'

Constance couldn't discuss her problems with Milva, much as she would have liked to. She smiled and changed the subject.

'So, you have rearranged the workbenches?'

Milva knew that she had gone far enough in intimacy. Assuming her most businesslike voice, she said, 'Yes, we now have four pairs and each one is responsible for one process. The shaping is done by Assunta's team and the trimming is looked after by Concetta. The best girls take care of the most important processes.'

'Well, judging by the figures, it seems to work,' Constance said happily.

'Yes,' Milva went on, 'it is working very well. So well that I thought a slight increase in pay would be a wise thing.'

Constance panicked. 'Oh,' she said, 'I don't think we are ready for *that*.'

'No?' Milva's look was quizzical. She knew the state of the books and was sure that a comfortable little profit was already being made.

She was right. Constance was astonished at how well the hats were selling in Florence. Things were going much better than Milva realised. Savognia had insisted at the outset that even a small business in Italy must have three sets of books, all telling a different story. One was shown to employees like Milva; one went to the tax authorities and the last – containing the true figures – was kept for the eyes of family and partners alone. It was this book that told Constance the gratifying story that she and

236

Ludovico were moving towards financial independence at a steady pace. She hated the thought of slowing it down by cutting into the profits.

'I would rather take on more hands,' Constance said. 'I'm planning to go to see the couturiers in Rome to see if I can persuade them to order. If I do it will mean a bigger production line.'

'Yes, I see that, signora, but these are your base workers who will be training new hands. They need a little more money if I am to continue to get the best from them, believe me.'

'How much?'

The sum mentioned by Milva was modest. Constance decided that it would be foolish to alienate her for a very short-term gain and so she agreed. She knew that Savognia would be distressed, especially as the decision had been taken without consultation, but she also knew that she could trust Milva's judgement.

Later in the day, she took a magazine from her bag, and showed Milva and the girls a picture of Rita Hayworth and Aly Khan.

'I wonder if it would be possible to make something like that in straw?' she asked, pointing to the star's hat. 'You know, something more high fashion.'

Milva squinted at it with great concentration. Straightening up, she said, '*Si*, I will work on it with Concetta and see what we can do.'

Constance found that being back at the factory made her difficulties with Ludovico hurt a little less. She loved watching the girls working; They're doing it for *me*, she thought to herself. This is all mine, and she was amazed and delighted at how skilled they had become under Milva's training. The woman herself fascinated Constance. She was a natural leader. '*Pens' un po*. Think a little,' she would say when one of the girls had a problem. The secret of her success with them was that she never provided the solution; she led them into finding one for themselves. That was why morale and self-esteem were so high.

Reflecting on the tensions caused by Savognia's bonus scheme that she had accepted without thought, Constance said to herself, How could I be so stupid? What does an aristocrat know of work? The person to ask is a worker.

Two days after her arrival, Milva suddenly said, 'You will soon be like your Princess Elizabeth, no?'

'What do you mean?' Constance asked.

'Presenting a baby to the world.'

'How did you know?'

Milva smiled. 'There are always babies in the country, signora. Being made, being carried, being born. There are no secrets from a country woman.' She looked closely at Constance. 'But it is good, no? And yet the signora looks sad.'

Constance blushed. 'Things are not always so easy, Milva,' she said.

'You tell *me*, a peasant woman? I know everything of the sadness of babies, signora, *everything*.'

There was a pause.

'And your husband? He is happy?'

'He doesn't know.'

'Then he must. You go back to Florence. I will see to things here.' Her voice became hoarse with intensity. 'Go, signora. Trust Milva. Go.'

Giancarlo called round to see Ludovico while Constance was up in Biaggibonsi. 'You need cheering up,' he said, 'I'll take you for a spin. Let's go into the country for lunch. Truffles and wild boar with a good Barolo. Come!'

Ludovico was glad of any diversion and hurried to get dressed. While he waited, Savognia glanced round the apartment, looking for clues to the way the couple lived and the true state of their marriage. He found none.

As they drove up into the hills to a favourite trattoria, Giancarlo asked, 'Have you seen anything of Carlo?'

Ludovico shook his head violently, wishing to end the conversation there.

'But he knows you are married, surely,' Giancarlo persisted.

Ludovico frowned. 'I'm sure he does. But I haven't set eyes on him since he went away.'

'Do you miss him?'

'Desperately.'

'I do not wish to criticise Maria-Angelina, my dear boy, but she was too severe – and quite wrong to involve you against your only brother. Don't you feel you might . . . ?'

'Never,' Ludovico interrupted. 'Too much was said, too much was felt for us to ever come together again. Besides, he destroyed the family honour. I cannot forgive that.'

Giancarlo said sharply, 'No more than your father did, surely?'

Ludovico turned to face him in the car. 'Giancarlo!' he cried. 'Have you forgotten what Carlo did? My father may have had his indiscretions but murder was not one of them. Surely you don't put him on the same level as Carlo?'

Savognia realised that there was no point in pursuing the discussion and quietly asked, 'You haven't told Constanza?'

'Of course not!'

'She thinks you have no brother?'

'Yes.'

'What happens when she finds out?'

'I do not think she will. After all, the one woman most likely to tell her simply cannot, can she?'

'Bettina is not the only gossip in Italy, *caro*. I wouldn't be so sure that this is a secret that can be kept for ever.'

Ludovico changed the subject. 'Do you think that this hat business will work?' he asked.

'I most certainly do,' his friend replied. 'Your wife is a very determined woman. And, I think, a talented one. She will not let it fail.'

'I thought it would be finished with the terrible end of Giulio, but I was wrong. It seems to have made her even more resolute.'

'He has become her martyr,' Savognia replied, 'burned to death for her. She cannot allow herself to fail now. How big a success she'll have remains to be seen but I can assure you, the hats have a very distinctive style. I would be happy to put some money into this little enterprise, you know. That's how sure I am of its success.'

Ludovico remained silent. He found his friend's certainty impressive, but also disquieting. He didn't want his wife to be a successful businesswoman. He knew that, if she were, he would take second place and he had no wish to contemplate such a situation.

'There was no inquest on Giulio.' It was less a question than a statement.

'No,' Ludovico replied innocently, 'nobody seemed to think it necessary. After all, how would they ever find out how the shed caught fire?'

'Don't you mean, who set it alight? Giulio's death was murder, just as clearly as Carlo's action was,' Savognia said. 'Not knowing who did it doesn't alter the fact. There should have been an inquest. I assume that your mother stopped it, for her own reasons.'

They drove on in silence.

'Are you going to tell me what they were?' Ludovico asked, staring straight ahead at the empty road.

'Yes,' his friend replied, 'I think you should know. Giulio was your father's bastard.'

Constance returned to Florence with three completely new hat shapes created by Milva and Assunta. She was as proud of them as if she had made them herself.

'Look what my illiterate girls have produced,' she said to Ludovico and Giancarlo, '*and* without a man to supervise them!'

Savognia was impressed. 'But these are most interesting,' he said. '*Most* interesting.'

240

'I cannot imagine why you're so surprised, Giancarlo. I told you we would do something to make Constanza Hats important. I think that this is just the beginning!'

Savognia carefully turned the hats over in his hands. 'They are very well balanced,' he said. 'Is one of your women a milliner?'

Constance laughed. 'Giancarlo, you *know* Biaggibonsi! Are you mad! My girls were working in the fields not so long ago.'

To her delight, Ludovico put his arm round her waist and said, 'You are very clever to get this sort of work out of those people. I've known them all my life and I wouldn't have thought it possible. I am proud of you, my darling. Very proud.'

# CHAPTER 10

Two days later, Constance travelled down to Rome, still without telling anybody about her pregnancy. Not even Ludovico knew. Despite Milva's certainty, she was still sufficiently insular to want the opinion of an English doctor before making it public. As well as showing her hats to the couturiers, she intended to visit Louise's doctor while she was there.

Louise put Constance to bed the moment she arrived.

'My dear! You look absolutely *exhausted*!' she exclaimed. 'What have you been up to?'

'Oh, I haven't been sleeping too well,' Constance replied guardedly, alarmed at how her emotions must be showing in her face.

'No worries with the business, I hope?'

'No, no. Just the opposite! Oh, Louise, I can't tell you how well the girls are doing. The hat shop keeps running out of stock! Milva's already looking for new girls. Isn't it exciting?'

Constance felt refreshed after a good night's sleep and was grateful that Louise allowed her to stay in bed until well gone eleven. After a slow and deliciously hot bath followed by a lazy breakfast on the terrace, she felt better.

Louise appeared with a bottle of champagne. 'This will cheer us up!' she cried brightly. 'It's the real thing, would you believe! I haven't had any since before the war. Jim got it on the black market, I'm ashamed to say.'

'Oh, Louise! How did you know we had something to celebrate?'

'Well, the business, darling. But is there something else?' Louise paused. 'Do tell, darling. What is it?'

'I'm pregnant.'

'Oh, my dear, how marvellous! I'm so happy for you! Actually, I *did* wonder last night when you arrived. I thought there was something. Have you told Nora? She'll be over the moon!'

Constance burst into tears.

'What on earth is wrong?' Louise asked in horror.

'Oh, Louise, I'm so unhappy. Everything has gone wrong.'

'You must simply *force* yourself to believe him, darling,' Louise said firmly after Constance had finished telling her about Gioella, 'otherwise you'll go mad and that won't do *anyone* any good. Least of all the baby. After all, you don't have any *proof* that he's still seeing this woman, now have you? I think that with the baby and all the hard work up at the factory and everything, you've let yourself get a little down and your imagination has run away with you. I can't believe it of Ludovico. You've only to look at him to see that he worships you, my darling, absolutely *worships* you.'

'I know,' Constance replied, 'but I'm not *enough* for him. I'm convinced that he's still seeing her.'

'You mustn't give way to these silly feelings,' Louise said, 'you must think positively – for the baby's sake.'

And that was the line she kept to for the rest of the visit.

The House of Portinari was the oldest established and most august couture establishment in Rome and despite her experience at Maison de Levantière Constance felt intimidated as she stepped through its grand doorway in the Via Condotti wearing a new red and cream silk dress and a black picture hat. Her heart beating furiously, she walked across the vast hallway to a desk in the corner, where a woman dressed in black looked up arrogantly as Constance approached her with the samples. She hadn't felt so physically awkward since the first time she had modelled for Monsieur de Levantière. She seemed to have lost all co-ordination, and she bitterly regretted how unprofessional she must appear, carrying the mismatched hatboxes that Savognia had sorted out for her at the last moment.

I'll have my own boxes for the next time, she thought crossly.

Her nerves were caused less by feelings of social inadequacy – although everything in the surroundings was calculated to create that effect – than by her deep involvement with her hats. She hated the thought that they might be rejected and, despite her fears, she had decided to approach Portinari first because if he accepted them, she knew that the rest of Rome would follow.

She was ushered into a small anteroom and the door was closed noiselessly behind her. The whole building was as uncannily silent as a country church, although, to Constance, the tiny room was more like a prison cell. She became increasingly nervous as the minutes ticked past and her confidence had almost evaporated when the door was gently pushed open to reveal the severe presence of the chief vendeuse, a white-haired woman dressed in the height of fashion. Constance had never seen such perfection. Every inch of the woman was immaculate, including her eyes, which were washed clean of anything like a human expression.

As she began to show the hats, Constance became aware of a softening in the woman's demeanour. Nothing as vulgar as enthusiasm but something not far from interest began to show in the deadness of her impeccably made-up face. Finally she spoke.

'Yes,' she said, 'I think that Signor Portinari would like to look at these. I will go and find him. Wait here until you are called.'

At that moment, the silence was shattered by a hysterical shouting somewhere in the depths of the building. It grew louder. Suddenly it was in the hall outside. A high-pitched voice, only just recognisable as male, was screaming abuse into the air.

'Where is that bitch? She is never around when I want her! How the hell am I meant to create a collection when my chief vendeuse disappears for hours on end? Find her! Find her, immediately!' And there came the unmistakable sound of a petulant foot being stamped.

The vendeuse had frozen at the first sound. When the tirade ceased, she crossed the small room without a word to Constance, and was out in the corridor in a second. Constance could hear her comforting Signor Portinari. She was incredulous at the woman's tone; the vendeuse sounded as if she were talking to a child of six, trying to soothe it after a temper tantrum. Constance's fear vanished as quickly as her confidence had earlier.

The door was pushed open and Signor Portinari stood there, red-eyed. Constance was struck by his elegance. He wore a faultlessly tailored dark grey suit with a discreet rose boutonnière. She found it hard to believe that this dignified-looking man had been responsible for the childish fuss of a moment ago. When he spoke, she knew there had been no mistake. His voice was high and querulous, belying his austerely grand image.

Paolo Portinari was the third generation of designers in the family and was recognised as the genius of Italian fashion. Constance was desperate for him to take some of her hats for his collection. Remembering what Bettina had said of America, she knew that Portinari would give her the right exposure. His was the only Italian collection ever reported in the international press.

'So,' Portinari said as he graciously extended his hand, 'you are the English wife of Villanuova who Savognia is always talking of. I believe you know my good friend Bettina Bonoccorsi. I had not expected someone quite so young.'

Constance blushed. The couturier stood expectantly before her.

'Come,' he urged, 'show me your wares.'

Constance could tell that the designer was impressed. He held the hats up to the light at every possible angle, examined inside the crowns and balanced the brims on his little finger. Finally, to her surprise, he placed one on his head.

Turning to her, he said, 'Yes, they feel right.' The vendeuse relaxed and the atmosphere changed. Constance waited. There was clearly something on his mind. Eventually he said, 'Forgive me, signora. It is a question of taste. I know that you will not take offence but, if you are to supply hats for my clothes, there is something I must say.'

Constance waited, her mouth dry.

'We live in the century of Le Corbusier and Chanel, signora. The century of simplicity.' He removed a tiny pair of scissors from his top pocket. 'May I?' he asked and, without waiting for her reply, took up a hat. To her horror, he began to snip away at the decoration. She watched in alarm as he quickly worked at removing and rearranging the trim. He held the hat up before her. It was transformed.

'In couture, signora,' he said in his high-pitched voice, 'less is more. Always.'

It was a comment Constance never forgot.

As he walked to the door, he turned almost as an afterthought and said, 'Yes, we will work together,' and left the room.

By the time Ludovico arrived in Rome for the weekend Louise's therapy and the triumph at Portinari had begun to work on Constance and he was delighted at the warmth of her welcome. All the tension between them seemed to have gone and he was struck by how radiant she looked. She seemed to glow with good health and contentment. He also detected a suppressed excitement in her and he had not been in the apartment for more than five minutes

246

before she was eagerly telling him what her aunt's English doctor had confirmed in his Parioli surgery that morning.

'No!' Ludovico cried. 'I cannot believe it. Is it possible? Oh, Constanza! This is marvellous news.'

He made to tightly embrace her but then, remembering her condition, nervously stepped back and kissed her with great gentleness. 'We must take very, very great care of you, my darling,' he murmured. 'Nothing, absolutely nothing, must be allowed to endanger him. He will be the new Villanuova heir.'

'Oh, Ludo,' Constance laughed, 'I'm only a few weeks pregnant. I'm not made of sugar. Don't start treating me like an invalid already!'

She hugged him tightly and went on, 'What makes you so sure it won't be a girl?'

'Oh,' he replied lightly, 'it couldn't possibly be. I am so masculine that my first child will naturally be a boy.'

Constance laughed.

'I mean it,' Ludovico insisted. 'Men who are all man produce male babies first.'

Constance laughed again, but looked at him uneasily. 'Don't make jokes,' she said. 'It doesn't matter what sex it is, as long as it's healthy and strong.'

Ludovico gave her a sharp glance. 'What do you mean – it doesn't matter? Of course it matters. The first-born Villanuova *must* be a son. An heir. It is always so. But,' he went on, his tone lightening, 'there is no problem. It *will* be a boy. You know how I am in bed, my darling; you know . . . my size. Of course we will have a boy.' He ended on a note of expansive confidence, as he held her hands and gazed proudly into her eyes.

Constance was stunned. How could his thinking be so primitive?

'Ludo, my darling,' she said kindly, 'it has nothing to do with how much of a man you are. That is not what determines the sex of a child.' She paused, rather uncertain as to what actually did determine it. 'Constanza,' Ludovico replied dismissively, 'you do not understand these things and you do not need to. All you must do is keep well and healthy and do nothing – I beg of you – *nothing* to put him in any danger.'

His attitude amazed Constance. She fought to contain her irritation at his crude superstition; she must let it pass. She was right to do so. Nothing would have shaken Ludovico from his conviction. He had spent too much time in the kitchens of his father's peasants when he was small, listening, unnoticed, to the women's talk of birth and death to ever be dissuaded from believing what he had taken in so eagerly – and certainly not by an English-woman.

In the months to come, Constance frequently remembered that morning in Louise's apartment. For her, it symbolised the huge cultural gap between them; Ludo, for all his education and experience of the world, thought in so many ways exactly as the peasants had done for generations. To her, such attitudes were unbelievable in a twentieth-century man.

'She insists that it will not affect the business at all,' Bettina told Monica. 'She intends to go on exactly as before. Ludovico and she drive up to the Marche once or twice a week and she seems to be coping perfectly well. In the last month, they will stay at the castle – he insists that the baby is born up there. That will be to please his mother, I would imagine. You know how desperately she clings to the Villanuova traditions.'

'And so does Ludovico, don't forget,' Monica interrupted, 'they are every bit as important to him.'

As her pregnancy progressed, Constance felt her energy level sapping. She tried to keep her spirits high by making plans, but she could do very little about nursery things because of Ludovico's absolute conviction that the child would be a boy and her equally strong premonition that it would not. She reluctantly gave in when Ludovico begged to have his first child born in his ancestral home,

248

but her heart sank at the prospect. The month at the castle was passed in a flurry of instructions to the estate carpenter for nursery furniture and wooden toys, and they spent many more-or-less happy hours arguing over the colours they should be painted. The ornate family cot had been brought down from the attics and placed in the painted gallery where, it had been decided, the birth should take place. Despite its name, it was a small room, brightly decorated with Victorian frescoes after Botticelli's 'Primavera'. Constance felt that there were rather too many angels fluttering around for her taste and imagined how Miss Hatherby would shudder at the harsh greens and violent blues of the landscape, but she agreed to have the birth-bed moved in there ready for the great moment.

'Every male Villanuova has entered the world on that bed since seventeen twenty-nine when my great-great-great-grandfather was born in it in Piedmont. We had estates there in those days. It was his father's bridal bed, but for many years now it has been kept exclusively for births.'

As Ludovico patted the ornately carved headboard, Constance rested her heavy stomach against the high mattress and wondered where female Villanuovas had been born. Ludovico sensed the question.

'In all that time there have only been two female Villanuovas. They both died.' He shrugged dismissively. 'We are a male line. That is why I am so certain, my darling.'

He slipped his arm around her shoulder. 'This afternoon I will have the linen brought in.'

Constance had seen the bedding already and found it exquisite: seventeenth-century linen sheets edged with thick frothy lace, pillowcases and a counterpane completely covered with embroidery of the Villanuova crest, with mythical beasts, giants, gods, flowers and wild animals in subtly coloured silks. The whole design was brought together by four-inch-wide cream silk ribbons that ran round the edges, slotted in and out of the lace border that was at least twelve inches wide on the counterpane, and nine on the pillows. Constance had never seen such workmanship. It seemed strange to her that a family who owned such beautiful things could tolerate the crude colourings of the painted gallery.

Even Ludovico seemed captivated by the beauty of the bedding. Running his hand across the embroidery, he explained the history of the workmanship.

'All done by nuns – originally for the bridal bed, of course.' He grinned. 'Poor things. I wonder whether they used to imagine what would go on under this cover.'

Constance was hardly listening. She was gently fingering the delicate needlework. 'It must have taken a lifetime,' she murmured.

'Oh, more!' Ludovico replied. 'This was work handed down by several generations of nuns – they had to give up when their eyes were no longer good enough for sewing of this quality. The counterpane took many, many years – but it is a work of art, no?'

'Oh, absolutely,' Constance agreed enthusiastically. 'It should be in a museum.'

'It is,' Ludovico grinned, '*our* museum. The museum to the greatness of the Villanuovas.'

He swung his arms expansively. 'This castle is our museum. Everything we are is here.'

Constance saw nothing of Maria-Angelina. She remained in her own darkened part of the castle, praying and doing her jigsaw puzzles – and, through her servant, receiving daily bulletins on the movements of her son and his wife. Constance found it unnerving that her mother-in-law was never seen, and she endlessly badgered Ludovico for information.

'What does she do all the time?' she asked.

'She prays – for me,' Ludovico answered flippantly, 'she thinks I have lost my soul – through you.'

Constance was indignant. 'I don't believe you ever had one to lose, so she can hardly blame me!'

Ludovico laughed. 'Don't think about my mother. She

said goodbye to the world a long time ago. But I know that she cares very much that you keep well so that he will be healthy. That is why they bring you so much fruit and honey.'

'I'll get as fat as a seal.'

'No, no, it is not for you. Your job is to make a strong baby.'

Although she was pregnant, Constance did not neglect the factory. Every day she drove down to Biaggibonsi and occasionally took Ludovico with her. He was there one afternoon when she became involved in a trivial disagreement with Milva over the colour of a trim.

'*Pensa un po!* Think, little one,' Milva said indulgently, 'Milva is right.'

Constance saw that her overseer was indeed correct, and deferred to her judgement. As they drove back up the valley, Ludovico suddenly turned on her, his eyes blazing with fury.

'Why do you let that woman speak to you like that? I can't believe the tone she takes with you. Does she forget that you are my wife and that I am a Castelfranco di Villanuova whose ancestors have ruled these lands since the days when peasants like her had no ancestors?'

Constance was shocked at the violence of the outburst. 'I trust Milva's judgement. She was right. I would have been ridiculous not to acknowledge the fact.'

'She is a peasant and an employee – and you have allowed her so much freedom that she has forgotten her place.'

'Her place? Milva Pecoraro is a friend of mine.'

'Friend?' Ludovico almost shrieked. 'Are you out of your mind? You have married an aristocrat, you do not *have* friends who are peasants – can't you see that?'

She tried to keep her temper. 'Ludovico, I can't believe what you're saying. This is the twentieth century. Stop behaving as if we are still in the Middle Ages. Milva

Pecoraro may be a peasant by your standards but she is a highly intelligent woman, whose judgement I trust.'

'Milva Pecoraro,' he sneered, 'do you know what that means – little shepherd! Is that what my wife wants – a little peasant shepherd to tell her what to do?'

Constance's temper snapped. 'It's not as bad as having a mother who tells you what you can and can't do! At least, thanks to Milva, we'll soon be out of *her* clutches!'

Ludovico's concern for her health made him stop the argument. He was terrified in case anything should go wrong with the birth. In fact, his nervousness was beginning to get on Constance's nerves. He could hardly bear to let her out of his sight and fussed around her all day. Although his over-protective behaviour irritated her and they quarrelled frequently over trivial matters, Constance was pleased that their relationship had reverted to its old intimacy. His anxiety made her wish it was all over and done with, but Constance blessed the baby because it had brought them together again. She felt entirely at ease with their relationship. She knew that Ludovico wasn't seeing Gioella. How could he be, when he never left his wife's side?

One afternoon, as they drove back to the castle from the factory, Constance said, 'Oh, my God, how tired I am of all this waiting. I feel as if I've been cut off up here in the country for a lifetime. I long to be in Florence again.'

'That would be quite out of the question,' Ludovico said in alarm. 'The baby's time is far too near for you to take risks driving all that way.'

'Oh, Ludo, surely one weekend wouldn't hurt?' she begged. 'I am going mad up here. I hate that dreary castle. Please let's go away for a weekend.'

Ludovico was deaf to her pleas. The next day, however, he said casually to her, 'You know, Monica is who you need. She'll cheer you up. I shall go down to Florence tomorrow and get her.'

'But that means you will be away overnight.'

'So? You have the servants . . . and my mother.'

'What if something happens and the baby starts?'

'Oh,' he laughed, 'that'll be all right. I would run and hide even if I were here. That is woman's work. You don't need me around for that.'

She could think of no argument to stop him and so it was agreed. Ludovico would drive down to Florence the next afternoon.

Less than an hour after he had left, the Principessa Maria-Angelina surprised Constance by sending a servant to inform her that she was expected to join her for dinner in her quarters that night. Constance was alarmed but knew that the invitation was a command, not a suggestion, and that no excuse would be accepted. At precisely seven-thirty, she was ushered into the Principessa's *salotto*. The door closed behind her and Constance stood silent and perplexed. The room was empty. As her eyes became accustomed to the gloom, she discerned the huge pieces of a half-completed jigsaw puzzle on the floor. She stepped forward to look at it.

'Are you interested in puzzles?' a deep voice enquired.

Constance gave a start and looked up. There on a platform at the end of the room stood Maria-Angelina holding a long ivory pointer, like a billiard cue. She was dressed entirely in black as she had been on their first encounter, but Constance was relieved to see that her face was uncovered this time. As the Principessa was helped down from the platform by her servant, Constance stood by the side of the jigsaw and glanced around. Her eyes gradually became accustomed to the light. The *salotto* was enormous and virtually unfurnished. She could see a large table by the curtained window. It appeared to be covered with bundles wrapped in silk. Suddenly the princess stood before her. Constance was shocked. She was looking into the face of Ludovico, the one that she would see when he was an old man. The princess had the same perfectly regular features, strong profile and long eyelashes. Constance could see that Maria-Angelina still had the remnants of what must have been an outstanding beauty in her youth.

No time was wasted in small talk.

'You will sit?' The Principessa motioned to the table. The servant had now lit the candles and Constance could see that her first impression had not been wrong. All the table silver and glassware were wrapped in white silk. As the servant shuffled out for the food, the Principessa unwrapped her cutlery and glass as if it were the most natural thing in the world. She dropped the wrapping at her feet and closely examined the forks. Maria-Angelina was convinced that all peasants were dirty and that the hands that prepared food must never be allowed to touch crockery, crystal or cutlery, which she believed harboured germs. She was equally convinced that outside her carefully controlled part of the castle, germs abounded. Although she waited daily for death, she took all proper precautions to remain alive and her servant was personally responsible for cleaning everything used at the Principessa's table. The moment the cutlery, crockery and crystal had been polished they were wrapped in their silk bags for extra protection, in case other servants might touch them. As Maria-Angelina believed that cooking killed germs, she never allowed anything raw to come to her table and insisted that, for extra safety, all food must be cooked for such long periods that it was eventually served as a tasteless, formless mess.

Constance unwrapped her own cutlery. She could feel the weight of the silence pressing on her but she was determined not to speak first. The two women faced each other in a battle of wills and it was only after the soup had been removed that politeness, curiosity or some other force finally compelled the Principessa to speak. It was not a moment too soon. Constance was on the verge of breaking out into hysterical giggles.

The Principessa's words, however, quickly dispelled laughter. 'You will not invite Ludovico's brother to be godparent to the child, I assume?'

The question stunned Constance. For several seconds she was unable to reply and the Principessa asked impatiently, 'You understand what I say? My son tells me that you speak Italian. Is it not so?'

Constance tried to recover her poise, which had been jolted by the hostility of the Principessa's tone.

'Yes, of course,' she stumbled, 'it's just that . . . I didn't know that Ludovico had a brother.'

'He does not,' the Principessa commented, confusingly, 'the man who was his brother forfeited the right to consideration as one of the family many years ago. He has been struck from the Villanuova records. He no longer exists. But I know Ludovico and his weakness. I would not be surprised if he tried to contact Carlo when the baby is born. He must not do so. I rely on you to make sure of that.'

Constance thought she might faint. Her palms were sweating and her head reeled. She did not know which she found more shocking, the icy venom of this woman who was talking of her own flesh and blood or the fact that Ludovico had kept her in ignorance of a brother and repeatedly claimed to be an only son. The mystery of the photograph was dispelled. No wonder the third boy had looked so like Ludovico. She remembered the three youthful faces smiling out from the arch their rackets made.

Despite her racing brain, she was conscious of how acutely Maria-Angelina was watching her.

'Principessa, forgive me,' she blurted out, 'I didn't know that Ludovico had a brother. He has told me nothing.'

'Then I shall,' the Principessa said, laying aside her knife and fork and motioning to the servant to remove the barely touched food. As she shuffled round the table collecting the plates, the women sat silent. Only when she had left did the Principessa speak again.

'Carlo was two years older than Ludovico – a strange,

wild child. The servants could do nothing with him. He was a wilful boy. His only pleasure lay in doing evil.'

She paused.

'He behaved not in the naughty way of children but in the deliberate way of the devil. The priests used to tell me that he had been touched by Satan's hand. I knew they were right. I had given birth to a monster. The devil has always envied the Villanuovas and tried to claim them as his own. He claimed Carlo at birth.'

Constance shuddered.

Carlo Castelfranco di Villanuova had committed only one unforgivable sin but it had turned his mother's mind, and thereafter he became in her eyes a creature of depravity, cursed from birth with the taint of evil. He had committed murder, worse, the murder of his own flesh and blood – he had killed his brother's child.

'Carlo lived in Florence,' Maria-Angelina said. 'His life there was dissolute and wild like that of his father before him. He met a woman as steeped in corruption as he was. Their behaviour was a scandal to all decent people. Not content with their own degeneracy, they set out to seduce Ludovico into their evil ways. He was seventeen and eager for the world. His father had already encouraged him to embrace the sins of the flesh. You might imagine how easily he followed his brother's lead.'

Maria-Angelina's eyes clouded with hatred.

'He thought he could turn his back on me, his conscience and the Church and remain unscathed. Ludovico always was a fool. It was Carlo who had the brains. My sons set up an unholy alliance with that degraded woman who shamelessly shared herself between them.'

She paused, watching Constance closely to see how she would react. Constance stared back at her, determined that her face would not betray how devastated she was at the thought that Ludovico could behave in such a way.

'When the woman confided in Carlo that she was pregnant,' the Principessa continued, 'she did not even know which of my sons was the father.' Her voice became harsh.

'Carlo has always spoken with the devil, and he did so then. He became convinced that the child was not his but Ludovico's.' There was another long pause. Constance thought the Principessa had finished. She could think of nothing to say to break the silence.

Maria-Angelina began to speak again, her voice slightly softer.

'Sometimes God gives a moment of goodness even to those completely steeped in sin. Carlo decided that he would claim the child as his, marry the woman – although he knew that she was little more than a whore – and never tell Ludovico the truth. He came here and told me everything. He begged me to give him money.' She faltered and Constance could see tears in her eyes. 'What could I do? I prayed. For three days I prayed, pleading for guidance. Then I knew what I must do. Carlo was damned for ever but I could at least save Ludovico. I agreed to release money on the strict condition that Carlo would never again speak to his brother and would take the whore he would marry and live with her far from Italy. He accepted my conditions – and yet, finally, he betrayed them, as I discovered later. He continued communicating with Ludovico and he and the woman went to London unmarried. The child was born. It was an idiot.'

She passed her fingers under her nose, paused and then began again in a voice breaking with emotion.

'He killed it. He smothered it with a pillow. Carlo took its life, without a second's thought.'

'What was it – a boy or a girl?' Constance asked.

The Principessa started and looked at Constance in surprise. She had almost forgotten the Englishwoman's presence.

'A boy . . . No one questioned, no one bothered over a tiny Italian corpse. The woman had been taken to one of those clinics in London that openly defy God's will and the Church's teaching. A place where destroying infants before birth is considered commonplace. It made no dif-

257

ference that this one was murdered after his birth. Carlo,' the Principessa's voice strengthened with hatred, 'was proud of himself for solving the problem so neatly. He told Ludovico of the deed. When Ludovico came here to tell me of the terrible thing done in London, I realised that he did not know that it was his son that Carlo had murdered. It was my duty to tell him and to extract the promise that he would never speak to his brother again.' Maria-Angelina looked directly at Constance.

'It was the beginning of the revenge I took on Carlo, a revenge necessary for the honour of the Villanuovas. I decided that after such dishonourable behaviour, there was no longer a place within our family for my elder son. He would never again enter this castle, speak to me, see his brother. He would, in fact, be amputated like a diseased limb before his poison could spread any further. I was determined that he would be cut off, thrown away and forgotten about.'

She looked at Constance.

'I banished him for ever.'

'How?' Constance asked, her voice betraying her horror.

'I removed every trace of him from this castello. Every trace. Clothes, books, personal mementos: everything that belonged to him. I had them piled in the centre of the courtyard and burned. His memory was consumed in that fire. I forbade his name to be mentioned by anyone in my employ and I made Ludovico give his solemn promise that he would never talk to Carlo again. For all his faults,' she ended with satisfaction, 'Ludovico has at least cared enough about our family's honour to obey my ruling.'

Constance staggered back to her apartment shocked and overwhelmed by what she had heard. Shortly after daybreak, she woke from a troubled sleep, immediately aware that something was different. The baby's kicks, to which she was accustomed, had changed to a fluttering sensation that was new. It's going to be today, she thought. Oh, please God, let Ludo be back in time. She lay perfectly still for the next two hours, conscious of her body as never before. Periodically the fluttering movements were punctuated by brief stabbing pains. She began to count the intervals between them. They grew shorter. She knew she must find help. There was no bell in the room. She made her way unsteadily into the corridor. The castle seemed unnaturally silent. Surely somebody must be awake, it's past seven, she thought, but the long corridor was deserted. The pains grew in intensity, doubling her up, but she was not afraid. She slowly dragged herself to the top of the stairs that connected Ludovico's rooms with the Principessa's wing. Holding tightly to the banister, she tried to walk down them. At the half landing, her legs gave way and her waters broke. Was there nobody about? Through her pain, she heard the sound of shuffling feet. The Principessa's servant was laboriously climbing the stairs towards her.

The old woman stopped in amazement at the sight of the Englishwoman crouching on the stairs, her face white and covered in sweat, but she knew immediately what must be done. After all, she had brought both the Principessa's sons into the world. She could do it again. Stooping over Constance, she said, 'Vieni! Come!' and helped her to her feet. Together they struggled to a small room on the angle of the landing. It was simply furnished with nothing more than an old oak day bed and a cabinet. The wooden floor glowed with years of polishing. Through her pain Constance wondered why she had never been in the room before, nor even been aware of its existence. The old crone helped her on to the bed, then disappeared. Constance called after her. She was afraid, both for herself and for the baby; she knew that she couldn't manage to deliver it alone and she was in desperate need of human comfort and assistance in any form.

She heard the shuffling feet through another violent contraction. The woman was back with bedding. She forced a rough linen sheet under Constance and then placed another over her. She brought no pillow. She disappeared again but returned within minutes carrying a small tin bath which she filled with hot water.

'Your time is near, signora, push, push, bear down, push.'

Constance did as she was told. She felt like an animal, straining and heaving. The veneer of centuries of civilisation disappeared. She was a primeval creature, gripped by the urgency of birth, determined that her baby would emerge intact and strong. She was aware of the woman's hands. Then she had an extraordinary sensation that something was being forcibly thrust out of her; the pain of the expulsion was excruciating.

Suddenly, she knew that it was done. She had given birth. She had produced a baby. Relief and disbelief swept over her. Then came the fear. Was it all right? What was the woman doing? She tried to raise her head, but couldn't. Suddenly the sheet was pulled from her and the old woman placed the baby on her stomach.

Its little body was hot against her skin. She cupped her hands around it, amazed at how small it was. It felt beautiful to her touch. She raised her head as the woman cut the umbilical cord. She had expected the baby to be covered in blood but, to her surprise, it was only bloody in the crevices and folds of its body. Although its skin was red and angry-looking, Constance thought it the most perfect thing she had ever seen. As her head fell back, the woman lifted the baby from her. Constance just had time to see that it was a girl.

The sun was high when Constance woke up. Her eyes took a few seconds to focus. She looked round the room. On the cabinet the old woman had placed a rough earthenware pot containing four yellow celandines. Constance felt tears come to her eyes at the poignancy of the gesture. But where was her daughter? There was no cot anywhere in the room. Panicking, she forced herself up in the bed. At that moment, the door opened and the old woman shuffled in. She carried a shallow rush apple basket. Lying in it was Constance's baby, tightly wrapped, sound asleep and very pink. Gently placing the basket on the cabinet, the old woman handed her the child. As she took her, Constance smiled with delight – a smile short-lived.

'I am sorry for your shame, signora,' the old woman whispered. 'Have patience. Next time it must be a boy.'

The words were like a blow to the heart for Constance. She remembered Ludovico's confidence – 'it will be a boy' – and was overwhelmed by her sense of failure.

Ludovico and Monica arrived at lunchtime. Constance heard Ludo running up the stairs, shouting excitedly, 'Where is he? Where is he?' He burst into the little room and rushed over to the bed. Seeing Constance's face he stopped in his tracks.

'What's wrong?' His voice was full of fear. 'Constanza, what's happened? Why are you crying? Tell me, what's happened to my son?' He was on his hands and knees by the bedside, shaking her in alarm. 'Tell me! Tell me!' He was almost screaming.

With a deep feeling of hopelessness, Constance pushed him away. 'You have no son: it is a girl,' and, sobbing, she turned her head from him.

Ludovico remained on his knees as if he were paralysed.

Quietly, almost to himself, he said, 'This cannot be.' His voice broke with emotion as he repeated, 'This *cannot* be.' He wept in despair. Clutching at Constance, he buried his head between her breasts. She held him tightly to her as he sobbed, 'I want my son! I want my son!'

'You bastard! You selfish bastard!' Monica's lip curled with contempt. 'Is that all you can say, after what she's been through?'

Ludovico paced the room, hardly aware of her and deaf to her comments.

'*How?*' he said, pounding the air with his hands. 'How could it have happened?'

He swung round. 'It was that woman!' he cried. 'She's

a witch! She deliberately put Constanza in that room instead of the painted gallery so that it wouldn't be a boy.'

'Don't be so ridiculous!' Monica retorted. 'I've never heard such primitive superstition in my life. What on earth is wrong with you? Your wife gives you a beautiful, healthy daughter and all you can do is whine because it isn't a boy! You Italians are incredible!'

'You don't understand Italy or Italians,' Ludovico shouted. 'The Villanuovas are a male line! Constanza has been bewitched!'

Suddenly, clutching at a straw, he said, 'I know what happened! It is not my baby! That evil old crone has changed it for another. That girl is a substitute, I tell you!'

Monica's temper snapped. She strode across to Ludovico and hit him hard across the cheek.

'Stop it! Stop it, I tell you! You madman! You're not worthy of Constance or your child!'

Ludovico stood, amazed, for a second. Then he fell into her arms, weeping like a baby.


'I shall leave him. I'll take her back to England,' Constance said to Monica. 'I think he's mad.'

For all her firmness with Ludovico, Monica felt it her duty to take his part.

'Don't be foolish, Constance,' she said reasonably. 'You have to make allowances for the Italian temperament. You know how extreme these people are.'

'He doesn't love me. What is the point of staying?'

'Oh, Constance, come! How can you say that?'

'He's a liar and a cheat. Imagine not telling me that he had a brother. He said he was an only son, Monica; he said that to my face. And don't think I don't know about Gioella, because I do, despite all his denials. What sort of a marriage can I have with a man like that?'

'But what about the business?' Monica asked.

'He hates that as well,' Constance said. 'It seems I can

do nothing to please him. Everything I try meets with his disapproval – or contempt – or indifference.'

After Monica had left her, Constance lay for hours thinking about her marriage. What sort of a thing was it, surrounded by endless betrayals, lies and disappointments? And yet, despite everything, she loved Ludovico as much as ever. Even more, she needed him. If only she knew how to help him overcome his problems. 'Please,' she prayed aloud, 'show him how to love me for what I am and who I am. Make him see that I cannot be like an Italian wife. And I cannot give up my hats. Please don't let him ask.'

It was Monica who reconciled Ludovico to the sex of his first-born. She took him up to the painted gallery, where Constance and the baby had been moved. Taking the child out of the eighteenth-century cradle, she placed her in his arms. It was a simple gesture and an unpremeditated one and it succeeded because of its spontaneity.

'Look how beautiful she is,' Monica murmured, 'look at her delicious little fingers. Isn't she *gorgeous*, Ludo?'

The baby looked up at him and stretched out its hand. 'Oh, look,' he said in delight, 'she's trying to touch me!'

Monica slipped from the room. With infinite care, Ludovico carried the child to Constance's bed. There were tears in his eyes as he asked, 'What shall we call her, our little principessa?'

Constance felt her own eyes grow moist. Oh, my sentimental, emotional darling, she thought, how could I ever live without you?

The baby was baptised in the family chapel, with Monica and Giancarlo as godparents. She was named Margharita Beatrice Alessandra Castelfranco di Villanuova – for no other reason than that Constance liked the roll of the words. Maria-Angelina did not attend the ceremony.

Constance longed to return to England to show off her

daughter to Nora and Miss Hatherby, but it was six weeks before she and the child were strong enough to travel.

She went with a heart still heavy with worry. Ludovico's hysteria over the birth of a girl child had been frightening, and the lies he had perpetrated about his family background seemed incomprehensible. Increasingly, Constance asked herself if her husband was unbalanced. His mother, after all, was mad. When I return to Italy, she decided, I shall get Giancarlo to introduce me to Carlo. I must find out what sort of man he really is. Even as she thought it, she knew it was impossible – Ludovico would see it as a betrayal. She couldn't risk alienating him – their relationship was insecure enough already and Constance didn't want it to deteriorate further. Although Ludovico had finally accepted his daughter, Constance felt that Margharita would in time be rejected, in favour of the male child she knew she must give the Villanuovas. But Constance loved her daughter deeply and fiercely, and was determined not to let this happen – and equally determined that Ludovico's hostility towards her hat business would not hamper its development. She would protect her child *and* her career – and both would be successful. She would make sure of that.

In Northumberland, Constance and Margharita were given their due share of compliments.

'She's gorgeous, darling,' Nora said expansively. 'As lovely as her name. What dark mischievous eyes she has! I must say, though, there's not much Simpson in her. She's all Italian, if you ask me.'

'She won't be,' Constance replied, 'I don't intend to let Margharita grow up like Italian women, doormats to their husbands, expected to close their eyes to God knows how many infidelities.'

Nora was on to the indiscretion immediately. 'Ludovico's not playing fast and loose, I hope,' she demanded.

'Good heavens, no.' Constance's reply was quick. 'What an idea! No, it's just that the more I see of Italy the more

I'm amazed at what women are expected to put up with in their marriages. You'd be appalled. The men call all the shots out there, believe me.'

'I hope you're not talking of Ludovico as well.'

'No,' Constance said, 'he's different. He's not even typically Italian.'

Could Nora tell that she was lying? No matter what, Constance was resolved to keep her doubts about Ludo to herself. She changed the subject.

Nora returned to it that night at dinner.

'How does Ludovico feel about having a daughter?'

'Oh! He's over the moon.'

'Really?' Nora's voice was distant. 'I always understood that Italian men wanted nothing but sons.'

'Yes, Mummy,' Constance replied sharply, 'but as I've told you, Ludovico is not a typical Italian. He loves her.'

Nora changed tack. 'How's the business?' she asked, looking at a point just above Constance's head. 'Has it started making any money yet?'

'Come on, Mummy, it's far too early. But it will. Don't worry: your investment is safe.'

'I wasn't thinking of that,' Nora replied, with dignity, 'I just wondered if you were still having to live off hand-outs from Ludovico's mother.'

'Not handouts, exactly. Advances against the estate.'

'Well, they sound like handouts to *me*. At least when the old biddy dies, Ludovico will finally have sole control of everything. That's one good thing.'

Constance knew that she had to tell her mother about Carlo.

'Not quite,' she said in a voice she hoped was casual. 'He has a brother, you know: he's the black sheep of the family and he's been sort of banished but I suppose he'll have to have his share of the money.'

Nora merely said, 'When did you learn about him?'

'Oh,' Constance said, 'ages ago. It's no great secret.'

'What's he like?'

'I haven't met him.'

Constance was thankful for the brevity of her mother's response. 'Black sheep, eh?' was all she said. 'It seems you've married into quite a rum lot, Constance.'

She rolled up her napkin and stood up from the table. The subject was not mentioned again.


Constance proudly showed Margharita off at Seaton Cramer Hall. Miss Hatherby was entranced. As they walked across the lawns together, she was startled when Miss Hatherby stretched out her hand and clutching her arm said urgently, 'You *are* happy, aren't you, Constance? Truly happy?'

'Yes, of course,' Constance said, 'you know how much I love Italy.'

'And your marriage? You have adapted to the different attitudes of the Italian male?'

Constance laughed. 'Well, I'm learning to.'

They walked a few more steps in silence. Miss Hatherby stopped.

'I have always felt a deep shame over Nicholas's extraordinary behaviour. It seemed so out of character. Did he never contact you again, even briefly?'

Constance was touched by her distress. She realised that her friend felt that Nicky had betrayed the family name. 'Please don't worry about it,' she said. 'It really was just one of those things. At the time I was devastated. I wanted to die, I felt so betrayed. I can look back now and think that, as things have turned out, it was for the best. I was too much in awe of him. It would never have worked.'

Miss Hatherby took her hand.

'You are happy, aren't you, Constance?' she asked again.

'Yes,' Constance laughed to cover her embarrassment. 'Why do you ask?'

'I must be sure that Nicholas's behaviour has not had any permanent effects.'

She paused and looked down at Margharita.

'Forgive me, Constance. What a foolish question. Of course you are happy. How could you fail to be with such a perfectly beautiful daughter. Now,' her tone brightened, 'tell me all about your life in Florence. How you live, where you live, who you know. . . . I want to hear everything.'

Her eyes sparkled with enthusiasm but that did not stop Constance thinking, she knows. I can't hide it from her. She always could see right through me. She knows about Ludovico. I'm sure.

For a moment, she thought of telling her friend everything but, remembering what happened when she tried to enlist her help over Nora's affair, decided not to. Ludovico was her problem and hers alone. She would find a solution without help from anybody. Looking at Margharita, she knew that she must. Too much was at stake now to let her marriage fall apart. I know I can hold on to him, she thought fiercely as she drove Nora's little car away from Seaton Cramer Hall, trying to avoid the potholes in the drive.

A few days after Constance returned to Italy, Giancarlo gave a luncheon party. It was full of elegant women and sophisticated men and Constance, who had spent two very quiet weeks in Northumberland, was in her element. Although she thought most of them vacuous and self-absorbed she admired their ability to talk lightly on any subject. It was a gracious attribute she was determined to acquire, and she knew that she could. As she moved around, confident in a lime green silk dress with a pencil skirt, she met friendly faces and welcoming smiles. I belong here, she thought happily, this is my true world now. In the thick of the crowd, she half noticed out of the corner of her eye a particularly tight knot of fashionably dressed women, all chattering and laughing at once. She moved towards them. Suddenly, she recognised one of the harsh, gravelly voices. At that moment, the group parted and she was face to face with Gioella, who, as always, looked marvellous, with not a hair out of place. She was wearing a silk shirt in swirls of pink, orange, purple, fuchsia and peacock; her black velvet pants were cut as perfectly as a Guards' officer's and her fuchsia lipstick exactly matched the colour in her shirt. Constance immediately felt fat and dowdy. Her confidence of a moment ago evaporated. Despite herself, panic rose and a lump formed in her throat as Gioella stepped towards her.

'Constanza!' She smiled broadly and put out her arms in a generously enclosing gesture. 'My dear, congratulations. I hear you have produced a daughter. How clever of you to break all those generations of boring tradition by not having a son.'

Constance could feel her face turning scarlet but she knew she had to take a stand. It was a crucial moment.

'Oh, I don't think I can take all the credit,' she replied swiftly, determined to play this woman off at her own game. 'I've told Ludo, Italian women are so easily satisfied that he had allowed himself to become slack. But now he knows how demanding Englishwomen are, he's promised to try harder next time. Talking of my husband, I must go and rescue him. He's sure to be trapped in a corner by some sex-starved socialite – and he can never resist a gift handed him on a plate. Still, Gioella, what man can? But I'm sure I don't need to tell *you*, my darling!'

And she walked away, modestly pleased with herself and feeling the laughter bubble up in her as she crossed the room. Although it was only a very mild put-down, she glowed with superiority and felt ridiculously smug.

'My God! You're looking radiant!'

Constance stopped dead. Standing before her was Nicky Scott Wilson.

'What on earth are you doing here?' she cried.

'Oh,' he replied, languidly, 'they've sent me to Rome to look after Italian sales. You know what it's like . . . everything in the art world is becoming so international these days.'

'No, no!' Constance interrupted. 'Not here in Italy, but here, at this party. Who brought you?'

'Nobody. Giancarlo invited me.'

'But how?'

'Oh, my father told him I was coming over. They met when Giancarlo came over to Cambridge. My father was a fellow of his college. You know how it is . . .' he ended lamely but then, regalvanised, added, 'but it's absolutely super to see you again, old girl . . . and looking so good. I hear you're married and have a baby. Well done, I must say.'

She didn't know what to say. Nicky's sudden appearance had been a severe shock. She felt the tears coming to her eyes. 'Oh, Nicky,' she said.

'Sorry about the long silence, Constance. Just one of those things. Still think about you a lot.'

'I'm sorry,' she said.

'Who's the lucky man?' he asked, looking round the room. 'Aren't you going to introduce me?'

'Oh, Nicky, I can't. Not now.' She turned her head away to hide the tears. 'Please don't ask me. Another time.'

She was saved by Monica. 'He *has* to be English!' were her first words to Constance as she joined them. She laughed. 'You both look so damned Anglo-Saxon, you could be bookends standing here.'

Without waiting for Constance, who had still not recovered her poise, she stretched out her hand to Nicky and said, 'Monica Peterson. Now say something and let me hear those marvellous English vowels. They always remind me of cigar smoke and panelled libraries that go back for centuries!'

Nicky rose to the occasion. 'Why do Americans always make fun of the poor old Brits simply because we have tradition! It's not our fault we've been around for so long. We couldn't give away a history like ours, even if we tried.'

Constance said, 'Monica, this is Nicky Scott Wilson,

an old friend of mine. I think you'll find him quite entertaining for an Englishman.'

She moved away, looking for Ludovico. She had to leave. She couldn't cope with Nicky now; she had to give herself time to think. Blessing Monica for appearing at the right moment, she leant against the doorpost of a small antechamber and stood on tiptoe to search for Ludovico over the heads of the packed guests. The door was half ajar and as her eyes raked the crowd Constance recognised a voice in the next room. It was Bettina Bonoccorsi. She was about to push open the door and ask her if she had seen Ludo when she was stopped in mid-movement by mention of her own name.

'Constance has no idea at all, poor darling, but the affair with Monica is becoming very serious, I gather. She's decided not to go back to New York and he demands to see her at least three times a week. He's cunning, of course – a Villanuova characteristic, I can tell you, when mistresses are involved – so Constance probably won't find out but I'm damned sure that Gioella will and *then* the fun will begin! She plays second fiddle to nobody!'

# CHAPTER XI

Constance watched her husband as he undressed. Not a mark on his flesh or a change in his movements to betray the fact that he had two mistresses that she knew of and God knows how many others. She could hear Giancarlo's diplomatic tones '. . . it means nothing, my dear, nothing . . .' Did she have to deceive herself into believing that it meant nothing to her either? If this was marriage in the Italian way, would she just have to accept it? What else could she do? Her thoughts were desolate. They had a child. But more than that, she had her pride. She would not admit to Louise or her mother that the whirl-wind marriage had turned sour. She had already had a glimpse of what her mother's reaction would be and she was damned if she would give her the satisfaction of knowing she was right.

She shifted on her pillow as she watched Ludovico brushing his teeth. He was wearing only his pyjama bottoms and she saw the muscles on his torso flick as he swept the brush back and forth with deft, definite movements. A deep sadness came over her. He was so beautiful and she loved him so much. She wanted to cry out, 'You are everything to me. You are the beat of my heart,' but she remained silent, sunk in her unhappiness.

Why had it all gone wrong so soon? Was she too cold for him? Maybe she didn't know how to respond. She felt sure that Gioella would know how to excite him and she could understand that. She was, after all, a beautiful and sophisticated woman. But Monica? Constance couldn't imagine what her husband could possibly see in her. Big-titted Valkyrie, she thought viciously, as Ludovico came out of the bathroom and climbed into bed.

By distancing her mind from her body she found it easy enough to allow him to make love to her. She was even able to respond. His urgency amazed her. You'd think he hadn't seen a woman for at least a month, she thought cynically. No wonder they all fall flat on their backs.

If I cannot make my marriage work at least I'll make my mark as a businesswoman, Constance vowed.

With the contract for Portinari, it had become obvious that the present operation at Biaggibonsi must be expanded and she and Milva had already worked out how it should be done. Increasing the hat production was a step forward but even so, every time Constance went to Rome to visit Portinari she felt unfulfilled. She needed more. She had evolved a secret idea during her pregnancy. She decided that it was time to try it on Ludovico.

Going through the invoices one afternoon at the castle, she said to him, 'You know, Ludo, we actually made a reasonable profit in the last two months.'

He was sitting reading the newspaper and didn't look up. 'Really?' he asked in a voice completely empty of involvement.

'Yes,' Constance replied. His lack of interest irritated her. 'In fact, if things go on like this we'll soon have to think about taking on more girls.'

'No room,' he said flatly.

'Well, we'll just have to move to somewhere bigger, won't we?' she said.

Ludovico finally looked up. 'Isn't what you have enough for you?'

'No, it is not. This is just the beginning. I've been meaning to talk to you about this for some time. Now seems as good a moment as any. I want to start designing clothes. I'm convinced I can. I know a certain amount

272

about the fashion business from my days at Maison de Levantière. I'm sure I could make a success of it.' Her eyes were alight with enthusiasm.

'I'm afraid you probably could,' Ludovico replied.

'What do you mean, you're *afraid*? How typical of you, Ludo, to try to dash my enthusiasm. You won't let anything disturb your cosy little world, will you? You'd rather I did nothing but just sit around all day. Just because you have no ambition, you can't bear anybody else to have it. Well, don't think your lack of interest will stop me. I intend to achieve something with my life – whether you approve or not.'

'Constanza,' Ludovico replied in exasperation, 'you have our daughter to look after. That should be enough. You cannot become so involved in business matters. Your first duty to our marriage is to be a good mother.'

Constance lost her temper. '*My* duty? What of *yours*? Do you think Margharita only deserves a good mother? What about her father? Do you think an erring husband makes a good father? Are you afraid that if you turn your back Monica might run back to New York? Why not bring her up here with you? I'm sure your mother would be very interested to meet her.'

Ludovico was shocked. 'What on earth are you talking about?' he demanded.

Constance had an unreal sense of calm and detachment. She was determined to let him know that she was aware of his affair with Monica, and to do so without losing her temper.

'Don't you think that the pretence should stop?' she asked him. 'I know all about Gioella *and* Monica. Florence is too small – and your friends are far too gossipy for you to be able to keep these things secret.'

Instead of defending or explaining himself, Ludovico retorted, 'What do you expect? Don't you think I have the right to seek comfort? What sort of a wife have you proved to be? You are more interested in a load of hats than you are in me. Don't you ever think that I need some care? If you gave me half the time and thought that you give to your business I wouldn't need to look elsewhere. You would rather talk to that peasant woman than be with me.'

'Ludovico, you cannot be jealous of Milva! I talk to her about the business – something you refuse to discuss.'

'Your place is with me, not down in Biaggibonsi all day.'

'I am not there all day.'

'I thought when you started this business you would set it up and then leave it to others.'

'I can think of no quicker way to lose my mother's money.'

'Your mother's money! Is that all you can think of? Does it never occur to you that I married so that I might have some company?'

'You can't seriously be suggesting that I spend all my days dancing attendance on you!'

'But I *want* you to dance attendance! Don't you understand! That is why you are here! That is what marriage is for!'

'Not for me, Ludovico,' Constance replied. 'You are my husband and shall remain so. But I am an individual and I mean to stay one. No matter what you do, I will always love you, but I will not be your doormat. I'm going to take charge of *my* life so that I can make a life for *our* daughter. We need money and so will she, so stop being an ostrich. If you don't like my business that is your problem, not mine.'

'You see, Giancarlo,' Constance explained over lunch, 'in a strange way I don't care about the infidelities. At least, not all of the time. What I cannot bear is his indifference towards the business because that is really an indifference to me as an individual. Despite everything, I still love him – but I am determined to be independent of him. I know I can design clothes – and I want to, more than anything in the world. But I need your help.'

274

Giancarlo was slightly embarrassed at Constance's intensity but her plans intrigued him. He was flattered that she wanted him to be part of them. He gave her his full attention.

'How much money do you think it will require?' he asked.

'Oh, I don't think the money is so difficult. What I need your help with, above all, is finding people who can work for me. Especially a good, practical designer who knows how to cut – who can make my ideas into clothes.'

Giancarlo was impressed at Constance's business sense and, though he felt slightly disloyal to Ludovico, he agreed to become a sleeping partner in the venture.

'You will share the profits, of course, and receive interest on the capital sum,' she said.

'At what rate?'

'What do you feel would be right?' Constance asked guardedly.

'Perhaps two and a half per cent?' he ventured.

There was a pause.

'Two and a quarter.' Her reply was decisive. He was surprised at her boldness but smiled in agreement. Giancarlo knew that money was important to Constance and, sensing that she wouldn't give way, declined to haggle.

'You won't regret it,' Constance assured him, 'and, please, don't worry about Ludo. I know I can cope with what we're going through. You see, I love him – and my love will bring us through.'

'I know he still loves you,' Giancarlo responded eagerly. 'These little affairs. They really don't – '

'I know, I know!' Constance interrupted. 'They don't mean a thing. I'll try to remember that,' and she smiled as she leant across the table and grasped Giancarlo's hand.

It was clear that a fashion business could not be based in the remote Italian countryside. Constance knew that she must find a property in Florence as a base for the firm, but first she and Ludovico needed somewhere to live in the city. Since the last days of her pregnancy they had been more or less permanently based at the castle. Constance hated its brooding atmosphere. Despite her happy memories of Santo Spirito, it was impossible to return there with a baby. Savognia managed to find them a small flat on the banks of the Arno, with a terrace overlooking the river. It belonged to a friend who had gone to South America for a year. Constance moved in with Margharita, a nanny and one maid, leaving Ludovico at the castle until she was settled in.

I wonder who he'll have up there first? Constance speculated, although she knew the answer. She had no doubt that Gioella would already be there. The thought pained her but she pushed it out of her mind.

Savognia had agreed with Constance that, although the dress business must be located in Florence, it would be madness to move the hat factory there when all the trained workforce was up in Biaggibonsi. However, she wanted Milva by her side. She went up alone to the Marche to talk to her.

'I know it's a great upheaval for you, Milva,' she said, 'but I need you to set up the Florence operation on the right lines. Please say that you'll come.'

'What of here, little one? Who will look after things here?'

'I wondered about Concetta.'

Milva considered for a moment. 'Yes,' she said slowly, 'she could do it, but I think that Rosa would be better. Concetta is creative and such a job would waste her talents. Rosa is not. She is reliable and thorough. She does not have the imagination to get us into trouble.'

Both women laughed.

'You are not married, Milva,' Constance went on. 'Do you think that some day you might wish to marry a village boy?'

Milva shook her head decisively. 'No, signora. I have five brothers, each one more stupid than the other. I have seen enough of men to know that Milva is much better off without them. It is my mother I worry about, signora. She is old and needs me.'

'How old?'

'Fifty-four.'

Constance was shocked at how quickly endless pregnancies aged Italian peasant women. She knew from previous conversations that Milva had four sisters as well as her brothers.

'But you could send her money. I would pay you well. And you could return to see her frequently.'

She could tell that Milva was attracted to the idea but something still held her back.

'I will give you whatever you want,' she said.

Milva looked directly at her. 'It would not work.'

'Why not?'

'Your husband, signora, does not like me. Up here it does not matter so much but in Florence it would.'

'My husband won't be involved in Florence, Milva,' Constance said, expressing a thought that had hardly been formed until now. As she spoke, she knew it was true: if a dress house were to be successful, it would have to exist quite separately from her married life.

She could tell by Milva's face that she would come and she returned to Florence in high spirits. With Milva as her right-hand woman the dress house *would* be a success, she was certain.


Constance was woken by the telephone. She picked it up quickly before it could disturb Margharita, asleep in the adjacent room. She had been in the new apartment only two days and few people knew her telephone number so she wasn't surprised to hear Ludovico's voice. He was at the castle.

'When are you bringing Margharita back?' he asked.

Constance suddenly felt sorry for him.

'Oh! I've almost finished here. Things are going so well. Provided we find a good designer we might just have a collection ready for next season.'

'How is Florence?'

'Oh, simply beautiful, my darling,' Constance replied enthusiastically. 'I took Margharita along the banks of the Arno yesterday and it was a perfect April day. You know, warm and sunny but fresh – like Northumberland in summer.'

'It's still cold here,' Ludovico replied plaintively.

Why are we exchanging these platitudes? Constance wondered. Why has he phoned? Perhaps Gioella has left and he's bored? Her heart gave a little leap at the thought that he might not have invited his mistress to the castle after all.

Before she could say anything Ludovico said, 'My mother fell from her platform yesterday,' adding hastily, 'she's all right. She didn't break anything and the doctor says there are no problems, but she refuses to leave her bed. She insists on seeing you.'

'Me? What on earth for?' Constance asked in panic.

'She won't tell me. She treats me like a child. Why does everyone treat me like a child?' Ludovico cried in frustration.

As she was dressing, Constance repeated the question. Why, indeed, did even she think of her husband as a child – immature, requiring instant gratification and shunning responsibility?

No one had ever wanted Ludovico to grow up. They had all loved him for the joy of his young looks. And now it was too late. He was stunted for ever. Not that she could condemn all the people who endlessly indulged him. After all, wasn't she insulting Ludovico more than anybody? As his wife, she should hate the thought of Gioella and Monica and yet now she couldn't. In a strange way that she was hardly prepared to admit to herself, she was grateful that they kept Ludovico out of her hair and enabled her to get on with the infinitely exciting affairs of business. When it's all set up, Ludo, my darling, she promised, I'll take you back and care for you. I know how much you need me to give you strength. I really do.

278

I won't let Gioella destroy you – and I won't share you with her or anybody. I'd rather lose you for ever.

The greater part of her newly acquired business woman's aplomb slid away from Constance as she drove through the huge arched entrance to the castle. Why do these walls make me feel so nervous? she wondered irritably as she crossed the cobbled courtyard, conscious that she was being observed by unseen eyes. Every stone of this castle breathes the Principessa Maria-Angelina, that's why, she answered herself crossly. Her anger was a way of keeping up her spirits. She was deeply unnerved by this call to the castle and dreaded what new revelations Ludovico's mother would make.

She hadn't long to wait. Within an hour of her arrival, she was called by Maria-Angelina's servant. She followed her, alone, to the Principessa's bedroom. With every step her heart faltered. As the huge door at the end of the corridor swung open, Constance was conscious of the close smell of the sickroom. The room was lit by a small lamp. The bed was so high that three steps were necessary to enable the Principessa to climb into it. To steady her nerves, Constance focused on the steps before allowing her eyes to rise to the bed and confront Maria-Angelina, who sat bolt upright against a pile of lace pillows, her eyes sparkling with an unnatural brilliance and her face flushed with high colour. As she was waved forward, Constance realised with a start that Maria-Angelina was wearing gloves.

The Principessa began to talk with great urgency and intensity. Constance was struck by how much slower her voice had become.

'I have called you here,' Marie-Angelina began, 'because there are things that must be decided. Family things.'

Has she had a mild stroke? Constance wondered, as the Principessa paused and pressed her gloved hands to her nose.

'But first, things must be known.'

Constance's heart sank.

'I am telling you because Ludovico would not understand. He thinks like a child. The Villanuova future must be placed in firmer hands. I will die soon. Not yet, but before the year is ended. It is essential that you understand the finances of the estates because it is you who must safeguard them.'

'But I don't want to,' Constance surprised herself by saying. 'They are Ludovico's responsibility. I have my business to run. I cannot do everything.'

'Business?' Maria-Angelina snorted. 'What is business compared with a hierarchy? The Villanuovas have been a dominant family in Italy for centuries and must continue so. Although it is a male line, most of the men have been tainted. Generation after generation have fallen victim to lust. The devil has them all by the tail. They surely perish as their time ends. But the Villanuova line continues, borne up and sustained by the women they marry and who shoulder the responsibility. We wives and mothers have a destiny that we cannot avoid. Do not think that you can hide from what you must do. I knew the moment I saw you that you were right for the task. God has cursed the Villanuova men with weakness, yet he has saved them by helping them to choose strong women. Even,' she added with disdain, 'foreign women.'

Constance looked at her coldly. She was determined that the future of her business would not be jeopardised, no matter what this woman might say.

'Hand me the ledger,' the Principessa ordered. Constance placed the heavy leather-bound book on the bed.

Opening it the old woman began. 'I intend to regularise the position. I will not countenance you living in a rented flat in Florence whilst Ludovico wastes his time up here. You must buy a suitable house and continue to live together. But you alone must control the money. I have never allowed Ludovico to have any real money in his hands because I always knew that it would cause mischief.

Nevertheless, there *is* money and you shall have it. Next, you must produce a male child, who will be a true heir to the Villanuova legacies. And he must be called Manfredo.'

Constance bridled. It was one thing for her mother-in-law to order her to breed, but to insist on the names of her children was altogether too much to accept. Maria-Angelina read her thoughts.

'It is the Villanuova tradition. All first sons are called either Ludovico, Carlo or Manfredo. Has Ludovico not even told you that? The names alternate. My husband, Ludovico's father, was the second son. His brother, the heir, was called Ludovico but he was killed in the First World War. That is why my husband inherited. Our first-born was next in line for the name Carlo and we called our second son Ludovico – although we could just as easily have used the name Manfredo – except that we knew that our grandson must be christened Manfredo, to carry on the tradition of the alternating three names for the first-born. So, you see, you must produce a male and he must be called Manfredo. I cannot believe,' she added disparagingly, 'that you are capable of producing only female children.'

'Does Ludovico have any say in this?' Constance enquired.

'Ludovico must be taught his duty,' Maria-Angelina replied, 'and it is you who must do it.'

There was silence and when she spoke again her voice had softened.

'Mistresses are the curse of the Villanuovas. They cannot be eradicated but they can be controlled. They must not be allowed to overshadow our duties. We, the wives who wait and suffer, have our role – and it is one that cannot be avoided. There *must* be a male heir,' she insisted as, languidly sniffing her fingers, she closed her eyes to indicate that the interview was over.

Constance was impressed. She knows everything that is going on, she thought, as she left the bedroom. Nothing escapes her – Gioella, Monica. I bet she knows everything about them.

Villa Andreoli was a mile above Giancarlo's house in Fiesole. Although it did not command the same fabulous views, there were tall meadows, wizened olive trees and dark pines enough to satisfy Constance's romantic dreams of the perfect Mediterranean landscape. From the moment Savognia took her to see it, she felt that Villa Andreoli could be a home. Walking the overgrown terraces, she looked down on the neglected gardens and visualised the cocktail and luncheon parties she and Ludovico would have. She was excited. Inside, the house was exactly right. A broad, marble-paved hallway ran throughout its length. Off it were the *salotto*, with its large double windows looking down across the valley; the dining room, with its seventeenth-century painted ceiling; and the library with its intricate marquetry woodwork. At the very end, a magnificent sweep of shallow marble steps branched out, leading to the bedrooms above. The building was down-at-heel, having been commandeered by German officers during the war, but structurally sound, and Constance was determined not only to have it but to furnish it with style and taste.

Ludovico became involved in the plans with an enthusiasm Constance had not seen since the early days of their marriage. As they combed the castle, deciding what pieces to take to the villa, she was constantly surprised by what she called the Savognia side of his character. Time and again, she was struck by his effortless taste and learning.

'Oh, no, Constanza,' he would say when she had picked out an item of furniture, 'it is too nineteenth-century. It is wrong for the proportions of the room.' She had to admit that he was always right.

'You should be in the antiques business,' she said to him after he had rejected a particular Venetian mirror because it was inappropriate for the paintings he had already chosen.

'Business, business!' Ludovico cried. 'No more business, I beg you, Constanza! It is all so boring, this business you always talk of. Why can't you enjoy things without always wanting to turn them into business?'

'But I thought you loved it when we started to get the hats made in the village.'

'Did I? That was different. We were enjoying ourselves. It was exciting but it wasn't serious. We used to laugh in those days. Now it's just business: very serious, all about money, nothing about enjoyment. Don't you see, Constanza, it is no longer fun.'

'I never wanted it to be only *fun*,' Constance said. 'You don't put all that work into something that is only a pastime. Can't you see that? It can't be fun if it is to be successful and if it isn't successful, why do it? Surely you can see that?'

Even as she asked, she knew the answer. Ludovico's smile was sad as he turned back to the job of selecting pieces for their new home.

Constance took some time to find the courage to face Nicky. Eventually, she invited him to Fiesole for lunch on a Saturday when Ludovico was at the castle. Looking at him now, she found it hard to imagine what she had once seen in him. He struck her as mannered and languid and his looks could not compare with Ludo's dark glamour. A ghost was laid. Nicky Scott Wilson was too bland and predictable to have held her attention as a lover. As they chatted over lunch, however, Constance warmed to Nicky as a friend. Like Louise, he held views predictably English. She knew that she could rely on him to confirm her sanity when she was thrown off guard by Ludovico's Italian logic. She decided to cement their relationship by broaching the subject neither had yet mentioned.

'Am I forgiven?' she asked.

Nicky half smiled. 'For what? Marriage?'

She nodded, not quite sure what it was she needed forgiveness for. Why did she feel guilty? She had done nothing wrong. Nicky had known perfectly well that she was going to join her aunt in Italy.

'I suppose that, despite all, when it came to the point, neither of us cared enough,' she said. 'We just let our love drift apart.'

'It all seemed to happen so quickly,' Nick said, 'and you were so angry that I had not mentioned my aunt. It made me feel hopeless,' he ended, lamely. There was a silence. 'I really loved you, old girl,' he murmured.

'And I loved *you*, then,' she replied.

'Was it a rebound job?'

'What do you mean?'

'Well, did you marry Ludovico in order to completely shake me off? You know, fresh start, and all that.'

'I married Ludo because I loved him, Nicky. There was no other reason.'

If Nicky was to be her friend, Constance knew that there must be no looking back. She wanted him to accept her as she was now.

'I can understand why,' Nicky said gallantly, 'he's a handsome man and everyone tells me that he's charming.'

Constance stiffened, wondering what else Nicky had been told.

'Who do you know in Florence – or in Italy, for that matter?' she asked, changing the subject. 'Who has Giancarlo introduced you to?'

She was interrupted by the telephone.

'The maid's out with Margharita,' Constance said, 'I'll have to answer.'

She crossed the terrace and went into the villa. She was away some time and, when she re-emerged, Nicky was shocked. She had gone deathly white and her hands were shaking. Before he had time to say anything she spoke in a faltering voice.

'That was Giancarlo,' she said. 'There's been an accident. Near the castle. Ludo is in hospital. He's not badly hurt – only a broken leg and concussion, but his passenger is dead. She was a friend of his called Gioella. Did you ever meet her?'

The accident had happened shortly after nine that morning. Gioella and Ludovico were returning to Florence to spend the weekend in Giancarlo's flat for one night, en route to join him on Capri. Gioella had recently bought a new sports car and Ludovico had persuaded her to let him drive. It was a beautiful morning and, once out of the village, they had stopped to let down the roof before continuing along the twisty lanes, down the valley and up the other side. Cresting the hills, Ludovico pressed hard on the accelerator as they rushed towards the next valley. He knew the road so well that he didn't bother to slow at corners. There was rarely any traffic on these roads, especially so early. Gioella's headscarf tugged in the wind but her dark glasses protected her eyes as she leant forward and fiddled with the controls of the car radio; it was the first one she had owned and it was her pride and joy. All she could get was a high-pitched crackling.

'Change the station!' Ludovico shouted.

'I don't know how to!' she yelled back against the wind. He leant over and began to fiddle but kept one hand firmly on the wheel.

As they approached a sharp curve, an old man suddenly appeared from a gap in the wall. He was leading a mule carrying panniers laden with straw. The mule ambled across the road. Gioella's scream made Ludovico look up from the radio, just as he had found the station. It was too late to stop. He swung the wheel to avoid hitting the mule's hindquarters and went straight into a skid. The car spun off the road, half climbed the wall and toppled back into a ditch. The impact with the wall threw Ludovico clean over it into the field but Gioella was trapped underneath the car as it skidded to a halt. Her neck was broken. In the eerie silence that followed the crash, the only sound the terrified peasant could hear above the aimlessly spinning wheels was a man's voice singing. Amazingly, the radio continued to play. Not stopping to

285

look at the bodies, he abandoned his mule and ran home to the village to the sound of Tony Dallara singing 'Come Prima', Gioella's favourite song.

When Constance arrived at the castle at midnight Ludovico was in bed, sound asleep, his head tightly bandaged, his leg in a splint. She was ushered into the bedroom by a nun. Constance assumed that she had been brought in to nurse Ludo on the principle that his brow should be smoothed by a surrogate hand of God.

'He has been given a sleeping draught, signora,' the nun whispered.

Constance ignored her. Her anger was aroused. Above the bed hung a crucifix with a rosary draped around it. Constance stepped forward, snatched it from the wall and, ignoring the nun's horrified gasp, threw it into the wastepaper basket. She wanted to shake the nun, who stood quaking before her, but merely said quietly, 'You may leave first thing tomorrow morning. I shall look after my husband from now on. Now you may go to bed.'

After the terrified woman had closed the door, Constance began to shake. She gripped the bedpost to steady herself. She could hardly bear to look at Ludovico with his bruised and cut face, the white bandage emphasising the unhealthy yellow of his skin in the artificial light. There were deep shadows under his eyes and as she looked closer Constance noticed a speck of dried blood on the lid of the left one. She took her handkerchief, spat on it, and gently rubbed it across the lid. Ludovico moaned slightly in his sleep but did not wake. Constance began to cry. 'Oh, my beautiful, broken Ludo. What have you done to yourself?' she sobbed.

She sat by his side all night, determined that when he opened his eyes she would be the first thing he saw. She didn't sleep. Contradictory and confusing thoughts ran through her head and she was unable to isolate and pin them down. She felt a guilty relief that Gioella was dead but was horrified at the manner of her death; shocked that Ludovico had been responsible for the accident but thankful that he had been driving, otherwise he might have been the one crushed under the car.

Shortly after dawn, Ludovico's eyes flickered open. She grasped his hand and just had time to whisper 'Ludo' before he slid back into his drugged sleep. Knowing that he had registered her presence, she was happy to leave the bedside and go to the bathroom to prepare herself for what she knew would be the inevitable call from Maria-Angelina.

It came even more promptly than she had expected. At seven thirty the Principessa's servant timidly knocked on the door and informed Constance that she was required.

Constance felt nervous but not intimidated as she made her way to the Principessa's quarters and stepped into the darkened room. Though she was lying in bed, Constance could tell immediately that Maria-Angelina was tense with rage. She began to speak even before the servant had left the room.

'How dare you defile the ancestral home of the Castelfranco di Villanuova family?' she demanded. 'How dare your blasphemous hands remove the crucifix placed above my son's bed at my express command? How dare you dismiss Sister Seraphina, whom I had personally instructed to tend my son?'

Constance could not control her own anger. 'I am Ludovico's wife,' she retorted. 'I don't need to ask your permission for anything that concerns my husband.'

'You are a guest in my home, uninvited and unwelcome. How dare you attempt to come between him and his God?'

'His God! Are you mad? Ludovico has no God. The only thing he worships is his prick. That and that alone, Principessa, and if you don't know that, you know nothing of your son. I am taking Ludo back to Florence with me and you can't stop me. He is mine now and his life is nothing to do with you!'

'Nothing! Nothing! How dare you speak that way to

me, you godless Englishwoman? I insist that he stays where he is.'

'I'm sorry, Principessa, he is returning to Florence with me. You can insist on nothing any more.'

The Principessa heaved herself up in the bed. 'Stop!' she cried. 'You must hear me. Ludovico must remain here until he is recovered. Not for my sake, but for yours. We do not know how seriously his head has been damaged. It could be dangerous to move him. Dangerous for your children yet to be born.'

'What on earth do you mean?'

'You recall what I told you about my other son, Carlo? The dreadful deed in the nursing home? You recall whose child it was?'

Constance felt afraid.

'There is a history of idiocy in the Villanuova line,' the Principessa continued, in little more than a whisper. 'Ludovico's child by that woman was not the first. My husband also had a bastard who was an idiot. He was called Giulio.'

She paused. Constance was shocked at the revelation but before she could speak the Principessa went on, 'You have still to produce an heir. I beg you, take no risk with Ludovico's mental health. The results could be terrible for you and for the Villanuovas. He must remain still until there have been tests.'

Constance knew that the woman was talking medical nonsense, but she was tired. Confused by the family deceits, treacheries and hidden history, she found herself agreeing to wait for a few more days before moving Ludovico.

Giancarlo appeared at nine thirty that morning. He had driven through the night. Constance took him straight to see Ludovico, who was still sleeping.

'He's been sedated,' she explained. 'God knows what that crazy nun has given him. Oh! Giancarlo . . .' and she told him of her row with Maria-Angelina and the fears for Ludovico's mental health.

Giancarlo did not comment. Instead he said, 'I must go down to Cadestino, in order to identify Gioella. I shall make arrangements for the body and then I shall return and pay my respects to the Principessa.'

Constance walked down to the courtyard with Giancarlo. He was about to step into his car when she said, 'Wait! I'm coming with you.'

His disapproval and embarrassment showed on his face. He flushed with anger but before he could say anything she had moved round to the passenger side and was opening the door.

'I want to see her,' she said.

'Constanza, this is most irregular and unseemly. Quite apart from her relationship with Ludovico, I do not think that you should be present. Women do not do this in my country. This is disagreeable work. Man's work.'

'Well,' Constance replied, stepping into the car, 'in my country women do what they feel they must, exactly as men do in Italy.'

Giancarlo started the car without a word.

The tiny hospital in Cadestino was faded and down-at-heel, as was the skeletal official from the coroner's office, who had dressed up especially in his dark suit to meet them. He was accompanied by the policeman who had gone to the scene of the crash – a man whose broad country face seemed to Constance only one stage advanced from imbecility. She and Giancarlo were ushered into a fly-blown little office with considerable deference. It was her first exposure to provincial Italian officialdom and its cringing respect for the social hierarchy. Both men seemed to enjoy grovelling before Savognia. No remark was made to him, no question answered, without his title being used.

When the preliminary discussion was over, Giancarlo turned to Constance. 'Constanza,' he said in English, 'I have to go to the body now. Please stay here, I beg you.'

The sincerity in his voice caught her unawares and she

was ready to agree, but he spoilt it by adding, 'It really is not for women.'

'I have as much right as you, Giancarlo.'

'Constanza, I do it merely because Grignano is in Chicago and the body must be identified in order that things can proceed. I know you will regret this.'

'I shall come,' she said firmly.

Savognia was right. The attempts to tidy up Gioella's body had been crude and inexpert. Constance took one look and, clutching her throat, stepped back in horror. She staggered into the corridor, dizzy and sick, and leant against the wall to steady herself. She thought she would faint. None of the men came to her aid. It was their way of showing disapproval of her temerity in trespassing on a male preserve. Constance would never forget the horrible angle of Gioella's head, nor her broken arms and shattered ribs. But the clearest and most shocking picture she took away was of the fingers. They had been snapped like twigs and their splintered bones stuck out like the prongs of a fork. Gioella's crushed wedding ring hung from a blood-stained finger. Constance knew that the image would haunt her for ever.

As Savognia drove her back to the castle in silence, Constance thought of Gioella's bruised and torn face with a mixture of pity and admiration. Even at nine o'clock in the morning in the remotest countryside, it had been made up as immaculately as if Gioella had been invited to a grand diplomatic reception in Rome. It seemed to symbolise the futility and the magnificence of the woman.

Less than a week later the funeral took place in the town in Piedmont where Gioella had been born. Although he was still suffering from dizzy spells and required sedatives at night, Ludovico was determined to attend. When Constance tried to dissuade him, he became hysterical and she gave in from fear that to deny him would do more harm. However, she insisted on accompanying him and this he accepted.

It was the first Italian funeral Constance had attended and she was impressed by its pomp and provincial grandeur. The church was full, and the narrow street up to it lined with old women in black, who had come to see the mourners and reflect on the grave's indifference to wealth and power.

Death betrayed the secret of Gioella's past. For all her sophistication and international gloss, Gioella di Grignano had been born a lower-middle-class provincial girl who had, by luck and beauty, leapt all social barriers. Her father was the local postman; her uncles were farmers, pig breeders and policemen. The family was overawed but gratified by the importance of the mourners – the princes, counts, industrialists and members of Parliament who shuffled awkwardly into the small church.

Constance entered between Savognia and Ludovico, whose head was still thickly bandaged. She put her arm through his to try to stop him shaking. As they sat silently waiting for the coffin, she looked round at the mourners. Her eye was caught by a man standing near the main door. He wore heavy dark glasses, yet Constance thought that she recognised him. She was about to ask Savognia who he was when the organ began to play and the service commenced. When the coffin was finally carried out and the congregation turned to face the door, the man was no longer there. Constance eagerly scanned the mourners' faces, but he was nowhere to be seen.

As they left the church, she became convinced that the man in the sunglasses had been as aware of her as she had of him.

'Did you notice a man in dark glasses?' she asked Giancarlo, as they walked down the dusty road to the cemetery.

'No,' he said, so quickly that she knew he was lying. Many of the mourners were in dark glasses; Savognia had clearly recognised the man she referred to. Why was he not prepared to acknowledge it? Constance knew without any doubt. The man she had seen was Ludovico's brother,

Carlo. She had the uncanny feeling that he came solely to look at her.

After the funeral, Savognia took a group of mourners to a restaurant for what Constance found a long and socially uneasy meal. She was trapped in a corner with Monica, listening to Bettina Bonoccorsi. Bettina drank whisky steadily throughout the meal. Constance noticed two bright pink spots appearing on her cheeks as she became increasingly argumentative with everyone around her. She suddenly turned to Constance with narrowed eyes and said, 'I feel so sorry for poor Ludo. How will he stand up in court? It looks very grim for him.'

Constance was alarmed. 'Court! What do you mean? Ludo won't have to appear in court, surely?'

'He killed a woman, didn't he?' Bettina replied harshly. 'What do you think the authorities will do? Pat him on the head and tell him not to be naughty again? I don't think so, my dear. No, little Ludo is in big trouble this time,' she went on vindictively, 'and it'll take a lot more than that famous boyish charm if he's to talk his way out of this mess.'

Constance was speechless at the hatred in Bettina's voice.

'He's always been able to wriggle out of his responsibilities far too easily,' Bettina continued. 'It's about time he was forced to live up to the consequences of his actions.'

'It wasn't his fault,' Constance almost shouted, 'the man's mule walked right in front of the car. There was nothing he could do.'

'Not at the speed he was travelling, I'm sure,' Bettina said, 'but we have laws against speeding, you know, just as you have in England.'

Constance was too distressed to reply.

'Bettina, I think you've said enough,' Monica intervened. 'You know full well that nothing will happen to Ludo and it has nothing to do with boyish charm. In

Italy, people of Ludo's class never have to face the consequences – even if there were any to face.'

She looked across the smoke-filled room. 'These sort of people don't have to worry.'

Constance recalled the servile officials who dealt with Giancarlo at the hospital. She knew Monica was right.

'Poor Gioella,' Bettina said, 'it's her I'm sorry for. What a way to end.'

'Women like Gioella always end badly,' Monica said, with what Constance considered shocking insensitivity considering her own relations with Ludovico.

'Not that badly, for God's sake, with their heads almost sliced off.'

'It was probably for the best,' Monica continued, as if Constance wasn't there. 'Her life was on the skids. Her infatuation with Ludo was like a sickness. She was self-destructive. She had no discipline. I've heard rumours that Grignano was going to kick her out.'

'It wouldn't have made any difference,' Bettina replied, 'she would have found somebody else to look after her.'

Her voice rose belligerently. 'I'll tell you what I damn well admired about Gioella, if you want to know. She started with nothing and she fucked her way to the top. And that's what I call style.'

There was complete silence in the room, then everyone started to talk at once, as Savognia crossed to their table and led the sobbing Bettina out of the restaurant.

# CHAPTER 12

Constance did not stay at the castle with Ludovico. She could not bear to be away from the business for too much time. She returned alone to Florence and it was ten days before Ludovico was brought to the city by Giancarlo. After seeing him into bed, Constance had a drink with Savognia.

'I think I've found your man,' he said.

Constance's mind flew back to the funeral and the mysterious stranger.

'And is he . . .' she began eagerly.

'Florentine?' Savognia said. 'No, he's a Neapolitan but he has worked in Rome – with Portinari, in fact. I don't know what he would feel about moving up here but I have no doubt that he is the designer for you. He is recognised to have enormous talent, but he's difficult. Actually, Portinari sacked him last year, after endless quarrels. Giuseppe Padone is a notoriously volatile character but he is also considered a genius.'

'How old is he?'

'Twenty-four.'

'How did you find him?'

'Oh, he's well enough known. He's a friend of Monica.'

'Do you think I should see him?'

'Yes, if you are prepared to accept that he will want a large measure of control.'

'Well, we can talk about that.'

To Savognia's irritation, Constance decided to meet

Giuseppe Padone alone. She invited him to lunch at Tre Bocce, her favourite restaurant, where she could be sure of a discreetly quiet table. Remembering Padone's reputation as a temperamental character, she was on her guard as she waited for him, having ensured that she would be at the table first. She was dressed entirely in black, in the hope that she would impress him as a businesswoman.

She was studying the menu when she suddenly became aware that a silence had descended on the buzz of conversation around her. She looked up, catching a glimpse of the woman at the next table who had stopped, fork in mid-air, and was gazing intently towards the door and the man who stood there. The waiter motioned him towards Constance's table.

As Giuseppe Padone approached, the eyes of everybody in the restaurant followed him. Although not conventionally handsome, he was dark and brooding, with a nervous intensity that acted like a magnet on the diners. His movements exuded a louche sexuality as, ambiguous and ambivalent, he strode easily across the restaurant. Constance felt that he could probably have anyone in the room he wanted – and something in his demeanour suggested that he knew it. As he neared the table, the looks also focused on her. Constance was aware of their hostility.

Giuseppe Padone stopped before her and gazed, unsmiling, into her eyes. The effect was devastating. He was every woman's dream of the half-starved, glowing-eyed Romantic poet. She shook his hand, noticing how soft – almost feminine – his touch was, and thought that Giuseppe Padone had a sensitivity at odds with his blatant sexuality. To her embarrassment, she could feel herself blushing . . .

As he sat down, Constance reached forward for her glass and in her confusion knocked it over. Swabbing up the water with his napkin, he grinned – and his face was transformed. The scowling seriousness vanished and he became a little boy, full of charm. Constance had been thrown completely off balance. She cursed Savognia for not warning her of what to expect, but she was being unfair to him. Giancarlo Savognia was probably the only person in Florence impervious to Padone's dangerous charm.

Constance knew that if she did not get the upper hand immediately, she would be lost. She started on business straight away.

'You know of my plans for a small fashion house, I believe, Signor Padone?'

'*Si.*'

Despite Constance's assumed air of sophistication, Padone's appearance had destroyed her confidence and the conversation could have floundered there and then had the waiter not appeared and given him a menu. Watching him study it, she was struck even more forcibly by his resemblance to a beautiful, nervous animal. She thought, This is a mistake, I must take charge before he does.

'What do you know of me, Signor Padone?' she asked.

'Nothing,' he replied, 'except that you are an English-woman and you make hats that Portinari thinks quite highly of.'

'Do you know my hats?'

'No.'

'But the Principe Savognia has spoken of them?'

'The Principe Savognia told me you were looking for a designer. That is why I am here.'

'That is not entirely correct. I need a collaborator. Someone who can interpret my ideas.'

He pushed back his chair. 'I am sorry, signora,' he said, as he made to get up, 'I am a designer, not a collaborator.'

'Please,' she replied, 'don't leave. At least let us talk and eat the meal we have ordered.'

He hesitated. She smiled.

'Of course,' he said, blushing slightly. 'I am sorry.'

'My hats are good,' Constance went on. 'I would like to use them as the basis for a collection of clothes. What do you think of that idea?'

'Do you really want to know?'

'Yes, that is why I asked.'

'*Mi scusi*, signora, but it is ridiculous.'

Constance could feel her cheeks burning. She said nothing.

'You are mistaken, signora. No fashion can ever start with hats. They follow the line of the clothes.'

'But I am known for my hats.'

'Really? Well *I*, signora, am known for my line.'

He lit a cigarette and blew the smoke across the table, making no attempt to avoid Constance's face. He grinned the same infectious, cheeky grin and it took the sting from his insolent gesture.

'Why don't you design the clothes yourself, if your hats are so good?'

'I have to run the business – and I have a small daughter to look after. My husband is recovering from an accident. I have strong ideas about how the line should be but I need someone who knows the technical side of dressmaking to help me, someone who knows how to cut and can tell the workrooms what to do.'

'I, signora, am not a dressmaker, nor a messenger boy. I am a tailor.' He stubbed the cigarette out neatly as the waiter arrived with their orders.

'That is perfect.'

'Yes, but above all, I am a designer – and that is the role you wish to keep for yourself.'

They ate in silence for a few moments. Constance liked Padone's integrity in making it clear what he wanted. And she found that she liked his personality. He was obviously strong. That was good. She liked strong characters and knew that they were essential for success in the fashion business. And yet, there was something about his intensity that made her wary. She tried to provoke him.

'Are you so arrogant that you would resent any criticism?'

'Absolutely.'

She could not help herself: she burst out laughing at his preposterous egotism. He laughed with her.

'*Scusi*, signora, but I am an artist. I cannot compromise. You see, we start from different points. You wish to make money, I wish to create beauty. We can both follow our own path if we work together but only if you have faith that my pursuit of beauty will make possible your pursuit of wealth. That faith – and only that faith – can stop you interfering. I am blunt, but you must know, signora, if you interfere with a designer you do not end up with a collection. You are left with a fruit pudding. Now, would you like to see my sketches?'

His aplomb unnerved Constance. He had taken complete control and she had no idea how to regain the upper hand. She nodded her agreement. Padone pushed back his chair and arrogantly sauntered across the restaurant to the reception desk where he had left his portfolio. Constance liked his walk. It was loose and fluid. The walk of a confident man, relaxed and yet in charge of his world.

'So,' he said, on his return, 'this is a capsule collection I have done to show you how I would work for you.'

'*With* me?' Constance's question was almost flirtatious.

'No, signora, *for* you.'

'What is the distinction?'

'Signora,' he said, almost as if speaking to a child, 'you must employ me and then leave me alone. I thought I had made it clear that in creativity there can be no co-operation. My responsibility is to the cloth. I must do honour to it – and you must approve, or sack me. That is what our collaboration would be based on. There is no other way.'

She recalled Savognia's words: 'He's hungry, Constanza; he has come from the bottom of the Neapolitan pile. If you can stomach his arrogance, he is our man, but it will not be easy, I think.' Turning the pages of the portfolio, she knew that Savognia was right. The designs were strong. They were sculptural and formal, with a seriousness that Constance found appealing. By the time she had reached the evening dresses, which were opulent without theatricality, she knew that Giuseppe Padone was exactly the man she had been looking for. He had already created the line that had taken only a nebulous shape in her imagination.

'Your husband, signora? He has design views also?' Padone's tone was patronising. He could tell how impressed she was with his work.

'My husband has his estate to run. He is not part of the business.'

'So, signora, it is up to you and me? Are we able to do it together? Do you like my work enough to accept my conditions?'

Constance bridled. 'Signor Padone,' she said, 'you forget that I am the employer. I think that *I* am the one who makes conditions. Now, supposing that we decide to go ahead – together,' she smiled, 'how much would you wish me to pay you?'

'Outrageous!' Giancarlo cried. 'Such a sum is absolutely, categorically out of the question, Constanza. We would be a public laughing stock.'

'I want him, Giancarlo. I know it's a lot to pay but he's worth it. He'll make our fortune. As for what people might say, I couldn't care less. Now, I think you'd better start drawing up Mr Padone's contract.'

She knew why Giuseppe Padone had demanded such a high salary. It was to put her in her place. She accepted it because, apart from his evident talent, and despite the spikiness of his temperament, working with this man would give her exactly the excitement she needed.

'You realise that he is a homosexual?' Giancarlo asked. 'Does that present a problem for you?'

'Not at all,' Constance replied. She was sure that Giancarlo was not entirely right. Her intuition told her that although Giuseppe Padone might sleep with men, he was also attracted to women. The speculative, half-seductive way he had looked at her over lunch did not suggest that he was a man interested only in men. There was something sexually dangerous about Padone. It excited her while alerting her to be on her guard.

Giuseppe Padone entered Constance's life at a period when she felt most vulnerable. Five weeks after Gioella's death, the coolness that had arisen with Giancarlo over her determination to view the body was still there. Constance wouldn't admit that her behaviour had been ill-advised and was determined that Giancarlo must learn to accept her as an independent equal if they were to work together. She knew that he would eventually come round, but she missed the warmth of their previous closeness.

The problems with Ludovico went much deeper. Gioella's death had brought Constance's marriage to a crisis point. She cursed its timing. By dying, Gioella had ensured that she would never go away. Her shadow would always hover over Ludovico, bathed in the permanent sunshine of her prime years – years that would never fade and sunshine from which Constance would forever be excluded. Ludovico seemed as incapable of breaking free of her memory as he was of turning his back on his guilt over her death. His fear of the coming court case kept her constantly in his mind.

'I think he's becoming a depressive,' she told Giancarlo. 'He does nothing but gaze into space all day. I feel terrible because I can't give him the time he needs. In fact, I feel guilty most of the time these days. I don't see nearly enough of Margharita – and Ludovico shows no interest in her at all. I wonder if we're right to be moving into a bigger business set-up at this moment. I don't know if I can cope.'

'Of course you can,' he replied. 'Once things are up and running, Padone will take over many of the day-to-day decisions.'

The thought did not entirely please Constance, who felt that if anyone were to take the weight from her shoulders it should be Milva, but she remained silent.

'As for Ludovico,' Savognia continued, 'you must give him time. He is still in shock.'

'He's dreadfully worried about going to court.'

'Oh, I don't think he should be. In my view, it will be an open-and-shut case. That foolish man with the mule was responsible for the accident. Any court in the world would uphold that. You can't just walk in front of a car and expect it to stop instantly.'

'But Ludo wasn't looking.'

'Who knows? Who can prove that? Were there any witnesses? No. You mustn't allow him to give in to these feelings of guilt. Quite simply, Constanza, Gioella's death was not Ludovico's fault. *Basta così.*'

Constance was heartened. Although she suspected that Savognia was wrong about the cause of the accident, she was aware of his influence and felt that ultimately that would prevail in court.

'There is no reason for you to feel guilty, Ludo, darling,' she said one morning when he joined her on the terrace for coffee. It was a hot, still day, silent apart from the muted sounds of the maid Rosanna in the kitchen below, cursing the cats in her broad country accent. On such a day, Constance found it hard to bear the forlorn and crumpled look on Ludovico's face. For all her sympathy, a little flash of Nora sparked in her head. His expression of hopelessness irritated her. She must do something to stop him wallowing in grief.

'It was an accident. A straightforward, unfortunate accident. Who could have known that crazy old man and his mule would suddenly appear out of the blue? There was nothing that you – or anybody else – could have done. You really must see that and stop blaming yourself.'

'I wasn't looking,' Ludovico replied flatly. 'I didn't see him. It was only her cry that made me realise – and it came too late. I shall never drive again.'

'Oh, Ludo! Don't be so silly! Of course you will drive again. As soon as your leg is better.'

'No, you are wrong. I cannot.'

301

'Ludo, darling. You mustn't think like this. Good God!' she exclaimed in exasperation. 'Do you think your life has been finished by one accident? Are you going to sit around and mope for the rest of your life because of something that couldn't be helped and can't be changed? I've never heard anything so self-indulgent. What about us? What about me? I have a life too, remember, even if I am just a woman.'

'Your life? You have your life already. We have no life any more, you and me.'

'And Margharita?' she asked heavily. 'What of her life?'

'I'm sure that you already have that worked out, Constanza, my dear – as you have everything. She will be turned into a perfect young English lady and taught to despise the Italian side of her heritage. But it won't matter,' he ended sadly.

'Of course it won't,' Constance snapped. 'She's female. It doesn't matter what she becomes, as long as she is aware that her role in life is to stand by and let men ride rough-shod over her while she closes her eyes to a thousand infidelities and deceptions.'

'Why do you have this hatred of men?' asked Ludovico angrily.

'I don't know what you mean. Hatred of men? I don't hate men, Ludo. What I hate is a husband who thinks he must chase every available woman he meets – and I shall do everything I can to make sure that Margharita does not end up in the same situation as me.'

'As you wish,' Ludovico said dismissively, and stood up. As he made to go down the garden, Constance leapt up and stood in front of him, eyes blazing.

'As I wish?' she cried. 'Don't you try to fob me off like that! We are married and married we must remain. I will not let Gioella destroy everything I have worked for. She's over! She's past! All the moping in the world can't bring her back. For God's sake, stop being so spineless! Why don't you, just for once, think about me and my feelings instead of always thinking only of yourself? I have needs too, you know. I love you – more than that bitch Gioella ever could.'

Ludovico's lip curled but before he could speak Constance went on. 'You can't just turn your back on me like this! I won't let you! It isn't fair! I will not stand by and let that woman destroy our marriage. I will not! I will not!' and she began to hit him, drumming with clenched fists against his chest. Catching her wrists to stop her, Ludovico pulled Constance towards him. Crying with frustration and rage she collapsed against him. He closed his arms around her.

'Oh, Constanza,' he sobbed, 'I wish I were dead. Why couldn't it have been me?'

He buried his face in her hair and held her tight. He was shaking. She lifted his head.

'Ludo. Please don't cry. I know we can start again. But you *must* let me help you. Please, please, my darling, don't shut me out.'

Ludovico's moods were unsettlingly unpredictable. On some days, he was deeply morose; on others he was almost his old self. The former far outnumbered the latter and it took all Constance's courage to stick to her resolve not to allow him to depress her or weaken her efforts to save their marriage. She was now more determined than ever. Since the accident, Ludovico, who could go for many hours without speaking to her, had insisted that they make love regularly. It was as if this was the only way he could communicate with her: in darkness, silently and urgently. He seemed to be using her body to wipe out his feelings of guilt. On many nights as he lay on top of her, spent and sweating, he would begin to cry. Her comforting always led to a second, even more passionate, love-making that Constance found immensely exciting. She was disturbed and upset by the difference between Ludovico in and out of bed. Making love, he was totally unselfish. Uncannily attuned to her needs, he knew exactly how to satisfy them, often bringing her to orgasm several times

303

a night. At those moments everything else was blotted out, even the business. She needed nothing more than the rhythm of his cock inside her – a rhythm that sent waves of sensation tingling through every part of her body. On sceptical reflection, she felt that Ludovico would make love to any woman just as expertly – hadn't Bettina said that it was all he was good for? – but while it was happening to her she was passionately and deeply moved by what seemed his overwhelming need of her.

There were times when Constance felt that she would splinter into little pieces, so many demands were being made of her. Ludovico's needs pulled her one way, the business and Savognia another, and her desperately inadequate attempts to find time for Margharita, a third. It distressed her that Margharita was such a difficult baby. She cried constantly and flew into a tantrum whenever her nanny tried to discipline her.

In an effort to get away from at least some of the problems Constance decided that, instead of Padone bringing his sketches for the first collection to Florence, she would travel to Rome to see him. She could visit Portinari and discuss the next hat collection but, above all, she would see Louise. She longed to talk face to face with her – especially as Jim's tour of duty was coming to an end and they would soon be returning to England. Also, she was convinced that she was pregnant again and wanted the reassurance of consulting her aunt's English doctor. She promised Savognia that she would stay in Rome no more than four days. There were so many decisions to be made about the new business that it would be unfair to expect him to take them alone. In any case, she wanted to be involved with *every* decision, no matter how small.

Louise was as delighted to see her as ever. 'My dear,' she exclaimed, 'you look marvellous! Business clearly suits you enormously!'

Constance told her of the problems that she was facing

with Ludovico and his changed personality since the accident.

'Well, you must give him time. After all, the inquest isn't out of the way yet. Naturally he's worried about it. Do be fair, Constance.'

'Oh, it's so much more than just the accident. He seems to have lost any interest in *life*. He is beginning to live in the past, Louise, he really is.' And she told her aunt about Ludovico's growing obsession with his ancestors.

'He'll end up like his deranged mother if he doesn't take hold of himself. She is so involved with the Villanuovas and their continuity that she seems to think of nothing else. The modern world hardly imposes on her life at all. I can't bear the thought of Ludo ending up like her. I just hope that this second child is a boy. I really think that is the only thing that could bring Ludo to his senses – and pull our marriage together again.'

'Oh, my darling,' Louise said, 'is it as bad as that? I'm so sorry. Does Nora know?'

'Good God, no! And I don't intend to let her! Just imagine her triumph if she knew I was in trouble so soon.' Constance paused.

'Actually, Louise, perhaps I've exaggerated. Things are not that bad. It's mainly that Ludo is still in shock. I know the new baby will change everything, especially if it's a boy.'

Louise laughed. 'Oh, darling, babies never change anything! They're not like vacuum cleaners, you know! They can't just suck up all the mess of a marriage, leaving everything spanking new – more's the pity!'

Constance was forced to agree, much as her aunt's comment had disappointed her. There could be no easy solution to the problems she faced with Ludo.

Giuseppe Padone's intensity was extremely unsettling to Constance. He had a particular way of looking at her that made her feel insecure and gauche. He was so much the master of his space that he threatened hers. Was it because they were meeting in Rome that Constance felt so strangely out of place with him? His behaviour was insufferably overconfident and yet it convinced her. She accepted his self-assessment and after she had looked through all the drawings, she congratulated him.

'That is not necessary, signora,' he said dismissively. 'Now let us get to work. We must put the drawings into groups, each of which must tell a different story in the show.'

Constance was lost, as he had intended. Padone laughed and said, 'It is easy. For example, woollen coats.' He rifled quickly through the pages, pulling out about thirty drawings.

'Now we subdivide, by colour, texture and shape. Each part of the show will consist of about ten pieces. They must tell a strong, clear story. It must be immediately apparent – buyers and journalists are very stupid.'

He laughed; he was enjoying himself. Constance relaxed, and soon they were working as a pair, talking excitedly. Constance realised that she was having a marvellous time.

'Signor Padone . . .' she said.

'Giuseppe,' he interrupted. 'You must call me Giuseppe.'

She hesitated, unsure that it was a wise move.

'Come,' he urged, 'your relationship with your designer must be an intimate one. Formal terms do not work in a creative world.'

'Very well, Giuseppe,' she agreed.

'And I?' he asked. 'I may call you Constance?' She coloured. How could she refuse?

'Yes,' she agreed, 'of course,' and she bent her head over the drawings, very conscious that he had noted the blush.

'It will work very well,' Constance told Savognia. 'Giuseppe and I understand each other.'

'Giuseppe?' Savognia frowned.

'I think it important that we avoid any unnecessary formality,' she said. 'It doesn't work in a creative situation. Christian names are much more relaxed.'

Savognia looked irritated. 'Well, Constanza,' he said coldly, 'it is up to you how you address your designer but he will remain Padone to me. I would have thought,' he added sharply, 'that it would have been wise for you also to keep a slight barrier of formality. After all, my dear, you are a very young woman and employees often take advantage of people they think of as friends.'

Constance was angry at the implication but decided to let the slur pass. To lighten his mood, she said, 'I have marvellous news, Giancarlo. I am pregnant.'

'What about the business?' he asked in alarm.

'Oh, don't worry! I'm only *just* pregnant. There are nearly eight months to go. By then Padone – I mean Giuseppe – will know how to keep things going.'

'I do hope your business life is not going to be endlessly punctuated by pregnancies, Constanza,' Giancarlo said.

'Oh, good heavens, no. This is almost certainly the last one,' Constance laughed.

Provided that it's a boy, she thought. Please, God, let it be a boy.


Constance returned to the castle to find the place suffused with a feeling of despair. Maria-Angelina was undoubtedly failing – deliberately and wilfully giving herself to death, in Constance's view – and Ludo seemed to drift through the days as aimlessly as before. She asked for him and was directed to the library. He was reading a small volume of poetry.

'Who is it – Dante?' she asked as she leant over the back of his chair.

'Hardly,' Ludovico replied. 'These are very bad poems written by my great-grandfather – and I mean, very bad.'

'Why are you reading them then?'

'I am searching for my ancestors. I want to know about them. I *must* know about them.'

Constance straightened up. 'Don't you know enough already?'

'No. For example, look at the dedication to this book. I never knew until I read it today that my great-grandfather wrote these poems when he was young. For his twenty-first birthday he planted a wood which was to be chopped down fifty years later to make the paper for this privately printed anthology. And that is what happened. He gave a copy to the library of every noble family in Italy – as well as the Vatican and the universities. What thoroughness. What foresight. What confidence.'

Where did it all go? Constance asked herself, as she looked sadly at her husband.

Without telling Ludovico, Constance sent a note to the Principessa asking permission to see her. An interview was speedily granted. The servant led her into the darkened room where nothing had changed since their last stormy meeting. Maria-Angelina sat up in bed, stiffly formal. She wore the grey gloves and her eyes burned as brightly as ever. As Constance had expected, her reception was cool. She came straight to the point.

'Principessa,' she said, with a slight flutter in her voice, 'do you recall how you asked me to do my duty by the Villanuovas and fulfil roles that are beyond Ludovico?'

Maria-Angelina stroked the tip of her nose and nodded.

'Well, I've thought about it very carefully – especially in the light of how Ludovico has been since the accident – and I think I can do so without putting my business at risk.'

Maria-Angelina looked away impatiently at mention of the business. It was the only time she took her eyes off Constance's face throughout the interview.

'But if I am to help the Villanuovas, they must also help me,' Constance continued.

The Principessa raised her chin and looked at her through half-lowered lids. She said nothing.

'I shall need money, Principessa.'

Maria-Angelina remained silent.

'You are aware,' Constance went on, 'that my business is expanding. The Principe Savognia is now a partner and we are to create our own clothes to go with the hats.'

Constance blushed. Why did she find it demeaning to talk of fashion to Maria-Angelina? She thought of Miss Hatherby and knew she would feel exactly the same with her. She dismissed her inhibitions and took the plunge, despite the growing coolness of the atmosphere.

'I need suitable premises in Florence, Principessa.'

Once it was said, she felt strong enough to defy the Principessa's silence. She waited . . .

Maria-Angelina cleared her throat and asked, 'How much?'

Constance decided to be oblique. 'I'm sure you know Palazzo Tondi on the river bank above Ponte Vecchio. It is for sale.'

Maria-Angelina knew it very well. It would be expensive. Would it be wise to advance money for such an investment? Before she decided, she needed to know more – what would Constance give in return?

It was a long interview – as it had to be. Constance was asking for a considerable sum; Maria-Angelina expected an equally considerable commitment in return. Each obtained her objective.

During the discussion, Constance began to learn, as she never had in her conversations with Ludovico, of the psychological importance of continuity to a noble family.

'All the past, everything it stands for – the privations, poverty, risks and gambles – has meaning only if it leads to a future,' Maria-Angelina told her. 'Families like the Villanuovas die if the continuity is broken.'

Constance recalled her mother describing her father's fervid belief in man's equality; she thought of Padone, whose existence had no meaning in Maria-Angelina's scheme of importance. She knew that the Principessa was wrong in her dismissal of those outside the narrow world of the nobility and yet, listening to this half-crazed woman talk about a family in which she still felt a stranger, Constance was unwilling to be the one to break the chain. She longed for the baby in her belly to be male even as she determined to make her daughter strong – strong enough to withstand the insidious Villanuova downgrading of women. Margharita, she vowed, would grow up to be a first-class person, not despite, but because of, her sex.

Constance had decided that she would still visit Biaggibonsi as often as possible – on the advice of Milva.

'You must not abandon them just because you have a new enterprise, signora,' she said. 'They need to know that you still care and that what they do is valued.'

After her interview with Maria-Angelina, she drove down to the village. As she pulled into the square she passed an open car driven by a man in sunglasses. Seeing her, he swung his car round and followed her. She parked and walked across to the bar. He did the same. Constance was shaking as he leant on the counter next to her and greeted her in English. She knew he was Carlo.

'So,' he said, 'you are Ludo's English wife who has so scandalised my mother.'

'I thought that you had nothing to do with . . .' she stammered.

'Of course not. But about this the whole of Italy is talking. Naturally, I hear these things.'

'Why did you follow me?' she asked.

'Curiosity.'

'Is that why you came to Gioella's funeral?'

He smiled. 'I am curious, but I am not agog to see you. I was at Gioella's funeral to pay my respects to a woman who had been a friend and whose effect on my family was not insignificant.'

Constance blushed. 'Why did you try to hide, then?' she asked.

'My little brother – and others – would have been

unhappy if they had known I was there. I could hardly spoil their day, could I?'

'What are you doing in Biaggibonsi? I thought that your mother had banished you?'

He laughed. 'My mother! She is crazy. You have heard about all that absurd theatrical business with my possessions? It means nothing. Italy is still a free country. She may have cut me off, but banish me from my own land she cannot do.'

Constance looked at him. She was struck by his close physical resemblance to Ludovico. When he laughed, Carlo looked exactly like his brother. She wondered about his eyes, but they remained hidden behind his dark glasses. He was aware of her scrutiny and smiled sardonically. 'How is he?' he asked.

'Not very well – he suffers from terrible depression. He blames himself entirely. Giancarlo Savognia says it was clearly the fault of the man with the mule but I simply can't convince Ludovico that that's the truth.'

'And you will not,' Carlo said, 'because it is not. Ludovico knows that. He is not so foolish as to be taken in by Savognia's bland reassurances.'

'Of course it wasn't Ludovico's fault,' Constance said. 'The man came out right in front of the car. What could Ludo do?'

'That is not the guilt that oppresses my brother. The death is just a side effect.'

He straightened up. 'I must leave you now,' he said. 'Do not be tempted to give my brother my love. He couldn't bear that.'

As he walked across the sunlit square Constance wanted to call him back. There was so much she needed to ask him; so much she longed to know. Then she shrugged, suddenly undisturbed by his abrupt departure. She knew that she would have the opportunity to ask him everything in the fullness of time.

When Savognia had first suggested its purchase, Constance hadn't realised the grandeur of Palazzo Tondi. Every inch of its fabric was aristocratic. Its vast dilapidated rooms were perfectly proportioned, with high windows and magnificent doors that reflected the nobility of the life previously led there.

'These are rooms that demand respect, Constanza,' Savognia said as they walked through them, their echoing footsteps startling the pigeons which had nested on the beams. 'We cannot partition them or make them pretty in a contemporary way. They are history, and so they must remain.'

'What about the frescoes? Shall we have them repainted?'

Giancarlo stopped in his tracks. 'Good God! What a barbarous idea, Constanza. They must remain precisely as they are. Nothing must be allowed to destroy the patina of decay.'

'Oh! I was only joking,' Constance laughed, but Giancarlo's anxiety was aroused.

'Promise me,' he said, 'promise me that you won't touch any part of the fabric.'

'How shall we furnish the rooms?' Constance asked, recalling Maison de Levantière's dainty little gold chairs and satin-covered sofas and thinking how foolish they would look in Palazzo Tondi's enormous rooms.

'I've been thinking of that and I have an idea,' Giancarlo replied. 'There is an ancient monastery in a remote part of the Abruzzi. It hasn't flourished since the last century and its numbers have so dwindled that the Vatican plans to close it. I went there some years ago, and I recall the furniture clearly. It was very simple but beautifully crafted. Monumental tables and high-backed chairs so heavy that two monks were needed to move them – you know the sort of thing. The scale would be perfect for these rooms. The furniture would look so . . . how can I say? . . . so noble. It would give the house the right sense of seriousness for the classic clothes that Padone is

312

planning. I shall talk to the Vatican and see what they are prepared to sell.'

Constance was excited about the furniture which, as Giancarlo had predicted, looked magnificently assured in Palazzo Tondi, but she was even more delighted by the heavy eighteenth-century fabrics that came from the monastery chapel. Green damask hangings of immense weight – thickly woven tapestry backcloths and marvellously rich silk cords and tassels – they were all that the rooms needed. They reminded her of the backgrounds of Titian paintings.

'It is unlike any other dress house in the world,' Giancarlo commented approvingly. 'It has its own personality even before a dress has been designed.'

Constance had slight misgivings. 'Is it too severe?' she asked.

'Not at all. Your customers will come from the highest echelons of Italian society. They will appreciate the strength – and yes, the breeding, I think we can say – in such assurance. The atmosphere is austere, but that is good. Maison Constanza Castelfranco is not a place for the flippancy of fashion. It will be a temple to the highest levels of couture.'

That's all very well, Constance thought, but people don't spend money in temples.

As Giancarlo organised the public rooms – persistently calling her to inspect a new treasure or approve the siting of a piece of furniture – Constance addressed the difficult question of working on the collection with Giuseppe Padone. Even before his first week was over, she conceded that Giancarlo had been right about their designer. Padone was undoubtedly a genius, but she had no intention of sitting at his feet, like some eager young girl. Maison Constanza Castelfranco was hers and she was determined that her will must prevail, no matter how subtly she might have to hide it.

Ludovico remained aloof in the Marche, refusing to become involved. Even when he came down to Fiesole, Constance could not persuade him to visit Palazzo Tondi. She found his indifference maddening. She wanted to shake him, to force him to take an interest in what was rapidly becoming the centre of her life. But she had neither the time nor the energy. She worked incredible hours. As each day continued through crisis, loggerheads and panic, her exhaustion grew. There were times when, arriving at Villa Andreoli as late as midnight, too tired even to sleep let alone eat the supper Rosanna had left out for her, Constance doubted that she had the stamina to continue. Giancarlo did his best to encourage her.

'It will be easier when the baby is born,' he kept saying but she wasn't fooled. Carrying the baby made her tired, but the real problem went deeper. It was inherent in the business. It was to do with the human unreliability of the fashion world. She was given endless bland assurances by everyone, from fabric suppliers and workroom heads to outworkers. Almost always the assurances were false. Even as they were made she knew that the promises would be broken. Nothing was ever delivered on time; nothing was done exactly to her orders. Constance realised that being a businesswoman was beginning to turn her into a cynical doubter, unable to accept the face value people put on themselves until she had tested the reality behind the façade. Much of the problem was caused by the kindness of the people who worked with her.

'They're all so damned charming,' she complained to Giancarlo, 'they feel they've got to tell me what I want to hear, not what I need to know. They'll drive me mad. All I want is the truth, and nobody will give me it.'

The two exceptions were Giuseppe Padone and Milva. As they worked together in the grand *salotto*, choosing fabrics for the sketches and breathing excitement with the birth of each new idea, Constance found herself relying increasingly on their professional honesty. Milva rarely spoke but the language of her body never left Constance in any doubt about her views.

The sessions were always dominated by Padone. When he was working, his personality became as austere as the furnishings and surroundings; he grew so engrossed in the problems he was solving that Constance knew that for long periods he completely forgot that she was there. She could accept this because once he had found the solution he never patronised her by telling her anything but the truth – even when he knew it would wound her.

'No, no,' he would say, if she opposed him over a particular colour or fabric, 'I cannot allow this.'

'*You* cannot allow it!' Constance would feel her nerves snapping and she would say something silly and untenable, ending lamely, 'It is what I require and it must be done.'

An argument would flare almost immediately and Padone would flounce out of the *salotto* in a rage, not to return that day. But as her trust in him grew, Constance learned to control her temper. She had to. In all professional matters, Padone was uncompromising. There was, for him, only one way. The correct way. Constance had to admit that he was always right.

Although *she* could accept this, Milva, who as Constance's assistant almost always witnessed the clashes, found them increasingly difficult to take. One day, after a comparatively mild display of temperament from Giuseppe, she exploded.

'Signora!' she cried. 'You must not let him speak to you like that! He is a peasant!'

Constance was shocked. 'Milva, never refer to Signor Padone in that way again! He is my designer and collaborator and you must show him the respect his position demands!'

Milva's face darkened. 'You are la Padrona. It is you who requires respect – and it is you who should *demand* it! You are not Italian, signora, I am. I understand people like Giuseppe Padone in a way that you never will. Men like that should not be trusted. They will betray you without a moment's thought. *Mi Raccomanda*, you be careful, little one. Be on your guard with men like Padone. Milva knows.'

And she walked out of the *salotto*, leaving Constance appalled by the grim vindictiveness of her tone. She'd been unaware of the strength of the resentment that had built up over such a short time, and she was perplexed. She trusted Milva and her judgement too much to lightly cast her words aside.

As her pregnancy followed its course, Constance took to spending the weekends at the castle with Ludovico. Despite the unease she felt at the Principessa's unseen presence, she welcomed the fresh country air which helped her to relax after the week of pressure in Florence.

Constance was happiest when left to herself, taking leisurely walks across the hills behind the castle, sitting on the high rocks and feeling the kicks of the child growing within her. The silence up there was all-pervading, she was completely alone and she was able to think and plan the complicated life she must juggle as mother, wife, businesswoman and overseer of the land that stretched below her.

One afternoon, she was returning to the castle when Carlo suddenly stepped out from a clump of trees. Although the day was overcast, he was still wearing his dark glasses. They gave him a furtive look.

'What are you doing, coming this close to the castle?' Constance asked him, looking around guiltily.

'I am here every day,' he replied. 'I watch you walking alone each weekend. Do you know that you talk to yourself?'

She blushed. 'Why do you come here?' she asked.

'Because I like to see you.'

'Me?'

'Yes, because you are the only Villanuova I *can* see. Why does Ludovico never leave the castle?'

'He's afraid. These roads hold too many memories for him.'

'Monica never leaves the castle either,' Carlo said.

'Monica?' Constance asked in surprise. 'What on earth do you mean? Monica isn't in the castle.'

He smiled. 'Not now,' he said, 'but during the week? Yes, most certainly.'

He moved towards her. 'Please,' he said, 'make Ludovico relent. He will never be well until he does. You think that he is grieving for Gioella. It is not true. He is trapped by the dark forces of evil released by our mother to keep us apart. He needs me, and I need him. Neither of us will ever know any serenity until the web is broken. You can do that for us, Constanza. You must make him understand that what I did was for him. I did it so that his young life would not be ruined. He must be made to see the irony in the way our mother is destroying his whole life – and mine also.'

His voice died away. Before Constance could focus her thoughts, he was gone.

In a daze, she sat down heavily on a pile of logs. The trees were spinning round her. Monica! Monica at the castle? It couldn't be true. She wouldn't believe it. What urge for revenge was making Carlo tell such lies? He was trying to destroy her marriage. Why? Because he was jealous. Of course, that was it. He was jealous of Ludovico and resentful that he was still the Principessa's favourite. She began to make her way back as fast as she could. She must question Ludovico and prove to her own satisfaction that Carlo was lying.

As she approached the castle, doubts crept into her mind. Bettina's words at the party came ringing back; she remembered how in their arguments Ludovico had never categorically denied that Monica was his mistress. Now she grew convinced that Carlo had spoken the truth. Monica was visiting Ludovico while she, Constance, was in Florence.

By the time she reached their apartments, she had made

up her mind to say nothing to Ludovico, and she left for Florence that evening just as she always did.

Constance telephoned Savognia. 'Giancarlo,' she said, 'I shall not be in the office this week. I feel so tired, I'm going to stay in Fiesole with Margharita. If there are any problems, I know that you and Padone can solve them. I really don't wish to be disturbed. I need a complete rest for a few days. Incidentally, do you know if Monica is in Florence?'

Was there a hesitation before he replied or was it merely her imagination?

'Monica?' Giancarlo asked. 'I think she's still in London.'

'In London?' Constance said. 'When did she go to London?'

'Some days ago. Why do you ask?'

Constance made a decision.

'Giancarlo, will you please come up here as soon as you can? I need to talk to you.'

She was determined to find out the true situation. If Giancarlo knew anything she would get it out of him, of that she was sure.

Savognia was nervous.

'Is there anything wrong, Constanza?' he asked when she had closed the *salotto* door behind them.

'Yes, I think there may be,' she replied. 'And I rely on you to tell me the truth. Before we even begin, let me make it perfectly clear that I will not accept lies, no matter whom you think you might be protecting.' She told him of her meeting with Carlo and what he had told her, about Monica.

Savognia hardly let her finish before bursting out, 'I cannot believe it! I will not believe it! Monica has no earthly reason to tell me lies and when she says she is going to London I believe her. Why Carlo is hanging around up there, I don't know but . . .'

318

'He's a desperately lost and unhappy man,' Constance interrupted.

'That is possibly true. I cannot say. I haven't spoken to him for years. The whole thing is a mystery. Why should he tell lies? He was never a mischiefmaker. In fact before the trouble he was always one of the kindest and warmest of friends. Why he should say such things now I do not know.'

'Almost certainly because they are true. Now listen, I need your co-operation,' Constance said. 'I am returning to the castle secretly. I've arranged for a chauffeur-driven car. If Ludovico telephones don't tell him where I am. Make up any excuse you like.'

Savognia's aristocratic sensibilities were shaken. How could Constance expect him to lie to his best friend?

She read his thoughts. 'You will be doing it for Ludovico's sake, and,' she added, 'the good of the business. I'm not prepared to let this situation continue.'

When Constance arrived, unannounced, in the small dining room of their apartments that night her presence caused consternation, as she had intended it would. Although she was shaking, she felt completely in control of the situation. If she were to lose her husband to Monica it would not be without a fight.

'Good God!' Ludovico cried. 'What on earth are you doing here? What is wrong? Has something happened? Where is Margharita?'

'Darling! What a fright!' Monica said. 'You could have let us know.'

Constance was impressed by her cool command of the situation. 'So that you would have time to creep away and hide? I don't think so. It's you I've come to see.'

'Me? What on earth for?'

'For a start, I'd like to know why you're having a secret dinner with my husband when you're supposed to be in London.'

As she spoke, Constance felt slightly self-conscious. It

would have been so much easier if she had found Monica in a negligée instead of a woollen dress or with her hair dishevelled instead of pulled back tightly in a chignon.

Monica stood up. 'Will you excuse us, Ludo?' she said laconically. 'This is girls' talk.' And she led the way out of the dining room, with Constance, whose assurance was rapidly evaporating, following behind.

'Really, darling, what can you be thinking of, bursting in like that, with Ludo in his present state?' Monica said sharply. 'You know how nervous and easily upset he is. Why on earth didn't you phone?'

'Why aren't you in London, that's what I'd like to know?' Constance answered.

'Sit down,' Monica replied. 'I told Savognia I was going to London because I didn't want him interfering and I especially didn't want him worrying you. You have enough to cope with already.'

Constance began to feel insecure.

'What is going on, Monica?'

'All right,' Monica said in a resigned voice. 'I guess I can't keep it from you any longer. You remember the Principessa's old servant who delivered Margharita? Well, she used to be Carlo's nurse. In fact, that room she put you in was Carlo's day nursery before Ludovico was even born. It may surprise you to know that although the old hen tends the Principessa so carefully she loathes her and has never forgiven her for what she did to Carlo. She keeps him informed of everything that goes on in this castle.'

She paused.

'Now Constance, I don't wish to offend you because I know how hard you're working to get the business right. I know that whatever spare time you have goes to Margharita, but I have to say that you've neglected poor Ludo terribly since the accident. You come up here every weekend, go for long walks and generally recharge your batteries. I don't blame you for it, but you hardly look at Ludo, let alone listen. He's crying out for help, poor darling, and you're preoccupied. You don't know how close to the brink he's been. So when Carlo – who loves Ludovico to distraction – phoned me, I knew that it was too much to expect you to help but I was damned sure *I* could.'

'Well,' said Constance, 'it all sounds very cosy. Erring wife too busy with her own life to worry about her husband. Mistress takes over. Everybody is happy. Who do you think you're fooling, Monica?'

To her consternation, Monica began to laugh. 'Constance,' she said, 'I don't think you should get too carried away here. I am not, and never have been, Ludo's mistress. What a preposterous idea!'

'So you say!' Constance replied. 'But I know differently. Please don't play games with me, Monica. I heard Bettina telling someone at Savognia's last party.'

'Bettina Bonoccorsi!' Monica laughed. 'Darling, you must be joking. Nobody takes any notice of Bettina Bonoccorsi. She's a mentally sick woman who loathes the Villanuovas and takes every opportunity to make up scandal about them. Nobody in their right mind would listen to a word of it. Really, darling! I'm surprised at you.'

She crossed over and sat next to Constance. 'Now, listen, and I'll tell you. I've been up here for the last two weeks – Monday to Thursday. Not because I wanted to sleep with Ludo but because he was on the verge of a nervous breakdown with this case coming up and I was frightened for him. I've tried my level best to help – and I think I have. He's much calmer now. But I am *not* sleeping with him and I am pretty damned sure that the only woman he has *ever* betrayed you with was poor Gioella. So, please, let us have no more of this.'

Constance knew that Monica was telling the truth. She felt ashamed of her suspicions, so easily aroused to jealousy. How could she have been so foolish as to jump to the conclusion that Monica and Ludo were lovers? There was nothing in what Carlo had said that could justify such a reaction. Constance had to admit that Ludo's secrecy and his affair with Gioella were turning her into an insecure, distrustful wife – and she didn't like it. I won't allow Gioella and the Principessa to make me into something I am not, she resolved. Their influence must be destroyed if Ludo and I are to have any hope of a happy life together. I'm going to make Monica a friend. I need her positive approach. She is full of generosity. Perhaps her goodness can make a better person of me.

Constance suddenly realised that what she had been most missing since she came to Italy was a true female friend – a more modern Miss Hatherby. Louise was a great comfort but she was in Rome and soon to leave for England; Milva was marvellous in her honesty and judgement but there were many things that could not be discussed with her, and Savognia (whom, she could see now, she had been trying to use as a substitute female friend) was far too self-involved and precious. No, it was quite clear that the gap in her life could be filled by only one person: Monica Peterson.

Constance went into labour on the weekend following her conversation with Monica. This time she was not alone. She not only had Ludovico, Monica was also with her. When her labour began, Monica had plenty of time to ensure that Constance was safely placed in the Villanuova birth-bed. 'You never know,' she laughed, as she helped Constance into the bed, 'there may be something in all these superstitions. This might just do the trick. Anyhow, darling, there's not much you can do about it now except push hard and keep your fingers crossed.'

Constance smiled, grateful for Monica's good humour and common sense. She admired her ability to put all the suspicion and ill-feeling behind her and carry on as if nothing had happened. She made up her mind that she would do the same.

After several hours of labour, Constance finally gave birth. When the baby was held before her by the nun who had, somewhat against Constance's will, been put in charge of things, she was overjoyed to see a tiny pink penis. Her relief at producing a boy was echoed by the nun, the Principessa's servant and the peasant woman who had been called in to help. Constance smiled at them and they smiled back. '*Piccolo, ma perfetto, signora*,' the nun said as she put the small bundle into Constance's arms.

Ludovico was delighted. For the first time in months he grinned his old grin. Constance realised that there was still hope. She *could* bring back the man she loved so much and who had seemed lost for ever in the memory of Gioella and the terrible accident.

'He is perfect, just perfect,' he said as he lifted the baby gently from her arms. 'And he has the Villanuova eyes, yes?'

Constance had to agree. They were startlingly like Ludo's. In fact, she realised with a pang, everything about the baby was Villanuova. There seemed nothing of her in this child.

'He is the first Manfredo in many years,' Ludovico continued. 'We must have a grand *festa* for him when you are well enough. We will have bonfires on every hill and roast a whole goat in each village to celebrate that at last the Villanuova family has an heir.'

His enthusiasm opened up the old wound. What a contrast to poor Margharita's reception, Constance thought. Well, I love her as much as ever and I'm determined that she won't be downgraded just because we now have a son.

Constance found the celebrations medieval but she had to admit that they were magnificent. Ludovico had planned everything. All that was expected of her was to present the boy for the adulation of the Villanuova tenants and friends – for whom it was as if her first child had never been born.

When she carried her son down to the castle courtyard, Constance was amazed at the transformation. All its grimness had gone. The walls were garlanded with white and yellow daisies – the colours of the Villanuova crest – linked by yellow and white ribbons which fluttered from the parapets. The pillars of the colonnade were wreathed in flowers and their plinths buried in bouquets. Everything was yellow and white, including the awning that the work-men had set up to cover the huge fire where two oxen were roasting, slowly turning in opposite directions on their spits. Most impressively, above the main door, thickly encircled by flowers, hung the family crest: a painted leather shield with a wild boar, chalice and port-cullis depicted on a primrose-yellow and white chequered background, framed in blue and white. It glittered exoti-cally as the evening sun caught the gold highlights.

Constance was immediately surrounded by a crowd of villagers, eager to see the heir. A huge man, wearing a hat made from a newspaper, pushed them aside and stood directly in front of her, a posy of yellow and white flowers clutched in one fist. He was the local butcher, there to supervise the roasting oxen. His face gleamed red in the flames of the fire and his vest was dark with sweat. Silence fell as, leaning forward, he ceremoniously placed a bloody thumb on the baby's forehead and marked it with the sign of the cross. Then, presenting the little bouquet to Constance, he said, with tears in his eyes, '*Auguri!* Greet-ings, signora.' The villagers all cheered.

Constance suddenly realised how much an heir meant to these people, how important it was to their confidence in the Villanuovas – and she felt humbled and ashamed that she hadn't understood it before.

Even the audience with Maria-Angelina that preceded the festivities was not as alarming as Constance expected. Easing herself up in bed, the Principessa took the baby from Constance's arms and, unsmiling, picked up a pair of silver scissors. Constance felt a split second of panic. What was the crazy woman doing? Maria-Angelina snip-ped a tiny piece of hair from Manfredo's head and placed it in a small silver box. Handing the baby to the servant, who nervously gave him to Constance, she then closed her eyes. Constance stood awkwardly by the bedside. Not

324

a word had been spoken to her nor, she realised, would be. As she left the room with the baby, she knew that to Maria-Angelina she was no more important than a brood mare, whose only valid function was to produce young – of the correct sex.

The celebrations began at eight o'clock, as the sun was sinking. Huge flambeaux had been placed in iron rings set high in the courtyard walls. Their tarry smell reminded Constance of the fishermen sealing their boats in Northumberland when she was a girl. As darkness fell, the flickering flames joined with those of the roasting-fire to create enormous jagged shadows, giving the courtyard a barbaric air. It must have been like this five hundred years ago, Constance thought as she and Ludovico stepped down from the great doorway into the crowds below. Their progress was slow. Everyone wanted to see the baby, shake the hand of Ludovico and give Constance a bouquet. Her arms were so full that Manfredo was literally lying on a bed of flowers – like Moses, she thought. Having eaten some of the roast oxen – which she found delicious – and drunk some of the strong red wine from the farm's own vineyards, they climbed into the car to visit the other villages of the estate. As they dropped down into the valley, Ludovico pointed out the fires.

. 'Look, Constanza! Look!' he said excitedly.

She became aware of brilliant haloes of scarlet flames on every hilltop. They came from huge bonfires, lit simultaneously to celebrate the Villanuova baby.

'They are for you, my darling, for being a good wife and bringing us a boy.'

Ludovico seemed unable to let the subject drop. 'Everyone is so pleased with you,' he said, as they were preparing for bed. 'We knew that you would do it, that there was no . . . no flaw in you. It is a cause of great joy to them.'

'I'm glad,' Constance replied coolly.

'I know how much shame you felt,' he said gently. 'And

I want you to know that I do not blame you for it. In the circumstances, it is only natural.'

'What do you mean, shame?' Constance's voice rose. 'Shame for what?'

Ludovico had drunk too much wine. He failed to interpret the danger signs.

'A daughter as first-born,' he rambled on. 'It's unheard of. The Villanuovas too – of all families. We are, after all, a male line.'

'If I'm told that just once more I shall hit someone very hard indeed!' Constance hissed. 'If anyone ought to be ashamed in our marriage it's you, for your reckless self-indulgence that made me – your lawful wife – a laughing stock whilst Gioella swanked round the length and breadth of Italy letting everyone know what you were doing. How could you treat me in that way? Don't you see how cheap you've made me look?'

'*I* have not made you cheap, Constanza,' Ludovico replied softly. 'You *are* cheap. You have married into one of the noblest families in Italy and yet you insist on dragging our name down with your vulgar little money-grabbing business. That is what everyone in Italy is talking about, not my harmless *amours*. That is why I can no longer be seen in public. I am a fool to all my friends. You have no idea how a woman in your position must behave. No wonder my mother has taken to her bed with grief.'

'If it weren't for my vulgar little business where do you think you'd be by now?' Constance cried. 'You dare to marry me without a penny to your name and then have the effrontery to criticise me for doing something about it? You must be mad. Did you really expect me to accept a situation where a grown man lived off the doubtful generosity of his mother – asking for his pocket money like a schoolboy? My vulgar little business has made you independent for the first time in your life, and don't you forget it!'

'What is to be done?' she asked Giancarlo wearily. 'I can't go on like this. I need a husband who will give me *support*. I find these fights exhausting – even more than his long absences from Florence and those terrible silences. It might be better if we were legally separated. At least I would know where I am. I can't give all my energy to him, Giancarlo, I know that I'll get nothing in return. He'll only drain me – he's totally self-absorbed. I won't put my business at risk for him.'

Savognia frowned. 'You are too harsh, Constanza. He is recovering from a deep shock. You must give him time.'

'Oh, I know, I know,' she cried, 'but someone must look to the future. I can't allow my children's lives to be blighted by the spectre of Gioella. In any case, how do I know what will happen when the Principessa dies? She says that things will be all right but this family is so steeped in lies and deception that I can't trust her. How do I know that she won't leave everything to the local cats' home – or even to Carlo! Nothing is too bizarre for her. Then what happens, if I don't have my vulgar little business to feed my children by?'

'Oh, come, Constanza, you're being theatrical.'

'I know I am, Giancarlo, but I cannot give up everything for Ludovico. Frankly, he isn't worth it in his present state – and never will be as long as he lets Gioella haunt him.'

'That is up to you, my dear,' Giancarlo replied gravely. 'You are the only person who can lay that ghost.'


Ludovico's happiness over the birth of his heir was short-lived. The celebrations had hardly ended when a summons was delivered. He must present himself at the court in Ascole Piceno where his case was to be heard.

'Now this time, darling, Ludovico *must* come first,' Monica said. 'I know that you're working very hard on the collection but you have to find time to help him. I'll give all the support I can – and so will Giancarlo, I'm sure – but you must remember that there's absolutely no substitute for you. Now, promise, darling – for every-body's sake – family first.'

Constance felt ashamed. The criticism behind Monica's words was clear enough. She must try to make her friend understand.

'My involvement with work is something in me that I can't change, Monica. And I don't want to. I don't think I could even do it for Ludo. That is the simple truth.'

'My darling, I don't think you have to change anything, except the emphasis. I think you'll agree that you have been rather obsessive about the business recently, and I fully understand why. You had to be, otherwise you'd never have taken it so far. Certainly, nobody – least of all Ludo – wants you to fail. But everything is going fine now. Surely you don't need to give it quite so much of your time, especially at this moment, when Ludo is under such strain.'

Constance smiled ruefully. She was positive that this was just the beginning and that she would have to work even harder after the first show in order to make the business a real success.

'After all,' Monica was saying, 'your family has the right to some of your time, darling. You're not just a wife; you're also a mother – and a real one now that you have a *son*.' She laughed and went on quietly, 'I know that it distresses Ludo that you see so little of the children. I'm sure you can do something about that too.'

She had hit a raw nerve. Constance felt guilty, and couldn't resist replying aggressively, 'Ludo wants me to be a little Italian woman, endlessly spoiling the children, playing with them and ruining them in the way Italians do. While they grow up to be monsters, I grow old before my time, fit for nothing more than making minestrone! No thank you. That is not how I see my life.'

'Oh, Constance, you're wrong about Ludo,' Monica replied. 'He wouldn't want you to be like that at all. He's proud of you. He just wishes you could be more domestic.'

'And don't you think I wish it, too?' Constance cried

in despair. 'Oh, Monica, you have no idea how hard I try. I adore the children – they mean everything to me – but they don't excite me in the way the business does. Not even the clothes do. Of course, I love clothes. I'm often moved to tears when I see the beautiful things Giuseppe creates but what *always* excites me is the business part – the planning, the manipulation, the decision making. I am a businesswoman, Monica. I suppose if I'm honest I love the power. It's like a drug. I become so totally absorbed in it that hours – even whole days – pass without me giving a thought to anything else. But that doesn't mean I don't love my children. I *do* love them but I can't give the time to them.'

She paused. 'No, if I'm truthful, I don't *want* to give the time to them. I can't focus on the way their little minds work. They're much better off with their nanny.' She bit her lip. 'Monica,' she asked, 'do you think I'm dreadfully wicked? I often think I am. It must be in the blood. You haven't met my mother and I certainly don't want to speak badly of her – after my father was killed, she had a difficult time, I'm sure, bringing me up alone. She did a good job, I suppose, but with all her efficiency she never managed to bring us close emotionally. She wasn't maternal. I think it must be a family flaw. Try as I might, I think I'm going along exactly the same path as Nora. I don't know what I can do about it.'

'I don't think you need worry too much, my darling,' Monica replied. 'It's terribly hard for an intelligent, achieving woman like you, whose brain is working at full speed all day, to come down to the level of young children. Your mind can't slow down enough to enter their simple world. In my view, you shouldn't feel guilty at all. Margharita and Manfredo won't need you until they start thinking. They have a good nanny. At the moment, they can be looked after by anybody. It's just that Ludovico feels that *nothing* about your family interests you these days. Your life seems to be so separate from theirs.'

She paused.

'Constance, can I ask you a question you might prefer not to answer?'

Constance nodded but said nothing.

'Is there somebody else?'

Constance was startled. She could feel herself blushing. 'What do you mean?' she asked.

'There's something about you that I've noticed recently.'

The two women looked at each other.

'Well, is there somebody else?' Monica repeated.

'I don't know. I'm sure that sounds very silly, but it's actually true. I've been spending a lot of time with Giuseppe lately.'

'Giuseppe? But he's only interested in boys, surely?'

'Well, that's what I'm not sure about. Everyone says so but I'm conscious of very strong sexual vibrations when we're together – even just working. I know that it's not my imagination.'

Monica was completely taken aback. She was unprepared for such a bizarre idea.

'But you aren't having an affair?'

'No, not even a little flirtation. It's simply that I find him very attractive.'

Constance looked her friend in the eye. 'I know exactly what you're thinking, Monica, and I know that you're probably right, but there is something magnetic about Giuseppe Padone.'


Constance entered the courthouse on Ludovico's arm, dressed entirely in black.

'Ascoli Piceno is an austere provincial town,' Savognia had warned her. 'Don't look glamorous or smart. They won't understand and it will do Ludovico no good. Wear something dark. Oh,' he remembered, 'and very little make-up.'

She followed his instructions to the letter.

The moment that they entered the building Constance knew that her precautions had been unnecessary. The corridor they waited in was as crowded and confused as a railway station: overexcited people jostled each other for elbow-room, lawyers listened to impassioned last-minute pleas or alibis, and the atmosphere was thick with cigarette smoke. To Constance, it was all as ruthlessly masculine as a bar in north-east England, a place where women were hardly noticed let alone considered. Savognia stepped out of the throng to greet them. He was accompanied by a fat and florid man in his fifties whom he introduced as Ludovico's lawyer and who barely nodded at Constance before enclosing Giancarlo and Ludovico in a two-armed embrace that completely excluded her. Yet another little area of life not suitable for the ladies, Constance thought. Not that she minded. She would put up with any indignity to help Ludovico win his case.

She stood at the back of the courtroom with Savognia as Ludovico was led before the judge. His lawyer had explained that the charge to be answered was one of involuntary homicide. Constance thought that it sounded very serious but Savognia assured her that the hearing was merely a formality. As there were no witnesses, it was impossible to decide whether Gioella's death had been caused by Ludovico's negligent driving or the peasant's sudden appearance in the road.

'It's really little more than a way of making money for them all,' Savognia had murmured, looking round the noisy, chaotic room with patrician contempt.

He was right. No conclusions about the cause of the accident could be drawn and Ludovico walked out a free man. Just as they were leaving, a small man in his late fifties blocked their path. He was bald and wore spectacles but, even before he spoke, it was obvious to Constance that he was wealthy. In the split second she had to look him up and down she noticed that his suit was immaculate and his shoes hand-made.

'Bastard!' he screamed at Ludovico. 'Dirty bastard! You killed her! You killed my Gioella!'

He spat in Ludovico's face and moved forward to hit him. Constance thought more quickly than anyone. She

331

stepped in front of the man, raised her hand to push him away and shouted, 'How dare you spit at my husband, you disgusting creature!'

She was considerably taller than he was and the man stepped back in alarm. She pursued him.

'Who on earth do you think you're talking to?' she demanded. 'My husband is the Principe Castelfranco di Villanuova.'

The man recovered himself. 'And I am Dottore Umberto di Grignano. Your precious husband murdered my wife.'

Constance was stunned. She suddenly remembered him from the funeral. She had an overwhelming desire to apologise but before she could reply Grignano had pushed her aside.

'You should be put in chains!' he shouted at Ludovico who stood, dazed and silent, before him. 'You know your guilt! You know it was your fault – and no corrupt court can take that away from you. You will have to live with it for the rest of your life – just as I must live without my darling!'

He burst into tears. Constance had a sudden urge to comfort him but, as if he had read her mind, Giancarlo gripped her arm and propelled her and Ludovico away from the man. As they pushed through the crowds at the entrance, Constance began to sob with shock. She allowed Giancarlo to bundle her into the car. As it drove away, she caught a glimpse of Carlo standing on the edge of the crowd. He looked inexpressibly sad.

Ludovico had remained ashen-faced and silent throughout the whole proceedings. He had shown no reaction to the judge's comments, Grignano's hysteria or Constance's distress. It was as if he were in a soundproofed bubble, isolated and insulated from a world he could not see. In years to come, Constance was to look back to that cold grey day in Ascoli Piceno as the moment when she finally lost the battle to keep hold of her husband. That was the day he slipped away from her for ever.

# CHAPTER 13

Constance peeped through the curtain. She could see Giancarlo, with his back to her, effortlessly stage-managing the seating, ensuring that the right people were placed in the front row without offending friends who had to be relegated to seats further back. She admired his cool aplomb and felt a prickle of resentment that Ludovico had failed to give her the same support. Despite agreeing to attend the showing of her first collection, he had not yet appeared, though the proceedings should have begun several minutes before. An urgent tug at her sleeve told her it was time to leave her vantage point and return to the dressing room. Well, she thought, we'll just have to start without him.

Though disappointed at Ludo's absence, she was gratified to see the cream of Italian society sitting in the tightly packed rows, surrounded by Europe's top fashion journalists. Such support, Constance was happy to acknowledge, was more for Giancarlo than herself. Respected for his social position as well as his understanding of fashion, an invitation from him, even to the busiest of people, was proudly displayed on the mantelshelf, and always accepted.

Constance took one last look. She suddenly noticed that Louise and Jim were in the third row. Then she saw the woman sitting next to Louise. It was Nora. Slipping through the curtain, she rushed to greet them.

'Mummy! What are you doing here? What a marvellous surprise!'

Nora was delighted at her reception. 'Louise and I thought it would be nice for me to see my daughter's first fashion show,' she said, 'and I knew that if I waited for *some* people to remember to invite me, I'd wait for ever!'

She was in a fine good humour and the words were not said unkindly but they made Constance feel guilty, nevertheless. Before she had time to reply, Louise said, 'I so wanted to give you a surprise! I knew you'd get the shock of your life!'

'I don't see Ludovico,' Nora said, looking around.

Trust you to notice! thought Constance. The moment was saved by Giancarlo who came up to the group and said discreetly, 'It is time, Constance.'

As she stepped into the dressing room, Constance felt excited but not nervous. She was buoyed up by a great confidence. She had known the night before, when she and Giancarlo had joined Giuseppe for the final rehearsal, that the show would be a success. The look Giuseppe had conceived was strong and pure. The day clothes were classic without severity and their line was lightened by frivolous floral hats. The evening dresses were deliciously, extravagantly feminine in the grand manner of the Belle Époque.

Standing by the curtain with Milva ready to check the outfits before they went out, Constance could almost feel the silent intensity of concentration that greeted the appearance of each one. To her surprise, the silence was broken by a smattering of applause at the entrance of the fourth outfit, a brown woollen suit with velvet collar and cuffs. It was narrow-waisted, with a pencil-slim skirt. Constance knew it was elegant but she hadn't expected such an immediate response from the audience. The normal rule was to wait for the end of each section.

When the last of the day-wear had been shown, there was an enormous round of applause, which was gratifying enough, but when the first evening gown whisked out through the curtain, the audience became increasingly excited. Near the end of the show, Giuseppe's favourite, a black velvet evening dress cut very low and hugging the figure, was revealed as the model slipped off a huge bronze satin cape lined with black swansdown. There was a gasp of admiration and the audience were on their feet, clapping enthusiastically. They continued to do so as the remaining three dresses were shown. When the wedding dress appeared, signalling the end of the show, the crowd began to call for Constance.

She glanced across at Giuseppe. He had been supervising the dressing of the models and he looked dreadful. His eyes were sunk deep in his head; his hair was matted and his shirt was stuck to his thin frame with sweat. Despite his unprepossessing appearance, Constance was overcome with loving gratitude for what he had achieved for her. She rushed across the changing room and threw her arms round his neck. Suddenly, Savognia was by their side.

'A triumph!' he cried. 'An absolute triumph! I have never known an audience show so much enthusiasm! It's like the first show of Christian Dior! Nothing like it has ever been seen in Italy!' His eyes were moist. 'Constanza! This is incredible!'

She suddenly came down to earth. 'Ludo?' she asked. 'Was he . . .?'

'Your audience is calling for you, Constanza,' Savognia said, ignoring the question. 'You must make an appearance. You must acknowledge their support.'

Dearly as she would have loved to keep the moment to herself Constance knew that the triumph must be shared with the man who had made it possible.

'But I haven't done anything,' she said. 'It's Giuseppe who deserves the applause.'

Savognia frowned. 'It is you they're calling for, Constanza. Please, don't keep them waiting. Noblesse oblige, my dear.'

'Noblesse oblige, indeed,' she replied. 'That's why I

insist that Giuseppe takes a bow. He's the one who has done it all.'

'Yes, yes. Very well,' Savognia agreed tetchily, 'but first you must go out alone. Then you may call out whoever you wish.'

Stepping out into the glare of the lights and listening to the cries of '*Brava!* Well done!' Constance realised something she had forgotten; something she had discovered about herself years before. She adored applause. She needed praise. She loved the limelight. As she accepted a bouquet of flowers chosen by Monica, her mind raced back to modelling at Maison de Levantière . . . pleasing Miss Hatherby with the dolls' costumes . . . colouring the line drawings in *Blackie's* for her father. All her life she had done things in order to receive acclaim. With it, she blossomed; without it, she faded. If only Ludovico would understand, she thought, as her eyes scanned the rows of seats, looking in vain for him. She was deeply hurt that he had let her down but determined that nobody, least of all Ludo himself, would ever know the sense of betrayal she felt at his failure to appear.

It was only her admiration for Padone that persuaded her to share the applause that she longed to keep for herself but she knew that she must. She turned back and pulled him out on to the runway to stand next to her. The applause faltered. Then the audience recovered and began clapping with renewed vigour: not for Padone, but for the courageous Englishwoman who had openly acknowledged her designer where others would go to great lengths to keep even his existence a secret.

Walking back through the curtain with Giuseppe's hand still in hers, Constance came face to face with Milva.

'Milva!' she cried excitedly. 'Isn't this marvellous! All the hard work was worth it, after all!'

Milva's eyes were cold. '*Si*,' she said, and turned away without another word.

A week after the show, Constance was alone in her office

checking over the orders when the telephone rang. She had been so absorbed in the figures that its sudden noise startled her. Reaching to pick it up, she noticed to her surprise that the time on her desk clock said nine thirty p.m.

That will be Rosanna asking what time I'll be back for supper, she thought. She was wrong. It was Ludovico.

'I expected you to be home by this hour,' he began petulantly. 'What are you doing?'

'I'm still working, of course; what do you imagine I'm doing? Are you at the castle?'

'Yes. Are you alone?'

'Of course; everyone else left ages ago.'

'My mother is dead.'

The baldness of the statement shocked Constance as much as the information.

'When did it happen?'

'This evening, at prayers. The priest was hearing her confession. She died in mid-sentence with her rosary in her hand. Isn't that beautiful? The doctor said that she had a huge stroke and can have felt no pain.'

'Where were you? Were you with her?'

'I was in the library. By the time they fetched me it was too late. It was all over.'

Constance drove up to the castle early the next day. She had spent a bad night, tossing and turning. She regretted her promise to Maria-Angelina that she would take over the running of the family fortunes. It's the last thing I need at the moment, she thought, as she turned the car off the main highway to begin the twisty climb up over the hills. She had no intention of not keeping her bargain but she was also determined that she would not allow the business to suffer through the pressure of Villanuova affairs.

As she drove through the arch into the courtyard, she was reminded of the last time she had been at the castle, several months before, when everything had been gay in yellow and white. It made her feel slightly ashamed that

337

she hadn't been there for so long. Her mood quickly changed to annoyance when she noticed that the massive portico was entirely draped in black crepe. It's absolutely Victorian, this enjoyment of death, she thought as she parked the car.

The door was opened by Ludovico, dressed in black. Constance was aware that he had been crying – and she found the fact so touching and his appearance so like a lost and hopeless little boy that she rushed into his arms, all his betrayals suddenly forgotten. 'Oh, my poor darling,' she cried. 'I am so sorry! So dreadfully sorry!'

He stepped back and gave her a quizzical look. 'Constanza, come! You hated my mother,' he said, not unkindly. 'You must be glad she is out of the way.'

'No,' she replied, 'you're wrong, Ludo, I didn't hate your mother. It was more that she never allowed me to love her. You know that. She didn't think I was good enough for the Villanuovas.' She smiled. 'Perhaps she was right. But I really *am* sorry. I know how much she meant to you.'

As they walked across the hallway, her practical streak emerged. 'Has the body been seen to?'

'Yes, by her servant.'

'Is the funeral arranged?'

'She will be buried in two days' time.' He paused. 'Would you like to say your last farewell?' His voice was tentative and he was clearly so afraid that she would say no that Constance took pity on him.

'Of course,' she said, 'but if you don't mind, Ludo, I would like to be alone.'

He seemed surprised, but agreed immediately.

The little servant was still doing her duty by the Principessa even in death. She shuffled along the corridor before Constance, opened the door and stood back respectfully. Constance heard the door close gently behind her as she stepped into the room. She felt suddenly uneasy at the thought of being alone with the body. A rustling movement from the bed startled her. Her hand went to her mouth to stifle a scream; for a wild moment Constance thought Maria-Angelina was rising from the dead. But it was only the movement of her personal priest, who had been kneeling between the candles at the foot of the bed. He stood up and, murmuring his apologies, backed out of the room, leaving Constance with the body.

She looked down at Maria-Angelina. It was the first time she had seen her without her gloves. The flesh on her fingers was a pale lemon, dimpled and puckered as if the hands had been in water for a long time. Constance was surprised at how deeply sensual Maria-Angelina's face looked in death. So, she mused to herself, it's not only from his father that Ludovico gets his sexuality. What terrible sacrifices and denials you must have made in your life, Principessa. I wonder how many times you were tempted and decided to cower behind your religion so that you would not fall. As she gazed at the face, Constance was fascinated. Had Maria-Angelina ever slipped? she wondered.

After a few minutes, she left the bed and walked to the door, boldly gazing round as she wouldn't have dared when the Principessa was alive. She had never properly seen this room. Even when Maria-Angelina had been alive dark shadows had seemed to creep from its corners into the centre, to shroud everything in mystery.

Constance made a decision. She turned from the door, walked back to the window and wrenched at the curtains so carefully sewn together many years before. Like the curtains themselves, the thread joining them was rotten with age. Everything came away in Constance's hand, in a flurry of dust. She gasped and choked as it rose around her. The light flooded in, catching the dust and bathing the Principessa's body in the golden glow of the strong afternoon sun. Constance was shocked at how tiny and powerless the body looked in the full light of day. How could I ever have been frightened of you? she wondered as she looked at the frail cadaver.

Fluff and dust from the rotting draperies rolled away

from Constance's feet and hundreds of spiders scurried for cover as she walked across the richly patterned parquet floor. As her eyes became accustomed to the light, she stared incredulously. The walls of the room consisted of intricate marquetry pictures. Hundreds of different veneers had been used to create magnificent wooden murals, depicting giants, columns, pastoral scenes, mythical animals and strange devils, which covered every inch of the walls. Constance realised that what she had assumed in the gloom was Chinese painted wallpaper was, in fact, work of the greatest Renaissance craftsmanship. Tentatively, she climbed on to the Principessa's platform and looked down at the half-finished jigsaw. It was the martyrdom of Saint Sebastian, transfixed by arrows. Constance shuddered.

Suddenly, she knew what she must do. Stepping boldly into the wide corridor, where the cowering servant waited for her, Constance walked its whole length, tearing down the rotten curtains that swathed all the windows and drowning the terrified woman's scream of horror with loud cries of *'Luce! Luce!* Light! Let there be light! There *must* be light! No more darkness! Light!' She threw open the doors of rooms undisturbed for more than twenty years, tore down the curtains and pushed back the creaking shutters. One set crashed into the courtyard below. Constance started to laugh. Hysterically screaming, 'Light! No more darkness!' she ran, shrieking with wild laughter, through every room, allowing the sunlight to flood in, before collapsing at the top of the stairs. Overcome with relief that the Principessa's reign was over, she burst into tears of gratitude.

'On whose orders is every window in this castle wide open?' Ludovico burst into the *salotto* angrily.

'Mine,' Constance replied coolly. 'The whole place reeks of decay. Some of those rooms haven't known fresh air for half a century, I'm sure. We must get rid of the stench of age before people start to arrive for the funeral. Ludo, stop looking at me like that. You know I'm right.'

'You are so wrong,' he answered slowly, 'that there is no point in talking to you. Desecration is all you seem to understand. Did you have to destroy her memory before she was even cold?'

They sat together in the *salotto* after supper. Conversation was sporadic and the atmosphere heavy. Constance longed for the next day, when Savognia and Monica would arrive. After a particularly long silence, she said quietly, 'I am sorry, Ludovico, if you feel that I showed disrespect for your mother's memory but life doesn't stand still. We must face the future.'

'I know it,' he replied, 'but let us get the funeral over before we make any decisions.'

'Your mother has given charge of the estate to me.'

'You? I cannot believe what you say!'

'I didn't want it, Ludovico. Please believe me. It is the price she made me pay for the money she put into the business.'

'You took advantage of a sick old woman in order to take my inheritance. Why? You have always hated everything about our heritage.'

'You're wrong, Ludovico. I never hated it – but I was determined to make us independent of it. And I have succeeded. In any case, the inheritance is really your brother's, surely?'

Ludovico remained silent.

'We must make a very important decision before the funeral, Ludo.'

'What is it?'

'Carlo.'

Ludovico stiffened. 'Carlo?' he asked. 'What decision is there to be made concerning Carlo? The final decision about Carlo was made by my poor mother.'

'You surely intend to allow him to attend the funeral?'

'I most certainly do not. My mother would never rest

in her grave if such a thing were to happen. Please do not even suggest it.'

Constance suddenly felt overwhelmed with weariness. This was a battle she couldn't fight alone. She knew that it must wait until the others arrived in the morning.


'Ludovico, you cannot deny your brother a son's right to take his farewell of his mother,' Giancarlo said reasonably. 'He must be allowed to see the body. And that means that he must come to the castle.'

'He must in any case,' Constance added. 'The funeral is in the chapel, so he will have to enter then.'

'You don't understand,' Ludovico said harshly. 'My mother banished him. She didn't want him to come to her funeral.'

'Banished him!' Monica interrupted. 'For God's sake, Ludo, stop being so medieval. People can't be *banished* in the twentieth century! He has as much right to enter this castle as you have. In any case, he is the first-born. Doesn't that give him all rights?'

'He has no more rights than you,' Ludovico said savagely, and turned away abruptly, leaving Constance and Monica gazing at Giancarlo in consternation.

'You must make him see sense, Giancarlo,' Monica said. 'Carlo is the first-born son. In justice this whole place should belong to him now. Ludo has no moral right to exclude him.'

'Carlo has to see his mother before the coffin is sealed,' Constance added, 'and obviously he cannot be banned from the funeral.'

'Think of the scandal,' Monica said.

Giancarlo shrugged. 'It would merely be yet another in a lifetime of Villanuova scandals,' he said philosophically. 'But you are right. I will persuade Ludo.'

He turned to Constance. 'It is better that I do so alone. We are two Italians so it is easier – and a man can more easily help a man make a moral decision.'

Constance swallowed her resentment of this argument and was glad to leave it to Savognia.

Ludovico agreed to allow Carlo to enter the castle one hour before the funeral service. He would be permitted to visit his mother's body and would then be taken to the family chapel to await the other mourners. He would leave immediately after the service.

'That seems so dismissive,' Constance protested to Giancarlo.

'It is as far as I can persuade Ludovico to go,' he answered with finality.

Constance was excited at the thought of seeing the two brothers together but full of trepidation on the morning of the funeral. As she waited at Ludovico's side for Carlo to arrive, she thought how beautiful her husband looked. Lack of sleep and emotional exhaustion had given him the pallor and intensity of a Shelley – shattered, broken and irresistibly vulnerable. She wanted to fling her arms round him and give him the comfort he needed but the atmosphere between them was so constrained that she dared not even slip her hand in his, knowing instinctively that he would withdraw. Ludovico stiffened as they heard the car enter the courtyard.

Watching Carlo climb the steps towards them, Constance was struck by how small he looked. As he reached the top step, he faltered, waiting for a sign from Ludovico. The day seemed to freeze. The seconds moved forward but everything else was still. Finally, Carlo spoke one word. Holding out his hand, he whispered, 'Brother.'

Ludovico remained motionless.

'Come,' Carlo said, stepping forward and embracing him.

Constance felt that the long, silent embrace would never end. When it did, she saw that both men were dry-eyed, although their faces showed the pain. Leading his brother into the hall, Ludovico said to Constance, 'We must go alone.'

She dropped back in confusion. Savognia took her arm and they silently joined Monica, following the two brothers at a distance.

For a long time the three of them heard no sound as they waited outside the Principessa's room. Then the silence was broken by Ludovico's voice. Straining to hear his words, none of them made any pretence at not listening.

'There can be no forgiveness, no reconciliation,' they heard him say. 'You are here today for propriety, not for pardon – and expressly against my mother's will.'

'Our mother did everything she could to keep us apart in life but only we can allow her to do so in death,' Carlo replied.

'No,' Ludovico replied, 'we have no control, even after her death. You are banished. Only *your* death can change that.'

'Please, Ludo,' Carlo pleaded, 'do not allow her to destroy the rest of our life. Can't we forget the past and all its mistakes? Will she triumph over us for ever?'

There was a silence. The listeners were startled as the door opened.

'Savognia,' Ludovico said, 'will you escort my brother to the chapel?'

As Carlo walked past them, Constance could not bear to look at him. Although his eyes remained secret behind their glasses, every part of his frame showed despair at his defeat. She could see that Ludo was shaking. She stepped towards him and grasped his hand. He did not move. She could think of nothing to say.

Monica came to their rescue. 'I think the other mourners will be arriving, Ludo,' she gently said. 'You and Constance must be on the steps to greet them.'

Constance gratefully led the way out of the dark hall and into the sunshine. There was no one in the courtyard. Suddenly, as if emerging from a daze, Ludovico let go of her hand and said, 'You know my brother.' She was startled and had no answer.

344

'How?' he asked.

'What on earth makes you think such a thing?' Constance replied. 'What did Carlo say to you?'

'I can instantly read my brother. He didn't need to say anything. I saw the way he looked at you. Not only was the look without curiosity, it was full of familiarity. How could you betray me in this way?'

'I have done nothing wrong!' she cried. 'I have not betrayed you. I met him in the hills – only once – and we talked briefly. That is all. I was curious. How can you accuse me when you were prepared to let me go through our entire married life without ever knowing you *had* a brother?'

'I did not – until you brought him back into our world.'

'Me? I have done no such thing! You said yourself that he had to be allowed to his mother's funeral – for propriety, not for me. Carlo is nothing to me. I barely know him – and for that *you* should feel guilt and shame. Don't try to shift them on to me.'

A row was averted by the arrival of the first mourners. Constance was seething with anger at the unfairness of Ludovico's attack and could hardly wait for everyone to leave so that she could have it out with him.

Ludovico wept during the funeral service. Carlo, standing at his side, did not. As the coffin was carried out of the chapel, Constance thought, So ends a woman who has destroyed both her sons. But then she thought again: the Principessa's influence had not ended with her death; Ludovico's rejection of Carlo made that clear. Constance found the thought deeply depressing.

As he left the chapel, Carlo stopped before her. 'Goodbye, Constance,' he said in English. 'We will not see each other again but please remember that, although I did wrong, it was not done for myself. Whatever happens in the future, never forget that.'

Constance felt the tears coming to her eyes. She half turned away. When she looked again, Carlo was gone, out of the black shadows of the hall into the blazing white light of the courtyard. Its blinding intensity seemed to have totally consumed him, leaving behind no trace.

Constance did not continue the quarrel with Ludovico. She realised that there was nothing to say – no words that could bridge the gap between them. Being an only child, Constance had always longed for a brother or sister. She couldn't understand what spell Maria-Angelina had worked to make Ludovico turn his back so completely on Carlo, a brother who clearly adored and needed him. She knew that Ludovico saw her meeting with Carlo as a betrayal for which she could not be forgiven.

As silence descended on the castle Constance took stock of her marriage. Apart from her promise to the Principessa that she would manage the estates, she knew that she couldn't leave Ludovico. She recognised that in an obscure way he needed her almost because of the sense of betrayal he felt over the business. At least it fuelled his anger and prevented him from spending all his time brooding over Gioella's death.

Did Constance need *him*? It was a question she tried hard to answer. Of course she wanted the children to grow up in a normal, balanced family but a father who cut himself off from the world and abandoned himself to melancholia was possibly worse than no father at all. The question she couldn't answer – the question that would have answered all others – was concerned with her attitude to Ludovico. Did she still love him? She simply didn't know. She knew, however, that she couldn't let him go until he had acknowledged her achievement – as mother, businesswoman and chosen successor to Maria-Angelina. If even her mother-in-law had been able to see her worth, how could her own husband remain blind to it?

Work was her salvation. Before she could begin to think about the estates, it was necessary for her to return to Florence and start working with Giuseppe on their second collection.

'It is crucial that we get it absolutely right,' he told her.

'After such a success as ours, there will be many people looking very closely to find the holes in the next one.'

'He's right,' Savognia agreed, 'the second collection is always the hardest. It must be even better than the first. After that people see that you have a rhythm and then they trust you.'

Already, Giuseppe had produced an amazing number of sketches. Looking at them, Constance could see his mind at work. They had the same powerfully individual hallmark of the last collection, but she admired the way he had moved forward. The new line was softer than the first one. The clothes were meant to skim, not hug, the body, and to Constance that slight relaxation of the shape made a striking difference. It was a younger, fresher look and seemed to her much more in the Italian spirit than the previous collection, which had been strongly based on the mood of Paris.

'He really is a genius, you know,' she said to Monica.

'Sure,' was the reply, 'but that's no reason to sleep with him. Einstein is a genius, but nobody wants to pop into bed with him.'

Constance laughed. 'Oh, Monica, how unfair to bring that up. Just because I said things in a moment of weakness. My relationship with Giuseppe is based on mutual respect. Please forget everything I said.'

'I already did,' Monica said, smiling knowingly.

Constance realised why she felt closer to Monica than she had to any other woman: she had generosity of soul. Her spirit was too big for her ever to take up moral attitudes. 'Would you like to work with us?' she asked on the spur of the moment.

'Work? How do you mean? The only thing I know about frocks is that they're never my size! What on earth could I do at Constanza Castelfranco?'

'I thought you might look after the public relations. And just be around to keep us all sane. You're always so cheerful and down-to-earth. We need you when things get tense.'

'Thanks a lot!' Monica laughed. 'You make me sound about as exciting as cream cheese.'

'Seriously,' Constance persisted, 'will you let me talk to the others about it?'

'Sure, I'd be honoured.'

Savognia had not spoken to Bettina Bonoccorsi for some time; he was surprised when she rang him at his home one morning.

'Giancarlo,' she said, 'how are you? I've heard nothing about you for weeks. I gather that your firm is doing marvellously. I'm so pleased. I knew Constanza and that rather strange young man would get on. You must be feeling very happy.'

'Yes,' he replied cautiously, 'the order books are looking very healthy.'

'I understand that you've been rather successful with actresses,' Bettina said with the slightest edge to her voice. 'Magnani, I believe.'

'Yes, she bought the black velvet with the swansdown cape.'

'Really? Who advised her to do that, I wonder? I wouldn't have thought that peasant bottom would look its best squeezed into anything as tight as that.'

'Constance tells me she looks superb in it,' Savognia retorted, stung by what was clearly meant as an insult to the House.

'Now Dietrich would look marvellous in something like that,' Bettina continued.

'Well, it's funny you should say that,' Savognia answered petulantly, 'she's coming to view the collection next week.'

'Good, good!' She waited.

'The great excitement is that Ava Gardner came yesterday and chose four outfits . . . and that new woman has been . . . Sophia Loren is it?'

Bettina was amazed how successful her technique was proving. This was how she usually obtained her information but she hadn't expected Savognia to be so easily trapped. He's so besotted with it all, he can't resist spilling the beans, she thought happily.

'Of course,' she went on, 'Constance won't just want actresses, darling. I mean, they're all right but she needs . . . you know . . .'

'Oh, don't worry, my dear,' Savognia interrupted grandly. 'They're literally queuing up! Doria Pamphili, Crespi, Ruspoli. If it goes on like this there won't be an Italian noble family that isn't dressed by us. Portinari will be furious!'

'A little bird tells me that Monica is working for you now.'

'Hardly working for us. More like helping us out – in a very *ad hoc* way.'

'Quite. Even so, I'm surprised, knowing what poor Ludovico feels about the business. Don't you think he'll see it as a betrayal?'

'Betrayal? Bettina, what on earth are you talking about?'

'Well, darling, considering their relationship, it could be thought a little odd.'

'Relationship?'

'Don't be naive, Giancarlo, it ill becomes a man of your years. You know full well what I mean.'

Savognia was shocked. 'Are you suggesting that there is something irregular in Monica's relationship with Ludovico?'

'Come, darling, everybody knows,' Bettina replied. 'Don't tell me you hadn't heard? All that time she spent up at the castle with him, alone? What do you think they were doing? Reading the Bible together? I don't blame Ludo. Poor devil, just as that dreadful old mother of his kicks the bucket, he discovers that his perfect English wife is really nothing more than a bossy bitch, obsessed with making money. Can you blame him for looking elsewhere for comfort? Just as the Villanuovas always have when things aren't going exactly the way they want.'

349

# CHAPTER 14

Giancarlo Savognia was deeply unsettled by Bettina's gossip. His first reaction was to try to put it out of his mind as a typical piece of Bonoccorsi malice. Yet he was unable to. Monica *had* spent a great deal of time alone with Ludovico; sex *was* the driving force and downfall of the Villanuovas, as their history showed all too clearly: it was perfectly possible that Bettina was telling the truth. He wondered if Constance had heard anything of the rumour. He wondered even more how he could get to the bottom of it. If it were true then they had been foolish to take Monica into the firm. He didn't care to think of the repercussions if Constance found out.

Shortly after arriving at the Palazzo Tondi to start work that morning, Giancarlo was startled to run into Monica in the corridor outside his office, at the opposite end of the building from Giuseppe and Constance's studio.

'Giancarlo,' she greeted him, 'may I have a word with you in private?'

'In private?' he asked. 'What about?'

'It's a personal matter, Giancarlo. I cannot discuss it in the corridor.' She looked pointedly at the door of his office.

'Oh,' he said in confusion, 'of course. Um . . . yes . . . do come in.'

Monica wondered why Savognia was behaving so strangely. 'You seem very nervous today, Giancarlo,' she said after he had closed the door.

'Not at all,' he replied, pulling himself together. 'I have rather a lot of things on my mind.'

Anticipating a rebuff, Monica said, 'I'm so sorry. I promise I won't take much of your time.'

'No, no,' he countered expansively, 'please go on.'

'Well, it isn't easy to know where to start, so I might as well plunge in at the deep end. It's Ludovico. He's becoming obsessed with the idea that Constance is betraying him.'

'Betraying him?' he asked in bewilderment.

'Yes, with Carlo.'

'Carlo! Good God!' Savognia looked so horrified that Monica wanted to laugh.

'Whatever can have given him such an idea?' he demanded.

'The funeral, darling, the funeral – he was convinced that they already knew each other by Carlo's reaction to her and then, being a Villanuova, he assumed that they *more* than knew each other, if you see what I mean.'

'Is there any truth in it?'

'Of course not. But I can't convince Ludo. I wondered if you would like to try. You know that he's more inclined to listen to you than any of us.'

'You are quite sure about Carlo and Constance?' Savognia asked cautiously.

'Absolutely. In fact, if there's any danger of her having an affair with anybody it would be much closer to home.'

Savognia raised his eyebrows.

'Actually,' Monica went on, 'Constance hasn't seen Carlo since Maria-Angelina's funeral and she's most unlikely to. He's gone wandering again and you know how obsessed she's become with work – and how infatuated she is with Giuseppe's . . . brilliance.'

The pause alerted Savognia. 'It is just his *brilliance* she finds fascinating, I hope,' he said.

Monica laughed. 'Well, I'm not so sure. You must have noticed how they behave together – and how frequently they *are* together.'

'Oh, my God, Monica,' Savognia cried, 'I really cannot bear all this sexual intrigue. What on earth is wrong with everybody?'

Monica laughed again. 'There's nothing wrong with anyone, although I do agree that it rather complicates life.'

'I couldn't care less about complicated lives,' he said. 'What concerns me is its effect on the business. There's quite a lot of my own money in this firm, you know.' In exasperation, he added, 'And what about the rumours concerning you and Ludovico? Perhaps you'd like to tell me if *they* are true?'

His tone irritated Monica. 'No, I would not, Giancarlo,' she replied sharply. 'My affairs are nothing to do with the firm of Constanza Castelfranco and I am not prepared to discuss them with you or anybody else here. Please understand that. Now, can I rely on you to knock this silly idea about Carlo out of Ludo's head, please?'

She stood up. Savognia knew that the interview was over.

'For summer, I want to do a "Barefoot Contessa" look for evening. We will need some marvellous silks,' Giuseppe said to Constance, 'the most beautiful that Como can produce.'

'I agree,' Savognia said, 'but production is still very limited and people like Portinari will have precedence over us.'

'It really is ridiculous,' Constance said. 'We're just as important as he is, 'for God's sake! Surely you can pull some strings, Giancarlo?'

'I can try,' he answered doubtfully. 'But the way to overcome poor materials is to embroider them. Very suitable for a "Barefoot Contessa" theme. In fact, if you compare us with the Paris couture houses, what we lack is really exceptional embroidery. It's so important for clothes at our level.'

'*Va bene*,' Giuseppe replied impatiently, 'but there is nobody in Italy who can work to the standard of Paris.'

'Quite,' Savognia replied, 'so what we must do is have our embroidery done in Paris. Lesage is our man. He is the best embroiderer in the world. I shall ask him to send us some examples of his work.'

When the samples arrived from Paris Giuseppe was more excited about the workmanship than the designs and declared that it would be better if *he* created the patterns for the Lesage workrooms to make up. He set to work immediately and produced ten drawings based on Moorish scrollwork, reflecting the Spanish theme of the collection. Constance thought they were marvellous but Giancarlo frowned when he saw them.

'I don't think that Lesage will be able to work from these without some guidance,' he said, 'and I'm certainly not capable of giving it. Can't you keep the spirit but simplify a little? Look,' he went on, holding up the first design that came to hand, 'this would require *paillettes* of at least a hundred different shades. Maybe if you removed the shadow effect . . . that would cut down the amount of work required.'

'And totally destroy the subtlety of the design.'

'I don't know about subtlety. I just think it's too complicated. Quite apart from the cost, the workrooms would need far too much advice and guidance. We have to be practical,' he added hastily, noticing how impatient the other man was becoming. 'After all, we are in Florence and they are in Paris. There must be compromises.'

'Creativity allows no compromise,' Giuseppe replied portentously. 'I will go to Paris,' he continued, 'it will take no more than two days to explain my intentions.'

The other two were well aware that a statement had been made. There was no possibility of questioning the decision, let alone disagreeing with it. It was decided, however, that Giancarlo would accompany Giuseppe.

'I think I should be there,' he said quietly to Constance

later, 'just to keep a check on prices. Hand work of this type can be very expensive and Padone might get carried away.'

Constance smiled. She had noticed before that Savognia was increasingly anxious that his investment should not be frittered away.

The day before they were to set out, Giancarlo went down with a cold. To Constance's intense annoyance, he behaved with what she had come to believe was the congenital Italian hypochondria when faced with the slightest snuffle, shiver or headache, and declared himself too sick to travel. She was never sick and thought impatiently, not for the first time, that most of the Italians she knew could benefit from spending a winter on the Northumbrian coast to give them some backbone. She immediately telephoned Albert Lesage, explaining the situation. He assured her that there was no problem. The moment he returned from New York he could see Giuseppe and Giancarlo.

'New York? How long are you going to be in New York?' she asked.

'Oh, two or three weeks. It is not decided. I have business – and then a little holiday.'

'When do you leave?'

'Four days' time.'

Constance thought quickly. This would completely throw out the timing of the collection.

'Monsieur Lesage,' she said. 'I think it better if we stick with the original arrangement. Signore Padone will arrive tomorrow, as planned, and I shall accompany him.'

They were staying at the Hotel Brighton in the rue de Rivoli. The double room Giancarlo had booked for himself was considerably superior to Giuseppe's, two floors above, and boasted a huge bed. As Constance settled in, she wondered whether Savognia had planned an assignation in Paris. The thought intrigued her.

The meetings with Monsieur Lesage in the tiny estab-lishment in rue de la Grande Batelière were an unqualified success. The two men fully understood and appreciated each other's skills from the beginning. Constance found the workrooms fascinating. She always loved to see the practicalities behind the illusions of fashion and was intrigued by the women painstakingly hand-sewing every bead and spangle on a design. On their second, and last, night she and Giuseppe dined alone at La Condonnerie, behind the rue de Rivoli. Giuseppe was relaxed at dinner and drank his French wine with enthusiasm.

'I love this city,' he said. 'You can smell fashion on every street corner. It is almost impossible not to be creative in an atmosphere like this.'

'Would you like to live here?' Constance asked.

'No,' he said firmly. 'It would kill me.'

'Why?'

'It would be like a carousel, going round and round, with no escape. There is too *much* creativity here. I would never stop. I would be like a dervish dancing wildly, faster and faster, until I dropped dead.' Constance laughed. 'Like Moira Shearer in *The Red Shoes*! What a bizarre picture that conjures up, Giuseppe!'

'No,' he said urgently, 'don't laugh! I mean it. Paris would kill me. It is *too* exciting.'

'It would be a magnificent way to die – sacrificed on the high altar of your art.'

'No, no,' he replied. 'I know precisely how I wish to die. *In flagrante.*'

Although Constance smiled, she refused to rise.

She had finished removing her make-up and was about to switch off the light when she heard a tap on the door.

'Who is it?' she asked.

'Giuseppe. I need to talk to you.'

Constance hesitated.

'Constanza, please!' he whispered.

She opened the door. Giuseppe was leaning against the wall, a bottle of champagne and two glasses held casually in his hand. His eyes were glittering and his hair was tousled. Constance thought he looked more like a wild animal than ever. He stepped in and she closed the door after him. He put down the glasses, reached behind her and locked it. Without pausing and with total confidence, he took her in his arms and pushed her against the bathroom door.

The force of his kisses pinned Constance against the door and the weight of his body pressing against hers forced it open. Their interlocked bodies fell into the bathroom. Constance knew that nothing would stop Giuseppe; the thought was unbearably exciting to her. She bit his neck like a wild thing. Groaning loudly, he pushed her back. She lost her footing on the tiles and slid heavily into the low-lying bath, still clutching Giuseppe tightly to her. She hit her head on the rim, the porcelain was icy on her back but she was unaware of it. As he fell on top of her he continued to kiss her madly, at the same time forcing his way inside her; his insistent movements pushed her body along the smooth surface of the bath, until her head was rhythmically banged against the tap. Tears came to her eyes but she didn't care about the pain. All she wanted was Giuseppe inside her, plunging deeper, harder, longer. That was the only reality. She longed for him never to stop. As his passion overwhelmed her, Constance's little cries of pain turned to moans of pleasure as she gasped his name over and over again.

Afterwards, they lay panting in the shallow bath, oblivious to the discomfort of their surroundings. When their breathing became calmer, Giuseppe spoke for the first time.

'Now you are mine. I will never let you go.'

She said nothing.

'I have wanted this for so long,' he whispered.

She tried to push him from her.

'Giuseppe,' she gasped, 'can you ease up a little?'

As he did so, she grasped a handle on the side of the bath to lever herself up. The handle moved and icy water began to spray on them from the shower above. Their screams of shock turned to hysterical laughter as they lay there, allowing the water to pour down on them, unchecked. Suddenly, before Constance knew what was happening, Giuseppe was inside her again, passionately, aggressively taking possession of her. As her cries of pleasure increased, and the water continued to cascade on to their slippery bodies, she knew that she could never let Ludovico make love to her again.

At the desk next morning, as they were checking out, Giuseppe took hold of the back of Constance's neck and pushed his hand up under her hair. It was a deliberately calculated sexual reminder that she was now his. Arching back her neck, she shuddered with pleasure. At that precise moment, she caught a glimpse of a face reflected in the mirror before her. It was Bettina Bonoccorsi. Constance knew that she had seen and understood Giuseppe's gesture. In a panic, she turned as Bettina walked over and said, 'Darling! *quelle surprise!* What brings you to Paris?'

'Oh,' Constance replied in confusion, 'business . . .'

Bettina laughed. 'So what's new, darling, it's *always* business with you!' She looked Giuseppe up and down deliberately, lowered her head in salutation, said coldly, 'Signor Padone,' and turned back to Constance.

'Just the two of you? My word, it *must* be business. Well, I wouldn't expect you to divulge your little secrets to me. You never know who I might talk to,' and, laughing merrily, she turned to go.

Constance noticed fearfully the calculating look in Bettina's narrowed eyes. She couldn't let her walk away thinking the worst.

'Are you in Paris for long, Bettina?' she asked.

'No, no.' Bettina smiled, enjoying the moment. 'I've just popped in to see what I can see. You know, keep abreast of friends. Find out what's going on. You know how I like to be in the swim. Well, darling,' she ended, 'I'd love to stop and chat but I have so many people to talk to that I simply must get on. I'm back in Florence tomorrow. I'll see you there. Be good,' and, ignoring Giuseppe, she swept out into the rue de Rivoli.

The journey back to Florence would have been a nightmare if Giuseppe's insistent love-making hadn't diverted Constance from the image of Bettina and the potential scandal she held in her hands. They had the carriage to themselves. Regardless of people passing in the corridor, Giuseppe pulled down the blinds and started to make love to her. Embarrassed at first by his recklessness, his passion was exciting, and when he finally whispered that he could wait no longer she willingly followed him down the empty first-class corridor and allowed him to lock them into the lavatory. There, deaf to persistent knocking on the door, Constance allowed him to have her, again and again.

I am wanton, she thought back in the compartment as the train trundled down from Bolognia, and she watched Giuseppe asleep opposite her. She smiled. She convinced herself that she could feel Giuseppe's hot sperm moving inside her. The sensation filled her with joy, and she began to lose her fear of Bettina's spite. He's the most exciting man in the world, she thought. Ludo has never made me feel like this – as if every atom of my body has been possessed. I can't give him up, no matter what Bettina does. She felt helplessly in his power, as if he had mesmerised her but in fact, she had mesmerised herself – by looking into the deep wells of physical lust he had opened within her, which, for all his prowess, Ludovico had never plumbed.

# CHAPTER 15

Four years after falling under the spell of Giuseppe's sexuality Constance became pregnant. Despite her conviction in Paris that she and her husband could never be intimate again, she had continued, sporadically, to allow Ludovico to make love to her. Nevertheless, she felt instinctively that this child must be Giuseppe's. Until very recently, she had resisted having his child and had taken every precaution against the possibility. Now she felt that the only way to bind Giuseppe to her was by having his baby.

It was inconceivable to her that the child could be Ludovico's and she expected that her pregnancy would bring a crisis to their lives. She was ready for it. After all, what she and Ludovico now had could barely be called a life. She knew that he felt she had sacrificed their relationship for her fame as the head of Constanza Castelfranco, but in her opinion he had given her no alternative. He had destroyed their marriage by refusing even to attempt to come to terms with her personality and needs. As her business had become increasingly successful, to compensate for the failure of her marriage she had fed on the power it gave her. It was the only thing that kept her self-esteem alive.

She admitted to herself – but to nobody else – that she loved being famous. Walking into a shop or restaurant, she was accorded immediate recognition and treated with respectful deference. It made her feel marvellous, though she knew it shouldn't. In the silent moments when she went over her life, she accepted that it was a weakness so deeply entrenched in her character that there was no fighting it. Instead she enjoyed it. Even more, she enjoyed being rich. Although she had never known poverty, life in Northumberland had been modest and Nora had treated money with respect. Now that she was in charge of her own finances, Constance liked being extravagant. She bought herself a white Mercedes roadster with red leather seats and a mahogany fascia, indulged the children with every toy she could find, even having them sent from Neiman-Marcus at Christmas and, as a final accolade of her success, had Portinari design her a full-length black mink coat, as he was famous throughout Europe for his furs.

She had failed to find the courage to tell Ludovico about Giuseppe and she quietened her conscience by convincing herself that he wouldn't care very much in any case. Theirs had become a marriage in name only. He spent almost all his time in the Marche. She hardly ever returned there. Even when the hat factory – now a thriving independent business in custom-built premises – required some attention she preferred to send Savognia or Milva to deal with it, according to the nature of the problem.

Her relationship with Milva had gone through a bad period shortly after Constance and Giuseppe had become lovers. Although they acted with extreme discretion, Milva guessed immediately and Constance knew it. She was conscious that she had fallen in Milva's estimation but her passion was too great to take any considered account of it. In fact, she was certain that Milva was the only person in on the secret and when she decided to confide in Monica she was shocked to find that she too was aware of what was going on.

'Darling,' Monica had said, when she told her about the coolness with Milva, 'what on earth did you expect? That she would say "Well done!" and pat you on the back? You're dealing with an Italian peasant here, remember – and a Catholic to boot! She thinks of you as aristocracy. After all, you're the daughter-in-law of the Principessa! You're a Villanuova in her eyes, and her people have been trained to view the Villanuovas as barely mortal. You're expected to behave like a goddess – and certainly not give way to anything as earthy as physical desire outside the marriage bed!'

'You sound like my mother! That's exactly what they would say up in Northumberland! I can't believe you're right about Milva. She's a highly intelligent woman.'

'Look, it has nothing to do with intelligence. It's about attitudes bred in the bone. That's what virtually *every* woman would say! I know all about the Seven Year Itch but, remember, Marilyn Monroe wasn't married and, in any case, it was the man who had the itch. No, say what you like, my darling, married women are not expected to take lovers.'

'But how did she find out?'

'Same way as I did. By using her eyes. You're right about Milva. She *is* highly intelligent. She's also very shrewd and *very* observant.'

'I just hope there won't be trouble, Monica. You know how much I rely on her – she's my right hand. I cannot have quarrels and atmospheres between her and Giuseppe.'

'Darling, that won't happen. She will behave perfectly correctly. Peasants are terrible snobs. She will treat him with indifference simply because he's a peasant too. No, you are the one she cares about.'

'Well, I don't know what to do.'

'The problem is that she's in love with you.'

'In *love*?'

'Yes. Head over heels. Not physically but in a hero-worshipping way. She loves your feminine strength that can dominate a male world. That's why she can't bear the thought of Giuseppe. It's the old feet-of-clay business. She cannot accept that you are anything less than perfect. You must tread very carefully. You could hurt her very deeply – and that, my darling, would be as unforgivable as it would be foolish. Remember that Milva will be with you for life.'

'And Giuseppe?' Constance asked in alarm.

'You tell me, darling.'

Constance was completely faithful to Giuseppe. In all the four years, it never entered her head to look at any other man. Such was not the case with him. His need for his own sex meant that right from the beginning he betrayed her consistently and frequently. At least three nights a week, he would leave her bed in Fiesole and return to Florence – for she never let him spend the night with her, fearing that the children would see him in the morning – to seek his own kind. He prowled the banks of the Arno searching for a young man to please him. Once found – and he never abandoned the search until somebody *had* been found – he would have him urgently against a wall in a black back street or take him to his apartment if he felt the need to play with him a little. Often, he would repeat the process several times in a night. Making love to his own sex was as natural to Giuseppe as it was crucial, so he hardly saw what he did as cheating of Constance and her exclusive love for him.

Everybody but Constance knew about Giuseppe's alternative nightlife. It was not so exceptional in Florence that it caused a great scandal. A little gossip here, a shrugged indifference to the frailty of humanity there, and that was all. *Her* relationship with him generated much more interest. Everybody knew, thanks to Bettina.

Even Ludovico. He had received a telephone call from Bettina almost immediately after her return from Paris. 'Now, Ludovico,' she had said, 'I know that the last thing you want is a telephone call from me but please don't hang up. For the sake of everything that happened so long ago and went so terribly wrong, please listen. I've just come back from Paris. It just so happened that I was staying at the Brighton, I usually do – it's nothing special but it's so handy for the Place Vendôme and the Ritz bar

– and, to my utter surprise, Constance was staying there too.'

She paused.

'Far be it from me to make trouble, Ludovico, but she wasn't alone. You can imagine my surprise. She was with that Padone man. Now, I'm not saying that there was anything *wrong* going on, dear, but they did seem so . . . well, close – so, when I . . . Ludovico?' The telephone had been put down at the other end.

Bettina was furious. Right, you spoilt little Villanuova bastard, she thought, if *you* don't want to hear, I'll make sure it gets round to people who will.

And she did, skilfully and speedily.

Naively, Constance assumed that because nothing was said publicly her affair with Giuseppe hadn't become common knowledge. The lack of gossip surprised her. She was certain that Bettina had fully understood the situation when she had bumped into her and Giuseppe in Paris. Why hadn't she told anyone? Even Savognia didn't seem to know about it. If he had, she was sure that his disapproval would have shown in a hundred different ways, some subtle, others petulant. Not that she would have cared. Giuseppe was rapidly becoming the most important person in her life, for whom no sacrifice seemed too great.

Ludovico knew that the castle was the correct place in which to end his life. He also knew the most fitting time. He chose to commit suicide on the night that his wife went into labour with her third child. Although she was in a clinic in London Ludovico had no doubt, as he sat alone in the silence of the remote Marche countryside, that Constanza's birth pangs had begun. And he was totally indifferent. The child was not his – as he was sure the whole world would know – and Constance was in London because both she and Ludovico knew that a bastard child could not be born in a Villanuova bed.

Ludovico was ending his life because he felt

inconsolably lonely. He had lost Gioella; his mother was dead; his brother he could not speak to; and his wife was indifferent to him, forever putting the demands of her business before his needs.

Even his children seemed distant and estranged. Margharita was wilful and headstrong, refusing to accept any guidance, and Manfredo was so timid and shy that often, watching them play, Ludovico thought that he should have been the girl. Frankly, he didn't know them and they didn't interest him very much. He felt that they shrugged him out of their lives as an irrelevance – as did Constance, who, apart from her absorption in the business, clearly no longer really wanted him in her bed. As his isolation grew, so did his sense of hopelessness in the present. Increasingly, he lived in the past.

He spent hours in the castle library, sunk in thought, recalling the carefree days he had enjoyed even before Constance had entered his life so dramatically. . . . the hot night when Gioella had seduced him on her husband's yacht, riding at anchor off Ischia . . . the first time he had shared a woman with Carlo . . . and even earlier times, when he was fourteen and his father had bought a whore for him in Naples and insisted on watching so that she would teach his son correctly . . . His mind travelled still further into the past, to the Villanuovas, the ancestors who had so dominated the present that his own life seemed only a brief and insignificant chapter contemplated in the immense time span of the family.

At least he had done the duty he was born for. He had produced a successor for the ancestors.

Apart from the ghosts of the past, Ludovico was alone that night at Castelfranco. The servants had taken Margharita and Manfredo down to the village for the traditional Midsummer *festa* and firework display. The only living creature left with Ludovico was his old gun dog. Sitting in the dining room, he looked round at the portraits of his Villanuova predecessors arranged along the walls in chronological order. Every head of the house was represented, each one looking remarkably like the others.

The line began in the fifteenth century with Manfredo the Magnificent, squinting bad-temperedly above an imperfectly pleated ruff, and ended with Ludovico's father, dressed with casual elegance, who gazed out with a look of relaxed and overwhelming conceit. Between these two extremes, it seemed to Ludovico, his ancestors showed every possible variation on the themes of temporal and spiritual pride. He pushed back his chair, stood up and allowed his gaze to move across their faces, realising for the first time that they all had the same eyes. Despite differences in shape and colour, the expression was identical. All had the same empty, distant and uninvolved stare. As he walked from one to another, their cool gaze began to unsettle him. What was the key to the ancestors he was so soon to join? Our problem, he decided, is that we are not part of life. We stand aloof and separate. We are self-absorbed – I can see it in the eyes of every one of them. We don't become involved with people on their terms, we expect them to join us on ours. And they never do, he concluded sadly, as he thought of how Constance, who he had assumed would fit into his mould, had been unable to adopt his scale of values or modify her attitudes to accord with his, always insisting on her independence of thought in everything.

The portraits also brought home to Ludovico how little he knew of the family which had been a part of his life from his earliest memories. He knew their names, their dates, what improvements they had made to the estate, what furniture they had acquired, what extra acres they had purchased – but he had learnt nothing intimate about them. They had not been of a contemplative or scholarly frame of mind; time spent in the study had been minimal compared with the hours spent in the saddle or the extra-marital bed. Few letters had survived and no diaries. Their thoughts had gone with them to the grave.

Ludovico felt let down by his forebears. They had left

him nothing against which to measure his own complex thought processes. For all the world, he decided, he was as spiritually unprovided for as the merest peasant. Certainly he knew what his grandfather looked like, which few peasants did, but his ignorance of his ancestor's thoughts and emotions was total. 'You left me nothing,' he murmured, and yet he knew that the heart of the family was in this ancient tumbledown castle in the remote countryside.

He stood in front of his father's portrait. It was a bad piece of painting by a fashionable Milanese portraitist famous in pre-war Italy but now totally forgotten. Ludovico and his father had been close and yet detached in a very Italian way. Their relationship consisted of shared secrets which were never confided. It was not important to put them into words. Every Italian father knows of his son's indiscretions. Even if the army of relations and friends who watch every move the children make do not tell him, he knows, because he was the same. Italian masculinity with all its traits and characteristics is immutable, because Italian femininity never changes. 'How different it would have been if you had lived,' Ludovico murmured regretfully.

He turned from his father's portrait, replaced his glass on the table, took one last look round the room as the gloom of the dusk settled on it and, opening the double doors of the dining room, stepped into the dark hall. He sensed his dog shuffle to its feet in response to his presence. As he began to walk across the marble floor towards his study a sharp light suddenly illuminated his way. It was followed instantly by the sound of an explosion. Good, he thought as he opened the study door, the fireworks have started.

He knew that the mayor and the local people would be hurt and affronted that he was not present tonight. Every year since his father's death he had walked round the sideshows, spent money and stayed to admire the fireworks that ended the evening. The tradition had carried on after his marriage. Even when Constanza had sulked and argued, 'Not again! Surely we can miss just one year,' Ludovico had always insisted that they drive up from Florence or the sea – wherever they were – so that after supper on the last day of the *festa* they could as a family walk down the dusty drive which separated the castle from the village half a mile away. Constance had no idea of the hierarchical symbolism of the event. For Ludovico, it was simply a duty which had to be performed, one of the very few he had ever acknowledged in his life.

In the study, he unlocked his desk where the keys of the gunroom were kept in a special drawer for which he alone had a key. Before picking them up, he unlocked another drawer and, taking out his old address book, removed the photograph of Giancarlo and himself taken with Carlo. As he looked at it, tears filled his eyes. 'My poor Carlo,' he sobbed as he slowly tore the photograph in half and let it fall on to the floor. He gazed down at it, lost in his thoughts.

Suddenly the silence was broken by the telephone on the desk. Ludovico knew it was a long-distance call. He sensed it was from London and was certain that it was the expensive private clinic in Bryanston Place eager to contact him with the news that his wife had given birth. He allowed it to ring. Its sound echoed out into the marble-floored hallway and seemed to ricochet round the empty castle, underlining the silence and the desolation in his heart.

The ringing finally stopped. By the distant flare of the fireworks Ludovico, closely followed by his dog, walked through the hall and down the stone stairs at the back to the corridor which led to unused pantries, ironing rooms, sculleries – and the gunroom. The long stone passage was pitch dark and he was forced to switch on the light. Its naked bulb barely lit the area. He had hoped to do everything in darkness and cursed himself for not picking up the guns while there was still some light. He unlocked the door, pushed it back and stepped inside. The damp smell

367

which permeated the castle below ground was even stronger here. Ludovico touched the wall with his fingers. It was running with water. Where is it coming from? he wondered. Franco should check these rooms, he thought with irritation. I must make sure that he oils and greases the guns properly before the winter . . . He stopped, realising the illogicality of his thoughts. He would be dead in less than an hour. It was the continuity of the Villanuovas surfacing again. He wanted to make sure that the inheritance would be handed on to his son in the same state as it had come to him. For a split second he toyed with the idea of leaving Franco a note with instructions, but shrugged off the thought. It would all be sorted out when he was buried.

He opened a small marquetry gun box and took out a richly engraved pair of belt pistols. They had been made for his great-great-grandfather by Il Negroni of Brento a hundred years ago. Ludovico knew that, despite the bore of having to prime them, these most beautiful of pistols were the only weapons worthy of the task ahead. He began to prepare them.

Ludovico walked slowly back to the dining room. The candles had almost burned down but there was sufficient illumination for him to make out the ten family portraits. Steadily, methodically and with a complete lack of emotion, Ludovico Castelfranco di Villanuova moved round the room and shot out the eyes of each of his ancestors in turn. The sound was deafening and by the time he had reached the portrait of his father the air was acrid. He disposed of his father and then, placing the guns to his mouth, he disposed of himself. In the last split second of life, as he pulled the triggers, his eyes locked with another pair of eyes, watching transfixed with fear, outside the dining-room window.

In the silence that followed the explosion all that could be heard was the terrified whimpering of Ludovico's dog down in the cellar where it had bolted, petrified, at the first shot, and the sound of the feet outside the window as they turned and fled.

# CHAPTER 16

Manfredo hated the noise and the crowds in the tiny village square. He stood close to Maria, the caretaker's wife, watching fearfully as Margharita pushed ahead of them, elbowing her way through the people, determined to see everything. Suddenly, he made up his mind. Turning back he began to force his own path through the crowds that were pressing at their backs. Ducking between legs, squeezing past stallholders and ignoring Maria's cries, he made his way back up the street that led to the castle gates. As he reached them, the first fireworks of the evening began. They shot into the air and burst into a mass of multicoloured stars. At the same time there was a loud explosion as the first of the evening's 'bangers' was let off at the far end of the square.

As he ran silently up the drive, Manfredo could hear the dogs in the surrounding farms barking at the reports that rang out and lit up the dark hills. He had a pain in his side but he was determined not to stop. As he toiled up the last steep slope to the terrace in front of the castle, he became aware of explosions in front of him, coming from inside. He ran along the terrace, past the front door, which was always kept locked, and round the side of the building.

He looked through the window. He could see his father through the clouds of blue smoke that hung in the air. He was holding two pistols to his mouth. Their looks met and Manfredo saw his father's eyes dilate with horrified

370

recognition as he squeezed the triggers. He turned and ran.

Bursting through the gate of the kitchen garden, Manfredo pounded up the hillside, beyond the line of trees that marked the end of the playing area for him and Margharita. The dry grasses and drought-dead plants scratched and cut his body as he jumped from boulder to boulder to avoid the snakes that Maria was always warning against. He ran, stumbled and fell, but crawled on, half blind with fear. Eventually he sank down on to the rough turf, exhausted, and passed out.

'What are you doing here?'

Manfredo's eyes jerked open as his shoulder was roughly shaken.

'Who are you?' the voice growled.

Manfredo tried to break away but he couldn't move in the tight grip that locked him. It was daylight and he looked into the face of a shepherd, rough, unshaven and burned by the sun. Manfredo was almost overcome by the man's smell: a mixture of stale milk, rancid sweat and dung. His clothes were matted with dirt and his breath stank of old garlic and wine as, pushing his face close to Manfredo's, he hissed again, 'What are you doing here?'

Before Manfredo could answer another man ran up. 'What have you found?' he yelled, then stopped dead. 'Tie him, before he runs,' he said.

It seemed only a matter of seconds before they had roughly bound Manfredo's ankles with coarse rope, making it impossible for him to move. Then they walked away for a short distance, their heads together, talking in low voices that Manfredo could not understand. As they talked, they kept looking back at him.

When they returned to him their faces had softened. They would have to treat the boy kindly if they were to collect a reward. They undid his legs and tried to talk to him but they could not persuade him to utter a sound, no matter what they said. He merely looked at them with

371

eyes large with horror and shivered whenever they tried to come close.

The air was silent except for the light sighing of the wind. The sheep were rhythmically cropping their way across the hills. Manfredo was lifted on to the back of the man who had found him and the shepherds began to follow their flock. His captor smelt foul and at first Manfredo struggled to ease himself away from his body, but soon tiredness overcame him and he slumped forward on to the back of the man's neck. Every now and again he woke and each time the smell seemed less unpleasant. As he half dozed in the sun, lulled by the rocking rhythm of the man's stride, Manfredo increasingly found his earthy masculinity comforting and strangely exciting.

They stopped for food in the late afternoon. The men offered him soft cheese, hard bread and rough wine. He refused them all. He still would not speak. The shepherds were joined by a third man. Although they talked quietly, Manfredo knew by the way they looked over at him that they were talking of his father. He heard the words 'lost boy' and the name of his village. He knew that his father was dead and he longed for his mother far away in England. That evening, around the fire, the shepherds tried to find out about him, asking him questions in their rough dialect. Manfredo could barely understand them and wouldn't answer. They tied his legs for the night but they gave him strong-smelling sheepskins to wrap himself in against the dew. He fell asleep to the sound of their voices, drunken now and totally incomprehensible.

Manfredo woke suddenly. It was still night. Very close to him a sheep was bleating loudly. He cautiously raised himself up, trying to make no noise. The scene that met his astonished eyes mesmerised him. He was horrified and fascinated at the same time, and never forgot those moments as he watched the drunken shepherds and the terrified sheep. The leaping orange flames of the fire were reflected on the sweat-glistening faces and limbs of the men and in the rolling eyes of the beast. The air was full of sound: the cries of the sheep and the drunken laughter and crude grunts of the shepherds. Although he wanted to, Manfredo could not look away from the extraordinary scene.

'I'm afraid I can get no reply from your husband's number in Italy,' the nurse said with what seemed to Constance a slight air of triumph.

'Who gave you permission to contact my husband?'

'Well . . .' The nurse was flustered by the direct challenge to her authority. 'It's normal practice . . .'

'I gave you that number in case of emergency. Why did nobody ask me before they started ringing it?'

'You were still sedated.'

The hostility of the reply was not so much in the tone as the delivery of the remark. The nurse's whole body seemed to arch with dislike as she spoke.

From the moment they had met at the reception desk of the clinic Nurse Sinclair had loathed Constance. Despite her considerable size, Constance looked not only elegant but glamorous in her pregnancy. She was wearing her mink coat, which shimmered expensively, and its obvious luxury irritated Nurse Sinclair. She had never seen anything so self-indulgent, nor had she smelt such an exclusive perfume, or seen such a stylish bag, or such beautiful shoes . . . As her practised eye travelled the length of Constance's body, Nurse Sinclair's contempt was excited by everything she saw. She felt sure that Constance must be a kept woman.

Constance was weary after her journey. 'If you would show me to my room I would be very grateful,' she said, her voice edgy.

Spoilt cow, Nurse Sinclair thought as she smiled a welcome and said, 'Of course. You look tired. Quite drawn. This way.'

'You wish to inform the proud father yourself, of course,' said Nurse Sinclair with the faintest smile and in slight acknowledgement that she might have been overzealous in ringing Italy. 'I will ask them to wheel in the telephone trolley. But you mustn't be long. It is almost time for his second feed.'

The baby had been placed in Constance's arms by the theatre sister with the words, 'He's a fine boy. You should be very proud. But he must be the last.'

Constance looked down at him groggily. It seemed that she had been in labour for hours. She had begun to think he would never come out, but there he was, looking quite hideous, in her arms. His face was a deep and angry red, his eyes were tightly closed and his dark hair stuck out at a variety of unlikely angles.

Oh dear, she thought wearily. Suddenly he lifted his arm and then stopped, remaining completely still in half movement. It was a gesture so reminiscent of Giuseppe that Constance immediately softened. As he snuggled at her breast, she thought the baby the most beautiful thing she had ever seen.

Constance rang Giuseppe's number in Florence. By what seemed a miracle there was only a short pause before it began to ring. Within seconds, she heard Giuseppe's voice.

'Constanza!' he said in Italian, his voice tremulous with excitement. 'Are you all right? Has it happened?'

'Yes, my darling,' she laughed. 'You . . . no, we . . . have a beautiful son. Oh, Giuseppe, he is so like you. He even moves . . .'

'A son! That is marvellous, my darling. You are so clever. I am proud of you!'

There was a pause. When Giuseppe went on, Constance noticed a change in his voice.

'Has Giancarlo called?'

'No, no one knows but you. You're the first, silly. Is there something wrong? Your voice sounds strange.'

'Constanza, there has been a dreadful accident. At the castle.'

'What? The children! What's happened? Tell me!'

'No, no, not the children. Ludovico.'

And Giuseppe told her everything, except about the disappearance of Manfredo. He lied when she asked if the children were safe. It was, he decided, something that only Giancarlo could tell her.

Constance lay perfectly still in bed. She knew that if she moved an inch she would be sick. Ludovico's beautiful face shattered and destroyed: she felt she would go demented if she thought of it and yet she couldn't stop herself thinking. It was like a nightmare. She was overcome by deep despair and shame; shame at the reason why she was lying in a nursing-home bed, shame at the failure of her marriage, shame at her inadequacy as a wife, shame that she was alive when Ludovico was dead.

'I killed him. I killed my beautiful Ludovico,' she moaned and, lying rigid, twisted her head from side to side in fruitless distress and anguish. Nurse Sinclair was shocked and insisted that Constance take a sedative.

When Giancarlo telephoned, Constance was in a deep sleep, so he talked to Nurse Sinclair and guardedly gave her an edited version of the events of the last twenty-four hours.

When Constance woke the next morning, she found herself surrounded by anxious faces. Nurse Sinclair, who had refused to go off duty, was there and, to Constance's surprise at such an early hour, so was her London doctor. He was now an old man, having been Louise's gynaecologist for years, and he was wise in the ways of grief. He held the baby in his arms, ready to pass him to Constance the moment the nurses raised her pillows. He knew that faced with death, the best therapy was life. Nurse Sinclair had told him what Giancarlo had said and he had decided that he would tell Constance himself about her lost son. She had barely time to assimilate the horrors of the story before Nurse Sinclair brought the mobile telephone to her bedside. It was Giancarlo telephoning from the castle. Without asking how she was or wasting time in small talk, he immediately put her mind at rest.

'We have found him. He is perfectly well, but shocked. We don't know exactly what happened because he won't speak to us, but I suspect he ran away because he was afraid of the fireworks. They were at the *festa* when it happened.'

'Where was he found?' Constance asked.

'He had run up into the hills where he was discovered by some shepherds. They took care of him overnight. They are after a reward, of course, but I will deal with that.'

'Giancarlo, please! Tell me what happened with Ludo? I'm going mad here.'

Giancarlo had his answer ready.

'It was an accident,' he said firmly. 'A hideous, tragic accident. I have talked to the police and they tell me that poor Ludovico must have been trying to clean the guns or maybe just examining them, when they literally went off in his hands.'

'But Giuseppe told me his head had been shot off,' she whispered into the telephone.

Giancarlo was furious at what he saw as the cheap sensationalism of a peasant mind.

'Nonsense,' he replied sternly. 'Constanza, you mustn't think of such things. I absolutely categorically refuse to allow it. It was a dreadful accident but accident it was and I don't think it helps you in any way to speculate on ghastly details.'

Constance leaned heavily on his strength. She felt certain that he was lying, but she allowed his words to comfort and lull her.

Later in the day, as she held her new baby to her, Constance thought sadly of the tragedy of her life in Italy. So much had gone wrong. She looked out of the window at the heavy plane trees that skirted the elegant square. She was conscious of the different quality of the light reflected from the stucco façades of the perfectly proportioned houses, softer and yet sharper than the light of Florence. She was aware of the London street noise, so much less strident and urgent than its Italian equivalent. She wondered why she had ever left England. This is my culture; this is a world I understand. I am part of it in a way that I cannot be out there. I like the strength and reliability here, she thought. Looking down at her baby son she made a mental vow. You are going to be my British child, she decided. You'll come to school here and learn about our history – Henry VIII and the Tudors. You'll be brought up in our traditions. You're going to have a British name. What are the names of the Tudor kings? Tudor . . . what a solid sound that has.

Within seconds, she had decided. That was to be the name of this, her last child, and she would ensure that he would live up to it in every way.

'Your mother,' Nurse Sinclair whispered, as she opened the door of Constance's room.

Nora walked in almost stealthily, not sure how she would find her daughter.

Constance had just woken from her afternoon nap. 'Oh, Mummy,' she said, beginning to cry, 'what are we going to do?'

Nora put her arms round her and tried to still her shaking shoulders. 'I don't know what you've done to deserve such a terrible thing,' she said in an attempt to comfort Constance. Determined not to cry, she went on, 'How could such an accident happen? Didn't he know about guns? Wasn't he a shooting man? I can't understand it.'

Constance shook her head in confusion. 'I don't know, I really don't know. The details seem so vague. At least they've found Manfredo.'

'*Found* him?' her mother asked in alarm. 'Found him?

Nobody told me he was even lost. What *is* going on out there?'

When Constance had finished telling what she knew, there was a silence.

'Well,' Nora said, 'one thing is clear. You'll all have to come back here. You can't possibly stay out there without Ludovico.'

Constance sat bolt upright in bed. 'Come back?' she said, forgetting her thoughts of a few hours earlier. 'What on earth do you mean – come back? My life is in Italy more than ever now; my business is there. I can never come back. What is there here for me now?'

'What is there over *there* for you, I'd like to know?' Nora countered. 'Think of the children, in Italy with no father. No, they must come back here to be properly educated.'

'Mummy, can't you see?' Constance asked in despair. 'The children are Italian, not English. How can I bring them back here?'

Before Nora could reply, there was a tap on the door and Nurse Sinclair walked in, holding the baby.

'Here we are,' she cried in a tone that was almost jolly, 'your bouncing baby boy and grandson.'

'Oh,' said Nora, taking him into her arms, 'he's the image of poor Ludovico. The image. He'll always remind you of him. What a comfort.'

Constance remained silent.

'What is he to be called? I suppose it must be Ludovico.'

'No, Tudor, actually,' Constance replied. Before her mother could comment, she went on, 'This one is going to be brought up English. I shall send him back here to school. He's going to live up to his name if I have anything to do with it.'

Nora was mollified. It would be nice to have one grandchild who thought predominantly in an English way, she reflected. Her pleasure was increased when Constance asked, 'Will you come back to Italy with me? I don't think I can go through it all by myself. I need you, Mummy – and so do the children.'

So many funerals, Constance thought sadly. It seemed no time at all since she had walked into the chapel with Ludovico, following his mother's coffin. Now she was following his. She walked up the aisle on the arm of Giancarlo. Out of the corner of her eye she noticed Monica, who was heavily veiled. Next to her stood Carlo. Constance had not expected him to appear, believing that he was still travelling. Monica had tracked him down – how, Constance didn't know. She was struck again by his likeness to Ludovico.

The funeral was attended by a vast and emotional crowd from the villages and estates around, many of whom Constance hadn't seen before.

She found the mass grief deeply harrowing and was glad that she had insisted on Manfredo and Margharita remaining at Villa Andreoli with her mother.

The introductions to the mourners, and their condolences, left Constance feeling drained. It was late afternoon before they finally departed. It had been arranged by Giancarlo (who had organised everything) that three people would spend the night at the castle. As well as himself and Monica, he had invited Carlo. Constance had been surprised when Giancarlo said, 'It is necessary, Constanza,' and was even more so when he told her that Carlo had accepted the invitation. She looked forward to the evening with a mixture of anticipation and dread.

On returning to the castle, Constance took Monica aside. She wanted to know about Carlo.

'Where has he been?' she asked.

'Oh, many places but for the last two years he has been in London.'

'London? Whatever for?'

'Don't all exiles end up in London? It has always been the staging post for wanderers and the dispossessed.

Anyhow, he loves the English – just as poor Ludo used to.'

'Where did he live? Did he have a job?'

Monica laughed. 'Of course not! He drifted, as the Villanuovas have always liked to do. I think he's had a very pleasant time, spending days in the British Museum reading room, warming his toes in the London Library. You don't understand Carlo. He is a cat. He loves comfort and warmth but he also enjoys the alley life. No loyalty to anybody but himself. Let's people impose only so far and then stalks off with his tail in the air, determined to keep his independence.'

'How did you know where to contact him?'

Monica laughed. 'I know Carlo very well,' she replied mysteriously.

Giancarlo had decided that the myth of the shooting accident must stand. That is what he had told Monica, Bettina and even Ludovico's brother. It was a lie that he couldn't go back on now despite the evidence of the shattered portraits. He was determined that Constance would never know that it was suicide and could see no reason why she should. He had ensured that the local police report clearly stated that it was death by misadventure and had managed to explain the portraits by hinting that Ludovico must have had some sort of brainstorm, caused by drinking. His story was given credence only because the alternative was too ghastly to contemplate. The one flaw in a tightly controlled fantasy was Manfredo. It worried Giancarlo that he was unable to find out whether the boy had seen anything or had been frightened into running off by the fireworks alone.

'Manfredo hasn't spoken to you?' he asked Constance at dinner.

The conversation, sporadic and jerky at its best, had hit a lull. It seemed to Constance that everything flattering and sentimental that could have been said about Ludovico had been repeated, several times over, by her guests and she was feeling dispirited by the sense of guilt and inadequacy that had settled on her.

She shook her head in despair. 'He has spoken to nobody. In fact, he seems literally tongue-tied.'

Good, Giancarlo thought as he said, 'Don't worry, he is in shock. He will come round if given time.'

'Poor dear,' said Monica. 'Does he realise that his father is dead?'

'We don't know,' Constance replied. 'Margharita won't say whether or not she told him.'

She felt weighed down by the psychological problems she would have to untangle for her children if they were to have any hope of a happy life. Monica, noticing her face, stood up and said, 'We must go to bed. Constance looks absolutely drained.'

Constance was exhausted, but she couldn't sleep. At half past midnight, sick of tossing and turning, she decided that a glass of scotch would help her to relax. Going downstairs to the small study where Ludovico kept the drinks, she noticed that a light was shining from under the door. Had Giancarlo forgotten to switch it off or was somebody still up? As she walked into the study, blinking in the light, her heart nearly stopped. Ludovico sat with his back half turned to her, staring straight before him. Her gasp made him turn, just as she was about to faint.

'Are you all right?' Carlo leapt towards her, startled out of his reverie.

'Oh, my God! It's you! What a fright you gave me! I thought . . . I thought . . .'

'What did you think? What? What?' Carlo cried anxiously.

'I thought . . . everybody was in bed,' Constance replied, recovering her poise. 'I didn't expect . . .'

'I am sorry. I just wanted to be alone and remember.'

'Of course,' she replied hastily, pressing her palms to her cheeks. 'I'm sorry. I'm half asleep. I'll leave you.'

'No!' Carlo replied. 'Please, talk to me! We might never have another chance!'

'Pour me some scotch, please,' Constance asked as she dropped into the nearest armchair. As Carlo did so she watched him, shocked again at his resemblance to Ludovico. His eyes, so frequently hidden by sunglasses, had so much of his brother in them that Constance was reminded of Ludo on the train to Florence, so many years before.

'I loved him,' Carlo said, his body hunched forward and his head in his hands. 'He was everything to me. When he was young I was so proud that he was my brother. All my friends – without exception – all my friends adored him. That is very rare in Italy, Constance, believe me. He was always full of fun . . . ready for everything.' He smiled. 'He always got what he wanted. Even with you, no? Savognia tells me that he wouldn't listen to reason until he had made you his wife. I know him. It was because he loved you so much that he couldn't bear to wait. Poor Ludo, he never could bear to wait. Whatever he decided to do, he wanted to do immediately. He never gave himself time for reflection. He was too spontaneous for that.'

'Why did he quarrel with you so dreadfully?'

'Oh . . . because he was like me, I suppose. I am quick – how do you say – quick to ignite, take fire – with passion, anger, amusement . . . I don't know what. So was he. We were like the branches of a young sapling. Our mother took an axe and split us apart. And just like a sapling, it killed us both, emotionally and spiritually. She told him bad things about me. But they were not bad . . . only they were made to seem so. He thought I had done this wicked thing against him but it was not as it seemed. He never understood because he gave me no chance to explain. I had hoped that when Maria-Angelina died we might . . . but there was no hope. You saw him at her funeral. How determined he was not to honour me with the smile of forgiveness.'

Constance sipped her scotch and thought how quaintly

beautiful the Italian expression was. 'Poor Carlo,' she murmured.

'No,' he replied, 'poor, poor Ludo. There was a deep disquiet in him at the funeral.'

'Well,' Constance replied, bridling a little, 'it was his mother's funeral, after all, and he loved her, even if you did not.'

'No,' Carlo replied decisively, 'her death made him sad – everybody could see that – but I saw something deeper . . . more permanent. His eyes were empty.'

Constance felt uncomfortable. She could think of nothing to say.

'I'm sure that he felt his life was over.'

'What do you mean?' she asked in alarm.

'He had stepped outside the process of living. He had nobody to run with any more. I was the only person and he had cast me out. Like a pair of hunting dogs, we were magnificent running together but lame and useless when separated and on our own.'

Constance was indignant. 'He was married to me, you know. Do you think that counted for nothing?'

'Absolutely nothing,' Carlo said, looking at her with a level gaze, empty of anger or hatred. 'He was a Villanuova in every inch of his skin. Marriages have never mattered to us.'

'He loved me,' she said sharply. 'No matter what you say. At least, until quite recently.'

'Of course. I know he did,' Carlo replied softly, 'but you were outside the Villanuova continuity. You counted no more than Maria-Angelina did ultimately. Men count with us – and he knew it. That is why what Ludo did to himself and to me was such a terrible thing. He killed me. I have been dead for years. Even though he loved me more than you can ever understand, he was prepared to destroy me – spontaneously and permanently. And he could never rescue me, though he must have desperately wanted to do so. That was why he knew that his life was

383

ended, just as mine was.' He sighed. 'Two lame hunting dogs,' he repeated, gazing into space.

There was a silence before Constance could pluck up the courage to ask, 'Do you think he ended his own life?'

Carlo looked at her. 'Yes, of course. But not in the way you mean. He didn't shoot his brains out.' He warmed to the lie. 'He drifted into an attitude of mind that made him careless. He allowed an accident to happen because it wasn't worth ensuring that it wouldn't. It didn't matter whether he lived or died. I understand that. He was right. It didn't matter – and it doesn't matter for me either. I could die tomorrow and it would be utterly unimportant.'

Constance was shocked. To her, life was a sacred thing and she couldn't imagine anyone calmly able to turn his back on it. No matter how hideous the difficulties, she found living a vibrant, exciting experience and she couldn't bear to contemplate Ludovico feeling such despair that death seemed even a possibility, let alone an attractive alternative.

Of course it was an accident, she thought fiercely, determined to block out the other explanation for his death.

# CHAPTER 17

'If I'd known how boring and exhausting preparing a collection was going to be I think I would have opened a pet shop instead,' Constance said to Savognia, with a weary smile, as they sat in her office having a quick sandwich lunch. The new show was less than a week away and they had spent all morning with Giuseppe in the cramped, overheated fitting room, making final adjustments to the clothes.

'He seems to work so slowly,' Savognia replied peevishly.

'Don't say anything, please, Giancarlo,' Constance said, with a nervous look at the door. 'He's tense and very tired.'

'Tired? What does he think the rest of us are? These fittings are interminable. He seems incapable of decision.'

'He is a perfectionist.'

'No, Constanza, he is a coward unable to make up his mind.'

Before Constance could reply, the sound of raised voices coming from the fitting room was followed by Giuseppe angrily calling her name along the corridor. With a despairing look at Savognia, she stood up and moved towards the door. At that moment, Giuseppe burst into the office, his face contorted with rage.

'Constance!' he screamed. 'What do you mean by telling Katrina that she can stop for lunch? How the hell am I to prepare a collection without a model, for Christ's sake?'

'Sit down, Giuseppe,' Constance said, 'Katrina must have a break – and so must you. Come and have a sandwich and some wine.'

She stretched her hand out to him. He knocked it away with such force that she lost her balance and fell heavily against the bales of fabric stacked against the wall.

'There's no call for that!' Savognia said, standing up. 'What is wrong with you, man? Have you gone mad?'

Giuseppe lunged forward and took hold of the lapels of Savognia's coat, ready to shake him. Constance leapt up to separate them.

'Please!' she cried. 'Please, stop! I can't take this. Stop!' The desperation in her voice pulled both men up short. 'Will you stop being so self-indulgent?' she went on. 'I'm sick and tired of all these male ego trips.'

She turned on Giuseppe. 'You think nobody matters but you. You have no consideration for anybody. You're like a child. I'm sick of you, too,' she said to Savognia. 'Always moaning and whispering behind Giuseppe's back. We have a collection to present in seven days' time. It has to be right; it has to be good and I'm determined that it will be. If you can't show any self-discipline, the pair of you can just get out now and leave it to me. I will not allow these childish tantrums to destroy my name.'

Both men were shocked and immediately subdued. They had never heard Constance so angry. Realising her strength, she said quietly, 'Now sit down, both of you. Giuseppe, I insist you have something to eat. Katrina will be back at two and until then you are doing *nothing*.'

Both men obeyed but Constance knew that the atmosphere had not been cleared. Savognia's pursed lips and Giuseppe's smouldering eyes made her dread the afternoon session, when they were due to check the suits.

The first two fittings passed without incident, the third took a little longer. Giuseppe kept repeating, 'Something's wrong, something's wrong. The jacket lacks balance.'

After a great deal of fiddling, he gave it three buttons instead of two and seemed reasonably contented with the result. But the impasse had renewed the tension and Constance wasn't surprised when the fourth suit was received in silence. Giuseppe glowered; Savognia's eyes glazed with tedium. The only sound was of Giuseppe tapping his pencil against his fingers. Suddenly, he snapped it in two and threw the pieces across the desk. Katrina gave a little scream. Nobody moved.

'What is wrong with it?' Giuseppe said almost in a whisper. 'What . . . is . . . *wrong* . . . with it?' His teeth were gritted and Constance could see the veins of his neck throbbing. I must clear this room, she thought but, before she could make a move, Giuseppe pushed back his chair and turned on her, his eyes blazing with anger and fear.

'Help me!' he cried. 'Why won't anybody help me? Tell me what is wrong with it! Am I expected to know everything? I am so tired, so tired.'

'Very well,' Giancarlo said, 'I will tell you what is wrong. It is vulgar.'

Constance swallowed hard.

'Furthermore,' Giancarlo continued, 'it is derivative. This is exactly the suit that the Countess of Toledo bought here last season. All you have done is add badly proportioned pockets that cheapen it. You are paid as a designer and your job is to produce original ideas, not decorative variations. Perhaps you could earn your money more convincingly if you cut down on your . . .' he paused, angrily searching for a word not too specific, 'your . . . social life a little and didn't arrive at work so clearly in need of sleep.'

All the aristocratic contempt that Savognia felt for Padone's lack of emotional control was apparent in his icily clipped delivery. Constance covered her eyes.

To her astonishment, Giuseppe did not turn on Savognia; nor did he start to shout. Without a word, he stepped forward, took hold of the pockets, which were loosely tacked to the suit, ripped them off and dropped them at Savognia's feet with a look of contempt. Then he walked silently from the room. Constance said, 'That will be all for today, Katrina, thank you. Be here at eight tomorrow morning, please.'

She waited until the model and the seamstresses had gone and she and Savognia were alone.

'Giancarlo, how could you?' she asked. 'How could you humiliate Giuseppe like that in front of the people whose respect he must have? Is that the noblesse oblige you are always talking about? Are you trying to destroy him? Before you do, remember that if you succeed you also destroy me, Constanza Castelfranco, and everything you and I have worked for. Can't you see how nervous and insecure he feels? Do you know nothing about the creative mentality?'

Savognia was stung. 'We are not discussing creativity, Constanza, my dear,' he replied. 'What is at issue is self-indulgence. We all have our parts to play in this firm and I don't see why one member of the team should attempt to dominate the others.'

'He is the designer, for God's sake!' Constance interrupted.

'Precisely,' Savognia replied. 'And, as such, he is expendable. There are vast armies of Giuseppe Padones out there, eager and hungry for a chance. I can pick up a Padone almost at random whenever we need one on the streets of Paris. That is something, my dear Constanza, that we should all remember – and especially him.'

'But I thought you admired him?' she asked in bewilderment.

'Indeed I did – and do. But I will not be blackmailed by an ego running dangerously out of control. Since . . .' He paused. 'I'm sorry, Constanza, but I must say this. Since poor Ludovico's death, Padone's arrogance has increased by the hour. Perhaps you can furnish an explanation . . . ?'

Constance rose to the challenge. 'Are you suggesting that sharing my bed has gone to his head? Well, I'd like to point out that Giuseppe was my lover long before Ludovico's death – and he is the father of my third child.'

Savognia was stunned by her directness. 'So, it is true?'

'Yes,' she replied, 'and furthermore, he will continue to share my bed. In fact, he is coming to live with me at Villa Andreoli. If that's what's having an effect on him then you'd better get used to it. Giuseppe is here to stay, but if he goes, I go and so does Constanza Castelfranco.'

And gathering up her files, Constance walked out of the fitting room. As she left she heard Savognia say, half under his breath. 'Sharing your bed? Yours and half of Florence's.'

Monica spent the weekend at Villa Andreoli so that she and Constance could work out the seating plan for the show, while Giuseppe continued with the fittings in Florence.

'God! It's so complicated,' Constance said, after a full morning's work had left them with over thirty people still to seat. 'Are you sure that we need to allocate so many seats to the American journalists?

Monica chuckled. 'They'll be there, I guarantee it. They're taking Italian fashion more and more seriously – and so are the buyers. Constanza Castelfranco is on the map now. Mind you, there'll be some who come hoping to push it off again, so it had better be another good show this time.'

Constance sat back. 'It is. Very good. So good that Giuseppe is terrified that they won't appreciate it.'

'If it's good, they'll appreciate it,' Monica said with finality. 'These press girls may be vindictive but they're not fools.'

'Why should they be vindictive, that's what I don't understand.'

'Well,' Monica said, after a pause, 'the arrangements at Constanza Castelfranco are a little unusual and, of course, they have been noted.'

Constance said nothing. They worked quietly for a while.

'Does Giuseppe have a wild social life?' Constance asked.

Monica was ready for it. 'In Florence?' she laughed. 'You must be joking!'

'Well, what did Giancarlo mean, do you think?'

'Giancarlo should learn to keep his temper and shut his trap, if you ask me,' Monica replied. 'I don't know what he meant. He's probably jealous. Maybe he isn't invited out so much any more.'

Constance decided to believe it for the moment, though Monica's explanation was unsatisfactory. Savognia's jibe had more to it than jealousy, she was sure.

'What is the situation with you two?' Monica asked.

'Who? Giuseppe?' Constance breathed in deeply. They were on the terrace and she found the hot sweet smell of the summer meadows shimmering below in the sun almost intoxicating.

'I want him to come here.'

Monica was puzzled. 'How do you mean? Not to live?'

'Yes.' Constance looked her straight in the eye. 'To live. As my lover.'

Monica was shocked. 'Are you sure? So soon?'

'You sound like Hamlet. "But two months dead". Monica, what difference does it make? It doesn't affect poor Ludo now and it's an affair that has been going on for some time, as you know.'

Monica was intrigued. 'Do you love him?' she asked.

'Love?' Constance replied. 'I don't think I know what that is any more. But I need him. God, how I need him. And he needs me. Do I shock you?'

'No,' Monica replied, 'but I wonder how much he needs you.'

'Don't you think he does?'

'I don't think that Signor Padone needs *anybody*, my sweet. He's totally self-sufficient.'

'You don't know him. He's vulnerable – like any artist, I suppose.'

'He doesn't like his ego bruised, I agree, but I'm not sure that he's all *that* vulnerable, darling.'

Seeing that she had annoyed Constance, she went on, 'Are you sure it can work in the long term? I mean . . . you know . . . what about the children?'

'Oh, I'll manage the children,' Constance replied. 'What bothers me is that everyone is so against poor Giuseppe and I cannot for the life of me see why.'

After lunch Monica brought the subject back to the children. 'You look tired, Constance,' she said. 'When this show is over you should go away.'

'Don't be silly,' Constance replied. 'I've already got a diary full to overflowing with appointments: so many fabric manufacturers that there cannot be one left in the whole of Como; button makers; that man who makes the marvellous artificial flowers. It's endless. I couldn't possibly get away.'

'What are Giuseppe and Giancarlo doing?'

'Oh, they'll be there as well.'

'So? Are you telling me that it takes three people to choose a button?'

Constance laughed. 'Darling, half the time even three people can't make a decision. It's a nightmare.' After a pause, she went on, 'Monica, do you think Giancarlo likes Giuseppe?'

'Why on earth do you ask?'

'Oh, it's just that he's increasingly cantankerous with him. Even if I wanted to go away, I wouldn't dare. They'd be at each other's throats the moment my back was turned.'

'I think you're wrong,' Monica replied. 'They're two very self-indulgent men who enjoy sparring. They're perfectly aware of the effect it has on you, and they know that you'll always sort out the problem. I don't know whether they like each other or not but I do know that they both take shocking advantage of you. It would do them good to have to come to terms with each other without always relying on you to paper over the cracks.'

'Giancarlo seems to resent the situation between me and Giuseppe.'

'I don't think he resents it,' Monica said, 'but I'm sure it affronts his *amour-propre*. You know what a hidebound old fuddy-duddy he is. Giuseppe is below the salt for him. A hired hand – and you know the old saying, you don't fuck the hired hands.'

Constance laughed uneasily.

'Of course,' Monica went on, 'you can't blame Giancarlo. He's under the pressure of the constant drip, drip, drip of La Bonoccorsi's acid tongue. She would corrode anybody.'

'What do you mean?'

Monica allowed her surprise to show. 'Really, Constance, you can't be that naive. You must know that she told the world about your Paris trip?'

Constance was shocked. 'But that was years ago!'

'She's found other reasons to gossip since then.'

'About poor Ludo?'

'Yes, and other things. It doesn't need much to fuel her poisoned pen.'

'Why is she such a bitch? What have I done to hurt her?'

'Oh, come on, Constance. You don't have to do anything to earn Bettina's hatred. You're richer than she is and much more successful; you have a lover in your bed and three children. Can't you see that that's quite enough? And, of course, you don't belong to the club.'

'What club?'

'Bettina is a crude, malicious bitch but she's an aristocrat. Like Savognia, she loathes the idea of a jumped-up Neapolitan back-street boy like Giuseppe having the whiphand. The aristocratic club is a very exclusive one. It may relax its rules to include people like you and me on sufferance but for the Giuseppe Padones of this world it's firmly No Entry. And Bettina never lets anyone forget it. That's why she is such a powerful influence on Gian-carlo.'

'Well,' Constance said calmly, 'Giancarlo had better *stop* letting her influence him. If he thinks he's going to freeze Giuseppe out, he's got another think coming. I've already told him that if Giuseppe goes, I go.'

'You'd never throw away everything you've worked for! What about the children? You once told me that they were the reason you worked so hard. Don't they count any more?'

She had hit Constance at her most vulnerable point. There was a silence.

'Since this is speak-easy time,' Monica continued, 'I might as well tell you what I think – and if you don't like it just hand me my coat and I'll go.'

Constance could feel her stomach contracting. She sat low in her chair and said nothing.

'Can I start by being corny?' Monica asked. 'I think you're an amazing woman. You've had the guts to build up your own business, you've coped with the sort of tragedy that would knock most of us sideways and you've made an independent life for yourself in a country notori-ously difficult for women. And you're still young. That's all marvellous. But you've paid the price – as one always must. Listen to Margharita and Manfredo down there in the garden. They're happy because they're with their nanny – the woman who is always there and won't let them down by staying late at the office. They hardly know you, their mother. Kids need security, Constance, the security of reliability – and that is what you aren't giving. The business always come first with you.' She smiled. 'OK. That's it. Kick me out now, if you like.'

Holding back her tears, Constance said, 'You're right. Every word you say is true. Do you think I don't know? I'm terrified of losing them.'

She leaned forward. 'Everything I've ever loved has been taken from me. My father. Nicky. Ludo. That's why the business is so important. It's mine. I control it.

393

Nobody can take it away from me. And the same goes for the children, but I just feel that there is no more of me to give at the moment. Their nanny is superb, and they're devoted to her. What more can I do? You once told me that it didn't matter who looked after them at this age. Why have you changed your mind?'

'Circumstances have changed, my darling, not me,' Monica said. 'You and your family have been through a terrible trauma and it has left its mark on you all. Look, we're talking about vulnerable little people. What happens now will affect them for the rest of their lives. Giuseppe is a big boy. He can stand on his own feet. So can Savognia and, if this collection is as good as you say, so can Constanza Castelfranco. You're backing the wrong horse. They don't need you like your kids do. You don't think you're very maternal. Well, I think that's bullshit. Give yourself a chance.'

She warmed to the argument. 'Really, Constance, for such a clear-sighted woman you can be so stupid sometimes. Those kids down there need you. Are you telling me that choosing some lousy buttons is more important than they are?'

'That's unfair. It isn't about buttons. It's about the whole business. I cannot trust those two – especially at the moment. I feel that if I turn my back they'll be at each other's throats.'

'So? Let them. Let it come out in the open. All you're doing is holding back the flood gates. Now, forget about the collection, stop worrying about those overgrown schoolboys and start thinking positively about your own flesh and blood.'

Monica was in full swing. 'Give yourself two weeks for the selling period after the show, then take the kids to Northumberland. You can recharge your batteries and grab your family before it slips out of your grasp for ever.'

'Don't you think Giuseppe should come as well?' Constance asked. 'After all, he's part of my family now.'

Monica leapt from her seat. 'Constance!' she cried.

'How can you be so stupid? You're talking of oil and water. The children and Giuseppe will never mix – he's not the family kind. Can't you see that if he goes with you he'll expect you to spend all your time mothering *him*? Aren't three kids enough? Just for once, forget him and put them first. You've got to get to know them before it's too late – or they'll never be yours.'

Constance was unconvinced by Monica's line of reasoning. She could see no sense in keeping her children apart from Giuseppe if they were eventually all to live together at the villa. Besides, she argued to herself, how can I do such a thing? He's Tudor's father. Even as she thought it, she recognised her self-deception. Tudor was too young to be part of the problem. The difficulty lay with Manfredo and Margharita and how they would react to Giuseppe being part of their lives. She realised with a feeling of hopelessness that the measure of her failure lay in the simple fact that she didn't know her children well enough to even guess at what they thought – not only about Giuseppe but about anything. Margharita was truculent and uncooperative; Manfredo spoke hardly at all.

Despite the good sense behind Monica's views, Constance would have continued to procrastinate had something not happened later the same day – something that shocked and frightened her, making her understand how dangerously blind she had become.

The two women were enjoying the evening sun that slanted across the terrace and lit up the valley below with a tawny glow. Despite their conversation of the morning, the atmosphere was relaxed. They were both tired, having spent the afternoon wrestling with and finally overcoming the problems of the seating plan, but they were content – with their work, the evening and each other. Monica was reading and Constance was trying to summon up the energy to go inside and ring Giuseppe, hoping that his afternoon would have been as successful as hers.

Suddenly the peace was broken by the sound of the children. Fresh from their baths and ready for bed, they were brought out by Rosanna to say 'Goodnight' while the nanny put Tudor to bed. They both began to run towards the two women. Constance sat up and held out her arms, ready to embrace them. To her horror, they ran past her and threw themselves at Monica, struggling to be first on her knee. Manfredo won and Margharita sulkily moved away from the group and stood alone.

'Rosanna,' Constance said sharply, 'you can take Margharita upstairs and then come down for Manfredo. Off you go, young lady. But say goodnight first.'

Margharita glowered and moved behind Rosanna. Constance was embarrassed and only too conscious of her earlier conversation with Monica.

'Margharita, say goodnight,' she repeated.

The child was aware of the sharpness in her voice, as was Monica, and with a mumbled 'goodnight' allowed herself to be led away. Manfredo snuggled into Monica, silently and vindictively triumphant. For a split second, Constance hated them both. She stood up and walked to the balustrade. Leaning on it, she flexed her fingers in an attempt to stop herself shaking. Regaining her composure, she turned in time to see Manfredo reach up and put his arms round Monica's neck and hear him say, with bell-like clarity, 'I saw Daddy.'

Although her instinct was to rush forward to him, Constance remained perfectly still. Monica didn't move. She whispered, 'Yes, my pet, what did you see?'

Constance prayed silently, Please don't let him stop. Let him go on.

Her prayer was answered. Twisting round in Monica's lap and hugging her tightly, Manfredo said, 'Daddy, all blood,' and began to cry.

After they had calmed him and put him to sleep, Constance and Monica went into the library.

'I need a drink after that,' Monica said.

'So do I,' Constance agreed, 'and a stiff one.'

They stood together uneasily, sipping their scotch. Both were wondering the same thing. What had Manfredo witnessed? Had he seen his father's corpse or had he merely overheard the servants discussing details of the tragedy? 'If only he would talk,' Constance said in despair. 'If only he would tell us what he saw.'

'He must have help,' Monica said, taking a huge swig of her drink, 'he's traumatised, poor darling.'

Constance had a distrust of psychologists and had no intention of consulting one, despite Monica's strong conviction that to do so was the only solution for Manfredo. He's my son, she thought to herself, and it's my problem. I shall solve it in my own way. She couldn't block out the horrible evidence of her failure. In her mind's eye she saw her children's faces as they raced past her, eager to give their love to Monica. Worse, she knew that she would always be haunted by the picture of Manfredo clinging to Monica, exactly as if she were his mother, she thought in despair. A pang of jealousy swept through her. But like Nora, she didn't believe in self-deception. She had always been ready to recognise her weaknesses and she knew that she had no right to feel jealous. If her children didn't run to her as their mother then it was her fault, not Monica's. She made a decision that, no matter what the cost, she would get them back.

He's my son, she repeated to herself, they are my children. No one is going to take my place with them. No one. I will not lose them. No matter what happens, I vow I will not lose them. I'll kill before I let them go.

# CHAPTER 18

All three children accompanied Constance to Northumberland. Things continued to be difficult with them. Manfredo would still barely speak; he was terrified of men and gave all of them except Giuseppe a wide berth; Margharita was aggressive, angry and spiteful, refusing to be crossed by anyone. Whereas Manfredo was gentle, with Ludovico's eyes and the tentative, wary movements of a frightened faun, Margharita was as bold as she was awkward. Constance had to accept that Manfredo was a true Villanuova, but the personality Margharita most resembled was Nora. Although she was only eleven, she was exactly like her grandmother in refusing to allow anyone or anything to get the better of her.

Despite his English name, Tudor was darkly Italian in appearance. Constance knew that he would grow up with the louche charm and romantic good looks of Giuseppe. He would be devastating to girls. Margharita was the most English-looking of the three. She had the same blue-grey eyes as her mother and her light skin and hair were the true Simpson colouring. As they sat in the train at King's Cross, waiting for the long haul north, Constance was proud of her children's physical appearance, even if their minds caused her so much concern. Despite her exhaustion, she was proud, too, of her own survival against formidable odds. True to her vow, she had no intention of sacrificing her children to her work, but she was equally determined not to lose the business – or Giuseppe – either.

I have the strength to keep them all, she said to herself, taking the sleeping Tudor from the nanny as the train pulled out of the station.

Northumberland had an instant effect upon Constance's spirits. In no time she felt her troubles slipping away. She and Nora took the older children for long walks every day, while the nanny looked after Tudor. The sleep that had eluded her in Italy came with increasing ease. In the days before the show there were times she'd thought she would go crazy. Head reeling and eyes tingling, she had found it difficult to keep her mind on anything. Even afterwards, her brain had felt fuzzy and only half alive during the day and had raced around impotently at night, churning up new problems and banishing sleep. Slowly, the cool tranquillity of the northern atmosphere unwound and softened her like a silken ribbon and she began to feel a whole person again.

Her relationship with Nora was better than it had been for years. It's almost like talking to Louise, Constance thought. In fact, Nora was so proud of her daughter's achievements in Italy that she was as near to being over-awed as her personality would allow. The mellow holiday atmosphere allowed Constance time to realise that the reason for their new harmony wasn't only that Nora accepted her as a grown-up, achieving woman; it was also that Constance herself now had the emotional confidence to resist the temptation to oppose her mother on every trivial point. Though disagreements continued to be part of their daily exchange, they were now more often the cause of laughter than anger.

'Let's go to Holy Island!' Constance suggested one morning.

They set out in Nora's car in high hopes. Constance had the happiest of memories of the peace of the island. She recalled its total silence when she was a child – a silence only broken by the occasional cry of a wading bird.

She wanted her children to run round the harbour and slide down the dunes just as she had as a girl.

'We might see a seal,' she told them as they drove across the causeway.

Nora had enquired about the tides at the tiny garage at Beal and they knew they had enough time to see the Priory before having a picnic lunch. One of the few things on which Constance and Nora were in total agreement was the ghastliness of picnics so it was not surprising that, sheltering in the cavities of the dunes from the remarkably fresh wind, they became increasingly irritated with each other.

The conversation turned to Giuseppe. Nora called him a spivvy little Eyetye.

Constance was outraged. 'How dare you refer to him like that? What do you know about him? Come to that, what do you know about anything in Italy?'

'He's like a horrible little rat!' Nora went on, determined not to give way.

'Oh, really? Well, it might interest you to know that I'm in love with that horrible little rat, so there.'

Nora was shocked. 'What do you mean, in love? He's queer! Don't tell me you didn't know? Even your stupid mother can see that!'

'I intend to marry him when I return to Rome,' Constance said with dignity.

Before Nora could reply, the children came running up. 'Mummy, look at the water!' Margharita called.

Both women leapt up, their quarrel forgotten.

'Oh, my God, the tide!' Nora cried.

'Quickly, children,' Constance called. 'Into the car!'

'We'll never make it!' Nora said.

'Yes we will, provided you put your foot down.'

Nora had never before been asked to do anything remotely out of the ordinary behind the wheel of a car but she did her best and the little vehicle tore across the sand, throwing up huge sprays of water from the wheels.

Suddenly, the engine spluttered and the car stopped.

'Oh, Mummy!' Constance cried in exasperation. 'You've wet the plugs!'

'*I've* wet them?' Nora replied indignantly. 'Who was it told me to put my foot down?'

'Come on!' Constance said, as she opened the car door. 'We can't stand here arguing. Look at the tide!' The water was already above ankle-level and coming in fast. By the time they had reached dry land it was up to Manfredo's waist.

Collapsing on the dunes, Constance began to laugh.

'I can't see what there is to laugh at,' Nora said crossly. 'You know that we're stuck here for the next five hours, don't you?'

Constance was becoming hysterical. 'Don't look so *stricken*, Mummy,' she cried. 'Look at the car!'

The little Ford looked so comical, abandoned to the sea, that even Nora began to join in the laughter.

Constance took the children to see Miss Hatherby who, although now old and physically slow, was as quick-witted as ever.

'Goodness,' she said, picking Tudor up from his pram. 'This little fellow's the odd man out. Quite a different stable altogether. I think he's a throwback to the Villanuovas' gypsy past,' she laughed. 'Dark little thing. What bright inquisitive eyes. Why did you give such a decidedly Italian child such a quaintly English name, I wonder, Constance? Were you trying to undo the evidence?'

Constance was nonplussed. How could Miss Hatherby know? She couldn't possibly. Unless Nicky . . . no, she was convinced that he and Miss Hatherby would never sink to gossip. Then she caught a twinkle in the old lady's eye: it was clearly nothing more than harmless banter, but Constance was unnerved.

'I'm joking, my dear,' laughed Miss Hatherby, 'he's a gorgeous little boy although you must admit he looks more Medici than Tudor. You should have christened him Cosimo.' She paused. 'Perhaps not. It would have been too apt. I think it a pity when names fit personalities and appearances too well. They leave no room for deviation, and that is so important for creativity. The artist must step outside the predicted path, don't you agree?'

Constance was entranced. Miss Hatherby hadn't changed at all since the days when they used to roam together through Seaton Cramer discovering its treasures. She was unique. Nobody Constance had ever met talked – or thought – like Miss Hatherby. Furthermore, her friend was as good-hearted as she was original. You'll always be important to me for what you gave me; without you I would not have been ready to face the world, she thought as the sprightly old lady put Tudor back into the pram.

'Do you think he will be an artist?' Constance asked.

'I don't know, but there is something about his movements,' Miss Hatherby said. She bent over Manfredo. 'Now, about this little chap I have no doubts at all. Look at those eyes – and the hands. He is full of creativity. Margharita, I think, will have your business sense. She is very like you – and, indeed, your dear mother. In fact, Constance, my dear, you have the perfectly balanced Anglo-Italian family.'

She stretched out her skeletal fingers and plucked urgently at Constance's wrist, 'Nurture them, nurture them, Constance,' she said. 'Do not allow them to throw away their talents.'

Suddenly swinging away and moving across the room to the cockatoo cage, now empty and forlorn, she said, 'That is the great sin! The only sin! God will forgive anything else but He will not forgive us for turning away from the gifts He bestows on us. Promise me, my dear, to drive them forward to achieve everything of which they are capable. Educate their sensibilities; do not allow their souls to wither.'

Constance had never seen her friend so passionate. Manfredo and Margharita were transfixed – whether with joy or fear Constance wasn't sure – and the skin at the nape of her own neck tingled. Constance knew that Miss Hatherby was right. She vowed that she would never betray her children's gifts. No matter what their talents, she would encourage them to use them to the full.

The children loved to be taken down to the small harbour to watch the fishermen mending their lobster nets and sealing their boats. The smell of fish and tar which hovered round the quay was full of memories for Constance, reminding her of the days she had spent down there with her father when she was a little girl. To her pleasure, Margharita made friends with the village girls who played near the causeway, collecting stones, turning dead crabs with sticks and generally loving and hating each other among the flotsam and jetsam. She was even more delighted to see that Manfredo was so intrigued by the fishing boats that he ventured away from her and Nora and watched, fascinated, as the men worked. They spoke to him in their kindly, gruff Northumbrian voices and, though he understood nothing they said, he was sufficiently confident to allow them to lift him aboard where he sat cross-legged on deck, solemn and silent, as he watched their every move.

By the end of the first week, a pattern had emerged. The daily trip to the harbour was the highlight of the morning. While Margharita played with the girls, whose leader, Nancy, became her special friend, Manfredo joined the fishermen, attaching himself to Jimmy, a tow-haired, rough-stubbled man in his thirties, whose weather-beaten face creased into a warm smile as he sang old Northumbrian songs and sewed his nets in tune with their rhythm. Constance and Nora sat on the seat presented to the village by the Wardleys and talked nostalgically of Constance's own childhood.

The afternoon was the time for the family walk. The favourite route was along the Heights, because the children enjoyed walking past the farm. For the first time since her father's death, Constance walked alongside the field where he was killed. There were no carthorses now but she could still pinpoint the exact spot where he lay. She saw again the stricken farm workers and heard with a shudder the words, 'He's gone.' It was that field, with all its memories, that shattered the idyll of the Northumbrian holiday.

The late summer hedgerows were already thick with low-lying blackberries and Nora suggested that the family should go on a special blackberry-gathering walk.

'I'll make some jam!' she said enthusiastically. 'You can take it back to Italy and have a real English afternoon tea.'

'Oh, yes, yes,' cried Margharita, her eyes dancing with excitement.

Constance picked up the spirit. 'What an excellent idea,' she said. 'If we find enough, maybe Granny will make a lovely blackberry and apple pie for us.'

The afternoon was warm, the berries abundant, the task pleasantly undemanding. Working with great intensity, Margharita filled her small tin twice as quickly as Manfredo did his. As she emptied it into the large wicker basket and dashed back to collect more, Constance thought complacently that her daughter was a true chip off the old block.

'Even though Manfredo isn't competing, she still has to be best,' she whispered to Nora who smiled and said, 'Just like you at that age. Anyhow, I'm not so sure that Manfredo isn't competing. Look at him.'

Constance had to agree that in his quiet way he was doing his best. Nora picked him up. 'I'll lift you over the fence. There are lots on the other side,' she said.

Constance felt a sudden superstitious fear. 'No, Mother,' she said. 'Put him down. There are plenty of blackberries on this side. I don't want him going into that field.'

Nora knew by Constance's tone and her use of the word 'mother' that her daughter was serious. Anxious not to cross her, she put Manfredo down, saying, 'Well, darling,

Margharita has already wriggled through the hedge. She's on the other side now.'

Without a word in reply, Constance began to run up the lane, peering through the gaps in the hedge until she found Margharita.

'Margharita, come out of there now,' she said, 'I don't want you on that side of the fence.'

Margharita looked at her mutinously and said, 'Why not? There are lots here. Nobody's been picking them.'

'We have quite enough already. Do as I say and come over here.'

'I can't get through,' Margharita replied slyly.

'Don't be so silly. How did you get over there in the first place?'

'Up there,' Margharita said, with a vague gesture.

'Then go back up there immediately. We're going home.'

'Just let me pick a few more.'

'Margharita,' Constance said, 'do as I tell you,' and, leaning over, she managed to grab her daughter's arm. Margharita immediately tried to tear herself free. Her movement pulled Constance into the brambles, which scratched her wrist. Tightening her grip on Margharita's arm, she yanked it sharply. Her daughter pulled away. The human tug-of-war was brought abruptly to a halt by a strange jerk of Margharita's arm. She gave a piercing scream. Constance let go and, as Margharita fell to the ground, she saw that her daughter's arm was hanging limp.

'You've dislocated her shoulder!' Nora cried in horror, as she came running up.

'I can't believe what I've done. I just can't believe it,' Constance said to her mother when they had returned from the hospital at Chollerton and Margharita had been put to bed. 'It all happened so suddenly. I honestly didn't pull hard.'

'My dear girl,' Nora said, 'stop torturing yourself. It was an accident. A chance in a million.'

'I can't bear to think of her little arm in that sling. Oh! Mummy,' Constance turned to Nora, 'what's wrong with me? Why am I such a failure as a mother?'

'Don't be silly,' Nora replied, 'she's going to be all right. There's no real harm done. I know she's in pain, poor darling, but there's no permanent damage.'

Constance allowed herself to be soothed but her feeling of hopelessness over her relationship with her children was not so easily allayed.

'Thank God you've already been to see Miss Hatherby,' Nora commented, 'I don't know what *she* would have thought if you'd appeared with Margharita in this state.'

Precisely, Constance thought. Despite what you say, you know that it's my fault and my responsibility.

It was only a green fracture. Margharita's young bones began to mend quickly and she was soon playing with Nancy again. One morning, they both approached Constance and Nora in the harbour.

'Mum's taking us to the fair at Chollerton and she says that Margharita can come,' Nancy said.

'What fair?' Constance asked.

'Oh, surely you remember the Harvest Fair?' Nora said. 'They have it every September. We used to go when you were little.'

Constance did remember, especially the crowds.

'Oh, I don't think so,' she said to Nancy. 'Margharita mustn't get her arm banged. I think it would be too crowded. But it was kind of your mummy to offer.'

'Oh, please! Please!' Margharita pleaded. 'You never let me do anything!'

'I think it would be all right,' Nora said quietly, 'I do think Margharita deserves a small treat after what she's been through.'

Guilt made Constance give way, and she reluctantly agreed, against her better judgement.

'I expected Margharita back from the fair before now,' Nora said casually.

'So did I,' Constance said. 'I do hope nothing has happened. I still think it was unwise to let her go. I remember all those crowds, pushing and shoving everywhere.'

Before Nora could reply, they heard voices in the drive. 'Oh, here they are!' Nora said with relief, getting up and going to the door. Constance heard her say, 'Oh, Mrs Heston, there was no need for you to come . . .'

The conversation continued in subdued voices. Constance went out into the hall. Her mother was talking to a round-faced woman with a careworn appearance, who was holding Margharita's hand. She gave Constance an anxious look. At that moment, Constance noticed Margharita's ears. The lobes were carrying small gold hoops.

'Oh,' the woman exclaimed flustered, 'I was just explaining . . .'

'Where did you get those earrings?' Constance asked Margharita.

'At the fair,' Margharita said, 'I've had my ears pierced!'

'I'm ever so sorry, Mrs Simpson,' the woman said to Nora, trying not to look at Constance. 'They were only out of my sight for a minute.'

'Who did it?' Constance asked Margharita.

'A gypsy lady. Then she gave me her own earrings to stop me bleeding. It didn't hurt at all.'


'There's no point in ranting and raving after the event, Constance,' Nora said over dinner. 'It's done and can't be helped. Anyhow, now that we've taken the hoops out, the flesh will grow over quickly enough.'

'For God's sake, Mother, that's not the point. Can't you see? Who knows what was on those earrings? The woman took them out of her own ears! Margharita's lobes are bound to go septic; I know they will.'

Constance was wrong. The ears healed up without any apparent after-effects.

It was the last night of the visit. The children were asleep and Constance and Nora were sitting on either side of the empty grate, enjoying the cooling air after a day that had been sultry by Northumberland standards. They were drinking cider. Both women knew how much of the old tension had gone now. They were no longer a defensive daughter facing an insecure mother who was desperately trying to be mother and father, as they had been for most of Constance's life. They had finally accepted the fact that they were on an equal footing. That did not alter the fact that they were still two strong-willed women, each determined to have her own way at the expense of the other.

'How I'm going to miss this,' said Constance, 'and the cool. It will be sweltering in Florence.'

'I don't know how you can bear it in the height of the summer,' Nora interrupted. 'I couldn't – simply couldn't.'

Constance felt a slight sting of irritation. It was all very well for her to criticise Italy but quite another thing when her mother did.

'Well, of course, we're up in the hills,' she said defensively. 'It's quite bearable really.'

'No breeze,' her mother continued aggressively, 'I couldn't breathe. At least we have a breeze up here.'

'Breeze?' Constance snorted. 'Howling gales for nine months of the year, is more like it!'

It was Nora's turn for irritation. Petulantly, she remained silent before turning to the subject she had decided not to raise again.

'Now, Constance, I hope I'm not to hear any more of this nonsense of marriage. You made one mistake out there and it sounds as if you're planning to make another. Look at me! I didn't rush off and marry the first unsuitable man to catch my fancy after your father was killed – and I've survived. You're like me. You're perfectly capable of living by yourself and taking responsibility for your own actions. You must see how unsuitable this Giuseppe would be. Think of the children.'

'You know, Mother, your ideas of marriage are very old-fashioned. You don't take a husband so that he can make all your decisions for you. I shall *always* think of the children but I cannot let them dictate every aspect of my life. That's the Italian way, not mine.'

Despite the success of the visit, Constance was happy to return to Italy. To her delight, just as Northumberland's empty spaces had cleared her head, so the cool autumn air seemed to have blown away the tensions at Constanza Castelfranco. Giuseppe was already deeply involved with the new collection. Giancarlo seemed more constructive than he had been for months. Constance could only assume that the new calm was the result of Monica's diplomacy.

'You've worked miracles with them,' she said at the end of the first day in the office. 'How on earth did you manage it?'

'Oh,' Monica laughed dismissively, 'I told them both a few home truths. Remember, I go back a long way with both these boys. I won't stand any of their nonsense.'

'What did you say?' Constance asked, intrigued.

'Not a lot. I merely let it be known that I wouldn't have you upset simply because they enjoyed acting like children. I pointed out how much they owed you. *Basta!*' She clapped her hands. 'I don't want to talk about them. Too boring – like most things to do with men!'

'I think I'd better go away more often,' Constance said. 'I can't believe how positive everything is around here.'

Monica laughed. 'Let's just hope it stays that way!' she said.

Early next morning, Giancarlo walked into Constance's office and closed the door.

'Constanza,' he said, 'I've done a great deal of thinking while you've been away, and I won't allow Padone to

409

come between us. Our friendship is too important to both of us.'

Constance smiled. 'Oh, my dear Giancarlo, Giuseppe won't come between us. He's like a child. All he wants is to be left alone to play with his clothes.'

'Constanza, I cannot turn my back on your personal life. I think our friendship should stand for more than that.'

Constance acknowledged the reproach. 'Giancarlo,' she said, 'you are my greatest ally – just as you were Ludovico's greatest ally. Do you think I can forget everything you've done for me – and, even more, for him? But you must stop listening to gossip. You know how much Bettina hates me – and how difficult she finds it to acknowledge Giuseppe's talent.'

'His talent is not in question. Do you think I would allow a foolish gossip like Bettina to affect my ability to appreciate genius? Come! What do you take me for? I know Padone is a good designer but there is a place for the Padones of this world . . .'

'Giancarlo! You are nothing but a snob!' Constance interrupted.

'Oh, no, Constanza. You are wrong. I am wise in the ways of the world. Padones only give of their best when they feel insecure – when they are afraid that they will be pushed back into the mire.'

'My God! You do hate him!'

'Nonsense. Constanza, *listen* to me. I know these people. Padone is a peasant. Brilliant as he is, he can be nothing else. The background forms the man. To try to change him will spell disaster.'

Constance counted to ten – rather quickly.

'I can see you're never going to forgive his behaviour in the fitting room. I'm sorry, Giancarlo, I had no idea that your self-esteem had been so badly bruised. However, I don't think that the incident gives you the right to call Giuseppe a peasant.'

Giancarlo was gazing away from her with Olympian disapproval. Constance thought how pompous he looked.

'Italy's problem is twofold,' she continued coolly, 'people think of nothing but tradition and children.'

'And do the English not?'

'England is a modern country. It keeps things in proportion.'

Giancarlo laughed cynically. 'You talk of Italian tradition! What about your ludicrous Beefeaters? Do they have a place in the modern world?'

Her temper snapped. 'Look,' she said, 'I sleep with Giuseppe; he is the father of my youngest son; he is my creative right hand. I demand that you respect him.'

'And him?' Giancarlo replied spitefully. 'Do you imagine that he sleeps only with you? If you do, then you are mad. I do not criticise him. What he does with his body is his affair – bodies aren't nearly as important as some people like to imagine.'

'What sort of people?'

Giancarlo snorted. '*Women*,' he said venomously as he turned to leave.


'Nicky! What a lovely surprise,' Constance said.

She meant it. A quiet evening at the villa had begun to drag and the telephone call was a welcome interruption.

'Where are you? I haven't heard a thing about you for ages.'

Constance felt a sudden need to confide her doubts in someone outside the hothouse world of Palazzo Tondi; she longed for somebody to understand and give her some encouragement. She arranged to meet Nicky for lunch the following day.

As she replaced the telephone, Monica's words came flooding back. Constance had told her of what she saw as Savognia's spiteful class war against Giuseppe. Her friend had surprised her by being totally dismissive of Giuseppe – but worse, she had hurt Constance by making her feel unworldly and naive.

411

'You really must grow up, Constance my darling,' she had said sharply. 'Stop imagining that Mediterranean life is like an English vicarage tea party, because it ain't. Giuseppe likes boys. Not as much as he likes you, I grant you, but pretty much. Nothing will change that. Look, I'm sure he's marvellous in bed. Bisexuals often are. Enjoy him. Love him. But for God's sake don't marry him. You would never know a moment's peace. It really is too silly.'

Throughout her life, Constance had countered opposition by determination. The more she heard of Giuseppe's unsuitability the more she convinced herself of the absolute necessity for him in her life. Nevertheless, in spite of her determination, it was with some trepidation that she set off to meet Nicky.

During the meal they chatted about inconsequential things and drank rather too much wine, but Constance noticed that Nicky was tense. A sixth sense convinced her that someone had already talked to him. Every time she tried to bring the conversation round to Giuseppe her courage failed her and she allowed their talk to swing away. They had ordered coffee before she finally introduced the subject, crudely and brutally, by asking Nicky directly if he liked Giuseppe. She was aware of a look of panic in his eyes as clearing his throat, he addressed the subject that had hovered, unspoken, between them for so long. Smoothing his hair nervously, he said, 'Actually, old girl, I was talking to Savognia about him just the other day. I do rather like Giuseppe. It's just . . . well, I know this'll sound frightfully pompous but . . . honestly . . . do you think he's entirely suitable to have around the children?'

Constance bridled. 'Do you mean socially?'

'Well, yes, in a way, but I was thinking more widely than that.'

He coughed. Constance was not prepared to let him off the hook. 'More widely in what way?'

Nicky gazed away. 'Come on, Constance,' he said. 'You know what I mean. You know the life that Giuseppe has led. You know how . . . ambivalent he is. Or, at least, was,' he added cautiously.

'Well?' she asked, trying to keep her voice even.

'I mean . . . how much do you know, really know, about Giuseppe? His background and that. Things rub off, you know,' he ended mysteriously.

'Oh, Nicky, how pompous. You sound just like Giancarlo.'

Nicky turned to face her. 'I don't want to spoil things for you. I just want you to be careful. I know men like Giuseppe. They can be very cruel – they're by nature predatory and follow only one law – the law of self.'

He leant forward and rested his elbows on the table. 'If you're afraid that he'll slide away again, back into the night, don't fool yourself that you'll chain him with a wedding ring,' he said quietly. 'People like Giuseppe have two sides, equally strong, and they must be satisfied. No matter how much you love him, it is all one-sided. You cannot satisfy the other side. It is impossible. Physically impossible.'

'Giuseppe, I think we should have a weekend away. Just the two of us. We've worked so hard – especially you – that I think we need to relax totally, away from telephones and all the other interruptions.'

Giuseppe gave Constance a quizzical look. 'Yes?' he asked. 'Do you think so? I feel perfectly relaxed.'

'Well, you're not,' Constance replied, ruffling his hair. They were in the studio and everyone else had gone. 'We need to talk, my darling,' she continued. 'We really do. I thought we could go to the castle.'

Giuseppe removed her hand from his neck and swung his chair round to face her.

'Constanza,' he said wearily, 'are you mad? That's Villanuova territory. We'll never be able to talk up there. Too many ghosts. Look, if you want to, we'll go to neutral ground.'

'What about the sea?' Constance asked.

'No,' he replied. 'Leave it to me. I know the perfect hideaway.'

'Where on earth are you taking me?' Constance laughed, as the car began climbing the steep Tuscan hills.

'Didn't you see the sign back there?' Giuseppe asked. 'Caprese Michelangelo – two kilometres?'

They came to a wall of thick mist, cutting visibility down to a few yards. Giuseppe slowly eased the car round the bends in the road. Quite suddenly, they burst out of what had been low-lying cloud and into the sun playing across the high meadows. Looking back, Constance saw the land below, as if through a jagged layer of cotton wool, as Giuseppe swung the car into the courtyard of the remote and solitary hunters' hotel where they were to stay.

Over dinner they finally talked.

'We're at the crossroads, Giuseppe,' Constance said, 'we must decide which way to go now. And please understand that I mean "we". I can't go alone and I can't carry you unwillingly with me.'

Giuseppe looked at her tenderly. 'Constanza, do you think I would do anything if I didn't believe in it? I can't believe that you know me so little.'

'I'm frightened of the future, Giuseppe. It seems so terrifyingly large and all-embracing.'

'What does?'

'Oh, moving into the international market, developing an American outlet – even doing a ready-to-wear line. Everything that people have been talking about recently. I don't know what you want. I don't even know what *I* want.'

'I know what you want,' Giuseppe said, with complete assurance. 'You want to be very rich and famous. I will make it possible.'

'How detached you are,' Constance said. 'You care only

414

for your creations. Nothing else matters to you, does it? Not even your own son.'

Giuseppe took a slow drink from his wine glass, his eyes on Constance's face. The tension grew. Finally, putting down his glass, he said, 'Why do you say that?'

'Because it's true. You seem more interested in Manfredo than Tudor. You hardly acknowledge that he is your son.'

'Because he isn't. You never gave me the chance to love him. You took him from me at birth, by naming him as you did. Even before you returned from London with him you had put up the Keep Off sign. Tudor Castelfranco di Villanuova. Very grand and impressive – and nothing to do with Padone.'

'Do you think he should know who his father is?'

'What! When he's destined to be an English gentleman? No, Constanza, you keep him. There are enough boys in my world already.'

The cruelty of his words goaded her. 'I've always been led to understand that there are *never* enough for you!'

'For Christ's sake, Constanza, you know my life. I've never made a secret of it. I can't help how I am.'

He threw wide his arms in agitation. 'There is something about me, I don't know what. Boys look; they want. I cannot resist. Eighteen – nineteen – twenty – they are more like women than men. I love their soft skin, their sweet smell. I admit it. I love it – but none of it is important. It's only bodies.'

'I wish Italian men would stop saying that. It's too convenient an excuse for self-indulgence.'

'And you think you have not been self-indulgent? You English are such puritans that you see sex as the only sin. Isn't too much ambition a sin when it excludes everything else?'

'To think I wanted you to marry me,' Constance said ruefully.

She was completely unprepared for Giuseppe's reaction. He threw back his head and laughed hysterically.

'Constanza! You cannot be that frightened of the future, surely? I've never heard such a crazy idea. Marriage! We'd be the laughing stock. Surely you can see that? Being together as lovers gives us style; married, we'd become pathetic. It's a ludicrous idea, my darling. What would you do, if you were married to me? You would drive us both mad. Your English sense of order would want everything to be proper – and our love can never be that. Don't you realise how quickly a wedding ring would kill our passion and bring in distrust and deceit? There is no one – believe me, Constanza, no one – I need as much as you. You are my strength. Emotionally, intellectually and physically, there is nobody in my life – and never will be – who can give me what you give. Without you I would die. My creativity would shrivel. But marriage would kill me even quicker – because that would shrivel my cock.'

'I don't see why, if you're telling me the truth.'

'I know, my darling. I know you do not see why. You are English and the English are so bourgeois when it comes to love. Don't try to understand. Just believe what I say.'

Constance knew that what he said was true. The mood between them had relaxed and lightened.

I will never get rid of him, Constance thought in bed that night as Giuseppe licked, sucked and bit her body in a wild passion that demanded a response from every inch of her flesh. Tiny depth-charges of desire seemed to explode beneath her skin as his tongue roved eagerly across and into every part of her, making her ready for the moment when he took her and she gave herself with total abandon. Afterwards they lay together, spent and sweating on top of the bed, and drifted into sleep.

Constance woke about an hour later, feeling cold. Getting up she went, half asleep, to the chest of drawers to find her nightdress. Suddenly she was aware that Giuseppe had slipped silently from the bed and was standing, trembling, behind her. He pushed her roughly against the chest of drawers. She heard him spitting on his hand. She was pinned against the furniture by his body. Suddenly, she felt an excruciating pain as Giuseppe's cock forced its way inside her. She screamed in agony but he did not stop. Pushing further inside her, he covered her mouth with his hand to stop her cries. The force of his passion lifted her feet from the floor as he took possession of her with rhythmic thrusts. After a minute he took his hand from her mouth, knowing from experience that her cry of pain would have changed to deep sighs of satisfaction . . .

When she came out of the bathroom, Giuseppe was sitting, open-legged and provocative in a chair, facing her. He grinned. 'Now you know why the boys all think me such a hell of a stud,' he said.

# CHAPTER 19

Constance had spent a lot of time since her return from Northumberland trying to decide what to do with the castle. She knew that Ludovico had always been right in claiming it was the heart and centre of the Villanuova family. Was it her duty to maintain it as such? Frankly, she didn't want it. The building was full of memories that she preferred to be without. She was happy in the airy lightness of Villa Andreoli and did not relish the cold shadows of Castelfranco. She wished the children to learn to love the leafy warmth and glowing colour of Fiesole. Although the Principessa had given Constance total control over the castle and the estates, she had done so only because she had banished Carlo. Constance was desperate to find a way of outwitting the old woman whose final wishes seemed like a curse laid over her life.

'Why can't I unbanish him?' she asked Monica. 'I mean, it doesn't mean anything legally. He is still the Principe and the castle is his ancestral seat, regardless of family passions and honour, surely?'

Monica laughed. 'Constance, for God's sake. How long have you been in Italy? Haven't you learned yet that passion and honour are the only things that Italian families care about? In fact, that's all they actually *are* about, if you think about it.'

Constance could feel herself turning pink. All right, she thought, I may not be terribly smart but I won't let this primitive thinking spoil my plans. I have enough on my plate already. She had to make Monica understand her imperatives, even if they did cut across Italian ones.

'I am right,' she insisted. 'The castle belongs to Carlo. I shall ignore all Maria-Angelina's silly mumbo-jumbo of banishment and hand it over to him. It's his responsibility, not mine. He can take care of the problems – until he dies or is ready to hand it over when Manfredo grows up.'

Her voice rose in desperation. 'I cannot take on the responsibility. I will not lose the ground I've gained with the children – well, with Margharita – just to satisfy a madwoman's will. Why couldn't she leave everything to the Church – she was such a devoted Catholic.'

'You know damned well why,' Monica interrupted.

'Oh, yes! God, yes,' Constance said bitterly, 'the precious Castelfranco di Villanuova continuity, carefully hoarded and preserved to hand down to the next male – always the male, of course. Never the female. Perish the thought! Well, if I don't succeed in getting Manfredo on my side there won't be a male to hand it on to. I will *not* sacrifice my children to soil and stones. I absolutely will not, Monica. I don't care if the Principessa passes a posthumous curse on me. I will not let her whims beat me – or my family.'

Monica laughed. 'Well, try to give it all to Carlo. He can only say no, after all. Not that I can see any reason why he should. You're right when you say that it belongs to him and if he didn't have such a sense of honour, he would have demanded it back by now, as his rightful inheritance. And the money. Don't forget that.'

Constance tossed her head. 'He can have it all. It's so tied up and entailed it would take thirty lawyers a lifetime to untangle it. I get virtually nothing in direct cash – everything is ploughed back into the estate. That's why poor Ludo had to go all over Italy with cap in hand, free-loading and begging his bed and board. The whole situation is medieval. Thank God I had the sense to start a business.'

'No, darling,' Monica corrected, 'starting a business is

nothing. What Ludovico should have thanked his lucky stars for was not that you started a business but that you made such a success of it.'

Constance's eyes shone. 'And I'm going to make an even greater success of it, I promise.' She caught Monica's hand. '*You* believe in me, don't you? You believe that it can be a success – a *real* success – so that I have something of my own to hand down. Something every bit as valid as the Villanuovas have. I know it will work – and continue. Margharita is like me. She'll be a marvellous business-woman some day. She has talent and I shall train it so that she learns from my experience. I can't just lay down the reins after all I've gone through.'

'You are not thinking of retiring already, are you?' Monica laughed.

'*Retiring?* I haven't *started* yet! I intend to found my own dynasty. And it will be stronger than the Villanuovas' because it will be founded on talent – my children's talent – not on privilege.'

'I know, my darling,' Monica said, 'you're going to make the Castelfranco name world famous. Sure, dump the castle and the Villanuova estates if you can. You don't need them; you don't need anybody. You're so strong.' Her eyes glittered with excitement.

Constance put her arms round her. 'Oh, Monica,' she cried, 'how marvellous it is to know that you, at least, have faith in me.'

'You can do *anything* – and you will,' her friend whispered, holding her tight. 'You'll get everything right – including the children – I just know it. I have absolute faith in you, and so does everybody else. You're like a steel bow – no matter how far you're bent you always spring back. That's why we all have total trust in you, darling.'

Constance disentangled herself from the embrace. 'Well, let's see. At least I'll try Carlo. I must speak to Savognia and arrange to meet him.'

'Yes, but alone,' Monica cautioned.

'Of course,' Constance laughed. 'This is Villanuova business – real insider dealing!'

Monica always seemed to know exactly where Carlo was, which intrigued Constance.

'Do you keep in touch with him all the time?'

'Good heavens, no! But he's known to everybody and, despite the terrible things in the past, everybody likes him, so when he's around the word soon spreads. Not that he's invited anywhere any more.'

'Why not?'

'People know that he won't come. Carlo has a handful of people on whom he totally relies. He knows that he can appear on their doorsteps at any time, without warning, and be taken in immediately, no questions asked. They are the only people he cares about.'

'Are you one of them?'

Monica blushed. 'Not quite, although I *am* very fond of the rogue.'

'But what does he *do*? Where does he go when he disappears for years on end?'

'Your brother-in-law is a bit of a mystic, you know, Constance. He is reputed to have special powers – the evil eye and all that nonsense. It's absolute rubbish but you have no idea how credulous the Italian aristocracy can be.'

'Oh, yes I have,' and Constance told Monica about Ludovico's unshakeable belief that the sex of a baby depended on the size of a man's cock.

Monica roared with delight. '*Exactly!* My dear, scratch the surface of that world-weary veneer of sophistication and they're all like it!'

'Including Carlo?'

'No, he's different. That's why he spends so much time in monasteries.'

'*Monasteries?*'

'Oh, yes. Maria-Angelina was not the only Villanuova interested in the soul. Carlo is an expert on religion. However, unlike his mother, it's all theory with him. He's interested in what he calls the intellectual basis of self-deception – which is how he views religion.'

'So he isn't religious at all, really?'

'Not a bit! Would *you* be if you had a mother like Maria-Angelina? It was because he saw what a destructive force it was with her that he became interested in the first place.'

'But where does he go?'

'Mount Athos, usually. But recently, before he went to London, he was in Constantinople, using the library of the Patriarchal Academy. He loved it because it's on an island – Halki, I think it's called – right in the middle of Constantinople. Ideal for Carlo: surrounded by people and yet distanced. Just like he likes life to be.'

Constance could not help comparing Carlo, ascetic and philosophical, with Giuseppe, so earthy and emotional. Maybe there is a difference between aristocrats and peasants, after all, she mused.


'The look at Constanza Castelfranco is assured and refined,' Constance read. She was going through the press cuttings of the last collection, and thoroughly enjoying herself. It had been a triumph and the order books were full. She searched out *The Times*. It was always the foreign newspapers that she read most anxiously. They, she knew, told the truth. Their reports were never as fulsome as those in the Italian press but Constance felt that they were more objective. Although she had never dared to ask him, she was sure that Savognia bought favourable Italian comment by various types of corruption and pressure. Although she knew it was probably necessary, she disliked the thought and, uncharacteristically, turned her back on it, not wishing to know.

'The Castelfranco line is now well established,' the *Times* report began. 'Earlier influences from Paris (especially Balenciaga) have faded and the long lean shapes of the daywear could come from no other house. Nor could the colours. Bronze and pink, salmon and forest green, chocolate and grey: these sophisticated combinations make Castelfranco clothes stand out uniquely in the general prettiness of the Florence shows. A bitter, oblique look gives this rather austere house the edge on all Italian competitors except the Rome house of Portinari . . .'

Rosanna tapped at the door of Constance's study. '*Permesso?*' she asked. 'May I come in?'

Constance put down the clippings, feeling cross about the reference to Portinari. She didn't like to be second to anyone. 'Come,' she called.

'Signora, the priest is here.'

Constance was irritated by the interruption and bewildered by the announcement.

'The priest?'

'From the children's school. He says he must speak with you.'

Mystified, Constance told Rosanna to bring him in. She stood up. 'Father Benedetti,' Rosanna said nervously.

A thin old man stood in the doorway, his black robes emphasising the sickly yellow of his skin. Constance thought he must be very ill.

'Please take a chair,' she said, thinking, Before you fall.

As the priest carefully settled himself in the only hard-backed wooden chair in the room, Constance couldn't help noticing his hands. Skeletally thin, the purple veins stood out like hideous lacerations. Constance shuddered. She had an irrational fear and dislike of priests, and this priest, in particular, seemed so strange that she thought how closely the face of good can resemble the face of evil. He began to talk, softly but passionately. It seemed to Constance that he was bringing a message from another world. She strained forward to hear him, aware of the veins on the back of his hands pulsating as he pressed his fingers together in a gesture of supplication.

'Your extraordinary son,' Father Benedetti was saying, 'has an air of piety, an inner calm, the like of which I have never seen. He is chosen by God, Principessa.'

The effect of the title on Constance was lost in her alarm at the priest's intensity.

'God has decreed that we must take the boy and prepare him as His shepherd on earth.'

'What on earth do you mean?' Constance asked, although she knew the answer.

'The priesthood, Principessa,' Father Benedetti murmured, 'the priesthood. It is God's will.'

'How on earth can you know that?' she said. 'He's only a child.'

'But a child with special powers.'

'What sort of powers?'

'He hears the Virgin.'

Constance could feel the hairs on the back of her neck tingling. She looked at the priest in horror.

'Such is his purity, She has chosen him,' the priest continued. 'As you must know, Principessa, he is separate. He is not like other children. The Virgin talks to him. He has told me. That is the sign.'

'I'm afraid that you're mistaken,' Constance replied. 'He is traumatised. When he was younger he saw something truly terrible and it made him withdrawn and timid. That is why he finds it difficult to mix. There is no other reason.'

'Principessa, *you* are mistaken. He must train for the priesthood.'

The desperate note in the priest's voice chilled her blood but Constance continued bravely, 'Father Benedetti, I am neither religious nor a Catholic. A life devoted to the priesthood is a life thrown away, in my opinion – or at least gambled away on a very slim chance of eventual returns. I am sorry,' she added, noticing that the priest was crossing himself. 'I shouldn't have said that but you must understand that I hold my views every bit as strongly as you do yours. I will not countenance the thought of Manfredo training to be a priest. Now or ever.'

'Signora,' the priest said, almost in a whisper, 'you do not understand the nature of your son's gift. It is a power within him and it must be harnessed – for good or evil. If he does not answer the Virgin, the devil will take him.'

Constance felt her skin prickle.

'There is a destiny within your son that you cannot deny. Even if you deny me, it will still find its way but it will emerge crooked and deformed.'

Constance felt that she would faint; she could hardly breathe. She knew that she had to get rid of the man before he said any more.

She rang the bell for Rosanna. 'I'm afraid that you must look elsewhere for disciples. Please forgive me.' And she stood up decisively, determined to end the interview. The priest left without another word.

Constance was terrified. Was the Church going to take her son away? Was the devil going to get him? Absurd as the idea was, she couldn't quite dismiss it. Superstitious fears raced through her head. She must speak to Carlo. As she was about to telephone Monica to find out where he was, Rosanna knocked on the door again.

'Signor Nicky,' she said.

Thank God! Constance thought as she told the woman to bring him in immediately.

'The Church never gives up, you know,' Nicky said with a smile when Constance told him about her visitor. 'That priest will hound you and do everything he can to wear away your resolve. And, of course, he'll get at Manfredo.'

'That's what I'm afraid of,' Constance said. 'Oh, Nicky, what on earth can I do? I won't have it, I simply won't have it.'

'Keep calm, old girl. There's no harm done yet. I think you should take him away from that school, for a start. I'm sure Italian schools give a good education but unfortunately it's all filtered through a religious haze. It's bound to be. Manfredo and Margharita are taught by nuns, aren't they?'

'Yes, and the priest.'

'Well, it's quite obvious that their influence will prevail.

I mean, quite frankly, does he *ever* talk to anybody at home?'

Constance bridled. 'Of course he does,' she blustered. 'He's much better now. He's a quiet sort of personality, that's all. There's nothing odd about him. But you know, Nicky, what happened to him would have its effect on anybody, let's face it.'

Neither of them found her words convincing but Nicky knew that there was no point in not accepting Constance's face-value assessment of her son.

'I know a woman here who might be able to help,' he said. 'Quite a close friend, actually. Teaches at Oak House, an international school. Have you heard of it?'

'Oh, Nicky, how marvellous! What's her name? Do you think she could get the children in?'

'I don't know. It's a very small show there but they're always strapped for money. If you actually paid the fees – which I gather most parents prefer not to do . . .'

'Pay the fees!' Constance interrupted. 'I'll make a donation to their funds! Look, I must meet this woman. I want Manfredo – and Margharita – out of the hands of those people at the convent as soon as possible.'

'I'll arrange a meeting with Sheena. I'm sure something can be done.'

'Oh, Nicky, I'd be so grateful. I'm terrified. Do you think he really hears voices?'

'Oh, I shouldn't be surprised,' he replied breezily, 'most fourteen-year-old boys do. It's all guilt, really. You know – or rather, you *don't* know – it's all part of the agony and joy of discovering how to beat off. All that dreadful secrecy. Most teenage boys are unbalanced by it. I really shouldn't worry. He'll grow out of it when he starts doing it with girls. Until then, let him enjoy it, guilty voices and all.'

'You're outrageous,' Constance upbraided him, but she laughed.

Although the staff at Oak House Academy was a shifting

body, Nicky's friend was an exception. Sheena McWatters was in her early thirties, had been at the academy for seven years and seemed set to remain in Florence. She stood out from the rest of the Oak House staff in two respects: she was beautiful, with a translucent skin lightly dusted with freckles, and she could speak Italian. She was also rather well dressed.

Constance asked Nicky to invite Sheena to lunch the following Sunday. To her surprise and annoyance, he came back with the information that Sheena had arranged to go to Milan for the weekend and therefore could not accept the invitation.

'Surely she can go to Milan another weekend?' she asked. 'I'm very anxious to get this whole thing settled.'

'She and her friends have booked seats at La Scala,' Nicky replied. 'They can't cancel now. Anyhow, it's only a week. She can come the Sunday after.'

Constance felt inordinately annoyed at having her wishes thwarted. 'Can't you persuade her?' she asked.

'You don't know Sheena!' Nicky laughed.

'Oh, well,' Constance said ungraciously, 'you'd better come as arranged. But make sure you bring her with you the following week. As she clearly has such a crowded social and cultural calendar you'd better book my humble lunch now in case she wants to flit off to Oberammergau or somewhere!'

Nicky laughed again, preferring to take Constance's words as a joke rather than the irritation of a woman who expects to have her own way and dislikes it when she does not.

Since the incident of the pierced ears, Constance had found it easier to deal with Margharita. Although they had many battles of will, Constance saw these as a natural and positive part of a growing relationship between mother and daughter. She was even able to convince herself that Margharita liked her, despite the shaming memory of the dislocated shoulder. Certainly, her daughter was prepared to talk to her now as she hadn't been previously.

On Sunday morning, Constance asked her, 'Do you enjoy going to school, Margharita?'

Her daughter gave her a suspicious look. 'Yes,' she replied non-committally.

'And Manfredo?'

'I don't know. Ask him. He's not in my class.'

'I know that, silly. I just wondered if he ever said anything to you.'

Before Margharita could reply, Manfredo appeared in the doorway and came across the terrace towards them.

'Just in time, darling!' Constance cried. 'Margharita and I are talking about school. I wondered how you were enjoying it.'

Manfredo frowned and made no reply. 'He's always being sent out of class,' Margharita said.

Instead of denying it Manfredo said angrily, 'I hate those nuns. They're always picking on me.'

Constance was surprised. 'I thought you liked school, Manfredo,' she said. 'Why do the nuns always pick on you?'

'I don't know,' Manfredo replied.

'Because he's dreamy,' Margharita volunteered. 'They're always saying he's dreamy and sending him to Father Benedetti.'

'And what does Father Benedetti say?'

'He talks silly,' Manfredo said, blushing and looking away.

'How?'

'He asks me things.'

'Well?'

There was a pause. Suddenly Manfredo turned back to her and said violently, 'I think he's nuts! He's always trying to make me say things. I hate him – and those nuns.'

'Yes,' Margharita said, changing her tune. 'Why do we

have to have nuns? They're always talking about God and penitence. I want to learn about history and things.'

'And so you shall, my darling,' said Constance. 'You will learn about *everything* so that I can be proud of you. And you, Manfredo. I want to be proud of you both.'

Giving Manfredo a smile, she added, almost as an afterthought, 'Would you both like to go to an English school here in Florence next year? Would you like that?'

'Yes! Yes!' Margharita's eyes were dancing with excited anticipation. Manfredo made no reply. But Constance was content to have planted the seed.

Later in the morning, Nicky arrived for lunch. Constance was pleased that he was alone; she wanted him and Giuseppe to get to know each other. As they were having pre-lunch drinks by the pool on the lower terrace, Nicky said, 'My word, Constance, this is the life. Can we swim after lunch?'

'Of course,' she replied, 'have you brought a costume? It doesn't matter, Giuseppe can let you have one.'

'Do you live here now?' Nicky asked him, casually.

'No, no! Like you, I am a visitor, only allowed here by special invitation,' Giuseppe replied with a roguish smile.

'Don't tell lies,' Constance laughed. 'You know you can come and go when and how you please.'

'Do I? I am not so sure.'

'You are always too busy down in Florence to bother to come up here. I have to beg and pray to get you here at all. You are looking, Nicky, at one of the world's most boring overworkers. He never wants to stop.'

Nicky laughed. 'Well,' he said, 'he must be mad. If I had all this, I'd never leave.'

Giuseppe smiled. 'But I don't,' he said. 'Everything you see is Constance's. My world is Florence, on the streets with the other peasants.'

Over lunch on the upper terrace, Constance couldn't help contrasting the two men. Nicky was still as nonchalant as he had always been, his gestures languid and limp, whereas Giuseppe moved as if his body were a tightly wound spring, coiled up for too long and ready to leap out at any moment. Strangely, it was Nicky who appeared diffident and almost feminine, despite his total heterosexuality, and Giuseppe whose manner was directly and forcefully masculine, seeming to give the lie to his sexual ambiguity. Constance wondered momentarily what she would do if Giuseppe found Nicky sexually attractive. It was merely a thought, not a fear. She could tell that Giuseppe was finding Nicky's relaxed personality increasingly difficult to understand. When the children had dragged Nicky off to the pool, Giuseppe said, 'Is he typical of the English?'

'Not entirely. He's typical of a particular sort of Englishman. But I've met Italians like Nicky.'

'Effete and lacking in drive? Yes, I know you have. I don't understand them, Italian or English. They are like cogs that refuse to mesh into life's machine, turning round and round and achieving nothing.'

Seeing Nicky through Giuseppe's eyes, Constance secretly agreed. How could she ever have found him dynamic and exciting? She smiled at the memory of how he had overwhelmed her in Surrey and realised how much she had changed since those days. Although she knew that Giuseppe was right, she felt bound to defend her friend.

'Well, I don't know about that. I can't believe that Nicky would be employed by Sotheby's if he wasn't achieving anything.'

'He has no energy. No spiritual energy,' Giuseppe replied. 'It's sad. His upbringing stands between him and achievement. He puts nothing into life so he gets nothing out.'

Constance thought of Ludovico. 'I think that is much more a characteristic of Italians than the English,' she said, 'I'm sure that Nicky works very hard in his way.'

Giuseppe gave her a cynical look. Blowing his smoke

430

towards her, he smiled provocatively. 'I wish he wasn't here.'

'Why ever not?'

'Because I would like to make love to you now.'

Constance felt a tingling sensation. 'He'll be gone by six,' she said. 'Then we'll see.'

He grinned. 'I don't think I can wait.'

Constance made no reply, but her eyes held his gaze.

'Does he have a girlfriend?' Giuseppe asked.

'Who? Nicky? Lots, I'm sure.'

'What about this woman he's bringing next week? Is she his lover?'

'Oh, I expect so,' Constance replied evasively, not wishing Giuseppe to know how unfamiliar she was with her friend's private life. 'Probably one of many.'

'I don't think so,' Giuseppe replied, 'he doesn't have the energy. Not that it matters.'

He stood up, put out his cigarette and pulled Constance to her feet. 'Why don't we slip upstairs?' he whispered, knowing that she wouldn't be able to resist him.

Constance listened. She could hear the excited laughter of the children who were playing in the pool with Nicky. With a pang, she realised how they still rarely laughed with her.

'All right,' she said, thinking, as Giuseppe led her indoors, that at least there was one thing she could do well. They plunged on to the bed and Giuseppe ravenously took possession of her. As her cries mingled with those of her children below Constance knew why she couldn't resist loving this man. It was his childlike intensity and sexual energy that were so completely overpowering.


Sheena McWatters was pleased but not overwhelmed by the invitation to Villa Andreoli. Assured and quick-witted, she knew that despite Nicky's protestations to the contrary she was there for a purpose. Conversation flowed at lunch, but Constance watched Sheena closely. There was a hard competence about her. Several times during that meal Constance had the uncomfortable sensation of being upstaged at her own table. For long periods, Sheena McWatters held the floor, dominating the conversation with her strongly expressed views. The archetypal bossy schoolmarm, Constance thought, displeased at having to put up with this boring woman who wielded power in an area she could not control. As she listened, she reflected with pleasure on the considerable scope of her own authority. She decided it was time she took a hand in manipulating Miss McWatters.

She smiled at her guest. 'How long have you been a teacher, Miss McWatters?' she asked.

'Oh, almost thirteen years.'

Constance was surprised. 'But why are you still at Oak House? Shouldn't you be a headmistress by now?'

'Well, I *could* be, of course. I'm more than good enough,' Sheena replied, without a touch of irony. 'But I'm not ambitious.' She looked across the terrace with the slightest touch of disdain. 'I expect you find that hard to understand. You obviously made up your mind what you needed and went for it. You don't get this without pretty single-minded devotion to ambition, I imagine.'

Only the thought of the children made Constance bite her tongue. 'I haven't shown you the pool, Miss McWatters,' she said.

'Oh, please, don't call me that. It sounds so schoolmistressy.'

Exactly, Constance thought but, taking her arm, she said, 'We'll leave these men to talk football, or whatever, Sheena, while we take a stroll.'

Once on the terrace, Constance lost no time. 'It must be a nightmare running an educational establishment in Italy.' She smiled conspiratorially, embracing Sheena as a fellow foreigner. 'How long have you been here?'

'In Italy or in Florence?'

'Oh! Either,' Constance laughed, caught off guard. She

had not yet taken control of the conversation and knew that she must.

'What do you miss?' she asked. 'The thing *I* most crave is proper poached eggs. I don't know whether it's the bread or the butter here, but they never taste the same.'

Sheena McWatters knew very well that she was being patronised. 'I've always loathed poached eggs, so I don't have your problem,' she replied.

Constance began to like her. She was strong. Sitting on a marble bench flanked by classic columns, Constance looked across the pool and up to the top terrace. How beautiful it is, she thought. Can this woman be such a pedant that she is blind to it? Sheena McWatters was thinking, I suppose she thinks that this Hollywood film set makes a bisexual boyfriend and two disturbed children worth it, poor bitch. The women turned to each other and smiled.

'Nicky's told you how keen I am to have the children go to Oak House next year,' Constance said pleasantly.

Sheena McWatters laughed. 'Well, that's one way of putting it,' she said, 'I rather thought that your keenness was to get them out of the Italian system and you were so desperate that you'd take any port in a storm.'

Constance laughed too, but uneasily. 'Oh, dear,' she said, 'is that how you see Oak House? You certainly aren't very good at public relations, Sheena.'

'Don't believe in them,' was the reply. 'Cream always rises and all the talking up in the world can't change sour milk. I can see you have a problem. I'm not going to knock Oak House but I think you should know that it isn't the most rigorous of educational establishments. We're more interested in developing character and teaching children to come to terms with their personalities. However, it's better than any Italian school in my opinion because we try our best to give pupils a broad, liberal education, whereas they're only interested in indoctrination. It isn't easy, there are so many changes of staff, but we do try.'

'And I'm sure you succeed,' Constance said hastily. The two women were silent.

'You saw the children at lunch,' Constance said. 'What do you think?'

'Can I be blunt?'

'Please.'

'Well, they're clearly both more or less disturbed. Margharita is obviously very wilful and determined and could do with some discipline. The boy . . .'

'Manfredo,' Constance interrupted, icily.

'The boy,' Sheena continued, 'seems very withdrawn. Not that they're unusual. Most of our pupils are one or the other. You see,' she smiled sweetly, 'they nearly all come from families where the adults are achievers. I'm not suggesting that this is the case with you but, with that sort of parent, the children are always the casualty, poor little things. That is why we concentrate on pastoral care – to counteract the damaging effects of brutal ambition.'

Constance had never met anyone so direct. She couldn't decide whether Sheena was being deliberately rude or was unaware of the bluntness of her manner. She swallowed hard, and managed a smile, adamant that her temper mustn't spoil her plans. She was determined to take Manfredo from the priest and she knew that Sheena McWatters and Oak House were her only alternative.

'I know that I can rely on you, Sheena, my dear,' she said, as she stood up and guided Miss McWatters round the pool, confident that she would have her way.

How can two brothers look so alike and be so different? Constance wondered as she talked to Carlo Villanuova.

'You amaze me,' he said, as they walked across the terrace of Villa Andreoli. 'You are like a completely new species here in Italy. The businesswoman is an American concept, not a European one, and I am frankly surprised that you've been able to go so far as you have.'

'Do you think I've reached my limit?'

'Hardly!'

'Do you approve?'

'Absolutely! I think you have done marvellously, I admire your determination not to be beaten by Italy's attitudes to women.'

'Ludovico never approved, you know.'

'Of course not. Ludo was a very traditional man and his horizons were limited.'

'Oh, I don't think so!' Constance said defensively.

'Constance!' Carlo said sharply. 'You are far too intelligent to trade in deception. Nobody loved Ludo more than I but that doesn't alter the fact that he was really rather stupid. He was like my mother – all emotion and no intellect. I am like our father who was worldly, cynical and detached.'

'Is it a good thing to be detached?'

'It is essential if one wishes to avoid being sucked into the morass of daily trivia. Remember, it is different for people like the Villanuovas. Unlike you, we have nothing to achieve.'

'Do you think that will be true of Manfredo?'

'No, he won't grow up a Villanuova. Sadly, I fear that I am the end of the line.' He paused and leant against the balcony. 'Actually, it isn't sad. It's good. The Villanuovas are tainted.'

'That is what your mother thought. She felt that you all gave in to lust too easily.'

Carlo laughed. 'The old obsession! My mother had a genius for missing the point!'

'So, what is the point?'

'Something I have devoted the whole of my adult life to find out. I have failed, of course, but I have learnt enough to know that there is something dark and destructive in all of us, which *might* include sex but is far more important. That is why the priest told you what he did. Manfredo will not be able to avoid his destiny.'

'You are surely not suggesting that he becomes a priest?'

Carlo shrugged. 'Why not? Is it any worse than some other form of self-deception?'

He looked at her. 'You are too practical to believe in witches, I imagine. Or too afraid to allow yourself to, perhaps?'

Constance didn't know how to reply.

'My mother was a witch, of that there is no doubt. I have abilities that are not normal. There is something strange and strong in that son of yours. By all means take him from the priest but don't fool yourself that by doing so you are taking him from his destiny.'

'*What* destiny?' Constance asked urgently.

'My dear Constance, if I knew that I would have solved the riddle of the Villanuovas and my life's work would be done.'

As they turned back towards the house, Constance slipped her arm in Carlo's. She felt she needed the support of this amazing man who could bring a form of comfort to her even as he told her things to make her despair.

It was time to bring up the subject of the castle. It was the reason she had invited Carlo out to the villa and told Giuseppe to stay the night in Florence.

'I need to talk family matters with him and you'd find it so boring,' she'd told him. 'It's nothing more than a business dinner.'

She was not sure that she entirely meant it. Carlo Villanuova, so like and yet so different from Ludovico, fascinated Constance and she hoped that by getting to know him she might understand Manfredo, who was so much more complex and difficult than his father had ever been.

Crossing the terrace, she turned to Carlo and asked, 'Why does Bettina Bonoccorsi hate me so much? I really can't see what I've done to deserve it, can you?'

'There are things about Bettina and the Villanuovas that some day I may tell,' Carlo said. 'Although it seems a ridiculous thing to say after all the gossip about you and Padone, it is in no way personal.'

Constance laughed. 'Really? God help me when it *does* become personal, then, that's all I can say!'

'Of course, she is a little jealous of your fame.'

'Oh, really, Carlo, what fame?'

'My dear Constance, you are a very successful business-woman, according to *Il Tempo*.'

'That's what everybody keeps telling me but all the evidence I can see is that it only brings more headaches. That's why I invited you tonight, Carlo. I hoped that you might be persuaded to remove the biggest headache of all.'

She told Carlo of the promise extracted from her by Maria-Angelina.

'I cannot cope with the castle and the running of the estate, Carlo, I have too much to do already. But they can't be left in limbo – everything will go to rack and ruin in no time.'

She paused. Carlo replied in a voice strangely distant and detached.

'When my mother banished me in that foolishly histrionic way,' he said, 'she knew that she could only fulfil her fantasy if I lived my part of it and allowed myself to be banished. I did so because she did the one thing that left me no choice. She turned Ludo so much against me that I couldn't face the thought of meeting him. It was for *him*, not her, that I played that ludicrous charade for so many years. During that time I came to loathe the castle and the Villanuova lands because they stood as witness to the hatred she had planted in my brother's heart.'

He sighed. 'Now you expect me to forget everything and take them from you because a promise you made in order to get your own way has become too inconvenient to honour.'

'I never wanted them!' Constance cried.

'No, but you took them – so that you could get what you *did* want: success that belonged to you alone. And you think you have achieved it, but my mother has won – as she did with me.'

'Carlo, you must help me. Can't you see that her promise was extracted from me simply so that the Villanuova

437

heritage would swamp my business? Can't you see how she plotted it all to ruin my life – exactly as she did yours? Even from the grave she is determined to try to destroy everything I've worked for. I can't let her do it. *You* can't let her do it to me, surely? Please say you'll help.'

'I will,' he replied, 'that is, if you will compromise.' He fixed her with his brown, dark-lashed eyes, and Constance found herself wondering, not for the first time, about Carlo Villanuova's sex life.

'What do you want?'

'This is what I will do. I will oversee the land but I will not become involved with that castle, so full of hateful memories for me. Manfredo is old enough to be aware of what he will inherit. And what of the other, Tudor? What is to happen to him?'

'School in England,' she replied decisively.

'I understand the others are to attend an English school here in Florence?'

Constance laughed. 'You're very good at keeping tabs on what is going on, Carlo, I must say!'

'Yes, I've had years of training. Come! What do you say? You take the castle. I have the land. Isn't that fair? Actually, fair or not, you have no choice. You must accept.'

'If that is your best offer?'

'My very best.'

'Very well. We'll shake on it,' Constance said, stretching out her hand. To her surprise, Carlo took it in his own, and kissed it.

Two days later Sheena McWatters telephoned Constance.

'You'll be pleased to know that we have a place for Margharita next term,' she said.

'And Manfredo?'

'No, I'm awfully sorry. That year is fully subscribed. The second year, which is where he would go in, is always full. We get so many Italian children at that age. Maybe when he reaches third-year age, like Margharita . . .'

Her voice tailed off. Constance had never heard such a half-hearted explanation. She knew that she must be firm.

'I wouldn't dream of having Margharita and Manfredo split, Sheena.'

'Really? They didn't seem particularly close to me.'

'I wish them to be educated in the same way.' Taking a gamble, she added, 'I'm afraid if there is no room for Manfredo then Margharita cannot come.'

'I do not think that is a very wise decision, if I may say so.'

'Possibly not. Nevertheless, it *is* my decision and I shall stick to it.'

Sheena McWatters was in a quandary. She hadn't mentioned Manfredo to her headmaster because she knew that the boy would be in her class and she was certain he would be a problem. If she lost Margharita and, more importantly, a parent who would actually pay the fees, her colleague would be furious. There was plenty of room at all levels for new pupils at Oak House.

She had to capitulate. 'Look,' she said, 'I'll see what I can do. I'll see if we can find a way round this problem. I'll ring you back.'

Constance smiled as she put down the receiver. She knew that she had won.

So did Sheena.

'Bitch!' she said out loud, as she slammed down the telephone.

That night, Constance made a point of returning to the villa before the children had gone to bed. She arrived as Rosanna and the nanny were bathing Tudor. As they soaped his body, his tiny penis became hard. Rosanna pointed at it excitedly.

'*Guarda, signora!* Look!' she cried. '*Maschio, veramente!* What a little man he is already!' She tickled the penis. 'Feel, signora!' she said. 'Feel the strength of the man.'

Constance laughed and thought of Ludovico. She had always known that it was in the nursery that all *his* superstitions had started. She wrapped Tudor in a towel and carried him to his bedroom, where Manfredo was reading a book.

'Come and say goodnight to Tudor, before he goes to sleep,' she cried. Manfredo came and stood solemnly by her side as she put Tudor to bed.

'When he grows up, can Tudor be my friend?' he asked.

'Oh, my darling, of course he can!' Constance said, bending down towards Manfredo. He put his arms round her neck and hugged her. The simple gesture seemed such a powerful breakthrough of trust and love that Constance was overwhelmed. 'Everyone will be my darling's friend as long as you speak to Mummy. Promise me.'

She held him tight. 'Are you afraid of the priest, my darling? Tell me.'

For some while, Manfredo did not speak. Constance continued to hold him, giving him time.

'I see my body,' he said in a whisper. 'When I'm in bed.'

Constance was tense with anticipation. For several weeks now, the nanny had told her that Manfredo had a sort of nightmare each night shortly after he had gone to bed.

'What do you mean, darling?' she asked gently.

'In my bed.'

She waited.

Manfredo began talking quickly and fluently. 'I am up on the ceiling and I see my body lying on the bed. Sometimes I think that I do not know how to get back in.' He buried his head in her lap and began to sob.

Constance felt numb. As she kissed him goodnight, she said to herself, No one is going to let you down, my darling. We're going to solve your problems. I won't let that priest destroy you. You'll go to Oak House with Margharita, that I swear.

After saying goodnight to Margharita, she returned to Manfredo's room. He was already asleep. She looked down at him with tears in her eyes. 'Oh, please love

Mummy,' she murmured, 'please love Mummy as much as she tries to love you. I *will* make it all right for you.'

# CHAPTER 20

Oak House worked wonders for both children. By the time the term was a few weeks old Margharita had lost some of her truculence and Manfredo was beginning to talk reasonably freely to Constance. She was overjoyed, and blessed Nicky for introducing her to Sheena. Tactless and socially inept as she was, she had nevertheless solved the problem and for that Constance felt genuinely grateful.

At the end of the summer term, she phoned Sheena and told her of her pleasure. 'I would like to do something for the school. Can you tell me the best way to help?'

Sheena knew that Constance was a rich woman. She was school librarian as well as teacher. There could be a lot of personal kudos in getting the library properly funded. The two women talked. Constance liked the idea of giving money for books. By the time they put their phones down both were satisfied. Sheena felt almost able to like Constance and Constance thought with gratitude how cheaply she had been able to buy preferential treatment for her children. A donation of a thousand pounds per year was a small price to pay.

'During the school holidays Margharita will be coming in to see what happens here. I want her to learn about the business because some day she will take over from me.'

Milva stood, unsmiling, and waited.

'As head of the workrooms, I think that you can show her what she needs to know, Milva. She will be with me

442

in the studio for a lot of the time but it is your area that is most important for her. She must be shown the practicalities.'

Milva shuffled her feet and looked embarrassed.

'What's wrong?' Constance asked in surprise. 'I thought that you'd enjoy teaching my daughter.'

'Oh, signora, so I would, but . . .'

'Well? Tell me, Milva. We've never had secrets before. I can't believe we are starting now!'

'It is Signor Padone, signora.'

Constance waited.

'And the boys.'

'What boys?' Constance asked with a sinking heart.

'Signora, Signor Padone is always employing young men that I know nothing about. Are you saying that you know nothing of it, either? If I had known that I would have spoken earlier.'

'Tell me about these boys, Milva.'

'Well, signora.' Milva paused for breath and then started speaking very quickly.

'For many months now, young men have been presenting themselves to me and showing a piece of paper from Signor Padone that says they have been given a job in the stores, or the packing department or even as cleaners. I naturally find them something to do but I get no work from them. They are always off in some dark corner with Padone, laughing and giggling and . . . I don't know what, but I *do* know that they are up to no good. They last about a week and then disappear.'

'What do you do then?'

'I wait for the next one, signora.'

'What sort of boys are they?'

'*Maleducati!* Rough street boys!' Milva said contemptuously, 'from Naples and Palermo! Savages! *Mi scusi*, signora, but most of them are *marchetti*, I'm sure!'

'*Marchetti?*'

'*Si, signora.* Boys who sell themselves on the streets of

Florence late at night. How can your daughter be exposed to scum like that?'

Constance looked at her watch. It was almost nine thirty. Damn, she thought. Where had the time gone? She had determined to be home before the children went to sleep. Now it was too late. Gathering up her papers, she switched off her light and walked into Giuseppe's studio. To her surprise it was in darkness. He must be in the showroom, she thought. As usual, they were the last two people in the building and she was conscious, as she walked down the main staircase, of how peaceful and confident Palazzo Tondi always felt when the scurrying feet and ringing telephones had been stilled. She loved the building, so austere and cool compared to the fussy femininity of most fashion houses. As she stepped into the grand *salotto*, which was the main showroom, the pale light from the concealed bulbs gave the faded frescoes an almost translucent quality. What a beautiful room, she thought and, not for the first time, blessed Savognia's prescience in insisting on a headquarters with such a unique personality that it seemed to impose its own dignity and style on the clothes of Constanza Castelfranco.

Mine, Constance thought with pride as she walked across the richly coloured parquet floor, all mine.

Her eyes fell on the design table – a sacrosanct area used only by Giuseppe, his sketcher and the head cutter. To her surprise, a folio of sketches had been left on it. Even more surprising, it was open and some of the drawings were lying on the table. Constance frowned. One of the things she had early learned about Giuseppe was that he was paranoid about secrecy and security. Having once worked briefly with Christian Dior, the most paranoid of all about piracy, he took great pains to ensure that his drawings were seen only by those for whom it was absolutely necessary. As she gathered up the sketches and replaced them in the folio, Constance thought how

444

uncharacteristic it was of him to walk out of the *salotto* and leave an open folio on his table.

Walking down the dark stairs in search of Giuseppe, Constance heard a noise from the cutting room. She walked towards the door. Thinking she heard whispering, she tried the door. It was locked.

'Is anybody in there?' she asked.

There was silence. She tried the door again. Still no sound. It must have been the wind, she thought as she continued downstairs.

She expected to find Giuseppe in the stockroom, his favourite place at this stage in preparing the collection. He wasn't there but Signora Anna was, checking over the latest consignment of embroidery from Lesage. Signora Anna was a powerful woman who ruled the stock cupboard as if it were her own kingdom; Constance felt that even she was allowed there only on sufferance. Nobody, with the exception of Giuseppe, dared touch anything in the stockroom except under Signora Anna's direction. She saw them all off, from pert young design assistants to chief cutters, seamstresses and fitters. The only person apart from Giuseppe who had free access was Milva, who came and went exactly as she pleased.

Constance looked round the tiny, stuffy room. It was a riot of controlled colour. Each bale of material was personally checked and labelled by Anna, who knew where everything was and to the nearest millimetre how much fabric was available.

'Signor Padone?' Constance asked her.

'*Buona sera, signora*,' Anna said, making to get up.

'Please! Stay,' Constance said. 'Isn't he here?'

'He *was*, signora, but he has just slipped out for a moment.'

Constance sat down next to Anna and started to examine the panels of embroidery.

Seconds later, Giuseppe burst through the door, looking flushed. 'Aren't they marvellous?' he said, his eyes bright with enthusiasm.

Constance picked up a panel. It was a beautiful blend of pale green and peach beading that slowly evolved before her eyes into stems of corn with little butterflies made of seed pearls.

'That's for "Harvest Home", the first of the chiffon evening gowns,' Giuseppe said. 'Look!' He leapt up, and scattering bales of fabric dragged out one of eau de Nil chiffon and one of peach. 'See how they work together,' he said, layering them on top of each other.

'Oh, Giuseppe, it's beautiful,' Constance said. 'Do you like it, Anna?'

'*Si, si, signora, molto,*' Anna replied, her voice gruff with pleasure.

They were interrupted by the heavy sound of feet clattering down the stairs.

'Who can that be? I thought everybody had gone,' Constance said.

'Oh, it will be one of the cleaning boys,' Anna said contemptuously. 'The lazy pigs are always late these days.'

Before Constance could reply, Giuseppe had distracted her. 'Look at *this* colour combination,' he said, leading her over to the bales of fabric, 'isn't it absolutely stunning?'

It was an hour before Constance could break up the fabric party. As they walked towards the main door of the palazzo, she remembered the folio.

'Oh!' she cried. 'We must go back to the *salotto*. You left a folio out and I didn't have the cupboard key to lock it away.'

Giuseppe stopped and turned to her in surprise. 'Folio – left out? I think you're wrong, Constanza.'

'Of course I'm not wrong,' she replied, 'I saw it – just before I came to the stockroom.'

Hastily bidding Anna goodnight, they turned back to the *salotto*. The folio was no longer on the table. Giuseppe smiled with relief. 'I knew you had imagined it,' he said.

Constance went pink. 'Giuseppe, I did *not* imagine it. There was a folio on that table. I *touched* it, for God's sake; I put some drawings back in it.'

'Well, what did you do with it? Where is it now?'

Cursing herself for not taking it with her, Constance began to search the room, whilst Giuseppe unlocked the folio cupboard and began to check the drawings.

'You're right,' he said in a small voice. 'Some day-dress drawings are missing.'

For such a creative man, Giuseppe was obsessively thorough. Each drawing was named and numbered and placed in its correct order: day dresses, suits, blouses, every item had its own folder. It was easy to check that a drawing was missing. Within a short time, it became apparent that key drawings had been removed from each folio.

'You know what this means?' Giuseppe asked Constance. 'Someone knows exactly the spirit and style of our next collection.' His voice rose. 'In other words, a *disastro*! We might as well stop now. All our line has been stolen.'

'Oh, no, Giuseppe, no!' Constance cried. 'It can't be true. They *must* be here somewhere.'

They were not. An exhaustive search produced no results. The next day the whole palazzo was turned upside down but no trace of the drawings was found. Giuseppe was in utter despair. 'Who has done this to me?' he kept asking. 'Who has betrayed me? Someone within this House is a traitor. Who is it?'

Constance called a meeting. Monica and Savognia joined her in her office but Giuseppe was too busy redesigning the collection to attend.

'Are we calling in the police?' Monica asked.

'Absolutely categorically not,' Savognia replied. 'This affair must remain a secret within the House. The police are hopeless and, in any case, we haven't paid them any money. They will do nothing. No, we must solve this ourselves.'

'But how?' Monica asked. 'We can't have a witch-hunt. Things are edgy enough already. How the hell do you think we can find the culprit in a set-up like this? It could be anybody – from you downwards.'

'Monica, don't be absurd,' Savognia said. 'If you can't say something sensible, I suggest you keep quiet.'

Within seconds, they were bickering nervously. Constance sat silent. I will not let some sneaky little traitor rob me of all I have worked for, she thought. After all the sacrifices I have made, nobody is going to take this away from me now . . .

She made up her mind. 'Please,' she said firmly, 'stop arguing, we're achieving nothing. Constanza Castelfranco is my company and it's my job to find out who has stolen the sketches. And I *will* find out – because if I don't everything we have all worked for is thrown away. As far as the world goes, nothing has happened. We must go on as normal. We have three weeks left and by then I know that Giuseppe will have a new collection. Now, we're wasting time here so I suggest that you both get back to what you should be doing. Leave the investigation to me.'

Her voice softened. 'And smile – we're going to survive.'


Constance called Milva into her office.

'Is the present cleaning boy a friend of Signor Padone's?' she asked.

Milva looked directly at her in the way she used to when they disagreed over the hats at Biaggibonsi. Constance knew that bad news was coming. Milva's body seemed to sag. '*Posso?* May I sit, signora?' she said, motioning to a chair.

Constance was shocked by the request. It was so unlike Milva who, even when relaxed, always retained her dignity by standing as if to attention.

Milva sat in front of her, twisting her hands in silence. Eventually, she started to talk, slowly and deliberately, without once taking her eyes off Constance.

'Signora,' she said, 'what I'm going to say will distress you but it is something you must know. Please forgive me if I embarrass you. It is not easy . . .

'You know, signora, I often stay late checking that

everything is in order and ready for the next day's work. Nobody knows I am here, usually – not even you.' She paused and then, making a great effort, continued, still keeping her eyes fixed on Constance.

'I see many things, signora. Many things that I do not want to see and that I have often tried to tell you of. I am ashamed to say that my lack of courage has now brought this terrible shame to your house . . .

'When you are safely in your office and the building is deserted and in darkness, Signor Padone enjoys himself. Forgive me, signora, but you know what he does, I need not say.'

Constance felt she must know for certain; must hear it from the lips of this dignified woman. 'Tell me,' she whispered.

Milva's reply was brutally short. 'He plays with them on the cutting table. Not just one night; *every* night, signora – until he is bored and sends them away.'

Constance felt sick. She wanted to say 'Are you sure?' but she knew the futility of the question.

The two women looked at each other. Milva's eyes were full of tears. 'I am sorry, little one,' she said as she rose to go.

Constance remained in her office for the next two hours, by which time she had drawn her conclusions. Nobody would steal drawings this close to collections time in order to copy the ideas; it was simply too late. The motive for the theft must be a personal one. Clearly, the drawings had been removed with the malicious intent of destroying Constanza Castelfranco. She was equally convinced that the betrayal hinged on Giuseppe and his sexual affairs. Forcing herself to face the reality of the man she loved, she was sure that he had been betrayed by one of his casual boyfriends. Who, and for whom? she asked herself.

The only way to find out was to face Giuseppe and have it out with him. Deep in her heart, she had known that some day his activities would provoke a crisis between them. It was something she had tried to avoid thinking about but now, in order to save her company, she was prepared to look it straight in the face, no matter what was revealed.

'Will you come to my office, please, Giuseppe?' she asked on the internal phone.

'What, now? I am up to my eyes with the collection. Can't it wait until tonight?'

'No, it can't. Please come now.'

Giuseppe was clearly angry at the interruption. He came in, eyes blazing. 'I hope this won't take long,' he said. 'You *do* know that I have a full collection to redesign, don't you?'

'It will take as long as you let it, Giuseppe,' Constance replied evenly. 'Who was the boy you were playing with in the cutting room on the night we discovered the theft?'

'Boy? what on earth are you talking about?'

'Please, Giuseppe, don't play games. I *know* you had a boy in there – as you do most nights when you think I'm safe in the office. You're right. We don't have time, so please, don't tell me lies.'

'It's that bitch Milva, isn't it? She's always hated my guts.'

'How dare you criticise Milva? She's worth ten of you. She has more sense and discipline in her little finger than you have in your whole body! Her loyalty to this firm and to me personally are beyond question. If you had *half* her integrity we wouldn't be in the mess we are now – a mess entirely caused by your disgusting self-indulgence.'

Despite her invective, Giuseppe would not budge. He refused to admit that he had been with a boy and the more he protested the more distanced Constance became. She was appalled by his cowardice.

Finally she said, 'Giuseppe, we must stop this charade. In future nobody enters this building without Milva's permission – absolutely *nobody*, do you hear? And anyone to be employed, no matter how menial the job, is seen personally by me. Is that clear? I will not allow anybody to destroy what I've worked so long for, least of all your

450

street boys! For God's sake grow up and start behaving like a man, not a spoilt teenager. If you don't, I warn you now, you'll go. I'll sacrifice you before I'll let *you* sacrifice my business.'

She meant it. For the first time, she began to think of the possibility of Constanza Castelfranco without Giuseppe. She remembered Savognia's words: 'I can pick up a Padone on the streets of Paris any time I like.'

They brought her comfort.


Giuseppe strode along the banks of the Arno in a white heat of rage, fuelling his anger with thoughts of revenge. How dare she speak to me like that? Who does she think I am, to take that from a woman? I'll show her who's important in Constanza Castelfranco! Sacrifice *me*? She must be crazy! Without Giuseppe Padone there *is* no Constanza Castelfranco! Everybody in Italy knows that.

He stopped for a cigarette. Leaning over the parapet, he gazed moodily down at the Arno swirling past as he contemplated what he saw as the injustice of Constance's attack.

Suddenly a voice said, '*Ciao*, Giuseppe. *Come stai?* How are you?' It was Manfredo.

'What are you doing here?' Giuseppe asked. 'Why aren't you at school?'

'We were let out early today.'

Giuseppe made a decision. 'Fancy a cappuccino?' he asked, taking Manfredo's arm and guiding him to a bar.

As he was paying, he looked along the counter and grinned at Manfredo, thinking what a very pretty teenager he had grown into.


Constance knew that the only way to stop a repetition of the theft was to find out who the drawings had been stolen *for*. I need help with this, she thought, I suppose I'm looking for a spy, God help me: somebody who can find out who Giuseppe's boy was paid by.

451

Three days after the discovery of the theft, Constance looked up from her desk in Palazzo Tondi to see Carlo standing in the doorway of her office, smiling confidently. 'I have come to take you to lunch,' was all he said.

Constance surprised herself by simply closing her diary and replying, 'What a delightful idea.'

She felt wholly at ease with Carlo. Looking at him, dappled in the sunlight which played through the vine-covered pergola of the unfashionable restaurant he had chosen, she smiled and, leaning forward, removed his dark glasses. He blinked and made to put them on again.

'Please,' Constance said. He left them on the table.

To her surprise, he ordered champagne. 'Goodness!' she cried. 'What are we celebrating?'

'Nothing at all,' he said, 'I just thought that you might need cheering up.'

Constance dropped her guard in astonishment. 'So,' she said, 'you've heard.'

'Heard?'

'About the theft.'

'So,' Carlo replied, slowly pulling the word out, so-o-o. 'That's it.'

'Do you mean that you didn't know?'

'Not specifically. But I knew you were in trouble. Why do you think I came?'

Constance was confused. 'How did you know? Who told you? It is meant to be a House secret.'

He laughed. 'How quickly you turn into the fiery little commercial lady! Don't worry! I know no secrets. But I *do* know you and I felt that you probably needed me.'

Constance looked into his eyes. She knew that he was telling the truth. 'I have needed you,' she replied, 'without really knowing it. Isn't that odd?'

'No,' he replied, 'not really. What's wrong? Why don't you tell me?'

Constance told him the story, repeating when she'd finished, 'How did you know?'

Carlo leant back, smiled mysteriously and said, 'The

Castelfranco di Villanuovas are a strange lot – as you should well know. Think of Marie-Angelina – and poor Ludovico, for that matter. They were disturbed souls. They were able to see too much of the other side.'

'Other side of what?'

'Life – or, more appropriately, death. We Villanuovas all have a sixth sense – an ability to see things others cannot. It is only a partial gift – a curse, if you like – because we have not been given the final gift of being able to understand what we see. We know things – and we don't know things. That is why we all go mad.'

'Was Ludo mad?'

'Of course. Look how he died. As for my mother . . . !'

'And you?'

'Not yet, but imminent.' He smiled. 'I knew you were in trouble but I didn't know what it was. Now that I do, I shall help you solve it – if you will allow me. I'm sure that you have already decided to do so entirely alone, but I hope that you'll let me help.'

'Who can it be who hates poor Giuseppe so much?' Constance said.

Carlo looked startled. 'Giuseppe?' he asked. 'What has he to do with it? He is only the designer. The person who has done this hates *you*, Constance, not a hired hand. I would have thought that perfectly obvious.'

Constance shivered. 'Who?' she asked in a whisper.

'Well, it could be Bettina,' Carlo speculated.

'Why?'

He looked away. 'It goes back long before you came to Italy but in any case you are too successful – and you've stolen Monica's affections.'

'Do you think Savognia . . . ?'

Carlo laughed. 'Of course not. He would never betray you. He's too stupid for intrigue on the Bonoccorsi scale.'

'I don't think he has ever forgiven Giuseppe for stepping out of his peasant place.'

'No, probably not,' Carlo agreed, 'but I know Giancarlo's snobbery very well, and he would think it the height of vulgarity to plot the downfall of a Neapolitan street boy. You see, Constance, from Savognia's point of view, there is no downfall to plot. No matter how well he does his job, Giuseppe Padone will always be a street boy to Savognia. I'm sorry to say so, but that is how he thinks.'

Constance changed the subject. 'If it's Bettina, what can we do to stop her?'

Carlo suddenly sat upright. 'I do not think that it ends with Bettina,' he said with conviction. 'She is just the go-between, the corruptor, the one who does the dirty work. What we must find out is who is paying her and why. And I know how to do it. I will talk to Pino. He's the obvious choice, I suppose. He wouldn't do it for you, but he will for me. He adores me.'

For a split second, Constance thought she could be listening to Ludo – the confidence of these Villanuovas!

'He has always wanted to sleep with me,' Carlo continued. 'He will do anything for that.'

'Oh, Carlo, do be careful!' Constance cried. 'I wouldn't want you to make that much of a sacrifice!'

Carlo laughed. 'Don't worry, Constance,' he said, 'no danger of that. It's hope and anticipation that gives one power over the Pinos of this world. Consummation would destroy that power even if I were into sleeping with men, something that doesn't interest me at all. Simply not my style.'

I wonder what is? Constance thought.


Carlo did not require long to find out who was behind the theft. Four days after their lunch, he walked into Constance's office, closed the door and asked, 'Are you worried about the future?'

Constance was mystified. 'What do you mean?'

'The future of the business.'

'No. Should I be?'

'Hasn't all this Swinging London thing affected you at all? Constanza Castelfranco is not exactly famous for mini-skirts, is it?'

Constance was stunned. Only two days before she and Savognia had talked about producing a ready-to-wear line because despite the loyalty of their private customers it was becoming increasingly clear that they could not survive on them alone. The idea was so fresh in her mind that she wasn't prepared to talk about it in any detail, even to Carlo.

'Obviously we have to move with the times but I certainly wouldn't say we were *frightened* of the future. There will always be a market for beautiful clothes.'

Carlo looked sceptical. Constance felt a little stab of irritation. What did he know about fashion? His present help didn't give him the right to tell her how to run her business.

Sensing her pique, Carlo smiled. 'It certainly bothers your main rival. Signor Portinari is a *very* worried man. He thinks the market will dwindle so quickly that Italy won't be big enough for both of you. And that is why he is employing Bettina to destroy you – aided and abetted by Padone's sexual peculiarities.

'So, the mystery is solved,' he ended, 'Pino has proved a very good little detective for us.'

'Who actually stole the drawings, that's what I want to know?' Constance asked flatly.

'Do you know an employee called Signora Anna?'

'Of course I do. She is our stock keeper.'

'Her son.'

Constance felt faint. 'I can't believe this,' she gasped. 'Did Anna know?'

'Oh, no, her loyalty is not in question.'

'But did she know about Giuseppe and her son?'

'Of course, she's an Italian mother, isn't she?'

'And she closed her eyes to what was going on?'

'No, not at all! She opened them wide with joy! She adores Padone. Anyhow, what an honour for the boy – and the family – to have pleased such a great designer. That's how she'll see it, I know. Apparently she thinks your Padone is almost as great as Leonardo!'

Constance was stunned. 'I'll never understand Italian women if I live to be a hundred,' she said. Her head was reeling. 'Please leave me, now, Carlo,' she asked, 'I need to think . . .

Left alone, she went over their conversation. Was Portinari right? Would one of them go to the wall? Even as she thought it, she knew that whatever happened it would not be her. As she began to list all the requirements for the projected expansion she found herself writing 'Designer' with a question mark. She did not write Giuseppe's name after it.

# CHAPTER 21

The new collection was ready on time. Constance thought it looked fresher and younger than previous ones and she was relieved that the setback of the theft had been overcome so professionally. Whatever his faults, she had to concede that Giuseppe had saved Constanza Castelfranco and she looked forward to the show with an equanimity that she could never have imagined three weeks earlier.

The rehearsal was a disaster. Everything that could possibly go wrong did. Nevertheless, Constance kept calm. She felt an emotional detachment that made her strong. Even when Giuseppe scrapped two dresses, insisting that they be started again from scratch, she merely smiled and nodded agreement. She was totally confident. She knew she had a real success on her hands.

For the first time ever, at Giuseppe's suggestion, Constance had allowed Manfredo and Margharita to come to the dress rehearsal. Arriving immediately after school, they came into the *salotto* rather nervously, sensing the excitement and tension in the air. As the show got under way, Constance looked across at them, their faces lit up by the catwalk lights. She was delighted to see that they both sat, entranced, watching every movement around them. Even at the frequent points when Giuseppe stopped the show and spent tedious minutes fiddling silently with a dress, their attention never wandered. Two and a half hours later, when Constance thought she ought to get them home, neither showed even the slightest flicker of boredom. She walked over to them.

'What do you think?' she whispered. 'Do you like the clothes?'

'Oh, they're beautiful, Mummy,' Margharita said, 'and it's such fun.'

'What do you think, Manfredo?' Constance asked.

He turned his dark, serious eyes to her. 'Wonderful,' he said quietly.

Constance felt a lump in her throat.

'I can't believe how blind I've been,' Constance told Monica. 'For all these years I've worried myself to death trying to balance the business and my family. Keeping them in separate compartments. Trying to juggle the different demands. It never entered my head to try and bring them together. Why didn't I think of it before? You wouldn't believe the change in them at the rehearsal.'

'I saw, darling, I was watching them. It was marvellous. But it wasn't just the clothes – although they clearly loved them. It was because you'd let down the drawbridge. You were sharing something that they've always instinctively known is very important to you, something that is the manifestation of your personality. The kids realised that those frocks up there on the catwalk were you – Mom. And they were as proud as hell of you.'

'Well,' Constance demurred, 'not quite. The collection is Giuseppe's.'

'Oh no it isn't. Do you think Giuseppe could do what he does without you right there? I tell you, Constance, it's high time you stopped all this ladylike humility. We *all* happen because of you. And that's what your kids finally realised last night. You have to involve them more. I can just tell that they love it. They're clearly chips off the old block.'

'I *do* hope you're right, Monica,' Constance said. 'Really, you know, I'm doing it all for them. Some day I hope that they will take over. I'm absolutely certain that

Margharita will want to be involved and I know that I can train her to be a good businesswoman. I can see that shrewdness in her – and the determination not to be beaten.'

Monica laughed. 'Now she *is* a chip off the Constance block. Nothing will beat *her* once she's made up her mind!'

'Actually,' Constance said, 'what she has inherited from me is the need for acclaim.'

Monica looked at her quizzically.

'I've never admitted it to anyone before,' Constance continued, 'but that's what it's all about. That's why people become successful – because they need approval. I guess I always have but it was modelling in London that made me realise how much I really loved applause. Does that sound awful?'

'I think it's the most natural thing in the world,' Monica said. 'But I'm not sure that it applies to Manfredo.'

'I'm not too sure where Manfredo will fit in,' Constance confessed. 'He's certainly no businessman, he's far too dreamy for that. He takes after his father, not me.'

'Oh, I don't know,' Monica said. 'He's very artistic. I'm sure he'll be part of the business some day. After all, I gather that he's already designing.'

Constance frowned. 'Designing? Manfredo? What on earth are you talking about, Monica?'

'Honey, Giuseppe told me. Surely you knew? He says his drawings are very good. Hasn't Manfredo shown them to you?'

Constance was stunned. All her joy of a few moments earlier was swept away. Why did Manfredo turn to Giuseppe with his designs and tell her nothing about them? Furthermore, what sort of a game was Giuseppe playing, not telling her about Manfredo's talent? She felt betrayed by them both. She knew that Monica could see how hurt she was. There was no point in trying to put on a brave face.

'We've all been so busy recently we've let a lot of things slip,' she said, trying to keep the weariness from her voice.

'Sure, I know,' Monica agreed, 'but it will all be over soon and then we can relax.'

Two shows were staged and at the end of each one Constance and Giuseppe received a standing ovation. The success of the collection frightened Constance. Just as she'd felt on top of her problems, Constanza Castelfranco seemed to have blown up in her face. She was besieged on all sides; important decisions needed to be taken – decisions that would carry long-term results. She couldn't forget what Carlo had told her about Portinari and his fears for the future. Were they fears that she should be sharing?

This was not something she wished to talk about with Giuseppe and so she turned to Monica.

'What would you say if I said I was thinking of doing a ready-to-wear line?' she asked.

Monica's answer surprised her.

'I'd say not before time. I wondered when you'd get round to it. It has been obvious to me for a long time that we have to start putting that first and couture second. There just aren't enough customers left for couture clothes.'

'And yet there's still plenty of money in Italy,' Constance said.

'It isn't a question of money. It's attitude. Women don't want highly structured clothes any more. Anyhow, they don't have time for all the fittings. No, the future is in ready-to-wear. Look at Yves Saint-Laurent. Even *he* isn't giving so much emphasis to couture.'

'But Giuseppe's heart is in couture, Monica.'

'So?'

'Well, he *is* the designer.'

'At the moment. But who knows what might happen? It's simple enough, honey,' Monica said, 'all you have to decide is whether you want to be successful or enormously successful. If the first, stay where you are. If the second, start another line.'

'Just like that?'

'Yes, more or less. It isn't any big deal. But there are certain things you must consider – even if you decide you want Constanza Castelfranco to stay exactly as it is. For starters, Florence is finishing as a fashion centre. We're in the sixties. Look how things are moving. You either choose Milan or you go to Rome.'

Monica had her own reasons for wanting Constance to choose the latter so she was delighted when she cried, 'Milan! You must be joking!'

It was the one city in Italy Constance loathed. For her it was dark and claustrophobic with a disastrous climate: too hot and humid in summer, too cold and foggy in winter. She found its anonymous streets hostile and confusing and the Milanese struck her as priggish and pedestrian. She was adamant that the company wouldn't move there. How could she exist in a place like that after Florence? It was impossible.

'I would go mad in Milan,' she said firmly, 'all those bourgeoise little biddies with their ghastly miniature dogs fouling the pavements.'

'We don't have to be in Milan,' Monica replied. 'We could be in Como, where all the fabrics are made. It could be very useful from that point of view.'

Constance visualised Como. It took her a split second to dismiss it. She recalled dripping trees, a mist hovering over the lake and surly waiters in overpriced third-rate restaurants. That was the memory of her last visit. She conveniently overlooked the golden October days when the sun filtered softly through a haze, just as she ignored the sparkling April mornings when the whole lake leapt up at you, shimmering with light. But she did not forget the prim, inward-looking atmosphere of the town.

'You must be out of your mind,' she said. 'I'd die of boredom. Anyhow, who would come to a fashion house in the country?'

'Darling, I don't mean that Constanza Castelfranco should be based in Como,' Monica said. 'What I'm saying is that you could have a villa on the shore, near Villa d'Este maybe. Or you could live in the hills, nice and peacefully,' she added mischievously.

'And travel into Milan every day? No, thank you. It would be impossible.'

'Then that leaves Rome,' Monica said reasonably.

'Are you sure?' Constance asked in despair. 'Do we have to move?'

'I'm positive. Florence is on the way out. I talked to all the buyers and the press this time. No matter what happens, we can't stay here – and Giancarlo agrees with me!'

'But *everything* is here,' Constance protested. 'They expect me to leave the villa, close the palazzo and uproot the children?'

'Yes,' Monica said, 'I guess so.'

Constance telephoned Nicky.

'I expect you thought I'd died,' she joked. 'I feel so ashamed. I haven't spoken to you for ages. I don't know what auction houses are like but the fashion world becomes more frenetic by the week. How is Sheena? Oh, good. We really must get together again soon. Actually, it's just occurred to me: it's Tudor's birthday. I'm planning a small party round the pool. He'd be so thrilled if you and Sheena could come. Yes, do. Ask her to give me a ring.'

Constance knew perfectly well that Sheena McWatters was far too independent to telephone her but she was so keen to pick her brains that she decided to ring her instead. If the move to Rome went ahead, which seemed increasingly likely, Constance would need her advice on appropriate schools.

Relations with her elder children were variable and seemed to fluctuate according to the tensions at Constanza Castelfranco. The relationship between mother and

462

daughter was tempestuous at the best of times; disagreements were never far away and Margharita's jealousy of Manfredo and resentment of Constance's involvement with the business resurfaced continually. Nevertheless, looking back at her own teenage years and recalling all her battles with Nora, Constance felt that their relationship was not too bad, and she tried to make allowances for Margharita's psychological difficulties, which were due to her figure. Whereas her brother was lithe and wiry, and her mother slim and elegant, Margharita was overweight – a disadvantage, as Constance tried to point out, largely of her own making. She was always eating. 'Just like an American teenager,' Monica had commented. Increasingly, Margharita preferred her own company. She would spend many hours in her room, listening to records and reading. If she sunbathed in the garden or swam in the pool, nobody dared approach her before calling a warning and allowing her time to put on her clothes. Constance found her irritatingly theatrical at times, but accepted that it was merely part of the growing-up process.

Her relationship with Manfredo was not so clear-cut. She hadn't been able to face talking to him or Giuseppe about the designing and she found their friendship strange and worrying. It wasn't that she feared Manfredo might become another of Giuseppe's boys – such a thing, she knew, was out of the question, but she felt that her erstwhile lover's influence on her son was slightly unhealthy. She knew, however, that she must accept it, at least for the time being. To try to break the tie that bound them, for any reason, would be too dangerous. Manfredo had improved so much socially that Constance wasn't prepared to do anything that might provoke a return to his previous state of withdrawal. She fondly recalled the day of the rehearsal. Undoubtedly, the improvement stemmed from then. She was intrigued by the idea of his designs and longed to know just how interested he was in becoming a fashion designer. It was information that could help her when she came to make the final decisions about the future of Constanza Castelfranco.

About Tudor she had no such difficulties. He was an enchanting little boy who was prepared to fit in with anything and anyone around him. Constance sometimes wondered if anybody so easy-going could grow up to be anything but lazy but she realised that there was little point in worrying. Had he been Ludovico's son she might have felt concern but she felt that parents like Giuseppe and herself would ensure an offspring energetic and hard-working. Anyhow, she knew that when he went to school in England – only a year away now – he would soon cast off his indolent traits.

As she dialled Sheena McWatters's number, Constance prayed that she would not have made arrangements to go to the opera or visit Etruscan remains – or do any of the things that, once organised, appeared fixed and immovable as cement to Miss McWatters. Constance resolved that, if she had, the party would be rescheduled. However, Sheena was free. Constance chatted inconsequentially with her for a few minutes without mentioning Rome. She didn't want the children to know about the move just yet. She was sure that they wouldn't be happy about it but equally sure that they would have to come to terms with it. The move became more inevitable in her mind by the day.

On the afternoon of the party, Constance drew Sheena aside and asked her if she knew a good school in Rome.

'St John's,' Sheena replied instantly. 'Why?'

'Oh,' Constance replied, 'I'm thinking of the children.'

Sheena's mouth fell open. 'You can't be planning to send them all the way down there?'

Constance laughed. 'Oh, haven't you heard our news? We're moving to Rome – family, business, everything. Lock, stock and barrel. The children will miss Oak House terribly. They've been so happy there.'

'Do they know?' Sheena asked, to hide her surprise.

'No, not yet. I don't want to unsettle them.'

'Awkward age to transfer them,' Sheena said, 'but business is business, and must come first, I suppose, for you.'

'For everyone, actually, Sheena.'

'When are you moving?'

'Not for three months, I would say. They'll have one more term.'

'Good. Taking Margharita away earlier would disrupt the school play.'

'School play?'

'Hasn't she told you?'

It was Constance's turn to be surprised. How could Margharita not tell her such a thing? Why did *everyone* want to keep secrets from her? To cover her shock and give herself time to think, she said, 'What is the play?'

'We're doing *Antony and Cleopatra*.'

'Goodness, Sheena, that seems rather ambitious!'

'Not really. Children are so advanced in international schools.'

Constance laughed. 'Not *that* advanced, surely?'

'Margharita is marvellous. We've only started the read-through but it's clear she is very gifted.'

'Oh?'

'She's going to make a very mature Cleopatra.'

Constance felt her cheeks go pink. 'Cleopatra? Isn't she a bit young for that?'

'Oh, but her range! Your daughter will be a great actress some day.'

Constance was flattered, but she laughed dismissively. 'I don't think so, my dear! In any case, a theatrical career can hardly be based on one school play.'

'She's excellent – I think you'll be surprised.'

'Oh, I'm sure she is. Margharita takes after me. She wouldn't dream of taking something on unless she could do it well. She's a perfectionist.'

Constance was intrigued at the idea of Margharita in the play. She couldn't imagine her standing up on stage. She decided to put the girl on a strict diet, so that she would look her best. If only she had told me herself, she thought.

'I don't suppose you've managed to get Manfredo up on stage, have you?' she laughed.

'Not quite! Do you think I'm a miracle worker? Anyhow, he'll be quite busy enough, I can assure you.'

'Busy?'

'Well, there'll be lots of costumes needed.'

'Is Manfredo doing the costumes?' Constance asked faintly.

'I really can't believe this!' Sheena laughed. 'Don't you *ever* have time to talk to your children? Their lives seem an absolutely closed book to you.'

Constance was silent.

To cover the embarrassment, Sheena said, 'We were all so pleased about his designs for your last show. How marvellous of Giuseppe to make up so many of his drawings into dresses. I gather that they were some of the most successful in the collection.'


'Where is Giuseppe? I must speak to Giuseppe!' Constance said urgently to Monica. 'Have you seen him anywhere?'

'Are you all right?' Monica asked. 'You look terribly pale.'

'I'm fine. I just want to find Giuseppe.'

'Last I saw of him he was down on the lower terrace with Manfredo.'

Without a word, Constance turned and began to make her way towards the steps that linked both terraces. As she reached them, she bumped into Carlo.

'What's wrong?' he asked, looking anxiously at her face.

'Have you seen Giuseppe?' she almost sobbed. 'I *must* speak to him – immediately.'

Carlo made to go with her.

'No!' she said, 'I must do this alone.'

She found him sunbathing with Manfredo, away from the rest of the party. 'Giuseppe,' she said as calmly as she could, 'please get dressed and come with me. I need to talk to you in private.'

He knew by her tone that she would brook no argument. He stood up and started to dress.

'I think that you should join the others, Manfredo,' Constance said sharply. 'You shouldn't be sunbathing over here away from the party.'

Manfredo stood up and giving her a resentful look said, 'I'll see you later, Giuseppe.' He sauntered insolently away.

'What is all this about, Constance?' Giuseppe asked wearily. 'What is wrong now?'

'I'll tell you what is wrong, you bastard! What do you think you're trying to do to my son?'

Giuseppe gave her a quick look.

'How dare you use his designs in the collection without my permission? Who the hell do you think owns this company? Just what are you playing at?'

'I don't know what you're talking about,' he replied dismissively, turning to go.

Constance stood in front of him. 'Don't you dare walk away from me! I demand an explanation! What are you doing with my son? What game are you using him for? Answer me!'

Giuseppe grabbed her roughly by the wrist. 'Are you mad?' he shouted. 'I'm not playing any game, you're the one who is playing games, Constance, not me. All I have done is give the boy some encouragement to build up his confidence. If you were any sort of mother I wouldn't need to. But we both know that you are no sort of mother at all. You never give your children a thought. You think only of your power. No wonder they're a mess. Thank God my son will soon be out of your reach. Maybe *he* can grow up without being screwed up by his mother!'

'What are you up to with Manfredo?' Constance repeated.

'Absolutely nothing! I'm trying to *help* him, for God's sake! Can't you *see* that?'

'*See* it? How am I supposed to see it when it's kept a secret from me – even though everybody knows except his own mother!'

Suddenly, they both became aware of Carlo. 'Constance,' he said, 'please stop. Everybody can hear you. This is not the time to behave like this. It is Tudor's birthday party, I don't think that you should spoil it. The place for you to settle your differences is at Constanzá Castelfranco, not here.'

He put his arm round her. 'Come,' he said, 'the others are waiting for you.'

She broke away from him and turned back to Giuseppe. 'Keep away from my children, Giuseppe Padone. Do you hear me? Keep away from my children!'


'I am *not* angry that Giuseppe used his designs, Carlo. You must believe me. I'm perfectly happy for him to help Manfredo. If he's any good, there is no one better able to develop his talent. I've looked at the dresses. They were the ones that gave the show a younger look. They *were* good. That's not what I object to at all. It's the secrecy that I find so hurtful – I deserve better from Giuseppe.'

They were sitting in the office. Several days had passed since the party and Constance had calmed down. She had asked Carlo to come in because she was determined to clear the air and she needed his guidance. The atmosphere between her and Giuseppe was affecting everybody and she was conscious that, as the stronger of the two, it was up to her to do something about it. She wanted to, very much. She was bewildered and needed to get to the bottom of the dramatic deterioration in her relationship with him and she knew that Carlo would give her disinterested advice.

'What have I done? Why is he treating me in this way? Is there a reason why he doesn't wish me to know what is going on?' Her voice reflected her weariness.

'There is probably nothing going on,' Carlo replied. 'You mustn't give way to paranoia, Constance. You are a highly successful woman, no one can damage you now. But you must realise that you found him out – *and* that he is an Italian.'

'What do you mean – found him out?'

'With the boy and the stolen drawings. Can you imagine his guilt over that? You know that the Italian male doesn't have a very robust ego. You reduced him as a man by exposing his weakness.'

'I did no such thing!' she replied indignantly. 'He reduced *himself* by having the weakness!'

'None of us is free of weaknesses, Constance, and most of us try very hard to keep them covered.'

'What am I to do?'

'Let him go.'

Constance was shocked at the directness of the reply. 'What do you mean?'

'He's finished here. You'll never work together in the way you used to – the way you *need* to if you are to continue a success. Anyhow, you've said yourself that he won't be so happy doing ready-to-wear. Let him go. You have lost him already.'

Was Carlo right? The question went round and round in Constance's head until she thought she would go mad. Maybe he was, but she knew that she could do nothing about it until after the move to Rome. She could not – *would* not – contemplate that without Giuseppe.

I must keep him for another three seasons at least, she decided, until we get on our feet down there. By that time it will be apparent whether or not Manfredo has any *real* talent . . .

The school play was a revelation for Constance. The standard that Sheena had managed to achieve was amazing. Even more amazing – and gratifying – for her was the extraordinarily sophisticated talents that she discovered in her children. She flushed with pleasure at the quality of Manfredo's designs. They were good, she could see it at once, they were *very* good. She had taken Giuseppe along with Monica and Savognia in an attempt to paper over the cracks in their relationship. She leant over to him.

'Did you help him?' she whispered.

'No, not at all,' he replied, 'he did everything himself. He insisted.'

'But these costumes are remarkable!'

'So is your son. I have tried to tell you but you won't listen to me!'

Margharita's gift seemed the more extraordinary for its unexpectedness. Constance realised with a shock that her daughter was an actress. Just that. Not a talented girl doing well in a school play but an actress who commanded the stage with her own authority. In the death scene at the end, the emotional maturity of her performance was so powerful that Constance was overcome by tears. As the curtain came down, Savognia leant across and said to Constance, 'My dear, what a triumph for the Villanuovas! If only Ludovico could have seen this night!'

Typical, thought Constance, all credit to Ludovico. None to me!

Despite her pride, Constance was frightened by Margharita's triumph. She was *too* good. And she had tasted blood. The blood of the first spontaneous applause she had ever known: applause meant solely for her and independent of her mother. Constance knew that she must act quickly if Margharita was not to be lost to her, destroying her plans for the future of Constanza Castelfranco.

As she walked through the palazzo shortly before the move to Rome, Constance thought, I cannot let all this end with me. I must find a way of getting her on my side. She cannot throw all this away for a career in acting – she cannot and she must not. The shock of discovering how talented her children were had galvanised her.

We've got everything, she said to herself. Everything necessary for success in the next generation. Just a few more years and we can be independent of the Padones of this world. We will be a true family firm. That is the Italian way: to keep it in the family. That is what I intend to do – and I will allow nothing to stop me.

# CHAPTER 22

Capri at the height of the season was not to Giancarlo Savognia's taste. He found the round of parties, the baking sun and the crowds quite frightful and showed his dislike by keeping the Savognia residence shut and silent throughout July and August. Giancarlo emphasised his indifference and superiority to the rest of Capri's villa-owning population by holding his last weekend party at the end of June. As the final gathering of what he called 'our own discerning season' it was always popular.

'Come now or not at all,' he urged his friends. 'After this weekend Capri is overrun by the Goths. All those Neapolitan day trippers, German package-tour groups and American matrons – my dear, it is utterly unbearable.' The more favoured guests were asked to arrive on Friday, the less important, on Saturday.

At ten thirty on the Friday morning Giancarlo and Monica were sitting together in the garden. She had come across to the island the previous evening with him.

'What time did you say Constance was arriving?' she asked.

'They're on the noon boat,' he replied languidly. 'But it could be late. We will wait lunch for them.'

A little frown stabbed his fastidious brow. He felt that Constance had got the better of him over her visit. The children were at Porto Ercole with friends. He was grateful that Constance had not asked to bring them to Capri. Like most middle-aged unmarried men, Giancarlo had no theoretical objection to children. He realised that the soundest of cases could be made for their existence and yet he loathed having them anywhere near him. What angered him was Constance's assumption that Giuseppe was included in the invitation and her insistence that he should accompany her.

Constance hadn't wanted Giuseppe for his company but because she was determined to carry on as if things were entirely normal between them while she decided what to do about Constanza Castelfranco. Capri was the melting pot of Italian gossip and she knew that to appear without Giuseppe would add fuel to the speculations that she was sure would already be rife. She was right. That Manfredo's designs had been shown was interesting enough to fashion chatterers, but the information was irresistible when it became known that Constance hadn't been consulted. Success like hers automatically brought a high level of jealousy in the neurotic world of fashion. The fact that she was a foreigner, married into one of Italy's oldest families, and to a husband who had died in mysterious circumstances, made many speak of her with malice. Moreover, her relationship with Giuseppe was well known – as were his sexual predilections. And, of course, it was noticed that Manfredo, despite his awkwardness, was growing into a pretty young man.

Oh yes, there was gossip. Constance – although ignorant of the details – knew that there must be speculation and she was prepared to go through the motions with Giuseppe in order to keep it under control.

Monica was well aware of how much Giancarlo hated being outmanoeuvred by women. She still recalled with pleasure his horror when he'd told her how, years before, Gioella had ordered him out of his own house, as if he were a little boy, and she suspected that Constance might well be capable of doing much the same thing if the occasion were to arise.

She put on her sunglasses and gazed across the table. As Giancarlo slowly turned the pages of *Il Mattino*, his face showing no interest in what he read, Monica thought how age was beginning to betray him. Despite the noble brow and marvellous nose, her host's face was that of a weak and disappointed man. When he was young his health and vitality had hidden the truth. Now it was beginning to show.

'Have you ever thought of growing a beard?' she asked casually. The pages continued to turn. 'It would suit you. You'd look like a cross between a Jesuit priest and Ali Baba.'

Giancarlo looked up, squinting in the sun. 'You mean a rogue, either way. What gave you such a bizarre idea, Monica?'

'I just thought how demonic it could make you look,' Monica replied in a tone that made it clear that she had lost interest. She got to her feet. The spaniels beside Savognia's chair leapt up, hoping for a walk. She had not taken four paces before a loud banging at the front door had the dogs barking shrilly. Giancarlo looked at his watch. Whoever was calling at this hour would get short shrift.

The visitor was Louis Brunet, who explained that he had walked up from his yacht to get out of the way of the crew. 'They're all so busy swabbing and polishing, they don't want me getting under their feet,' he laughed.

Louis was a great favourite of Savognia and he brightened up considerably at the sight of his French friend's impeccable little figure. Louis was dressed precisely as the gin-palace yachtsman should be. His white linen trousers were immaculate; his white and red striped jersey and sparkling plimsolls were spotless; his whole appearance seemed to dazzle with light. Everything about him had a newly washed feeling of cleanliness, but the most noticeable thing about Louis Brunet was his hands. They had never been used for anything very strenuous: picking up a leather-bound volume; lifting a glass of wine; unbuttoning a woman's blouse or slipping off a young man's underpants. They were the hands of a voluptuary and as he talked, they fluttered, as Bettina had once remarked, like caged doves making love. Louis was extravagant – in manner, voice and gesture. Despite his diminutive size, his good-humoured personality filled the garden room. He instantly dispelled the faint irritation that had settled on Monica and Giancarlo. Louis Brunet was welcome wherever he went because he was an entertainer.

'Divine morning, my dears,' he exclaimed, 'just *un peu chaud*, but it promises a delicious sultriness for the evening.'

As he kissed Monica, he rubbed his hands up and down her back. Louis exuded a strong sexuality, all the more powerful for its ambiguity. Although he loved women – 'I am French, no? It is natural. It is in our blood' – he was not immune to the charms of young men – 'it is so amusing – a bum, yes?' Either pleasure was taken with such innocent zest that it was impossible to adopt moral attitudes. He was accepted by all the Capri set as an endearing showman, and his peccadillos were indulgently accepted and endlessly laughed at.

'My dears!' Louis said. 'You'll never guess who I met this morning. Carlo Villanuova! I haven't seen him on Capri for years – not since all the trouble. I took a cognac with him in the Quisisana. He tells me he is not invited to any of your parties now, Giancarlo.'

'He isn't invited to *any* parties,' Giancarlo replied. 'Not that he would attend, even if he were. What is he doing on Capri?'

Louis looked vague. 'I have no idea,' he confessed.

At that moment, the dogs began to bark again. 'That will be Constance,' Monica said. Giancarlo went into the house to greet her and Giuseppe.

Louis turned to Monica. 'Constance Villanuova, of Constanza Castelfranco?' he asked.

'Yes, and Giuseppe Padone, her designer.'

'Padone? Good heavens! I knew him years ago. He used to come across from Naples. A very handsome boy.' He turned expectantly, leaving Monica to think that 'come across' was an appropriate expression if Louis had befriended Giuseppe.

Constance had heard of Louis and was delighted to be introduced. His reaction to her was gratifyingly fulsome.

'I *adore* your clothes,' he said. 'So rigorous and yet so sensual. They have – how can I say? – Italian spirit controlled by English logic. They are magnificent. I have a very special friend in Marseilles – the sweetest little Persian boy – and, believe me, my dear, when he dresses up to go out on the town he *always* wears his favourite cocktail dress – a Castelfranco – black with jet on the bodice – so chic. He'll die of jealousy when he knows I've met you!'

Everybody laughed. Constance was aware that Giuseppe alone seemed ill at ease. Before she could say anything Louis went on, 'My dear, I've just met your brother-in-law.'

She was nonplussed. Who was he talking about? Seeing her bewilderment, Louis said, 'Carlo. Carlo Villanuova. He *is* your brother-in-law, surely?'

Everybody laughed again.

Constance covered her embarrassment by saying, 'Oh, Carlo! I thought you'd discovered another Villanuova secret. I don't think I could cope with any more long-lost brothers.'

There was a silence. To cover it, she turned to Giancarlo and asked, 'Is he one of your guests?'

'No, I didn't know he was on Capri until Louis told me. He never comes to the island now. Hasn't been for years. I can't imagine why he's here.'

'Do you think he's following me?' Constance joked.

To her surprise, Monica said sharply, 'You're becoming paranoid, Constance darling. After all, Italy is still one of that diminishing group of countries where the individual is free to come and go as he likes. Carlo has as much right on Capri as we do.'

The conversation moved on but the tone of Monica's voice remained with Constance.

Lunch was simple but on an opulent scale. Various early summer visitors from other villas and yachts joined the party and sat at the large table under the sun umbrella. Louis Brunet made a point of sitting next to Constance. As his bright little eyes flicked up and down, back and forth across the table, noticing everything, he talked non-stop. Most of his conversation was in the form of questions and he frequently did not wait for the answers.

'So?' he said. 'You and Carlo are friends? Good, good! And Monica?'

'Monica?'

Louis Brunet's eyes swivelled nervously across the table. Laughing, he said, 'I am going *mad* with all the excitement of this lunch! I meant *Bettina*.'

His tone did not entirely convince Constance. 'What about her?' she asked.

'Is she still at daggers-drawn with the Villanuovas?' Without pausing for a reply, he prattled on, talking clothes, people, travel – anything at all as long as it required no thought. Smiling, nodding, occasionally speaking, Constance played his game while watching Giuseppe and thinking about Monica.

Giuseppe knew that he was not welcome at Savognia's villa; he was well aware that he was only a member of the house party because Constance had insisted. He found the atmosphere of the luncheon uncomfortable and was relieved when somebody suggested swimming. The informality of the pool made him feel less conspicuous and he gained confidence from knowing that he looked much better in a swimming costume than any of the other guests. Constance watched him, as he swam and dived with a vigour none of the others could match. Her eyes were not on him alone, however: she noticed Louis and Monica gossiping and laughing under the umbrella and felt slightly jealous of the easy familiarity between them.

After his swim, Giuseppe stretched out next to Constance and fell asleep. She tried to read but, feeling restless, got up and drifted into the villa. The dogs, lying in the shade, looked up.

'Do you want a walk?' she whispered. They cocked their ears.

On an impulse, Constance let them out of the front door. She would take them for a quick stroll up to the piazza while everybody slept.

When she arrived there, she found herself in the thick of a great commotion. Crowds of people were pushing each other forward in an effort to reach the far corner where there was clearly something going on. There was such a crush that she called the dogs and set off back to the villa. Opening the street door and popping them inside, she was about to follow when her curiosity overcame her. Quietly closing the door, she set off, back up the narrow street.

As she reached the crowded piazza, the people parted. A policeman was pushing them aside to make way for two stretcher-bearers. As they struggled through, Constance realised to her horror that the man they were carrying was Carlo. His face was deathly white, streaked with blood from a gash in his head, and his body was twisted in agony. He was wearing only a bathing costume. One of the stretcher-bearers was holding a beach towel to Carlo's left shoulder. It was saturated with blood and huge drops brushed on to Constance's skirt as they passed her.

'Wait!' she cried, grabbing at the policeman. 'Wait! What's happened? This is my brother-in-law! What's happened to him?'

Her frantic cries arrested the procession; the crowds seemed to shrink away from her for a second before closing in again to hear her words. The policeman turned.

'Do not delay us, signora, this man is seriously hurt.'

'What's happened to him?' she repeated.

'He was swimming too far out,' one of the stretcher-bearers said, 'he was hit by a speedboat.'

'Oh God!' she cried. 'Will he be all right?'

'Not unless we get him to Naples quickly, signora,' the policeman said, beginning to push the crowds back again.

Constance looked down at Carlo. His movements had stilled. His lips were blue.

'Wait!' she cried. 'My friend – the Principe Savognia – he has a speedboat. I must get him.'

The pool party was just beginning to wake up when Constance burst on to the terrace.

'Giancarlo!' she cried desperately, 'Come quickly! There's been a dreadful accident! Carlo,' she sobbed, 'Carlo! He's been hit by a boat! They need your speedboat, Giancarlo, before it's too late. He must be got to Naples quickly.'

Before anybody had time to react, Louis Brunet's voice made them all turn. He was holding Monica's inert body against a table.

'Quickly,' he screamed, 'somebody help me, please. She has fainted.'

The guests chattered aimlessly and endlessly about what had happened. It was their way of filling the hiatus until Savognia and Brunet returned. Constance couldn't bear it. She went up to the separate room she had insisted on and locked the door. Sinking on to the bed, she was relieved that she was alone.

She was profoundly shaken by the accident but more so by her reaction. She knew that she was in shock and couldn't understand why. She had come to trust Carlo over the last few months; she liked him and was grateful for his encouragement and interest in the business, but the grief she felt reflected something deeper. It was as if the tragedy had uncovered something lurking unsuspected under the surface, rather as a tidal wave shifts the sands to expose a long-hidden treasure.

Why? Constance asked herself. What is Carlo Villanuova to me?

She thought of Monica.

Why had she fainted? Wasn't that even more of an

overreaction than the grief that she herself was feeling? Why should Monica take it so badly? What was Carlo Villanuova to her? They had known each other for years, but surely they were nothing more than friends.

Constance went over the scene in her mind. She had remained with Monica while Savognia and Brunet had organised the boat to take Carlo over to Naples. Although clearly very distressed, Monica had made a great effort to recover her poise. She had succeeded sufficiently to convince the rest of the party, but a doubt still remained in Constance. She recalled the hostility of Monica's comment when Louis had said that Carlo was on Capri.

Was Monica jealous of her? More worryingly, was *she* jealous of Monica – and, if so, why?

Savognia looked drawn and exhausted when he finally returned from Naples. He had been away for six hours. To his guests' enquiries he wearily replied, 'It was all ghastly, truly ghastly. I have never seen such chaos as in that hospital in Naples. No one had the authority to do anything! I had to telephone the chief of police, would you imagine, to get any action at all. Carlo could have died. He lost three pints of blood while we were kept waiting. This country is a disgrace. A disgrace to Europe. Naples should be given to North Africa.'

Louis Brunet confirmed the chaos and said that he was certain that if Giancarlo had not been with the stretcher party, Carlo would have died.

'He was saved by the power of the Savognias,' he claimed extravagantly.

'How serious is it?' Monica asked.

'There is a bad gash in the shoulder and some damage to the bone but that will be cured. What nobody seems to know is how serious the blow to his head will be in the long term.'

Constance thought of Ludovico – and Maria-Angelina's chilling words after the car accident. 'There is a history of idiocy in the Villanuovas,' the old woman had whispered.

Could a blow to the head inflict permanent damage on the brain?

The house party disbanded on Monday afternoon. By that time, Carlo had been taken off the danger list and there was talk of his being moved to a hospital in Rome later in the week.

'Is that where he lives?' Constance asked Giancarlo.

'Yes,' he replied, 'as much as Carlo Villanuova can be said to live anywhere. Since his mother so ruthlessly destroyed his past, he has lived entirely in the present, refusing to put down roots anywhere. The moment he feels that he is becoming anchored, he moves on.'

Constance couldn't help wondering whether the fact that Carlo lived in Rome had anything to do with Monica's insistence that it was the place to relocate the firm. Because she so hated the thought of Milan, Constance had willingly listened to her even though she had known as well as Monica that the future fashion capital of Italy would inevitably be in the North. Well, she thought, it's too late to change now. Rome it is.

She couldn't deny a feeling of excitement from the knowledge that Carlo was living there and hoped that he would not become restless and move on too soon.

It hadn't taken Constance long to decide on the new Roman headquarters for Constanza Castelfranco. Savognia had suggested various palazzi in the area of Via Gregoriana, Via Frattina and the Spanish Steps. She visited them all and finally decided on Palazzo Barbiano, in Via del Babuino, right at the foot of the Spanish Steps. Constance fell in love with the palace at first sight. It was a fine example of seventeenth-century grandeur. Broad, shallow steps led up from the courtyard hidden from public view by the huge double doors closing off the street. At the top of the steps was a narrow balcony with tall palms in pots. Constance thought that they looked as old as the Mediterranean itself – and certainly as ancient as the fragments of Roman sculpture embedded in the wall behind them. The colour of the wall – a blotched and faded terracotta – reminded her of the hide of an animal and she was amused that above the doors which led into the main hall there was a sculpted head of an elephant. Savognia told her that Barbiano legend insisted that the likeness was taken from Hannibal's favourite elephant and it was such a preposterous idea that it delighted her.

Indeed, the impressive beauty of the whole building delighted Constance, but what brought her the greatest pleasure and convinced her that this could be a happy successor to the dignity of Palazzo Tondi was its equally perfect, if less austere proportions. Her monastery furniture would be perfectly at home here and she knew that she would be too. She loved the scurrilous reputation of the statue of the baboon after which the Via del Babuino was named. The statue, battered and worn, was halfway down the dark and narrow street between the Spanish Steps and Piazza del Popolo. Savognia explained to her that it had for generations been one of several spots where Romans had posted political satires, attacks on the Church and denunciations of the civic authorities, or simply their comments about life in general to amuse passers-by. Constance decided that she liked the idea of being part of this Roman free-for-all. She approved of the independence of spirit which so matched her own.

She also approved of the superb first-floor rooms. The *piano nobile* consisted of several salons surrounding a central well. They made a perfect square, one side of which was entirely taken up by the huge *salotto* which the Barbiano family had used as the ballroom. Its parquet floor had worn to a rich tawny patina, and its enormous mahogany doors with their rich gilt decoration and severe classical cases stood out powerfully against the riot of Etruscan decorative devices which covered the walls. They carried the eye up to the room's true glory, which had made the Palazzo Barbiano a legend in Italy. The ceiling was as rare as it was magnificent. The only one in Rome painted by the Venetian master Tiepolo, it was considered one of his finest works. Known as 'The Departure of Antony and Cleopatra for Alexandria', it showed the amorous pair stepping into their triumphal car surrounded by cherubs, negro attendants, courtiers and assorted wild animals. Constance loved it as much for its controlled and organised exuberance as its fabulous colours, which seemed to her as fresh as the day they had been painted. This magnificent ceiling would be the focal point of her business. It would be here that she would show her collections to the foreign press and buyers just as she had in Florence.

Constance visited Carlo one afternoon after a discussion with her architect about alterations to Palazzo Barbiano. Giuseppe and Monica were still working in Florence, Giancarlo was on holiday in London, so she had come to Rome alone. On the spur of the moment, at the end of the meeting, she decided to take a taxi to the private nursing home where her brother-in-law was recuperating.

'I am the Principe Villanuova's sister-in-law,' she told the nurse at reception. Instead of being ushered into a ward, as she had expected, she was told to wait. After a few minutes, Carlo came walking down the corridor towards her. His arm was in a sling, but otherwise he appeared perfectly well.

'Carlo! How different from the last time I saw you! You had us all so worried.'

'Bad blood,' he smiled, 'it always recovers,' and, taking her arm, he steered her out into the small garden to a bench bathed in the late-afternoon sun.

"I think I owe my life less to bad blood than to you, actually,' Carlo said, as they sat down. 'If you hadn't seen me and called Savognia, I would surely have died in that dreadful hospital.'

They chatted for some minutes before Constance raised the question she had come to have answered.

'Why did you go to Capri that weekend?'

Carlo stood up and paced before her, exactly as Ludovico had years earlier in the Boboli Gardens.

'I could tell you a very convincing lie,' he said, 'or would you prefer the truth?'

'The truth, of course.'

'Are you quite sure? Do you know why you are asking the question?'

'What do you mean?'

'Every question is asked because there is need for a specific answer – and we do not always like it if we get a different one.'

'Please don't play games with me, Carlo. Why were you on Capri?'

'Because I wanted to see *you* – or, at least, look at you from afar.'

'*Me?* Don't you mean Monica?'

'No. I mean *you.*'

He sat down again. 'For months now I have tried to be everywhere you are. You'd be surprised at how often I've succeeded – and you've been quite unaware of my presence.'

'Are you spying on me?' Carlo shook his head. 'Where does Monica come into this?'

'She tells me where you are going.'

'So you *are* spying!'

'No.' He took her hand. 'Now, Constance, remember that you wanted an answer to your question? Well, it's simple. I love you and I intend to marry you. That's why I was on Capri.'

Constance stood up. 'This is preposterous. How dare you ask Monica about my whereabouts?'

'I do not.'

'But you just said . . .'

'She tells me. I do not ask. She is quite unaware.'

He's mad, Constance thought, like his mother.

As if reading her thoughts, Carlo said, 'We Villanuovas are very strange. I've told you – we have a sixth sense.'

'When do you meet Monica?'

'Oh, all the time. She is my mistress.'

'You're lying,' Constance cried, 'she would have told me.'

On the train back to Florence, Constance went over the evidence, which pointed overwhelmingly to the truth of Carlo's claims. She felt deeply betrayed by Monica. How could her friend have kept silent about her lover in all their intimate conversations? Furthermore, why *should* she if there wasn't something going on between them? The more she thought about it, the more absurd the situation seemed. Why should Monica have Carlo if what he'd said about loving her, Constance, was the truth? In her heart, Constance knew that he wasn't playing games, but she was frightened. If Carlo loved her, why was he making love to Monica? Was he like Ludovico, another victim of the Villanuova priapic curse?

By the time the train arrived in Florence, Constance had decided that if Monica wasn't prepared to raise the subject, neither was she. They would go on exactly as before. She couldn't trust Carlo sufficiently to risk a confrontation with her best friend. Maybe he *is* mad, she thought. Perhaps the blow to his head has had an effect. To her horror, she found herself hoping that it had, at least temporarily. She took comfort from the thought that he might not know what he was saying. She found the idea of Carlo making love to Monica deeply upsetting.

'I hate St John's. I don't see why I should go. I'm old enough to leave. Why can't I go to drama school?'

Constance had heard it so many times before from Margharita. She felt weary.

'Margharita, I'm not saying that you can't go to drama school. I have *never* said that. All I insist upon is your getting an education first. You must go to university. If you go to an American one you can major in business studies and you can do as much acting as you like in your spare time – but at least you'll be learning something useful. What if you *don't* make it as an actress? What then? All that time and effort would be totally wasted. If you do a business course, you have something that you can fall back on. It's only sensible. Surely you can see that?'

'I don't need to be sensible. I *will* make it. Can't you see that acting is the only thing that I want to do with my life and nobody will stop me doing it? *Nobody!*'

The words were like a blow to Constance's heart but she refused to let it show. She knew her daughter. Margharita would become obdurate if she suspected the extent of her mother's determination not to let her become an actress.

Her tone became conciliatory. 'If it's what you *really* want, my darling, then fine. But I know that Daddy would have expected you to have a proper education first, just as I do. *Then* we'll see.'

Margharita said nothing more to Constance. She preferred to talk to Monica, who was much more sympathetic.

Constance also preferred her to talk to Monica. 'For God's sake, Monica,' she said, 'do try to talk some sense into her. Let's be frank. She's simply not the stuff that great actresses are made of. Look at her figure, for a start.'

'That's nothing,' Monica replied, 'she'll start dieting when she has a *reason* to diet – like, for example, getting on to a drama course.'

'So,' Constance frowned, 'you're on her side?'

'No, not particularly. I'm just trying to be rational. Majoring in drama is just as good an education as anything else. Why don't you let her try?'

'How can I take that risk? She might be as good as she thinks she is and then what happens to Constanza Castelfranco? I – no, *we* – haven't put in a lifetime's effort to see it die with me. She's the second generation – the most powerful of all. And one thing I *have* learned from Italians is that the most successful firms keep it in the family.'

'You're forgetting Manfredo.'

'Oh no I'm not. Giuseppe says he's going to be a very good designer. That will be his job. He could never manage a company. Could you see him as a businessman?'

'Tudor?'

'Oh, goodness, no. I expect Tudor to go into the diplomatic corps or something like that. I don't want *his* expensive education wasted on the fashion world. His life must be completely different.'

When Constance did a sudden volte-face and agreed to Margharita studying drama, it wasn't due to a change of mind. It was an act of expediency. Constance knew that any further opposition to Margharita's acting career would build a wall between them that would take years to break down. But she had not moved an inch from her original position. Constanza Castelfranco had been tailored to continue in the next generation with Margharita at its head – and that was what Constance was determined would happen.

When she had explained her position to Carlo he had delighted her by taking her plans for the future of the firm very seriously, although he did not entirely support her on the question of how necessary it was to involve Margharita early in her adult life.

'You are young, Constance, you have many years left before you will want to hand over control of the business. In fact, you will only do so when you are old and tired. Before that time, you couldn't bear to let *anyone* – not even Margharita – take all the decisions.'

'Not *all*. But it would be nice to have somebody to share them with.'

'But you *do*! You have Monica – and Milva.'

'Yes, I know, Carlo, but they're not *family* – and they're both older than I am. They'll want to retire long before me.'

'This talk of retirement is bizarre. Margharita will have got acting out of her system long before that.'

'Oh, do you think so?' Constance asked hopefully.

'Of course. Acting is a very cruel profession for women. It is only possible for them when they are young. Already by thirty they are losing ground and by forty nobody wants them. There are simply no parts. I guarantee that, if you let Margharita study drama, she will be in the business, doing what you want, by the time she is thirty-two. I *guarantee* it!'

Because she needed to, Constance believed him and gave way.

The morning of Constance's fortieth birthday dawned a perfect Roman day. The April sky was as clear and unblemished as a lark's egg; the air was empty. Sitting on the terrace with her cappuccino and looking across to the pines on the Pincio, Constance though how lucky they were to have the whole top two floors of Palazzo Barbiano as the family flat. The children's area was on the floor below, as were the reception rooms. The top floor was devoted to her suite and the largest terrace in Rome's historic centre, complete with pots of oleanders and bougainvillaea, trellised alcoves and classical statues. Even on the hottest of days, it was a cool, green oasis and the French doors of her bedroom opened immediately on to it.

She rubbed her hand sensuously between her breasts, already warm with the sun's rays that filtered through the rose trellis, and, stretching, stood up and went into her bathroom. She had a quick shower, dressed and was ready to be away. This was a morning that she wished to have to herself and she was determined to be out of the building before anyone knew. Feeling free, like a naughty school-girl cutting a class, and wanting to laugh out loud, she ran downstairs, past the workrooms. Using the narrow twisting stairs of the staff entrance, she startled two seam-stresses having a gossip and a cigarette in the doorway as she burst out on to Vicolo Orto di Napoli, narrow and black with shadow. She turned into Via Margutta, one of her favourite Roman streets, so full of the echoes and ghosts of early English travellers that Savognia had said that the Romans used to call it and this whole area of the city the 'ghetto degli Inglesi'. Suddenly, she began to run, feeling a marvellous sense of freedom and power. She laughed and waved at the young men and old women in the street, thinking, I am so lucky to be living in this marvellous city!

As she climbed the Spanish Steps Constance watched the gardeners water the huge tubs of azaleas that climbed, a mass of colour, right to the top, leading the eye to the double façade of the church of Trinita dei Monti, shimmering pink in the early sun. She thanked God that she had mustered the courage to leave Florence and start a new life here. It was as if the decision to do so had acted as a punctuation mark, bringing to a close the unhappiness and confusion of her life since Ludovico's death. She realised now that it was a punctuation mark that she alone had been able to provide. And now, a new paragraph – no, a new chapter – of her life had commenced.

Constance dropped down into Piazza del Popolo and looked with appreciation at the twin churches of S. Maria di Monte Santo and S. Maria de'Miracoli. How she loved this square, despite the noise of the traffic, exacerbated by the screeching of too many cars trying to park in too little space. She began to walk along the Corso. She had decided that she would have a coffee in Caffè Greco, in Via Condotti, a place she normally avoided as pretentious and living on its past. She entered the plush darkness of the long narrow rooms, sorry to be out of the sun but relieved that, as it was early, it was empty of the usual crowds of tourists and Roman loungers. Constance wasn't sure why she had chosen Caffè Greco. In her view the staff were the rudest in Rome. She sat for several minutes watched by the surly-looking waiter standing at the other end of the room. His contempt and indifference irritated her and she flicked her wrist to bring him to her side. He spoke in English. 'American coffee or hot chocolate? A Danish?'

'No,' she replied in Italian, 'an espresso and water.' The waiter shambled away with a fraction more urgency in his step.

At the sound of her voice, the only other person in the room, hidden behind a bottle of mineral water and a copy of *Il Messaggero*, moved slightly. He slowly lowered his newspaper. Constance was conscious of being watched by a bearded man in dark glasses. He stood up and walked towards her.

'Signora Constanza?' he queried, removing the glasses.

'Good heavens,' Constance exclaimed, immediately recalling the voice, 'it's Pino, isn't it?'

'*Sì! sì!* Who else?'

'I didn't recognise you with your beard. How handsome it makes you look.'

'Oh, Constanza, I cannot tell you how pleased I am to hear you say that. I grew it to please . . . you know . . . someone whom I don't care to please any more. I have been having terrible doubts about it. In fact, I almost shaved it off this very morning. Now, I shall keep it for ever.'

Constance laughed.

'But,' Pino went on, 'what a coincidence! I met your son just the other night . . .'

'Who, Manfredo?'

'*Sì.* Now *there's* a handsome young man. What looks he has – so *nervoso*, so *ascetico*, so . . . so *sexy*. He will surely break many hearts.' He clutched his chest histrionically. 'He already has mine. I adore him. You don't mind that I say so, no? It is only a joke. But,' he flapped his hand flirtatiously,' *do* put in a good word for me!'

Constance laughed uneasily. 'Where on earth did you meet Manfredo?'

'Oh,' Pino replied, 'Louis was having one of his little parties. Giuseppe brought him.'

'Louis? Louis Brunet? But he doesn't live in Rome. Where were you?'

'Oh, he stays with La Bonoccorsi when he's here. He

490

has a small flat in the Palazzo Tronci. Didn't you know? His parties are famous.' He giggled. 'Although probably not with the ladies,' he added.

'Anyhow, I must tell you that your handsome Manfredo was the centre of attraction. You can't imagine. Everybody found him totally irresistible.'

Constance was hardly hearing him. 'The party was at Bettina's?' she asked faintly.

'Yes, but not in her rooms. In fact, she is not in Rome at the moment.'

'Did you say Giuseppe was there?'

'*Si, si.* I've said – he brought Manfredo.'

To celebrate her birthday, Giuseppe took Constance to dinner at Ranieri, her favourite restaurant, where he had ordered a special menu of all the dishes she loved best. They hadn't been alone together for a long time and Giuseppe hoped to use the occasion to put an end to the coolness that existed between them. Above all, he wanted to end the evening in Constance's bed, which had been denied him for so long. At the end of the meal, he gave her a Cartier box. She opened it. Inside was a diamond and ruby clip and a card. On it he had written, 'For Constanza, who amazed me when I met her, still does and always will, from the man who cannot live without her'. Constance read it, closed the box and said quietly, 'Thank you. But you shouldn't have.'

'Why not? You are worth it,' he smiled.

'Worth what – a handful of expensive stones or a pack of lies?'

Giuseppe stopped smiling. 'What is wrong?'

'I need some explanations, Giuseppe,' she replied.

'What is going on?' he protested. 'Surely we can forget business for this night at least?'

'This is not about business. Why did you take Manfredo to Louis's party when you know I want you to keep away from him?'

'I don't know what you're talking about,' Giuseppe

protested as he nervously lit a cigarette. 'I haven't been to a party at Louis's for years.'

'Please don't lie to me, Giuseppe. I know that you have and that you took my son. Why?'

Giuseppe remained silent.

'*Why*, Giuseppe?'

He stubbed out his cigarette and immediately lit another. 'You don't know your son at all, do you?'

'What does that mean?'

'I took Manfredo because he begged me to and his mother was too busy for him to ask. He's frightened of you. He senses your coldness.'

'*Begged* you to? Manfredo? He'll hardly speak a word to anyone, let alone go to a party. I have to resort to threats to get him to come to his *own* birthday parties. What are you talking about?'

'He talks all right, if the audience is to his liking.'

'Giuseppe, will you please explain, before I go crazy?'

'Not tonight. Please, not tonight.'

'I won't leave this restaurant until you tell me,' Constance said, sliding the Cartier box back across the table to him. 'Let me have a *real* birthday present: truth, just for once.'

'It all goes back to the night of your husband's suicide.'

Constance's heart sank; she could feel a tightness in her throat but she said, as calmly as she could, 'His accident.'

'No, Constanza, his *suicide*. Your husband deliberately shot himself and Manfredo watched him do it.'

Constance said nothing for a long minute. Finally, she managed to ask, 'How do you know? Who told you?'

'Manfredo, of course.'

Constance remained motionless.

'He was frightened by the fireworks in the village and ran home. He reached the window just in time to see him press the triggers. He ran away. He thought it was his fault.' Giuseppe paused. 'The rest you know,' he ended shiftily.

She knew it wasn't finished. 'There is more. Tell me.'

'There is no more. He ran away. He was found. *Basta*.'

'You are not telling me the truth. What else happened?'

'Oh, Constanza, it is all so long ago. No purpose will be served.'

'Please!' she begged. 'I *must* know. How can I help him if I don't know?'

Giuseppe lit another cigarette. He looked across the restaurant, avoiding her eyes.

'He saw . . . something . . . that night . . . that greatly affected him,' he said, choosing his words carefully.

She was silent. Had Manfredo had a religious experience? she wondered. She remembered how Father Benedetti had talked to her when Manfredo had been at the Catholic school. Giuseppe's next words killed that idea.

'It was not pleasant . . . in fact, it must have been shocking for a little boy.'

'What?' Constance said. 'For God's sake, Giuseppe, *tell* me!'

He leant forward and put his head in his hands. Finally, looking up at her, he said, in a whisper, 'It was the shepherds. They were drunk. Manfredo woke to find them fucking a sheep.'

'Oh, God,' she gasped, 'what did he do?'

Giuseppe looked down. 'That is the problem. He was frightened, but he was also excited. Those rough, primitive shepherds who knew no better had a permanent effect on him. He spent his childhood thinking about the incident and when he reached puberty he went out looking for his equivalent of those shepherds.'

Constance felt sick but she had to ask more. 'How old was he when this started?'

'Oh, it was only a few months ago. No, perhaps a year. Certainly, not until we came to Rome.'

'And his friendship with you? What is the explanation of that? And how long has that been going on?'

'We are two of a kind, Constanza. We share the same creativity – naturally he turned to me. Don't question our friendship. I have never touched him – you must believe that.'

Constance turned away. 'I cannot believe anything you people say. He's a child. What is wrong with you men? Taking somebody of that age to Louis's disgusting party. I really can't believe it.'

'He is no child, my dear, no innocent, but a precociously experienced young homosexual. He *has* made passes at me, but you have to believe me when I tell you that I've always rejected them. *Always*.'

'And at Louis's?'

'Look, Constanza, Manfredo is young, he needs sex. At least at Louis's he meets people a bit above the level of field peasants.'

'How *could* you take him there?'

'I went with him to protect him. Can't you see that?'

'Some protection,' she sneered. 'So this is what's been going on while I was working myself into the ground? I can't believe that you would do this to me.'

'I simply tried to regularise a situation already in danger of running out of control. Look, Constanza, your son has been up to *everything* while you and I were working late. He's known – in fact, he's *notorious* – in every gay haunt in this city, including some extremely unsavoury ones. Don't turn on me because I led him to the safety of Louis. At least I accept what Manfredo is – and so must you, if you want to help him. Don't you understand? He's gifted. He might even be a genius. Certainly, he's a better designer than I will ever be. But you have to accept the flip side. He is *what* he is because of *how* he is. If you care at all about him, you must understand that.'

Constance felt hollow. In her distress, she turned to Monica who amazed her by saying, 'Do you mean to tell me you didn't see it coming? Sorry, Constance, but I can't believe your naiveté.'

Constance lost her temper. 'What the hell do you mean, "naiveté"? He doesn't mince; he doesn't talk like Pino,

494

he doesn't move like Louis! How the hell is a mother supposed to *know*, for God's sake?'

'Look, it's not just by crude pointers that you can tell that somebody's gay. Giuseppe doesn't look gay – or bisexual or whatever he calls himself – but there are other signs. Has Manfredo ever had a girlfriend? Have you ever heard him pass a comment on a girl? Do men who spend all their time designing dresses normally have red-blooded desires? Dress designers are like interior decorators, for God's sake. The sexuality goes with the job – with few exceptions, in my opinion. But what's the big deal? Every man in the world can't be straight. Just think how boring that would be.'

'I'm not listening to this fatuous stuff, Monica. It's evident that you're not a mother or you could never talk so calmly. You may consider me old-fashioned and provincial but *I* think it's disgusting. I'm sorry.'

'Well, I just hope you don't let your disgust force a barrier between you both, after all the worry you've had about not being able to communicate with him. In my opinion, that *would* be tragic. The poor guy is going to need all the support he can get. The last thing he wants is to have his own mother turn against him.'

Constance knew that Monica was right. She could never turn her back on Manfredo – she loved him. Furthermore, she needed him. She was now finally convinced that Giuseppe Padone could not remain as her designer. Only one thing made her hesitate. Was Manfredo good enough to take over or should she be looking for somebody else to design the Constanza Castelfranco ready-to-wear range upon which she had set her heart?

# CHAPTER 23

Italy seemed all deviousness and duplicity to Constance. For the first time since the opening of the small hat factory, she couldn't concentrate on the daily running of the business. She found it hard to care about what was happening around her and she increasingly left to others decisions that she – and she alone – would have made previously.

One afternoon, when she and Milva were checking the order book, she suddenly felt the onset of tears.

'Signora!' cried Milva in alarm. 'What is wrong? Why do you look so sad?'

With a sense of relief, Constance finally broke down and told her loyal friend of all her problems, including the revelation about Manfredo.

Milva's face went white. 'That Padone!' she hissed. 'I would kill him for you with my bare hands if you would only say the word!'

The venom in her voice made Constance shiver. She knew it was genuine.

'I'm sorry to speak so, signora, but he is scum and always has been! Oh, how many times have I wanted to denounce him to you as the worthless rogue he is – but I couldn't find the courage.'

Constance didn't want to hear. She raised her hand to stop the developing tirade.

'I don't know what to do,' she said.

'You must go away, little one. To rest. You must go

back to your own people. To your family. To your country.'

'I *have* no country. Italy should be my country and yet I feel more like a foreigner than when I first came here and knew no Italian and understood nothing. I thought I'd learnt to understand but I think I know less about the Italians now than I ever did.'

'The Italians! The Italians! What are they? There *are* no Italians. There are people, only people, and they can be good or bad whether they are British, German or whatever!'

Constance knew Milva was right.

'Go to your mother, little one,' Milva said softly, 'she will make you whole again.'

Constance knew that she was not strong enough – she could only face Nora when she was feeling confident. Besides, she felt that the only way out of her introspection was to give, not take. She decided that she *would* go to England – but to see Tudor, now in his second year at school. As she wanted the visit to be a surprise, she didn't tell him she was coming.

Hiring a car at Heathrow, she drove down to Wiltshire, and arrived in Devizes in time to book into a local hotel, take a bath and go down to the dining room for supper. She wasn't prepared for the awfulness of the food served to her any more than for the respectful pride with which it was presented. Pushing it round her plate, she watched the other diners in amazement – they gave the appearance of people thoroughly enjoying what they were eating. Their zest saddened her. She thought of the Italians and the care and reverence they devoted to food. I could never come back to England now, she thought. I don't understand the English any more. How can they put up with a meal like this and actually relish it? They are bizarre.

Dining alone is always depressing but that night its effects on Constance were devastating. She was riddled by guilt over her inability to juggle all the different elements that constituted her world; a guilt not assuaged by Monica's regular assurances that she was doing a better job than most people could. She knew that her continued involvement with Giuseppe was wrong for her, the business and the children but self-preservation made her cling, if not to him, then to the *idea* of him. As for her children, apart from the inadequacy she felt over Manfredo and Margharita, she realised that she barely knew Tudor. Monica called him 'the little stranger' and Constance knew that she was only half joking. He came home for holidays three times a year, and each visit confirmed Constance's fear that, because of the very Englishness she had vowed at his birth would be his, he would soon have little, if anything, in common with her older children. Whereas they were bilingual and slipped easily between Italian and English, even in mid-sentence Tudor was already losing his fluency. Giuseppe thought this a deliberate betrayal on her part, and she wondered, not for the first time, if she had made a wrong decision.

In an attempt to cheer herself up she asked for a double brandy with her coffee. What will Tudor say when he sees me? she mused. He probably won't even recognise me. For a split second she wondered if *she* would recognise *him*. Smiling ruefully at her pessimism, she ordered another double brandy and took it up to her room. She sat and watched television. Poor as the programmes were she had to admit that they were very much better than in Italy. She was too restless to watch for long: she needed to talk to somebody in order to calm her nerves. If she telephoned Nora, she would be expected to go north; she decided to ring Italy and talk to her other son.

Both sleeping figures were roused by the telephone. One sat up, the other rolled away and pulled a pillow over its head. The ringing continued. Cursing, the first figure crawled out of bed and, stumbling over the dressing table, picked up the telephone.

'*Pronto*. Hello.'

'Giuseppe?'

'Constanza!'

'What on earth are you doing there? I thought you were in Como?'

Trying to keep the panic out of his voice, Giuseppe said, 'Where are you, for Christ's sake?'

'I'm in Wiltshire. In England. Where did you think I was? Why are you at the villa? Why aren't you in Como?'

'Oh . . . well . . . the car broke down. I had to turn back. I'm going up tomorrow.'

'Where's Manfredo?'

'Manfredo?'

'Yes, *Manfredo*. Where is he? I want to talk to him.'

'I . . . I think he's asleep. Why don't you ring tomorrow?'

'Are you all right? You sound strange.'

'Fine! Never felt better. Just a little tired.'

'But what about Como?'

'Tomorrow, tomorrow. It's late here and I must get back to Florence. Goodnight.'

'Give my love to Manfredo.'

Giuseppe walked across to the bed. 'Your mother sends her love,' he said, slapping the naked bottom protruding from the sheets. The second figure rolled over, arms opening voluptuously, and whispered, 'Show me.'

Next morning Constance had a headache. The smell of frying sausages that permeated the dining room was nauseating and she set off without eating breakfast. Driving through the narrow Wiltshire lanes she began to feel better and, by the time she arrived at the gates of Hopedale School, she was excited. She reported to the office and waited while the headmaster's permission was obtained for her to see her son. A prefect escort (a pink and blond pastiche of an English schoolboy, Constance thought) was allotted to take her to the games field where she was faced with a seething mass of seemingly identical small boys playing rugby. The game was stopped, Tudor was extracted, and the prefect respectfully faded away. Tudor stood before her, muddy and hot, blushing with pleasure. Constance noticed that his knee was cut but, realising that to mention it would be social death for her son, she allowed him to go and change while she stood on the touchline wondering what benefit public schools could possibly see in the vicious tussles taking place on the field before her.

The headmaster had given Tudor an exeat on the proviso that he be back at Hopedale by six. When Constance told him the news, Tudor's face fell.

'Oh,' he said, making no attempt to disguise his disappointment, 'I'll miss art.'

'Oh, dear,' Constance asked, 'does it matter?'

'No,' said Tudor, putting on a brave face, 'it's just that we're doing a mural and I only hope that nobody does my part because I'm not there.'

Constance felt inadequate to this and decided to change the subject. They drove into Devizes, where she realised with a sinking heart that she had no idea how to entertain her son. It was now twelve thirty and a cold drizzle had begun to fall. She noticed with relief a pub with a sign outside reading, 'Hot Snacks and Lunches'.

'Let's have an early lunch and then we can go to the cinema,' she suggested.

The bar was deliciously welcoming and warm, glowing with copper and brass. Thank God, Constance thought as she went up to the counter for a menu.

'I'm sorry,' said the barmaid, nodding in the direction of Tudor. 'He can't stay in here.'

'Why ever not?'

'Under age. We've got a garden for children.'

'But it's raining!'

'I'm sorry. He can't stay in here.'

They found a tearoom. Tudor had beans on toast,

Constance nibbled a toasted bun. As they ate, the conversation languished and died.

'Would you like to go to the cinema?' she asked. He said yes so politely that she knew he lied. With a heavy heart, she said, 'Or would you prefer to do art? You still have time.'

'Can I?'

'Come on.'

She drove him back to school in silence, her sense of failure complete. Returning the car at the airport, she discovered that Tudor had left his cap on the back seat. The discovery filled her with despair. It seemed to pinpoint her inadequacy as a mother. A *real* mother would have noticed and wouldn't have let her son return to school incorrectly dressed. She wondered if Tudor would be given detention. Should she phone the school and say it was her fault?

They were already calling her flight. Holding the pathetic little maroon cap in her hand she boarded, reflecting on the futility of the day. You're only good for business, she told herself. You should leave your kids alone and let them grow up without you. They don't need you and they don't want you. Forget them and get on with what you know you can do. The thought did nothing to cheer her up any more than the recognition of a fact that she had known subconsciously for a long time. She was a stateless person. That was the position to which her ambition had brought her . . .

Incapable of understanding the Italians and bored and irritated by the English, she felt despairingly that not only did she belong nowhere – there seemed nobody at all who really belonged to *her*.

'Monica, you can't imagine how ghastly it was. He was so polite and proper, and so distant he made me feel a complete stranger. And then I forgot his cap!'

'Well,' Monica replied, 'I wouldn't worry too much. I gather they no longer boil little boys in oil for being incorrectly dressed! And as for him being proper, I should damn well hope so too, after all the money you're spending. Isn't that what English public schools are all about? Pardon the pretensions of a humble American but surely that's where the stiff upper lip starts? How can there be any place for sentimental mums in establishments like that? You shouldn't have gone.'

'No, Monica, you're wrong. *He* shouldn't have gone. I shall bring him back to Italy.'

'Don't be so self-indulgent! He's not a pawn on a chess board, you know, he's a little boy. A human being. You can't take him away from his friends.'

'But how do I stop him growing apart from us?'

'Well, darling,' Monica said, 'isn't that what you intended when he was born? You've set your course. For Tudor's sake, you have to stick to it.'

Constance looked so desperate that Monica took her in her arms. 'Look, stop worrying. You know you're strong enough to hold them together. Just let them get the growing up over and then you can sort them out. Tudor's doing fine. Let him be. He won't let you down.'

Whether or not Monica was right, there was little Constance could do about Tudor at the moment. Getting Margharita and Manfredo involved in the company and planning a strong future for it were the important things to be dealt with now. Constanza Castelfranco was her anchor and her lode star; she believed that, provided the business was a success, everything else could slot into place. She had to; it was the only thing over which she seemed able to exercise any real control. Without it, I am nothing, she said to herself. With it, I am everything I want to be – and everything I want for my children.

Walking through Campo de Fiori one morning in late October, Constance met Louis Brunet. At first she did not recognise him when he spoke to her, then she realised that it was indeed Louis – but Louis subtly changed. There was something not quite pristine about him.

502

Although his suit wasn't crumpled, it was not pressed as immaculately as a Louis Brunet suit should be; his tie wasn't stained but it did not glow with the freshness appropriate to a Louis Brunet tie. Even his teeth seemed less dazzling than before.

Since Pino's revelation about the party where Manfredo had been a guest, Constance had changed her opinion of Louis Brunet. She no longer saw him as one of life's innocent entertainers. Irrational as she knew it to be, she couldn't help blaming him for Manfredo's sexuality. Their conversation was brief and rather cool. Although he toddled off round the corner with his usual dandified walk, Constance felt that his personality had lost something indefinable. As she bought some flowers, she realised what was missing. He's lost his raffishness, she thought. In fact, he looks quite careworn. She set off for Via del Babuino vaguely wondering what had changed Louis Brunet's fortunes.

At three o'clock on the same day, the internal telephone rang in Constance's office. It was Savognia. He had just returned from lunch at his club, Scacchi, and wanted to come and talk to her.

'Can't it wait, Giancarlo?' she asked. 'I have hundreds of calls lined up for this afternoon. Why don't we see each other for coffee tomorrow morning?'

'Constanza,' he replied, lowering his voice, 'this is too urgent to wait. Cancel your calls. I've just learnt something at Scacchi that could finish us all. I don't wish to talk in your office. Can I speak to you in your apartment, alone? I'll be there in five minutes.'

Despite the gravity of his tone, and the seriousness of his expression when she let him in to the apartment, Constance couldn't help smiling at Savognia's appearance. He looked as if he had just walked out of the members' enclosure at Goodwood. He wore a tweed suit, pale green waistcoat, pink and green tie and suede desert boots.

'Giancarlo,' Constance laughed, 'you look outrageous!

Whoever heard of an Italian looking like that? And isn't that a Garrick Club tie? I didn't know you were a . . .'

'Please, Constanza,' Giancarlo interrupted, 'where can we talk?'

'Wherever you like. What on earth is wrong?'

'The terrace,' he said, ignoring her question. 'We will not be overheard there.'

When they were seated in an alcove as far as possible from the apartment, Constance said, 'Really, Giancarlo, you are so *nervoso*. What's going on? It's cold out here.'

'I've just been lunching at my club. You know how everybody goes there – members of Parliament, the top people in the police – everyone.'

Constance knew perfectly well that Scacchi was the grandest and most exclusive club in Rome and wished that Savognia would get on with his news.

'News breaks there,' he went on, 'before anywhere else in Italy. Well, my dear, there is an enormous scandal brewing. It will rock the whole country and almost certainly bring down the government.'

So, what's new? Constance thought.

'Pier Paolo Pasolini was murdered last night,' Savognia said.

'Good God! The film-maker?'

Savognia nodded gravely.

'Where?'

'On Via Ostiense.'

'What happened?'

'He went to meet a pick-up and was attacked. A gang of street boys ran over his head with his own car.'

Constance shuddered.

'You knew that he was a homosexual?'

She nodded, dreading what was to come.

'With a penchant for very rough trade?'

She remained still.

'It seems,' Savognia said slowly, 'that his death might have been planned – with the connivance of the boy. It is thought it might be part of a right-wing plot. The prime targets are homosexuals.'

'Targets?' Constance asked in bewilderment.

'Too many homosexuals in Italy are left-wing. There is great fear in America that the Communists might come to power here. That the Americans will not allow. I'm sure this whole witch-hunt is funded and fuelled by the CIA in order to weaken the Communists' standing in the country.'

'But what has this to do with us?'

'A huge vice ring has been discovered here in Rome,' Savognia continued, ignoring her question. 'It is to do with the priests.'

'The priests?' she said, in disbelief.

Savognia rounded on her. 'Please stop repeating my every word, Constanza,' he said tetchily. 'Here in Rome there are certain so-called charitable houses run by unorthodox religious orders, which are nothing to do with the Vatican, of course, and do not seem to be attached to any recognised religious body. They befriend the young men who run away from the south – mainly Calabria and Sicily – and end up in Rome looking for a job. Of course, as they are illiterate peasants, they find no job. Some beg, but most become whores. They live in and around Stazione Termini. You must have seen them, Constanza. Eventually, these so-called monks contact them, give them food and a bed and set them to work for their living – as male prostitutes. The Church – the Catholic Church – and some right-wing organisations have been checking these houses for years. They have lists of men who use the services provided . . .'

'Not Giuseppe?' Constance interrupted in panic.

'Of course not!' Savognia said harshly. 'Padone is a peasant, a survivor. He can spot trouble a mile away and knows how to keep clear of it. The people who are attracted to these damned young men are the rich and privileged, arrogant enough to think that poverty and

505

degradation are there to be exploited. People like Pasolini, Louis Brunet – and Manfredo.'

'Manfredo?' Constance asked in horror.

'Yes, my dear, Manfredo. His name has been listed.'

'Oh, my God! What will happen?'

'When the press get to know, they'll go mad with joy. It'll be like bear-baiting.'

'But he's only seventeen!' she cried.

'Age is not important,' Savognia said, 'we're not talking about vice. That interests nobody. Who cares what two peasants do together? But when an aristocrat rolls in the slime, *everybody* wants to know. That is why Manfredo has endangered the name of Castelfranco di Villanuova and put at risk our whole business.'

'But what has he done?' Constance asked.

'I suspect that he has done very little,' Savognia replied. 'Apparently there are boys' clubs where people like him meet the sort of young man we are talking of – the sort who will do anything for a few lire. He's been along to these places a couple of times – but probably more out of curiosity than anything else. Your son is weak but not, I think, depraved. Of course, the baying mob hardly distinguishes between the two.'

'Oh, Giancarlo! This is ghastly! What are we to do?'

'Well, Constanza, it's a very dangerous situation but I think I can do something to keep his name out of it. You see, there are some big people involved – really big – and I think that little Manfredo Castelfranco di Villanuova can probably be lost in all the scandal. After all, what is he – nothing but the spoilt sprig of a once-noble family. Of course, the Villanuovas are known for sexual impropriety. If some zealous hack made the connection between him and his grandfather – one of the country's most notorious roués in the thirties – then more interest would be shown . . .'

Constance could tell that Savognia was enjoying himself. 'Oh, my God, Giancarlo!' she said.

'It will cost money, of course.'

'What will?'

'Keeping it quiet.'

'Anything! I don't care how much!'

'Constanza, you mustn't panic. Imagine if someone heard you speaking like that? How they could exploit you. No. There is a going rate for silence. I shall undercut it slightly.'

'Oh, Giancarlo, *do* be careful. I'd rather you took no risks.'

Conscious of the fact that for the first time in many years he had the upper hand, Savognia said graciously, 'Just leave it to me. However, I cannot do it all alone. Now this is what you must do . . .'

The next day Constance drove Manfredo to the castle. The journey seemed long because it was made in silence. As they climbed the winding roads across the hills, Constance felt her depression deepen. Sitting next to her was the young man she called her son but who was almost a total stranger. She had no idea what was going on in his mind. She didn't know whether he hated her or loved her; feared or despised her. Her heart sank even further as they drove under the grim walls of the castle and the memories of Maria-Angelina came flooding back. She hated returning there but it was the only haven she could think of when Savognia had said, 'He must be got out of Rome immediately. If my plan is to work, young Master Manfredo must disappear until things calm down.' As they unpacked the car, Constance remembered Savognia's face. He, at least, was obtaining some perverse pleasure from the situation.

The castle had been shockingly neglected under her stewardship. Constance could not deny her betrayal of Maria-Angelina's wishes. It was evident wherever she looked. Manfredo, she could tell, was appalled at the dilapidation revealed as the servant took them round the following morning. She dreaded walking into the dining room. Manfredo had not seen it since the night of his father's death. To her surprise, he began to talk the moment they walked in.

'He was standing right there. I had just got to the window when he pulled the triggers. I couldn't believe what I saw. It was like a dream. The room was full of smoke from all the shots he had taken at the family portraits. It was so dark and smoky, it was just like seeing something under water.'

He suddenly turned to Constance. 'Why have we stayed away? This is our home. This castle,' he raised both hands in an embracing gesture, 'is *us*. It is the Villanuovas. This is our continuity. Without this, what are we?'

Standing in that forlorn and abandoned room, Constance looked at him and saw Ludovico – the Ludovico she had loved so long ago. Manfredo was right, and by talking to her with a passion and directness she had never heard before, he exorcised the spirit of Maria-Angelina. It had, she wryly conceded, taken a male Villanuova to do so and she recalled with irony the old Principessa's words, 'We are a male line. Females do not count . . .'

As the days went by and their intimacy prospered, warmed by their shared enthusiasm for the restoration of the castle, Constance saw increasingly clearly what she had been unaware of in Florence. Not only was Manfredo a Villanuova to the core, he had Ludovico's taste and natural sense of style. As their confidence developed and their conversations grew more relaxed Constance remembered Miss Hatherby's words, 'About this little chap I have no doubts at all . . . he is full of creativity.'

Manfredo was like someone transformed. Not that his strange silences, odd moods and difficulties in communication entirely disappeared – they were still very much part of his personality – but what brought joy and hope to Constance were the sudden flashes of animated enthusiasm, the excitement in his eyes as he began to take in the full glory of the interiors and the quality of the workmanship in the castle's fabric – even the determination with which he overruled her suggestions about matters of restoration. 'This is yours,' Constance had told him on the first day, at the end of Franco's tour. 'You are the first-born son. Castelfranco is your responsibility, to hold in trust.' Manfredo accepted his responsibility as naturally and gracefully as she knew Ludo would have done. At the end of the week, she felt that she could return to Rome knowing that he was not only safely hidden away from the incipient scandal, but fully occupied in restoring the Villanuova home. She sensed that an artistic and creative talent was blossoming within her son that would restore him, too.

Sitting with Manfredo in the dining room on her last evening at the castle, Constance began to talk of her past. She told Manfredo of the death of her father, her meeting with Ludo, their life together when they were poor and living in Santo Spirito; she described the hat factory, she told him of Maria-Angelina. She couldn't stop talking.

Finally, she wound down and Manfredo spoke.

'I'm in hiding, aren't I? I've been banished from Rome just like my uncle was banished from here.'

'It's for your own good, darling,' Constance said, 'until the scandal dies down.'

'I feel like a coward.'

'Don't be ridiculous. What is courageous in having your name dragged through the mud? It could ruin us all.'

'Don't worry,' Manfredo said sharply, 'I'm sure it won't affect Constanza Castelfranco. Your investment is safe.'

'*Our* investment, Manfredo. Constanza Castelfranco belongs to all the family, just as much as this castle.'

She was hurt by his assumption that her first concern would be with the business but she knew that, from his point of view, it was a legitimate one to make. Legitimate but out of date. Since her trip to England to see Tudor, Constance had realised that a business that failed to take the whole family with it was not worth having at all. That

509

was why she had determined to fight to keep them all together.

'This should be our home again,' Manfredo said.

'Do you think so? But it needs so much work. Why don't you decide how you would like it, while you're here? It has to be restored. It might as well be restored to the taste of its eventual lord and master.'

In the pause that followed, Constance thought of Tudor, being educated like a little lord. 'I don't know about you being banished,' she said, 'but I do sometimes feel that poor Tudor has been banished to cold, grey England. I wonder if this should be his last term at Hopedale?'

'What does *he* think?'

With a shock, Constance realised that she had no idea.

Shortly before Christmas, the Camera de la Moda Italiana held its annual gathering of Italy's fashion clans. Designers, models, photographers, journalists and all the rag, tag and bobtail fashion followers of Italy appeared at the industry's party of the year, dressed to kill, ready to flirt and eager to gossip the night away.

Although she hated it, Constance knew it was an occasion that she must attend: never more so than now when the industry was so nervous about the witch-hunt against homosexuals and when people were actually beginning to talk of revolutions and coups – even of the possibility of reinstating the monarchy in Italy.

She arrived alone and drifted through the crowd, overhearing snatches of talk as she went. One in particular caught her attention. Two Milanese journalists were discussing the arrests and the fact that Portinari had hurriedly left Rome. She couldn't help herself. She broke into the conversation.

'Where has he gone?' she asked.

'Turkey,' the first journalist replied.

'Is he implicated?'

'And how!' said the second journalist. 'His pretty little

playmates have lost no time in doing the dirty on him. It was a case of get out or be behind bars.'

'But what of his business?'

'That's certainly finished. Can you imagine his type of customer putting up with a scandal like this? No way!'

'But . . .' Constance floundered, '. . . they can't be all that surprised. He was a very effeminate man.'

'Sure. Everybody knew he was a faggot. That isn't the problem. It's getting *caught* being a faggot that makes the shit hit the fan – and, boy, has it, this time!'

Constance lost no more time. Making her excuses as soon as she could, she began to search for Savognia. She had to speak to him and find out what was really happening. She found him in an anteroom, talking to Bettina. They looked up nervously at her approach.

'Bettina has been telling me the most dreadful news,' Giancarlo said, turning to greet Constance.

Before she could say anything, Bettina began, with a look of hatred, 'Louis has been arrested.'

'Louis Brunet?'

'Who else?' Bettina said contemptuously.

'They are trying to link his parties to the vice ring,' Giancarlo said. 'The two things are totally separate, of course, but by connecting them the police can make poor Louis a scapegoat and keep the politicians happy. Things look very bad for him.'

'He's a sick man,' Bettina said, 'he can't cope with prison. He'll die if we don't get him out.'

'Boys have sworn that his parties were arranged for them to make contact with clients,' Savognia said. 'All lies, needless to say, but sufficient for the police. He will only get off if someone testifies that they were ordinary parties to which Louis invited only personal friends.'

'Someone like Giuseppe,' Bettina suggested, giving Constance a searching look.

'What? Stand up in court?' she cried. 'You must be mad. Think of the publicity! Giuseppe could never do that. Imagine the effect it would have on the business.

511

I've just been hearing that Portinari is probably going to be finished by this ghastly affair and I have no intention of allowing Constanza Castelfranco to go the same way.'

'What effect do you think prison will have on poor Louis?' Bettina asked angrily.

'Ask Pino to testify,' Constance said desperately. 'He's a friend of Louis Brunet.'

'Pino!' Bettina laughed. 'He hightailed it to Los Angeles at the first hint of trouble. He won't be seen around here for a while, I can tell you! Of course,' she added cunningly, 'there's always Manfredo. He was a frequent enough guest.'

'You keep my son out of this,' Constance said. 'He has nothing to do with any of this squalid business, do you understand?'

'Ask your boyfriend, darling – or should I say *ex*-boyfriend?' Bettina spat out. 'He can tell a different tale.'

'You vulgar, gossipy bitch,' Constance retorted, 'I won't stand here and listen to this. Keep your innuendoes for those creepy gays you spend so much time with!'

'I may spend time with them, darling,' Bettina replied, 'but at least I'm not crazy enough to jump into *bed* with one of them! You disgust me, Mrs High-and-Mighty! Your lover and your son are up to their balls in this mess and you won't let them do a thing to help poor Louis in case it endangers your precious little fashion house!'

'You're damned right I won't. After all the sacrifices I've made, do you think I'll risk Constanza Castelfranco for that pathetic old queen? You must be mad. Louis Brunet can rot in hell for all I care. After all he's done to try to corrupt my son, do you think I would lift a finger to help him? If so, you must be mad!'

Savognia had considerable sway with the policymakers of Italy. His influence was based not on politics but on the power of his class. In other words, he didn't have to prove anything. Because he was who he was, he had the ear of all the men who made decisions in Italy – who were by no means always politicians. He used his contacts discreetly to ensure that Louis Brunet was released from prison. Constance was relieved but she was wise enough to accept that nothing Savognia did could alter the hatred for her that Bettina now professed quite openly. Her invective included attacks on Manfredo, which hurt Constance much more than all the vindictive remarks aimed at her.

'I just wish she could be silenced,' she told Carlo over a dinner *à deux*. True to her promise, she invited him to dine quite regularly when he was in Rome. He seemed to spend increasing amounts of time there and he and Constance saw each other frequently. They normally chatted about Villanuova business and discussed how things were going on the estate and at the castle. They never talked of Carlo's love for Constance and his avowed intention of marrying her. It was as if, having made up his mind, he was prepared to wait until *she* was ready to take it further.

Carlo was impressed with Constance's encouragement of Manfredo's restoration efforts and talked enthusiastically of a big party or dinner to mark their completion and the reopening of the castle as a family home.

'Would you come?' Constance asked in surprise.

'Oh, yes,' he answered.

'I thought you hated the very atmosphere of the place?'

'Yes, but you've just told me that Manfredo has transformed it. No more doom and darkness, you claimed. Surely, by sweeping everything away, he must have destroyed the last traces of my mother and her era?'

'Yes,' Constance agreed with enthusiasm, 'yes, he has certainly done that. It is so light and fresh now. Maybe you're right. We might think of a party in the spring when the weather is kinder. You know how cold the winters are up there.'

'How much longer is Manfredo to be incarcerated?' Carlo asked.

'I think that is not quite the best word, Carlo.'

He bowed to the criticism. 'The scandal seems to have died down,' he went on. 'Aren't things back to normal?'

'Yes, I think they are – or would be, if La Bonoccorsi would shut up.'

'Is she being difficult?'

'Difficult! She's determined to drag our names through the dirt at every opportunity.'

'Yes, but no one takes any notice of her.'

'At the risk of sounding like my mother,' Constance laughed, 'mud thrown, sticks – and I don't like it.'

'How quaint the English language is!' Carlo laughed too, but he decided that something *could* be done to stop Bettina's tongue.

Ever since his mother had destroyed every one of his possessions, Carlo Villanuova had travelled light. Having survived the trauma of being stripped of his past and deprived of his memories, he was determined never to let such a thing happen to him again. He made a point of owning virtually nothing. When his few clothes wore out, they were given to the poor; a book once read was handed to somebody else; no photographs were taken; pictures were enjoyed in public galleries or private homes; they did not hang on his walls. Not that Carlo Villanuova could be said to have walls. He rented accommodation on short leases; visited friends for long periods and was, in effect, the nearest thing to a gypsy that a civilised man can be. He had one possession, however, that he valued greatly. He had preserved it since the days of his disgrace. It was a letter – no, not even that, a brief note – written in haste and distress.

Bettina was getting ready to go out to lunch when her servant brought in a card on a silver salver. She picked it up and read the name. A frown crossed her brow but she nodded and said, 'Show him into the *salotto* and say I will be there in two minutes.' She finished her make-up, picked up her gloves and walked downstairs to meet her visitor.

'So,' she said, throwing open the door of the *salotto*, 'why have you come?'

'To silence you,' Carlo said.

'Is that your greeting?' Bettina asked.

'I don't think that you wish me to waste time in small talk any more than I wish to do so, Bettina.'

'Why are you here?' she repeated.

'I have told you.' He paused. 'I have your letter.'

'Letter?'

'The one you sent from London, begging my help.'

'So you kept it? After all your promises!'

'Yes, it is one of the few things I have been allowed to keep in my life.'

'What are you going to do?'

'When you confessed that you had murdered Ludo's baby and begged for my help, I gave it, even though it destroyed my life. I promised not to expose you and I kept my word. Even though it cost Ludovico and me our happiness. I even let him go to the grave ignorant of my innocence and your guilt. It was a simple question of honour. I think you have forgotten about honourable behaviour, Bettina, and I am informing you of the existence of your letter for nothing more sinister than to remind you of how people like us must behave. I am not threatening you. I am not intimidating you. But you must know that the opprobrium heaped on my head merely because of a *suspicion* of murder is nothing compared with the reception a signed proof of *actual* murder would receive. I know you will be sensible and think before you talk in future. I'm sure that, like me, you would prefer our letter to remain what it should be – a personal memento for the two of us. To make public such secrets is in nobody's interests. But I must warn you. You destroyed my brother's child because you couldn't bear the shame of an idiot baby; you will not be allowed to destroy his widow merely because you cannot face the failure of your own life. That is all.'

'What do you expect me to *do*, exactly – become her closest friend?'

'No, I expect you to maintain the silence that the dignity of your breeding requires and the vulnerability of your position demands. I'm not joking, my dear. I have the letter and I will use it, if you force me to do so. And remember, Giancarlo won't come to your aid as quickly as he did with Louis Brunet.'

'All right, I get the message. Just tell me *why*. Why are you so concerned with your sister-in-law's good name?'

'Because I intend her to be my wife.'

Bettina's eyes dilated.

'And if you tell anyone what I have just told you, Bettina, I will *finish* you.'

# CHAPTER 24

The moment she heard her Aunt Louise's voice on the telephone, telling her of her mother's accident, Constance knew that the news was worse than it sounded, even though Louise was full of reassurances.

'There's nothing to worry about,' her aunt said briskly. 'She's slipped and broken her arm. It isn't serious but she was a little shaken up so the doctor has decided to keep her in hospital for a couple of days.'

'Why should they keep her in?'

'Because she lives alone, I suppose. But you mustn't worry, darling. Chollerton has a nice little hospital – I went in to see her this afternoon and she's *fine*.'

'Do you think I should come over?'

'Good heavens, *no*! What would you do? She's in excellent hands and when she comes out I can look after her.'

'Oh, Louise, that would be too much for you.'

'Well, we'll cross that bridge when we come to it. Now promise me that you won't worry.'

But Constance *did* worry, and within a month her fears were realised. Nora had a stroke and died without recovering consciousness.

Constance decided to return to England alone for the funeral, meeting Tudor and taking him with her to Northumberland. He was at Heathrow with his housemaster. Constance was distressed at how similar they looked although Tudor was immaculate in his school uniform and the housemaster's suit looked as old as its owner. There was something distant and alienating about their well-mannered appearance and even more well-mannered attentiveness that Constance found disquieting. Their lack of spontaneity compared poorly with the rumbustious personal interaction of the Italians who had travelled on Constance's flight. Although their liveliness had irritated her, Constance found it a thousand times more attractive than the propriety of the pair standing before her.

She thanked the housemaster for accompanying Tudor and, formally taking possession of her son, gathered him to her. She half expected to have to sign for him.

To break the tedium of the journey, they had lunch on the train and Constance allowed Tudor to share her bottle of red wine. It relaxed them both.

'So,' she asked, 'you really like England?'

'Oh, yes,' he replied eagerly.

'And school?'

'Yes,' he replied with slightly less enthusiasm.

She knew from his reports that Tudor was not academic. 'And after O-levels?' she queried.

Looking her straight in the eye, he said with great force, 'I do not want to go to Cambridge.'

'Oxford?'

'No. Nowhere. I've had enough of school. I don't want to go to university. I want to be a painter.'

Constance was delighted – and surprised. She had assumed that Tudor's choice of career would be as stuffy as his education had proved to be. She smiled as she recalled her thoughts of a diplomatic career for him and was pleased that he had come up with a much more exciting idea.

'But first I want to get out into the world. To travel,' Tudor insisted.

'What a good idea,' Constance said, 'but you should begin by getting to know England and Italy, don't you think? They are your two countries, aren't they, and they're both perfect training grounds for a painter.' And she told him about the painters who took the Grand Tour to Italy in the seventeenth and eighteenth centuries and returned to paint the English landscape with eyes freed by the colour and light of the Mediterranean.

'You can have the best of both worlds, my darling. In fact, you have your *own* two worlds.'

A few miles south of Berwick, north of the long sweep of Bamburgh's white sand, a more varied and beautiful beach runs below the dunes. Its beauty is a secret from the hordes who cross to Holy Island, trudge to Dunstanburgh and swamp the tiny village of Bamburgh. It is a private, local place. Constance went there on the day after the funeral. She went alone, leaving Tudor to explore the Georgian walls of Berwick.

She needed to cry and knew that tears would come with blessed relief on those windswept dunes. Why have I come here so rarely? she asked herself as the sandpipers took wing at her approach and skimmed low across the waves in tightly packed convoys. Now it's too late; there's nothing left to come for. But as she walked, leaning slightly into the wind and welcoming the first spots of rain, she knew that she was wrong. Nora had gone, but Northumberland remained. For the first time, she thought of her own death. This is where I want to grow old. This is where I want to die. I cannot lose this place. Sitting in the coarse grass and watching the rain moving in from the sea she thought, again for the first time, of the possibility of retirement. I'm going to spend more time here, she resolved. After all, Margharita and Manfredo will be able to take over in a few years' time. I can train them. They won't always need me.

Acknowledging that her mother's house in Cramer was too small and primitive for her to use even as a holiday base, she took Tudor to the estate agent in order to put it on the market. In the car, she told him of her plan to buy a bigger property. 'I do think we should keep a toehold here, don't you?' she asked. 'After all, it's our family county and the only place in England where we have any allegiance – or even meaning, really.'

'I think it's a great idea,' Tudor agreed. 'I love it here. It's so wild and unspoiled. It's very strong, after Italy. Do you know what I mean?'

Constance knew precisely, and warmed to her son's perception.

'I love all those rich Italian colours but in the north the tones are more subtle,' Tudor continued. 'There's a different light.'

'Oh, Italy can be subtle as well, you know,' Constance corrected him. 'The most beautiful dawn I have ever seen was an Italian one.'

And she told him how Ludovico had woken her near La Spezia to show her the ethereal Mediterranean sunrise. Tudor was enchanted. She also told him of the remote beauty of Northumberland and evoked for him the colours and textures that she had loved so much on her walks with her father. 'I was so *young*,' she said, 'and yet I can still see everything he showed me – so clearly. You shall have a studio up here so that you can paint in our own county. I promise.'

Two days later she drove Louise and Tudor out to the Old Parsonage in Wrothburn, a moorland village about ten miles inland from Cramer. It had just come on the market and was an amazing house to find in dour Northumberland. Light-hearted and even witty, it had once been part of the Tweedsill castle estate. It must have been an alien growth even at the time of its building, in the early years of Victoria's reign. Like the castle, now turned into a hotel, the Old Parsonage was an exuberantly Gothic affair. From pointed widows and obelisked turrets to heavily studded doors and deeply sweeping verandahs, it was architecture confident of its style and breeding. To Constance it was pure enchantment and she was determined to have it. Passing the castle, shrouded in sombre trees, she turned the car off the road, drove downhill for about a mile and had the gratification of a gasp of delight from Louise as the house came into view. Though it was raining and the house stood empty, there was nothing sad or depressing about the Old Parsonage. Its white woodwork sparkled against the grey walls and it presented a welcoming face to them as they drove up.

'Oh, how *pert* it is!' Louise laughed. 'My dear, you absolutely *must* have it.'

And she did. The house was bought and became hers before she had even given herself time to think of what she would actually do with it.

Constance felt that she could not return to the south without walking by the sea once more. She needed to be alone with the elements. Arranging for Louise to take Tudor to Alnwick to see the castle, she set off early so that she would have the desolate coastline to herself.

Despite the recent funeral, it was not her mother but her father who was in her thoughts. She had walked these dunes with him so often when she was young. Today the memory of those happy times seemed especially vivid.

There was a rising wind and, feeling cold, Constance stopped and tried to tie her scarf around her head. Every time she thought she'd managed to catch the end the wind would take it and snatch it from her hand. It reminded her of how she used to stand impatiently whilst her father wrestled with her woollen scarf as he tried to tie it in the teeth of a gale.

*Quick, Daddy, I'm freezing!*

*All right, all right. I'm doing my best.*

Constance felt that she could hear Will's voice as clearly as if he were standing at her side. The thought comforted her as, having finally fixed her scarf, she reached the top of the dunes and surveyed the magnificent sweep of sand that stretched before her. The wind was so strong and the dunes so exposed that she could hardly stand. She looked towards the sea. The tide was coming in fast and the waves were crashing on to the beach in a swirl of greyish-yellow foam. Further out from the shore, she could see other waves breaking impotently on the surface of the sea, their white underbellies being swallowed by the heaving grey water below. The violence of the scene excited Constance and she felt her spirits rise.

*I'll race you to the water.*

*Oh, Daddy, wait.*

*Come on, Constance.*

The voices of her memories were caught and carried away on the wind as Constance plunged from the dunes down on to the beach. The little eddies of dry sand that she had noticed from above actually reached much higher than she had realised and the wind blew them spitefully against her legs. As she began to stride towards the shoreline they stung her flesh.

*Daddy, they're hurting.*

*No, no, Constance. Just a little pinprick. Keep walking.*

And she had because she believed everything her father said. Trotting by his side, the fine particles of sand did seem to hurt less after he had spoken. As Constance recalled his words, the memory had the same effect. Just as he always used to say they would, her legs stopped stinging.

'I so wanted you to be proud of me,' she spoke out loud. Above the shrieking wind and the crashing of the waves as they hurled themselves at the shore, she seemed to hear her father's voice, as she had so many times during her life.

*You can do anything you like, Constance. Nobody can stop you – only yourself.*

He had been right. She had done what she liked and nobody *had* stopped her. Nora's determination, Ludovico's infidelities, Maria-Angelina's deviousness, Giuseppe's betrayals: she had fought and beaten them all. Nothing had been able to break her spirit. 'And nothing will.' The wind snatched the words from her mouth and hurled them into the sky, in defiance of the storm. Out at sea, Constance could see the lowering clouds being tossed towards the shore. She knew that she would get soaked if she stayed. She had time to get back to the car before the rain started if she set off now.

She couldn't bear to. The elemental rage breaking around her was too magnificent to leave. She turned. Following the shoreline, she started to walk towards an outcrop of black rock a quarter of a mile along the beach on which the waves were crashing, splintering in fountains of yellowy-white spume tossed fifteen feet into the air. The wind behind her, Constance strode towards them, her pulse racing. Of course, her father would be proud. She had achieved, hadn't she?

'And I have every intention of going on achieving,' she shouted into the wind. 'Every intention.' She began to half run, half skip as the wind lifted her body and propelled her along. She laughed out loud with exhilaration. The storm was reaching its crescendo. Fierce raindrops began to strike her face. Within minutes, she was soaked but she was oblivious to any discomfort. 'I love this place,' she cried out loud as she scrambled over the rock to get closer to the breaking waves.

She knew that she had been right to buy the Old Parsonage. I need this wild country. I should have returned much more. In future I will come back at least once a year, She felt sure that her father would have been pleased with the decision and the thought warmed her. As the lashing rain obscured the beach, she looked back towards the dunes. She could hardly see them. She chuckled. Any Italian caught in this storm would think her crazy to plan on spending her time here. No, she knew one Italian who would understand, who would enjoy it as much as she. Carlo would love this. She felt a pang. She would love to be sharing this with him – as well as with her father's memory.

Turning from the shore, she began to walk back towards the dunes. Thoughts of Carlo made her realise how much she had changed. She looked back at her life in Italy – over twenty amazing years that she still remembered in vivid detail . . . She recalled her fear when she thought that Ludovico had abandoned her after their first night and the terror she felt with the old woman in black who could not understand her . . . Ludovico's cock and its soft silky skin . . . Maria-Angelina at their first meeting . . . she had understood nothing the old lady had said but Constance would always remember the uncanny stillness of the Principessa, even when she talked . . . and that strange smell, neither sweet nor bitter, that always permeated her room . . .

The rain had eased and out to sea the sky was lightening. Constance was so wet she no longer cared. Finding herself a place out of the wind, she snuggled down in the rocks and enjoyed her memories.

So much seemed to have happened. She had loved Ludovico and yet she had deceived him . . . was it a subconscious need to revenge his betrayal with Gioella . . . ? Even as she thought it, Constance knew the answer . . . Giuseppe had not just overwhelmed her, he had swallowed her up in a frenzy of sexual passion . . . she would never forget her feelings on that night in Paris . . . it had been as if she were exploding . . . every atom of her body torn apart by his lust . . . And it had meant nothing to him, she thought ruefully. I was just another body. I could have been another boy. What was it Giancarlo always said? . . . Bodies aren't very important . . . Well, she'd learned the hard way that they were all that mattered to Giuseppe. As long as they were available, he would have them . . . What destructive force had made her turn her back on reality and refuse to see the obvious evidence . . . why had she been obsessed with him? She thought with shame of how she had even put him before her children.

The thought of Margharita and Manfredo made her anxious. Could she hold on to them? That Manfredo was going to be a brilliant designer she had no doubt. Even Giuseppe said he was outstanding. It was her son's sexuality that frightened her. He had survived one scandal, thanks to Savognia, but how many more would his strange, twilight life produce? Why was he homosexual? Was it her fault? Perhaps she was too dominant. Clutching at a straw, she convinced herself that Manfredo's sexual attitudes might be a delayed adolescent reaction. After all, the trauma of Ludovico's death had clearly retarded his emotional growth. She began to see a light at the end of the tunnel. If she made him her designer, surely the increased responsibility would help him to grow up. Maybe it could help him to turn his back on the gay world. Why shouldn't he mature into a normal man? Carlo was always saying that being attracted to men was not the Villanuova style. Surely he was right. I'll talk to Monica and see if we can find him a girlfriend, she decided.

The idea caused her to pause. How strange that she had thought of enlisting Monica's help and not Margharita's. It was a measure of the failure of her family that brother and sister knew so little of each other and cared even less. I shall change that, she vowed. Thoughts of Margharita forced her to face her greatest problem for the future. She knew that her grand plan needed her daughter. Without her there could be no long-term future. And yet, she had seen Margharita's outstanding acting talent. How could she lure her away from the stage? Would it be wrong even to try? I *know* that she can be a business-woman, she said to herself. She's more like me than she – or anyone else – imagines. She would be marvellous at running the business – and she would love it. She recalled Carlo's philosophical solution. Maybe he was right. Well, she'd let Margharita act. She would even encourage her. But only if Margharita promised to take an interest in the business. Then, she thought, some day when I'm ready to come back to Northumberland for good it will all become hers. That will be my revenge on the Principessa and all her talk of the Villanuovas being a male line. She smiled with satisfaction.

What of Tudor? Did he have any of his father in him

or was he all hers? She wanted him to belong to her alone . . . Giuseppe could have no part of him. 'Three men in my life – only three – and every one a shit,' she said out loud. What had Nicky wanted, all those years before? Had he only been after her virginity and having lost his chance, decided that it was not worth making any real effort after she had returned north? How devastating she had found his silence. She could remember her bewilderment even now. Those nights spent tossing and turning, wondering what she had done, why he had abandoned her . . . blaming herself, convinced that there was something wrong with her. 'What a fool I was,' she murmured.

She remembered her sick feeling at Savognia's luncheon on realising that Gioella had been – and still was – more than just a friend to Ludovico. How vulnerable she had felt . . . how eagerly she had been prepared to swallow his lies . . . those protestations of purity that she made herself believe. 'God, how I loved him,' she sighed.

She thought of Carlo. Suddenly, feeling cold, she shivered. Had she lost him? Had his love dwindled into mere friendship? Why had she not made the break with Giuseppe at the time when Carlo had offered her his love in the hospital in Rome? 'What was wrong with me?' she asked, remembering her fears about his relationship with Monica, and her inability to see what she really wanted. But now she knew. Carlo was good; he was the only man she had ever met who automatically put her first; he understood her. Why had she hesitated? Was it because she was afraid of the Villanuova temperament? Had she feared that he would let her down, as Ludovico had?

'I've had to share my love too many times,' she said, thinking of Ludo and Giuseppe. Yet even as she said it, she knew that Carlo was different.

She felt cold. Standing up, she brushed the wet sand from her legs and began to walk back towards the car.

Although the rain had stopped, the wind still blew. The clouds were barrelling across the sky, one on top of another, each one a different shade of grey, and each grey a unique mixture of yellow, brown, purple and green. They were so beautiful that Constance stopped to look at them. Suddenly, behind her, over the heaving seas, the clouds parted and a shaft of sun streaked across the sand towards her. As it reached the dunes it turned the sea-grasses a fantastic, brilliant green, tipped with gleaming yellow. At once, everything was alive with sparkling, moving colour.

'I can't leave,' Constance cried. 'I can't walk away from this. Not yet.' And turning, she began to scramble up the dunes, heading back towards the sea. I must see the sun on it, she thought, as she reached the top.

Standing there, she surveyed the scene. The wind tugged and tore at her, the sea crashed in below her. The waves were lit from behind by the low-lying winter sun. Hitting the shore, they broke into a million pieces that caught the light like crystal. Constance began to run towards the shoreline. Half way down the beach, something along the shore caught her eye. She stopped. Shading her eyes, she could see a figure walking towards her. It seemed little more than a speck in the vastness of the scene and, for a split second, Constance had the most extraordinary sensation. Distant as it was, the figure was familiar.

Her father.

That's who it reminded her of. Her father. Who was it? As she stood, the figure began to run towards her, waving excitedly. She took a few steps towards it, leaning into the wind, so cold that it almost took her breath away. Who was it? The figure kept running towards her.

Suddenly, she knew. She began to struggle towards the man running to meet her. The wind resisted every step, tears came to her eyes, her face was numb but she would not stop. 'Carlo!' she cried but the wind tore the word from her mouth and tossed it over her shoulder. 'Carlo! Carlo! How did you know?'

He was less than ten feet away; the wind propelled

him forward at alarming speed, every part of his clothing flapping madly around him. Then he was there, holding her. Laughing, crying, kissing, they sank to their knees in the sand.

'Oh, Carlo! How did you know?' Constance cried.

'I had to come.'

The wind buffeted and howled around them as they held each other. The sun had gone, swallowed by more storm clouds, and the rain began to lash down again. But they were totally unaware of anything but each other.